The Girls of
Mulberry Lane

ROSIE CLARKE was born in Swindon,
but moved to Ely in Cambridgeshire
at the age of nine. She started writing
in 1976, combining this with helping
her husband run his antiques shop.
In 2004, Rosie was the well-deserved
winner of the RNA Romance Award
and the Betty Neels Trophy. Rosie
also writes as Anne Herries and
Cathy Sharp. Find out more at her
website: www.rosieclarke.co.uk

ROSIE CLARKE

The Girls of Mulberry Lane

ⓐ

First published as an ebook in 2017 by Aria,
an imprint of Head of Zeus, Ltd.

First published in print in the UK in 2017 by Aria.

9 7 5 3 1 2 4 6 8

A catalogue record for this book is available from
the British Library.

ISBN (PB): 9781788540995
ISBN (E): 9781786692573

Typeset by Divaddict Publishing Solutions Ltd.

Printed and bound by CPI Group (UK) Ltd,
Croydon, CR0 4YY

Head of Zeus Ltd
First Floor East
5–8 Hardwick Street
London EC1R 4RG

WWW.HEADOFZEUS.COM

The Girls of
Mulberry Lane

Chapter 1

'Here you are then, Peggy, love,' Jim Stillman said and set the box of fresh leeks, cabbages and potatoes on her kitchen floor. The smell of the leeks was strong and made her feel hungry. 'That's the last from Percy's allotment. Afore he died, he asked me to clear it before the next man took over and give you the produce.'

'Thanks, Jim.' Peggy Ashley smiled at him. 'I'll miss Percy's veg, because it was always so fresh and there were never worm holes in the potatoes.' Her eyes stung with tears because she would miss her stepfather's cheery smile even more. His death the previous month had hit her hard. 'I can't believe he's gone.'

'Nor me, love,' Jim said and moved his cap to scratch his bald head. 'Well, you won't miss the veg because I'll be bringing you some every week now. I've always got plenty left over and I'd rather give it to you than see it waste.' He gave a rumbling laugh. 'I caught that young Tommy Barton digging potatoes from Percy's plot this mornin'. Give 'im a cuff round 'is ear but I let him take what he'd dug. Poor little bugger's only tryin' to keep his ma from starvin'; ain't 'is fault 'is old man got banged up for robbin', is it?'

Tilly Barton, her two sons Tommy and Sam and her

husband, lived almost opposite the Pig & Whistle. Mulberry Lane cut across from Bell Lane and ran adjacent to Spitalfields Market, and the folk of the surrounding lanes were like a small community, almost a village in the heart of London's busy East End. Tilly and her husband had been good customers for Peggy until he lost his job on the Docks. It had come as a shock when he'd been arrested for trying to rob a little corner post office and Peggy hadn't seen Tilly to talk to since; she'd assumed it was because the woman was feeling ashamed of what her husband had done.

'No, of course not.' Peggy smiled at him. A wisp of her honey-blonde hair had fallen across her face, despite all her efforts to sweep it up under a little white cap she wore for cooking. 'I didn't realise Tilly Barton was in such trouble. I'll take her a pie over later – she won't be offended, will she?'

'No one in their right mind would be offended by you, Peggy love.'

'Thank you, Jim. Would you like a cup of coffee and a slice of apple pie?'

'Don't mind a slice of that pie, but I'll take it for my docky down the allotment if that's all right?'

Peggy assured him it was and wrapped a generous slice of her freshly cooked pie in greaseproof paper. He took it and left with a smile and a promise to see her next week just as her husband entered the kitchen.

'Who was that?' Laurence asked as he saw the back of Jim walking away.

'Jim Stillman, he brought the last of the stuff from Percy's allotment.'

Peggy's eyes brimmed and Laurence frowned. 'I don't know what you're upset for, Peggy. Percy was well over eighty. He'd had a good life – and it wasn't even as if he was your father...'

'I know. He was a lot older than Mum but... Percy was a good stepfather to me, and wonderful to Mum when she was so ill after we lost Walter.' Peggy's voice faltered, because it still hurt her that her younger brother had died in the Great War at the tender age of seventeen. The news had almost destroyed their mother and Peggy thought of those dark days as the worst of her life. Her stepfather had got them through it somehow and she'd always been fond of him, something Laurence had never understood.

'Have you seen my paper?' Laurence asked, obviously not listening to a word she said. 'I haven't finished the crossword yet and I think I've solved the last clue.'

'Do you mean the Sunday paper?' Peggy frowned as she tried to remember. 'I think that went out yesterday.'

'Damn!' Laurence glared at her. 'You know I've asked you not to throw out that paper. I like doing the crossword. Now I'll never know for sure...'

'Oh, the page with the crossword is in the top drawer of the dresser. I always save anything with a crossword for you.'

Peggy turned away, as her husband rushed to the tall oak dresser that took up most of one wall of the kitchen and was set with all the crockery she'd lovingly collected over a lifetime. He pounced on the sheet of paper with glee. Her eyes filled with tears, because Laurence just hadn't understood how upset she was over Percy's death. He'd never cared for Percy and hadn't particularly liked Peggy going round there to help him out as he'd become frail in the last months of his life. They'd had words over it a couple of times, and when Percy died Laurence had been relieved, and, she'd suspected, even pleased that she wouldn't be going to visit any more – and that hurt Peggy.

Laurence had filled in the clue and was crowing over it as he cut round the piece of newspaper and slipped it into an envelope with a stamp. 'Put this in the box when you go shopping,' he said, leaving it on the kitchen table. 'A lot of times the first prize isn't worth having because it's so easy loads of people win, but I'll be surprised if many get it this week.'

As Laurence went out, clearly cock-a-hoop at having solved the puzzle, Peggy stared after him in resentment. Didn't he know she was still grieving for her stepfather?

She took some trays from the oven and set them on the long pine table in the middle of the kitchen. It was a big kitchen, with lots of cabinets and spaces for her cooking utensils, and a lovely cool larder to store her foodstuffs. In fact the pub was a good place to live and Peggy had been happy working here for all of her married life and she'd thought she always would be, but Laurence had hurt her with his indifference over Percy's death.

It was stupid to brood over it. Removing her apron, Peggy took her purse and her basket. Fluffing up her blonde hair dressed in a pageboy style, she put on some fresh lipstick and smiled at her reflection in the mirror over the sideboard. Her eyes were blue but they looked sad, perhaps because of the permanent ache in her breast these days, an ache caused by the loss of Percy and Laurence's attitude. She would visit her friend Maureen at her shop at the other end of the lane. Maureen always made her feel better, because however hard things were for Peggy, her friend always had worse to put up with and she never stopped smiling.

'I'll take two tins of that ham while you've got it in stock,' Peggy said. 'It's Canadian, isn't it?'

'Yes; Dad always gets this from the wholesaler when he can, because it's popular,' Maureen replied and her smile lit up her pretty face. She had dark brown hair, which had recently been cut into a stylish bob by young Ellie at number nine, which was two doors down. Ellie's boss had only recently taken over one of the derelict shops in the lane, and they were already busy, because of the cheap prices. 'Dad has been buying in extra tins recently, filling the stock room, just in case...'

'You mean in case there's a war? Oh, I do hope it won't happen, Maureen. You're too young to remember what it was like last time, but I can and it makes me shudder to think of another one.'

'I do remember some of it.' Maureen's soft grey eyes showed concern. 'Mum was frightened of the Zeppelins and I know some of her friends were killed by one of those dreadful things. What I remember most, though, was the street party we had when it was over.'

'Yes, you would be just old enough to remember that,' Peggy said. 'I remember all our brave boys marching through the street, laughing and thinking it would be over by that Christmas and believing they were off for a marvellous adventure. Most had never been out of their own village or town before and they had no idea what they were in for.'

'Mum's brother Tim was gassed in the trenches... He came back but he was never the same, so Mum said, and he died three years later.'

'Yes, poor lad. I knew Tim well. Your mother looked after him, God bless her soul.' Peggy shook off the bad memories. 'Well, we shan't stop it by moaning about it. Are you coming to the church social on Friday night?'

'I'd love to, Peggy, but I'm not sure my father will let me.'

'Oh, Maureen love, why do you put up with it?' Peggy shook her head as she picked up her change and wicker basket. 'You're twenty-three now and he can't stop you going out. You're a fool to yourself if you let him.'

'It's just that he suffers from a bad chest and he gets so upset if I leave him on his own at night. He's been like it since Mum went. Last time I went out he upset himself so much that I had to call the doctor round.'

'It's emotional blackmail, that's what it is,' Peggy told her sternly. 'Do you want me to have a word with him, love?'

'No, thank you. My gran would do that if I asked. She's the only one he ever listens to. I'll see if he's in a good mood. Sometimes he goes to play cards with one of his friends and then he doesn't mind if I go – as long as it is with you or Anne. He approves of Anne more, because he says she does a good job at the school.'

'I suppose he thinks I'm a wicked woman because I run a pub.' Peggy laughed as Maureen flushed. 'Hit the nail on the head, have I? Never mind, love. Your gran will sort him out. Hilda Jackson always did know how to keep her men in line.'

*

Maureen smiled as she left the shop. Peggy was Maureen's closest friend, but even she didn't truly understand. Henry Jackson had played on his daughter's sympathy after her mother died, taking advantage of her grief to manipulate her.

6

'I can't manage without you, Maureen pet,' he'd said, tears streaming down his cheeks. 'If you leave me to go off with that feller of yours I'll just lie in bed and my death will be on your conscience. I need you and your ma would expect you to take care of me... with my chest the way it is.'

'Oh, Dad, don't do this to me,' Maureen had begged. She'd been promised to Rory Mackness, a young man she'd met at Peggy's pub just a few months before her mother died, and she'd been saving for her wedding, but her father had told her she must break it off for his sake. 'It isn't fair... it just isn't fair...'

'Do you want your father's death on your conscience, girl? Maybe if you'd stopped home with your ma a bit more and not gone gadding off to dances every night she wouldn't have left us.'

Maureen's throat tightened at the memory. It was so unfair of her father to blame her, to make her feel guilty because she hadn't been at home when her mother became suddenly and fatally ill. Perhaps if she'd been there to fetch the doctor she might not have died – but her father had been out too. Still he blamed Maureen, not himself, even though he was the one who had bullied her mother time after time, making her life a misery.

In the back of her mind, a little voice told Maureen that her mother was probably better off out of a life with her complaining and, sometimes, brutal husband. When Maureen was a child Ma had explained the bruises on her arms, and once her cheek, as being accidents, but as she grew up Maureen had suspected that they were the result of violent arguments between her parents. If only she'd been stronger three years ago! If she'd married Rory sooner and not bothered about saving for a nice wedding and a few bits for their home, her father couldn't have forced her to come back and look after the shop or him if she'd been Rory's wife.

Maureen had known Rory wouldn't let her go if she'd told him the truth and so she'd said she wasn't sure about her feelings, that she didn't want to marry him, and how she'd regretted that mistake, because Rory had tried to change her mind by kissing her and she'd so nearly given in, and then when she didn't he'd walked off in anger and she hadn't seen him since.

'What are you daydreaming for?' Her father's voice interrupted her thoughts as he walked through from the back room. 'Buck up, Maureen. If you've no customers to serve you can check on the stock room and make a list of what we need. I'm going to the wholesaler tomorrow and I'll need to know first thing.'

'Where are you going?' Maureen asked as he walked towards the door.

'None of your business, miss. If you know what's good for you, you'll do as I ask or…'

'Or what?' Maureen wanted to ask. She was pretty certain her father wouldn't hit her, because if he did she would walk out on him. Maureen wasn't her mother; she wasn't tied to her father other than by ties of duty and compassion. What no one understood was that Maureen genuinely felt sorry for him. Although she knew he feigned sickness whenever she defied him, he did have a weak chest and she believed he did feel remorse and distress over his wife's death.

'I'm going to the church social with Peggy and Anne on Friday night,' Maureen said before he could exit the shop. 'If you don't want to be on your own I'll ask Gran to come round.'

Maureen drew a deep breath as her father's eyes shot her a sharp glare. If looks could kill she'd be dead; however, a customer entered at that moment and he went out without a word. No doubt he would have something to say when he returned that evening, but Maureen had decided she wasn't going to back down this time. Peggy was right; it was time she had some say in her own life.

Maureen never closed for long at lunchtime, because her father said they couldn't afford to miss customers; instead, she snatched a bite of the sandwich she'd made early that morning whenever she got the chance. She had a kettle in the back room, but seldom had time to make a cup of tea and sit down with it.

She prepared to serve her last customer of the day, who had popped in for an evening paper and a packet of Woodbine cigarettes. He was a pleasant man, attractive in his own quiet way, and in his early thirties.

'That will be one and sevenpence, please, Mr Hart,' Maureen said and wrapped the small twist of barley sugar he'd asked for at the last minute. 'And how is your little Shirley?'

'She's been poorly again, Miss Jackson,' he replied sadly. 'Missing her sainted ma I dare say, though her granny does all she can to help the child – but my mother ain't getting any younger.'

'I expect she finds it hard looking after a small child, but she'll do her best,' Maureen sympathised. 'We all need our mothers, Mr Hart, no matter what age we are.'

'And that's a fact,' he said and looked more cheerful as he nodded his head to her and went out.

*

Maureen's father was sitting in his chair smoking his pipe when she went up that evening. He glanced at her when she entered but didn't speak. His silence didn't worry her, because she was used to his moods. He ate the meal she put in front of him without a word and then left her to wash up, going downstairs and out of the back door. Maureen knew he would have taken his key, as he did when he went out to the pub twice a week. Henry Jackson never drank to excess; he was too mean to waste his money on drink, though if he was offered a whisky by someone who wouldn't expect him to buy them one back, he would take it.

Having washed up and tidied the kitchen, Maureen relaxed in her mother's comfortable rocking chair and took out her knitting. She bought her wool from Mrs Tandy in the lane. She was a widow and very chatty and she let Maureen buy an ounce of wool at a time, putting the rest by for her. Maureen liked to knit, especially things for babies, and she was making some bootees, a bonnet and coat for a baby whose mother was struggling to support her. Anne Riley had told her about the family; they were good friends, even though Anne was a few years older, and had known each other since school. The young widow was called Sally Jones and had three children, all under five. Anne had the eldest daughter in her class at school and she'd discovered the child crying one day because she had no food and no money for her dinner.

'I shared my sandwiches with her and gave her my apple,' Anne had told Maureen when she'd popped round for a chat. 'I've been to the house and seen for myself what the trouble is. Sally is struggling to cope. She just can't afford to give Milly her dinner money.'

'There's so many in the same boat, Anne – what can we do to help them?'

'Well, I'm going to try and find a free nursery for the younger ones so that Sally can do a few hours' work – and I thought I'd ask Peggy to have a whip round at the pub. Sally hasn't even got a full set of clothes for the baby.'

'How old is the baby? I've got patterns and I'll make some clothes for him and the other children if you give me their sizes.'

Maureen had just cast on the back of the jacket when she heard the bell ringing downstairs. She went downstairs to the shop, peering out into the darkness before unlocking the door.

'Who's there? We're closed.'

'Not to me, love,' her grandmother's voice came back loud and clear. 'Let me in, love, there's a good girl.'

'Gran!' Maureen pulled the door wide, smiling as the little white-haired woman entered the shop. 'What are you doing out at this hour?'

'I'm not in my dotage yet, girl,' Hilda Jackson said strongly. 'My neighbour Martin Porter came round to tell me – they've carted yer dad off to the 'ospital. Had a fit and collapsed in the Royal Oak bar, so they tell me. Martin's a decent chap and offered to come and tell you but I said I'd do it.'

'Oh no.' Maureen's heart sank. 'Dad wasn't speaking to me tonight. I told him I was going to the church social and he's been in a mood ever since.'

'That's Henry all over; his own worst enemy,' Hilda said and shook her head in disgust. 'His father was much the same, but I wouldn't 'ave it. You put up with too much. Most girls of your age would have gone off by now – and it's time you were married, lass.'

Maureen turned her head aside, hiding the sorrow in her soft grey eyes. She pushed back the dark hair that waved off her forehead and just brushed the collar of her blouse in a neat bob; she was used to hiding her feelings.

'He'd never manage alone, Gran.'

'I doubt he would, but I could give him a hand – and if he wasn't so mean he could take on a lad to help.'

'He says the shop doesn't make enough money...'

Hilda snorted. 'Take no notice of him,' she said. 'He's even tighter than his father was – and my Ron had a nice bit put away when he died. He left me my share of what he had – I'll give him that – and the business to Henry. If he'd left it to me, I'd have turfed Henry out long ago. He should do his share, Maureen.'

'I don't mind,' she replied and smiled at the elderly lady who refused to show any sign of giving in even though she was now into her seventies. 'I'd just like to go out with friends sometimes.'

'As you should.' Hilda nodded. 'We can't do much about it now, love, but you leave it to me. You go to your church social on Friday. I'll be here if he's home by then – and I doubt there was much the matter with him. I reckon he brings those fits on himself.'

Maureen made no reply, though she knew her gran was speaking the truth – but Henry Jackson did have a weak chest; the doctor had told Maureen so when he was ill after her mother died.

'It isn't likely to kill him, Maureen,' Doctor Bond had told her. 'It means he may have difficulty getting his breath sometimes, but if he's sensible and doesn't get into foolish tempers he should be all right.'

The trouble was her father was a stubborn man. He was sometimes ill in the winter, though with careful nursing was up and about in a week or so, but his breathing could be erratic and when he was in a temper he seemed to hold his breath until he went red in the face and passed out.

'What am I going to do, Gran?' she asked, emotionally. 'If I'd been here that day perhaps Mum wouldn't have...'

'Is that what he told you?' Hilda looked fierce. 'He's worse than his father I reckon – it was Henry that made your poor mother's life a misery. I warned her to stand up to him when she married him, but she never could. Doris was a gentle soul and she loved you. She would never have tried to hold you back.' She took hold of Maureen's arm and looked into her face. 'Listen to me, love. If you let him that father of yours will make your life a misery. Your mother's death wasn't your fault – and if Henry should die, well, it's his time and that's all there is to it. If need be, I'll move in myself and keep him right.'

This last was said so fiercely that Maureen burst out laughing at the thought of the diminutive lady cracking the whip at her father.

'Oh, Gran, I do love you,' she said. 'Come upstairs and have a cup of cocoa and then I'll walk you home.'

'I've locked up tight,' Hilda said in a voice that brooked no argument. 'I'm staying here with you until your father is better again – however long it takes.'

Chapter 2

Peggy listened to the customer's account of how Henry Jackson had collapsed at the Royal Oak, a few streets away. He seldom chose to drink in her pub, possibly because she had no sympathy with his tantrums and disapproved of the way he took advantage of Maureen.

'I bet it was all staged just to get his own way over something,' she told Laurence as they went upstairs later that evening.

The bar was wiped down and the glasses washed, rinsed and left to dry, because Peggy never left things unfinished. She polished all the tables and benches and the floor was mopped every morning, both in the bar and the toilets, which were always left filthy by uncaring customers. Sometimes, Peggy thought the men who left chains un-pulled, urine on the floor and the seat, vomit and paper all over, had been brought up in a barn. These days she had a bit of help with the cleaning, but Peggy was a fair-minded woman and she shared the dirty jobs equally with her daily help, although Nellie had told her she didn't mind what she did.

'I've bin charrin' all me life, ducks,' Nellie had announced when Peggy asked her if she was willing to clean toilets. 'I reckon I've seen everythin' you can show me an' a bit more.'

She'd gone into a cackle of laughter that made Peggy laugh with her and they'd got on like a house on fire ever since. It had been months before the details of Nellie's sad life started to reveal themselves, because she'd never complained; her tragic widowhood in the previous war, the way she'd had to clean at all hours of the night and day to keep her two children and herself were not told so much as popped out in conversation. Nellie was in her fifties, having met and married the love of her life when she was nearly thirty; for most of those thirty years she'd looked after a sick mother and two younger siblings, so when the chance to marry came along she'd taken it. However, the Great War had erupted before her daughter was born, which happy event had been due to a wonderful visit home in 1916, when Dick told her how much he really loved her. That visit gave Nellie her biggest taste of happiness, because when her husband was sent home after being shot in the chest he was never the same, and she'd lost her beloved Dick to his injuries a few months after the war ended, only to discover that she was having her son.

'Never mind, ducks, he'll always be young an' 'andsome to me,' she said when Peggy sympathised. 'I'll never 'ave to watch him put his false teeth under the kitchen tap.'

Peggy admired Nellie's bravery and her will to keep going despite the odds, even though her son and daughter were now both in jobs of their own.

'My Pete's gorn and joined the Army, daft lad,' she'd told Peggy one morning when they sat over a cup of tea. 'And my Amy's thinkin' of joining the Wrens or some such thing after Christmas.'

'Well, I suppose they think there's more chance of a better life than they'll get round here.'

'An early grave that's what my boy will get if we have another war and that lot in Germany are spoiling for it if you ask me.'

Peggy smiled and passed her a plate of homemade shortbread; it was buttery and delicious and her family loved it.

'You spoil me, Peggy Ashley,' Nellie told her with a grateful smile. 'I reckon it was me lucky day when I came here for a job.'

'I was lucky to get you. Some of those young madams I've had in the past don't know how to do a fair day's work.'

'Comin' 'ere's like a holiday fer me, love, and alus 'as been.' Nellie grinned at her. 'Like another daughter you are, Peggy Ashley, and I'll 'elp yer all I can.'

Peggy smiled inwardly. Nellie was old East End and worth her weight in gold, the salt of the earth as her stepfather would've told her. She was lucky to have such friends; they made up for so much... but for the moment she needed to get on with her work.

*

'Tired, love?' her husband asked as she undressed that evening and sat before the dressing table to cleanse away the little bit of make-up she wore in the bar. She'd brushed her hair, which tended to curl naturally, and her blue eyes were clear and bright. 'Everyone was talking about those cheese and leek tarts you made this evening – but if the work is too much we could stop doing so much food...'

'We get a nicer crowd in since we started serving decent food, Laurence. The last thing we need is the sort that drink themselves silly, every Friday and Saturday night.'

'We've certainly made more profit since you started

cooking.' Laurence still looked doubtful. 'I don't want you gettin' too tired, love. I shouldn't know what to do if you were ill...'

'Well, you needn't worry on that score.' Peggy put her arms about his waist. He was still nice and firm, not a scrap of extra fat anywhere on his muscular body, and she liked to touch him. He'd always been the best-looking bloke in the lanes and she'd noticed him when she was still at school and he was working for his uncle in the pub; they hadn't known then that he would inherit enough from his uncle to take it over himself after the war. 'I get tired, but no more than normal and I'm as fit as a fiddle. I was thinking about Nellie... she's had a hard life, Laurence.'

'Yes, I expect she has.' He looked at her indulgently. 'You've got a big heart, Peggy Ashley. You'd take in the world's waifs and strays if you could. Who was that pie for I saw you taking over the road earlier? The Barton family, I imagine – so who else am I helping to support now?'

'You've seen those romper suits I made for Sally Jones, I suppose. I told you that she lost her husband in an accident, didn't I? Our kids never had to go without a thing.'

'That's because we both worked hard,' he reminded her. 'It wasn't easy and you had to carry most of the load while I was recovering from the war.'

'I was just thankful that you came back to me,' Peggy told him and lifted her face for his kiss. 'I do love you, Laurie – you know that, don't you?'

'Yes, I know,' he told her and bent his head to kiss her passionately. Peggy responded with warmth, her body springing to life as they fell to the bed together. Their bodies fitted instinctively, because they'd grown used to pleasing each other over the years and had enjoyed a healthy love life.

Peggy was often surprised that she hadn't had more children, but perhaps it was that bout of mumps Laurence had had just after their son Pip was born.

'Laurie, you won't have to go if there's another war, will you?' she asked as they lay side by side, content in the warmth of their bed.

'I don't think there will be,' Laurence said. 'I know they've got sandbags round all the important buildings up West, and I know they've dug trenches and talked about sending the kids to the country, but I think it's all hot air. The Germans were humiliated last time; I don't think they'll risk it again.'

'It might be just the reason they will,' Peggy said fearfully. 'Hitler and his jackbooted army of kids make me shudder. I saw one of his rallies on the Pathé News the other night at the flicks and it frightened me.'

'Well, if they like marching and saluting and yelling their heads off it keeps them out of trouble.' Laurence nuzzled sleepily against her neck. 'Have I ever told you how good you smell, Peggy love?'

'Go on with you,' she said but she knew he'd already fallen asleep. Laurence was lucky like that in having the knack to just shut his eyes and sleep. Peggy knew she would be awake for ages. Talking to Nellie about her son and daughter signing up to the forces had unsettled her, because Peggy had a son of sixteen and a daughter of eighteen and she didn't want Pip to join the Army or any of the other services. Janet had a good job on the East India Docks in the office of a firm that repaired ships, and she'd started courting just a few weeks ago. She'd asked if she could bring her boyfriend to the Christmas Eve party, which had become quite a social event, because they closed the pub to outsiders and all the regulars were invited for free food and drinks.

Peggy thought about Christmas as she lay beside her husband and listened to him snoring softly. She was a lucky woman to have a good husband, lovely children and a business she enjoyed, besides some real friends. She'd sensed that Laurence was restless for a while now, which was probably what made him snappy with her sometimes. He'd always had a short fuse, but any arguments had been made up quickly in bed, yet of late... something was changing and Peggy couldn't decide why.

*

Laurence woke as the first rays of a rosy dawn touched the window. What was that old proverb? Red sky at night, shepherds' delight; red sky in the morning, shepherds' warning... it would probably be a bitterly cold day and they might even have some snow before nightfall.

Shivering, he reluctantly eased himself from the comfort of his marital bed. This was the worst part of his day, when he had to get out of that lovely warmth and go downstairs to make up fires and get the place a bit cosier for Peggy when she came down. He'd need to check that the oil stove he'd put in the outside lavatory hadn't gone out and let the water in the pan freeze. It had happened one winter when they first moved in and he'd had a hell of a job to get it unfrozen and ready for their customers when they started to come in.

The lunchtime trade was usually very busy and Peggy would be working in the kitchen all morning, getting ready for the hungry men who came in looking for a snack with their beer. They were a different crowd from the evening lot, often travelling salesmen, office workers and delivery drivers snatching a break. A few women from the local businesses popped in for a sandwich; they normally had a cup of tea or cocoa rather than alcohol. The girls from the factories came at night, either in a group of five or so, because there was safety in numbers, or with their boyfriends. At night was when the real trade was done, Laurence thought. He'd often wished he could open up just for the evening, but the brewery would have had the licence off him straight away if he'd tried; that was the trouble with being tied to one firm, but it had always been a Greene King pub and Laurence couldn't afford to buy it and turn it into a free house.

The cobbles in the yard were covered with a sheen of white, but it was frost and crunchy under his feet rather than ice. He sighed with relief when he saw the toilet hadn't frozen and left the heater turned down slightly. In the meantime, there were fires in the kitchen, sitting room and the bars to be lit. Peggy liked everywhere warm and so did he – and he dreaded to think what they would do if fuel became scarce.

Laurence had dismissed his wife's fears that a war was on the horizon, because he didn't want her to worry, but he was anxious himself. He and Peggy had built this place up from next to nothing and it would be a shame to see it all go. If the war did happen it was going to be a lot worse than the last show. The Zeppelins had terrified people, but there was bound to be far worse in store this time. Laurence knew there was a possibility that he would be called on to fight for his country. He was forty-three but that wasn't considered old these days, and if things got bad they would call up men of his age.

He frowned as he thought what it would mean for Peggy if he had to fight. She already did more than her share, cooking, cleaning and serving drinks. Could she keep the place going if he had to leave her to it? Pip would help a bit until he went to college and Janet gave her mother a hand in the bar sometimes, but Peggy would still find it hard to run this place alone.

Laurence had hoped to retire when they were in their mid-fifties. He'd been putting a bit by for years, but he didn't stint his wife or his children and the savings pot wasn't by any means big enough yet. He couldn't afford to give up, which meant that Peggy would try to struggle on if he had to return to the Army.

One thing he was certain of; he wasn't going back unless they forced him. Laurence grimaced as the memories flooded back of lying in muddy trenches with his boots soaked through and chilled to the bone, as dying men cried like babies for their mothers and everyone else just endured. He didn't think that any man who'd seen the horrors of that war would ever forget it. All they could do was push the memories into a tiny corner of their minds.

Shaking his head to clear it of unwanted pictures, he finished making up the fires and then went off to have a wash and a shave. Maybe he was worrying for nothing. He should put the idea of war right out of his head and think about Christmas. Peggy would want her usual party in the pub for Christmas Eve and despite regretting the loss of a night's trading, Laurence couldn't deny her. She wasn't asking for a week's holiday at the sea; he'd offered her the chance to go with the children when they were smaller, but she never wanted to take the time off.

'Mornin', Mr Ashley,' Nellie said, coming into the back yard when he opened the gate ready for the brewery delivery. 'Nippy, ain't it? I reckon as we'll 'ave a bit of snow afore nightfall.'

'I shouldn't be surprised if you're right. Only a couple of

weeks to Christmas so I suppose we should expect it...'

'Don't remind me,' Nellie said with a cackle of laughter. 'I ain't got me shoppin' done yet – and I want to give my kids a good one this year. Pete's joined up and he'll be orf straight after – and Amy's daft enough to do the same.'

'Peggy has invited you all to her Christmas Eve party?'

'Gawd bless you, love,' Nellie said. 'She made sure I knew we was all invited. Your Peggy is a lovely girl, Mr Ashley.'

'I know,' he agreed. 'Come on in and put the kettle on. We'll all have a cuppa before we start.'

Laurence was thoughtful as he strode into the pub kitchen and stoked up the fire again. Nellie's son had got in early but a lot of others would flock to join up if the news over the next few months got worse. He hoped Pip wouldn't want to join up as soon as he could, though it was what he'd done himself as a young man; he'd been nineteen when it started and joined up as soon as possible, by which time he'd already started courting Peggy; they'd married on his first leave after he was sent overseas, though the kids hadn't come along until after the war.

Laurence had plans for his son, who was clever and could easily go on to college and make something of his life. He himself had settled for being landlord of the Pig & Whistle at the corner of Spitalfields Market and thought himself lucky at the time, but Laurence had a keen brain and often wished he'd been able to make more of his life; he certainly wanted more for his son. He wasn't exactly sure what, but something in an office away from the dirt and grime of the East End – an architect or something to do with aircraft. Pip had always liked planes and had quite a few he'd made out of balsa wood hanging up in his bedroom. Yes, a nice safe job was what Laurence wanted for his son, not lying in a filthy ditch with water soaking into your boots and the rats gnawing at the bloated bodies of men who had been laughing with you hours before. Laurence had seen enough of life in the trenches and he prayed it wouldn't happen to his son.

Laurence had had hopes of college as a young man, but his parents couldn't afford to send him, and he'd made damned sure his son was going to get the chance to stay on at school and take the entrance exams. He might be just an East End landlord, but if Laurence had any say in it, his son was going to do better for himself.

'Where have you been?' he asked as Peggy walked into the kitchen yawning. 'Nellie and me have got the kettle on. We thought you wanted yours in bed like a lady of leisure.'

Peggy ignored his sally and went to investigate if her oven was warm enough. 'I'm going to make some scones and soda bread this morning,' she said. 'I'll do a warming vegetable soup to go with them this lunchtime.'

'That will go down a treat,' Nellie said. 'With food like yours, Peggy, it's no wonder the pub is always bursting at the seams. We was just sayin' about it being nearly Christmas. I'm going to buy a goose this year if I can manage it. I want to give my boy a good memory to take with him.'

'Morning, Dad, morning, Mum.' Pip breezed into the kitchen wearing his school uniform and carrying a satchel over his shoulder. His dark hair was too long and brushed his collar, but it suited him and he was the image of his father as a young man; a bit like Clark Gable, Peggy always said. Pip was munching a piece of toast covered in dripping, which he'd made himself in their kitchen upstairs. 'Did you pack me any sandwiches, Mum?'

'Yes, they're in the cool pantry,' she said and smiled as her son pressed a greasy kiss to her cheek. 'There's a bit of shortbread and an apple as well as your cheese and pickle.'

'You're a star,' he said and then glanced at Nellie. 'I saw your Pete last night, Mrs Maggs. He told me he'd joined the Army. I wish I was old enough but I have to be eighteen and that's ages away. I hope they don't finish the war too quick.'

'It hasn't started yet,' Laurence said sharply, 'and I doubt it will so you can put the Army out of your mind, Pip. You're going to college.'

'If I pass all my exams over the next year or so,' Pip grinned. 'But there's bound to be a war, Dad – and it's the RAF I'll be joining. I want to fly…'

'You'll need all your exams for that,' his father said, feeling relieved, because if Pip's heart was set on flying he would have to finish his schooling before he joined up.

'Yes, I know.' Pip gave him the engaging grin that had half the young girls in the area in love with him. 'I'll stay on at school and go to college unless there's a war, Dad – but if it happens they'll need me and I'll join the RAF and train as a pilot, if they'll have me.'

'You should do as your dad says. With your brains you could design aeroplanes, better ones for the future,' his mother said fondly. She was trying to hide her anxiety but Laurence knew her too well, and so, he suspected, did Pip as he grinned and shot out of the back door.

Janet entered the kitchen as her brother left. She was smartly dressed for work in a slim tweed skirt and a plain grey coat, her fair hair curled neatly into a short bob. She had her mother's looks and an even better figure, her greenish-blue eyes deep with mystery as they swept over the people assembled in the kitchen.

'Have a cup of tea before you go, love?' Peggy offered but Janet shook her head.

'Mike is waiting to walk me to work,' she said. 'I've had the dregs of the tea you made upstairs, Mum. Pip drank most of it as usual...'

'I'll soon make you one.'

'Some of us have to go to work,' Janet said and threw a mocking look at her father as she flounced out of the room.

'You just watch your lip,' he barked, but Janet didn't bother to answer.

'That girl is asking for trouble,' Laurence said darkly, but actually he admired his bold, beautiful daughter and liked it that, though she looked like her mother with her honey-coloured hair that got lighter in the sunshine and greenish blue eyes – Peggy's eyes were bluer in his opinion – Janet took after her father in other ways. Janet wasn't afraid to say what she thought and nor was he. They didn't often quarrel, but there were lots of sparks when they disagreed.

'I expect she likes to get off a bit early so that she can walk with Mike,' Peggy said. 'I would sooner she hadn't got serious so quickly, but she's eighteen.'

'And she'll be a year or two older before she gets married so don't encourage her to think otherwise,' Laurence said. 'She's much too young to be wed.'

'I was married before I was twenty,' Peggy reminded him.

'You were different at her age.' Laurence looked stubborn and Peggy turned away to get on with her baking. He smiled to himself as he went through to the bar to start polishing glasses. Peggy knew better than to argue on that score, be-cause Laurence wasn't having his daughter go through the struggle he and Peggy had had to make ends meet when they were first wed. It wouldn't do Janet any harm to wait until she was at least twenty...

Chapter 3

'I've brought you some grapes, Dad,' Maureen said, smiling at the man sitting up against a pile of pillows. He didn't look ill but she could see he was fretting at being stuck in hospital. They paid into the doctor's panel and the treatment he was receiving at the hospital wouldn't cost him anything, but he would probably get a small bill for food and a night's stay. 'How are you feeling now?'

'Did you bring me a clean shirt?' her father said brusquely. 'They took mine away to wash because I spilled beer on it when I passed out – and I want to come home.'

'Has the doctor told you you can leave?'

'What is it to do with him or those interfering nurses? If they think I'm staying in here for a week and paying for the privilege they've lost their minds.'

'Oh, Dad, you were really ill last night; the doctor told me they want you to stay in for a couple of nights' observation.'

'I'll bet they do. I can't afford to be wastin' money like that, girl.'

'Would you rather be dead?' Maureen asked calmly. 'Because the doctor says you may have had a little heart attack and he wants to do some tests.'

'That's all nonsense. It was just me chest like normal... and you brought on me attack, always gadding out and never thinkin' of your poor old father...'

'That's not true,' Maureen said, but she spoke softly, not wanting to upset him. 'I only go out occasionally. Besides, Gran is staying with me and she'll be there to look after you if you're home tomorrow.'

'Not if, when,' he muttered and moved his legs beneath the blankets restlessly. 'I'm not stopping another night in this place. You go home and bring me that shirt and ask them what they've done with my clothes.'

'I expect they're in a locker somewhere. I'll ask, but you should have those tests, Dad. You don't want another attack, do you? Next time it might be more serious.'

He glared at her but inclined his head, giving in but refusing to acknowledge she was right. 'Bring the shirt anyway. I'm coming home tomorrow whatever they say.' He paused, then, 'So what did you come for?'

Maureen silently counted to ten. 'I just wanted to see you were all right and to tell you I'm managing fine. Gran is helping me and I went to the wholesaler myself and bought what we needed.'

Her father looked less than grateful as he barked, 'Where did you get the money and what sort of terms did you get? They'll cheat you as soon as look at you, girl.'

A nurse walked by carrying a used bedpan covered by a cloth, but the smell was unpleasant and Maureen understood why her father didn't want to be in there any longer than he had to.

'Oh no, Mr Stewart was very nice. He was sorry to hear you had been taken ill and showed me all the best bargains – and he gave me the same terms as always. I took the money out of the tin in your desk.'

'Oh, did you?' he said and his face went an alarming shade

of red. 'I'll thank you to keep out of my private stuff, miss.'

'I've put the invoice there for you to see and I returned the change,' Maureen said, unruffled. 'Don't upset yourself, Dad. I got some pink salmon cheap and I've sold most of it already.'

'I bet you didn't put enough on it,' her father grumbled. 'Just because you get something cheap doesn't mean you sell it cheap. You've no sense in your head at all, girl.' He plucked at the bedclothes agitatedly, as if he wanted to throw them off.

'I asked Mr Stewart and he said to sell it at our normal price so I did – we got one and sixpence on each tin, Dad. I thought that was good.' It was an excellent mark-up as they often got less than sixpence on tinned stuff and only pennies on biscuits and most other goods. Only the expensive chocolates they sold very occasionally for Christmas or birthday presents made more. Her father knew it too; she could see he was left with nothing to say until he added in a disgruntled tone, 'Let's hope it wasn't contaminated then...'

'Oh no, Mr Stewart assured me that it was perfectly good. He'd bought a big load from a new supplier at a special price, and he was selling it cheap to his regulars, but some people were still paying an extra shilling per tin.'

Her father made a sound in his throat that might have been satisfaction or disgust. Maureen hadn't expected him to approve of her purchases, but at least after that he listened in silence with only the occasional nod, when she told him that Mr Stewart had recommended they stock up on tins and sugar while they were readily available.

'I bought two dozen tins of golden treacle; it's useful for sweetening if you don't have sugar.'

'If I left you in charge you would bankrupt me in a month,'

her father grumbled when she'd finished, but Maureen knew he was satisfied as she bent to kiss his cheek as she wished him goodbye.

'I'll come again tomorrow.'

'Don't close the shop... wasting time...'

'It's all right, Gran can cope for a little while,' Maureen assured him. 'Now stop fretting and let the doctors do their work, Dad. We want you fit and well and home again.'

Her father grunted and Maureen left him. She was glad to be out in the fresh air again, because the ward had smelled predominantly of disinfectant but there was an underlying odour that hung about in the air of sickness and urine. The nurses and cleaners did their best, but it was always the same, especially in these older hospitals. The small windows were high and the walls painted with dark cream gloss paint, which made them easier to wash, but added to the jaded air where the paint had chipped off.

'Good morning, Miss Jackson. Have you been to see your father?'

Maureen looked at the man in surprise. She hadn't expected to see him here in the hospital grounds. 'Yes, I have, Mr Hart. I hope your family is well – no one in here?'

'Oh no.' Gordon Hart smiled at her concern. 'I just came to pay my bill. For my wife's last illness... she was here for a few days and they gave me time to pay. I could have got it free if I'd applied for assistance, but I'd rather pay for my lass's stay here. They were real good to her.'

'Yes, I'm sure,' Maureen sympathised with him. 'It must be difficult for you, Mr Hart. Coming here after...'

'Yes, and no. I'm over the shock of it,' he said and smiled at her. 'People are all so kind, and you've been a good friend, to my wife before she died – and to me. My mother always

29

tells me you never fail to ask after us when she comes in the shop.'

Maureen blushed as she saw the warmth of his approval. 'I like to ask after all my customers,' she said shyly. 'I expect you have to get back to work?'

'I'm on the evening shift today. It was nice speaking to you, Miss Jackson.'

'Oh no,' she said on impulse. 'Call me Maureen, please. Your mother always does.'

He looked pleased and tipped his cap. 'It's Gordon,' he said. 'I'll see you soon – Maureen.'

She was blushing, because she couldn't imagine what had made her be so forward. Never before had she asked a male customer to use her name, though some of them did; the bolder ones flirted with her when they came in at night to buy an evening paper or a packet of Woodbines. Maureen usually gave that sort a quelling look that kept them in line, but she rather liked Gordon Hart, and she'd felt so sorry for him losing his wife. She supposed he was in his thirties, at least ten or so years older than her, but he still had a youthful stride and he wasn't bad-looking when she thought about it. He had dark hair and eyes that looked warm and lit up when he smiled, and his mouth was generous and full, not tight-lipped like her father.

Gran was waiting for her when she got back to the shop. She was tidying a pile of magazines; people often spent time looking through them, but only a few actually bought them. Most just had a crafty look at the pages while Maureen was busy serving someone else.

'How's your father? Miserable as sin, I dare say.'

'Yes, he is – worrying about what they're going to charge

him, but the doctor says he has to have tests on his heart, so he has to stop in whether he likes it or not.'

'Gives us a bit of peace for a while.' Her grandmother smiled wickedly. 'Oh, there was a young man in here earlier asking for you – tall, very dark hair and soft grey eyes. He was a soldier by the looks of him...'

'Did he give his name?' Maureen could think of only one man who resembled her gran's description.

'Rory, I think he said; just popped in for some cigarettes, while he was in the area. Told me he used to live a few streets away, but he's based down south at the moment. Must be one of your old school friends I should think, because he asked how you were and if you still worked here.'

'Oh...' Maureen hadn't known Rory was in the Army. She'd heard nothing of him since he'd married a girl called Velma, whose mother lived in Thrawl Street. 'Yes, I went out with him a bit before Mum died. He married a girl I knew at school.' Maureen's heart was thumping as she went into the back kitchen to fill the kettle. If only she'd been here when Rory came in... and yet even as pictures of his handsome face crowded her mind and a feeling of aching longing filled her, she knew it couldn't matter less. In fact, it was probably for the best. Nothing had changed in Maureen's life and anyway, Rory was married.

'Pity you weren't here to see an old friend,' Gran said, coming in behind her to cut a few slices from the bread. 'Do you want a sandwich, love – or would you rather have a piece of toast to warm you up?'

'I'll have a sandwich,' Maureen said as the shop bell went. 'I'd never get to eat the toast while it was warm.'

When she went through to the shop she saw Peggy waiting to be served and another woman she knew only slightly. The woman didn't always shop there but popped in when she'd forgotten something. She asked for two candles and a box of matches and left looking disgruntled at the price of ninepence.

'She was telling me her gas meter had gone wrong,' Peggy said. 'I bet all it needs is a couple of bob but she probably spends all her money on other stuff and she's waiting for next week's wages off her old man.'

'She doesn't often shop here, because she wanted credit the first time but I said we didn't give it.'

'You're probably the only shop she doesn't owe money to,' Peggy said and then caught herself up. 'Oh, I shouldn't have said that, Maureen. It was mean of me, but she tried it on with me too – her and her husband.'

'We had some nice pink salmon in yesterday.' Maureen changed the subject. 'I've sold most of it but I kept a couple of tins under the counter in case you fancied it, Peggy.'

'Laurence likes the red best,' Peggy told her, 'but if I make sandwiches with lettuce and cucumber, he'll never know the difference. Thanks, love, pop them in my basket – and I'll have a pound of cheese; that's still my best seller in the bar, with my own pickle. I'm going to make a cheese flan tomorrow and some cheese puffs – that should keep them going while I'm at the church social in the evening. Are you comin'?'

'Gran says I am.' Maureen smiled as she added the rest of the items on Peggy's list to her basket. 'You'll have a lot to carry, Peggy.'

'Oh, I can manage; it's not far.'

'If Dad would have a boy to help he could deliver daily.'

'I shouldn't want that,' Peggy said. 'I like doing my

shopping. I'm going to the market on the way home. There's a good fishmonger on a Thursday.'

'Yes, I bought some skate on my way back from the hospital,' Maureen told her. 'Gran loves it cooked in black pepper butter with green capers, and I thought it would be a treat for us. She's helping me while Dad's unwell.'

'It's a good thing you've got her. You know me and Laurence would help whenever we could, but your gran is a good 'un.'

'Yes, she is,' Maureen agreed as she took Peggy's money. 'I'll see you at the church social tomorrow then.'

'I tell you what, Anne and me will call for you – about half seven?'

'Yes, lovely,' Maureen agreed. 'Thanks, Peggy. I'd much rather come with you two.'

'Much better,' Peggy said, picked up her basket and left.

Gran came through from the back with a mug of tea and set it on the counter. 'Drink that while it's hot, love. That Peggy Ashley is still a good-lookin' woman. You'll be all right with her and Anne Riley for company. It's what you need, my girl – more company and Anne is nearer your own age.'

'She's twenty-eight,' Maureen said, 'but Peggy never seems middle-aged, does she?'

'It's keeping the pub I expect, keeps her mind lively.'

Maureen nodded as she sipped her tea and mentally reviewed her clothes. Women wore nice dresses to the church social, and there was usually a bit of dancing, and she only had one decent dress. It had hung in the wardrobe since the last time Rory had taken her dancing at the Hammersmith Palais. She hadn't felt like wearing it after their split, but it was a waste and nothing else was good enough; she ought

33

to have bought a new dress before this, but it hadn't seemed worthwhile...

*

Maureen looked at herself in the deep emerald green dress with its full swirling skirt and almost took it off again. She was a different girl in this, younger and carefree, and it reminded her too much of Rory. Yet nothing else in her wardrobe was special, because she hadn't bothered to buy anything much for years. The blue dress she'd been wearing on the rare occasions she went anywhere had a nasty stain on the skirt. Her father had spilled beer on it when she'd put it in the kitchen to iron, and she'd never been able to get the yellowish-brown mark out.

Taking a deep breath, Maureen lifted her head. She wasn't going to change out of the best frock she had; determination not to give in to this useless longing for the past came to her aid and she looked for the pale cream suede shoes she'd worn with the dress. They were lying at the back of her wardrobe, also unused for three years.

Maureen took her purse and went through to the sitting room, doing a little twirl for her grandmother. 'Will I do, Gran?'

'You look a proper treat, love,' she said and then they heard the bell ring. 'That will be your friends. Off you go, love, and have a good time.'

'Thanks.' Maureen kissed her soft cheek, grabbed her coat and went down to join her friends in the street.

'It's chilly tonight,' Peggy said and Anne greeted her with a smile. 'We'll soon be in the warm though. I'm looking forward to this evening.'

'So am I,' Maureen said and linked arms with her friends. 'I love the Christmas feeling everywhere now, don't you? Most of the shops have their decorations up. Dad won't let me do a proper Christmas window but I usually manage a few sprigs of holly and a bit of cotton wool just to look like snow.' They paused to look in the window of Mrs Tandy's wool and baby shop; she'd decorated it with a crib surrounded by some ancient figures of the shepherds and a silver star hanging overhead. 'Look, she has the same things in every year. I remember them when I was a kid...'

'I suppose she can't really afford to buy anything new, because I doubt if she makes much out of her shop. If you want to see some lovely displays you should take a bus ride up the West End on a Sunday and walk round; it's all sparkle and glitz and the toyshops are wonderful with their grottos and Santas,' Anne said and shivered, squeezing Maureen's arm against her. 'It feels cold enough for snow. My room is never warm. I'm thinking of finding somewhere else to live but it's not easy to find a decent room at a price I can afford.'

They walked up the lane, passing the new hairdresser's shop, which had holly and tinsel in the window, the lawyer's office, which never seemed to open, the derelict bakery that everyone grumbled was an eyesore and the cobbler's, two doors down from Peggy's, crossing over there to the corner of Crispin Street.

'It's rotten having to live in digs,' Maureen sympathised.

Anne's parents had both died when she was young and she'd been brought up by her Uncle Derek and Aunt Irene. Aunt Irene had died while Anne was away at college training to be a teacher and although she visited her uncle at least once a week, mostly on a Sunday, she lived in a bedsitting room in a house near the school.

'It's a pity your auntie died,' Peggy murmured.

'At least I have my independence,' Anne said, 'and I'm near the school. If I lived with Uncle Derek, I'd have to catch a bus every day and he's a bit of a fusspot. His housekeeper looks after him and we have dinner together most Sundays. I cook and give Mrs James the day off to be with her family.'

'You're better off on your own even if your room is chilly,' Maureen said. 'At least you can come and go as you please...'

'What are you doing for Christmas?' Peggy asked them. 'You're both invited to my party, of course. Shall you go to your uncle, Anne?'

'I have every year,' Anne said. 'One of my college friends asked me to spend the holidays with her in the country, but I'd feel bad if Uncle Derek was alone...'

'You're nearly as bad as Maureen,' Peggy laughed as they approached the welcoming lights of the church hall. 'Here we go then; I'll bet you won't be cold tonight, either of you.'

Maureen followed her friends through into the large room where the social was being held, feeling a buzz of excitement as she heard laughter and happy voices. The large room had been decorated with paper chains and silver stars, and was the kind of affair that people brought their children to; some groups included grandmothers and grandfathers, as well as children as young as four and five. For the moment they were all settling into their seats or, in the case of the younger men, fetching drinks from the bar. Soft drinks for the women and a half of beer for the men themselves, but nothing stronger. The idea was for everyone to have a good time, but drinking alcohol wasn't encouraged.

In a little while some of the older women would play games with the children, and the men would go off to the next room and have a game of darts or dominoes, and then someone would put some records on and the younger men and women would have a dance at one end of the hall. For a start they would just chat and grab the chance to meet people they normally seldom saw, and then last of all, the tombola draw would begin for prizes. It was the signal that the evening was over and afterwards people began to drift away into the cold night. This being Christmas the tickets were two shillings each and the prizes included a goose and a bottle of sherry as well as lots of smaller things, like a bar of chocolate and some packets of sweets. It meant that almost every family ended up with a little prize of some sort. The stalwarts of the church committee worked hard to fund these treats. However, it was the goose and the sherry that attracted interest and Peggy bought three tickets, one for herself and one each for her friends.

Maureen tried to give her the money, but Peggy wouldn't take it; it was her treat and she also bought them all an orange juice, before taking her seat amongst the card players. Men and women played whist and gin rummy for counters and there was a prize of a large box of chocolates for whoever ended up with the most counters at the end of the evening.

Maureen and Anne both refused the offer to join the card players and sat close by, half an eye on what Peggy was doing and half an eye on the children playing team games. There was a lot of enthusiastic shouting from their end of the hall and after a while Maureen got up and wandered down to watch. The children were playing Blind Man's Bluff and there was a lot of laughter as they stumbled around trying to catch someone. One little girl was running round excitedly but unable to catch anyone until she came to Maureen, who didn't try to avoid her. She clutched her skirt, gave a shout of triumph and tore off her blindfold.

'Got you,' she said. 'You're "it" now.'

'Oh no…' Maureen shied back. 'I wasn't playing…'

'You've got to now, because you're "it",' the girl said and Maureen realised it was Shirley, Gordon Hart's little girl. As she hesitated, he came forward and took the blindfold from his daughter. His eyes were laughing as he motioned to Maureen to turn round.

'You were fairly caught, Miss… Maureen,' he told her and placed the scarf round her head so that it covered her eyes. Then he spun her round three times and gave her a gentle push. 'Off you go and catch someone…'

Maureen couldn't help smiling. It was ages since she'd played this game and she was suddenly caught up in the spirit of it, darting this way and that and making a grab at thin air until she started to use her ears and was able to detect giggling to the side of her. Making a swift swoop, she caught a young boy and was able to pass on the blindfold. As she began to get her bearings again, she heard the music start and then Gordon Hart was at her side.

'I didn't know you were coming this evening.'

'I wasn't sure,' Maureen said, smiling. 'Dad is still in the hospital and Gran is at home.'

'You look lovely,' he said, a faint flush in his cheeks. 'Would you like to dance? It's a barn dance and I can manage that…'

'So can I,' Maureen said. 'I can just about waltz but I'm not much good at the tango or some of the other fancy steps they do down the Palais.'

'Nor me,' he said. 'Me and Shirley's ma always had a couple of dances at the social, but we never went down the Pally. It wasn't my style – or hers really.' The Palais or Pally, as everyone called it, was Sam Harding's *Palace de Dance*, a posh name for a rather run-down dance hall that served drinks in the bar every night of the week and often had popular singers to entertain the regulars.

'Thanks, I wouldn't mind dancing,' Maureen said and took the hand he offered.

Gordon did the barn dance well enough for it to be enjoyable. He might not think of himself as a dancer but he was light on his feet and she enjoyed the set of three dances they did before everyone stopped for a breather and another drink.

Gordon fetched a drink for them both and came to stand beside her as she re-joined Anne. Peggy glanced across at them and waved. She looked pleased with herself and a few minutes later, she gave a crow of triumph as she won her hand yet again and gathered up her counters. She gave them in to be counted and came to sit with Maureen.

'I thought I'd let someone else have a go,' she said. 'I could do with a drink, what about you, Anne?'

'Let me fetch you both one,' Gordon offered and went off before they had time to answer.

'Nice chap, Gordon Hart,' Peggy said. 'It was sad him losin' his wife like that – so young...' She shook her head as they watched Shirley skip up to her father and saw him buy her a drink with a straw and a lollipop on a stick. 'She seems happy enough though.'

'Shirley is bright,' Anne said and looked at the father and daughter thoughtfully. 'She was a bit reserved to start with, but that was because she'd just lost her mother, and she's fine now.'

Gordon was bringing back drinks for all of them on a tray. He handed them round and then placed the tray on a side table.

'It was nice to see you, ladies,' he said. 'Shirley is getting

39

a bit tired. I'm taking her home as soon as she's finished her drink.'

'Not stopping for the draw?' Peggy asked.

'Oh, I'll get my winnings if I'm lucky,' he said. 'My mother is stopping on with her friends for a bit, but Shirley's had a little cough so I think I'll get her back to bed.' He finished his drink. 'Goodnight then, Maureen. I'll call in the shop tomorrow.'

'Goodnight, Gordon,' Maureen said and was conscious of her friends' eyes on her. 'Thanks for the dance and the drink.'

She watched as he walked to collect his daughter and the two of them left the hall together. It was a pity he'd had to go home so early, because she wouldn't have minded another dance with him.

'Oh, they've started the music again,' Anne said and looked longingly at the dance floor. Her toe was tapping in time to the beat and Maureen was about to ask if she wanted to dance with her; it wouldn't look out of place, because quite a few women danced with each other or with their children, but just then a young man in a soldier's uniform came up to them and her heart jumped as she looked up and saw it was a man she knew. He'd hardly changed in the three years he'd been away, and the look in his eyes made her feel breathless.

'Maureen,' he said in the deep voice she recalled so well. 'I didn't expect you to be here. I asked Aunt Sarah and she told me you hardly ever come...'

'Rory...' Maureen gasped. 'Gran told me you came into the shop...'

'Yes, I was just passing. I'm on leave and I've been visiting my cousins... would you like to dance?'

Maureen stood up, her mouth dry and her heart

thumping wildly. She was shocked to see him here when she'd been imagining him far away, and she wouldn't have expected him to ask her for a dance, because of the way they'd parted in anger.

'Thank you,' she said. 'I can just about manage a waltz.'

'And the barn dance.' Rory smiled wryly. 'I remember I was trying to teach you the tango... but I dare say you've forgotten?'

Maureen swallowed hard. This wasn't fair! It hurt to be reminded, to hear him speak as if it was just yesterday, and they had been nothing more than friends.

'No, I haven't forgotten,' she said in a whisper and her heart jerked as his arms went about her. For a moment Maureen closed her eyes and it all swept back: the nights when Rory had taken her dancing or to the flicks and then walked her home in the dark, making the most of their precious time together. He'd asked her to marry him almost as soon as they met, but she'd insisted on saving for the white wedding her mother wanted her to have – and then it was all suddenly too late.

Tears caught at her throat and stung her eyes, but she held them back. She should never have agreed to dance, she thought wildly. It was just laying up misery for the hours when she was alone. Rory was married and this was wrong. Had she been braver she would have torn herself from his arms and left him then and there, but she couldn't bring herself to make a scene. She thought he might say something but he didn't, simply holding her close in the way he always had, as if nothing had happened.

As the music ceased Maureen drew away from him. She breathed deeply to steady herself. 'That was nice, thank you – but I'd better get back to my friends.'

'Was that your husband and little girl I glimpsed you with earlier?'

'I'm not married, Rory,' Maureen said softly. 'I told you I wasn't ready to marry, but the truth is I can't marry anyone...'

'Why?' He gripped her arm as she would have left him. 'I've always wondered why you did that, Molly.'

'Don't.' She nearly choked as he said the pet name only he had ever used. 'Please, don't call me that – and let me go.'

'Not until you tell me...'

'My mother died and my father needed me,' she said, knowing it was what she should have told him three years earlier. 'I have to look after the shop and him.'

'You could have done that and married me,' he said and she could see the veins corded in his neck. He was so angry. 'If you cared... why just let me think you didn't?'

Maureen shook her head helplessly, because she couldn't answer. 'It hardly matters now, does it?' she asked. 'You didn't take long to replace me.'

'No, I didn't,' he said and released her, a strange look in his eyes. 'You're right. It hardly matters now...'

Rory turned and walked away, leaving Maureen staring after him feeling as if she wanted to scream or run to him. Yet she knew that was stupid because nothing could change the facts. She'd allowed the man she'd loved – still loved – to slip from her life because she'd been traumatised by her mother's death and her father's demands. He hadn't waited to discover why but had gone off and found himself another girl and married her.

'Are you all right, love?' Peggy asked as she went and sat down next to her. 'What did that soldier say to upset you?'

'Don't you remember him?' Maureen said faintly. 'He's

Rory... you remember we were nearly engaged...'

'He broke it off after your mother died.'

'No,' Maureen sighed heavily. 'That was my fault. It doesn't matter, Peggy. It's over and he married someone else.'

'Yes, I remember now,' Peggy said. 'What did he mean by asking you to dance when he's married? Is she here? His wife...'

'I don't know. I think they moved away after they married.' Maureen shook her head. 'Really, it doesn't matter.'

'I wish I could believe that.' Peggy looked doubtful. 'You still care; I can see that, Maureen. I bet it was your father's doing, wasn't it?'

'No, of course not,' Maureen said but she didn't sound convincing to herself. 'Well, he said he couldn't manage without me and...' She broke off, fighting the tears. 'Don't talk about it, Peggy. Listen, they're going to draw the tickets now...'

Peggy nodded, but Maureen knew her friend wouldn't leave it there.

The caller started drawing tickets from a drum and the prizes were claimed. Giggling children ran up to receive packets of sweets, a tin of biscuits and some of the pink salmon that Maureen had sold recently, and then the bottle of sherry. A number was called and Gordon Hart's mother went to claim her prize. Now only the big prize of a goose from the local butcher was left and the anticipation was sharp; there were gasps of disappointment when Peggy's name was called out and some muttering.

'Wouldn't you know it? She hardly needs it. Some people get all the luck.'

Peggy went up to receive her prize, which was an envelope

containing the voucher for a plump Christmas goose. She ignored all the comments and returned looking as pleased as punch.

'Nellie will be tickled pink with this,' she told Maureen. 'It's the reason I bought the tickets. She was hoping to buy one for her family this year and now she won't have to.'

'That's generous of you,' Anne said. 'I bet she'll be delighted with that, Peggy.'

'I know she will.' Peggy ignored a few dark looks as the friends went to retrieve their coats. 'I couldn't be more pleased. Besides, my Laurence prefers a turkey given a choice. I've got a cockerel and a turkey ordered for us, and another one for the bar.'

'We're having a cockerel too,' Maureen said. 'Dad won't eat turkey, says it's too dry, and goose is too fatty for him. It was a choice of a cockerel or a bit of beef and Gran likes a cockerel at Christmas. She makes a lovely chestnut stuffing.'

'Yes, we like that, too,' Peggy said with a sigh of pleasure. 'It won't be long now, girls. I'm really looking forward to the party. You tell your gran and your father to come to the party too, Maureen. We always have room for a few more on Christmas Eve.'

*

Alone in her room that night, Maureen sat before her dressing table and brushed her hair. Grey eyes looked sadly back at her. She felt as if a cloud was hanging over her and yet earlier, when she'd danced the barn dance with Gordon, she'd been happier than she had been for a long time. Why did Rory have to turn up and spoil things? Why did he ask her for a dance when he could just have ignored her?

44

He must know it was hopeless and far too late for there to be anything between them?

If Rory had ever cared for her, why had he got married so quickly? He'd sworn she'd broken his heart, begged her not to give him up – and then before she'd hardly had time to catch her breath she'd heard rumours that he was married and moving away from London.

It was all her father's fault! He'd made her feel guilty, responsible for his life and made her almost a prisoner in his shop. A flicker of resentment swept through her but she thrust it away. She knew he used his ill health to blackmail her, yet he was her dad and she couldn't just desert him.

She flicked away a stupid tear and got up, walking over to the bed and flinging back the covers. It was ridiculous to regret the past, foolish to wish that she'd told Rory the truth that night, explained to him the guilt and the need to help her father through their shared grief. Would Rory have waited if she'd begged him to? At the time she'd thought he would get angry and demand she keep her promise to marry him and leave Spitalfields, because Rory had always had ambition. She'd known he didn't want to settle for the life most people had round here. Perhaps he'd always intended to make the Army his life? Maureen didn't know. All she knew at the moment was that there was a huge ache inside her that wouldn't go away.

Chapter 4

Peggy looked round the bar at her friends and family. She thought how good it was to see that all the people of the lane had come to share Christmas with her and her family. There was Bob Hall from the cobbler's next door but one, and Mrs Tandy who ran the wool and baby shop at number seven; Mr Martin from number eight with his wife and son Deke and Jack Sawston, his wife Mary and son Robin – they had the bakery just round the corner from Mulberry Lane, but were such friendly people and regulars at the pub, that she'd invited them too. Maureen and Anne and Maureen's gran were there, and Alice Carter from number ten. Alice never missed a free drink, but she was always a good friend to anyone that needed help so Peggy was pleased to see her there. Mick Dobson had come with his three sons and two daughters, most of whom worked on the Docks in one capacity or another, and Ellie from the hairdresser's at number nine; she didn't live in the lane, but had done Peggy's hair the previous day. And there were also quite a few others from the surrounding lanes, some of whom Peggy wasn't strictly sure she'd invited.

She'd decorated the place with red paper chains and bunches of holly and a couple of helpfully placed sprigs of mistletoe for those who were courting or wanted to be. Christmas cards from customers had been pinned to one old oak strut behind the bar and there were red cloths on each table. A large bench stood at one end of the big room and was loaded with plates of food: cold ham, pink salmon with cucumber and corned beef sandwiches with dishes of pickles. Sausage rolls, cheese pastries and a huge pork pie, of which there was only a very small piece remaining, had occupied the other dishes, now largely empty. Peggy had made a big fruit cake, which she'd covered with nuts and glacé fruits and also a sherry trifle, and of course, her special mince pies.

The drinks had flowed all evening, beer for the men and sherry or a lemonade shandy for the ladies, with the occasional port and lemon or a whisky for those who asked.

'You put on a good do, Peggy,' Hilda Jackson said when Peggy came round with the mince pies again. 'I've eaten enough tonight to last me a month of Sundays.'

'Maureen won't let you get away with that,' Peggy told her. 'She's cooking a cockerel especially for you.'

'I know and I shan't let her down,' Hilda said and gave a cackle of laughter. 'I reckon she's got an admirer, but I'm not sure if she knows it yet.'

'What do you mean?' Peggy was mystified.

'He came into the shop this morning and gave me a little parcel for her – asked me to keep it as a surprise for her until tomorrow...'

'Oh, and who was that?' Peggy asked warily.

'Gordon Hart. I reckon he's sweet on our Maureen – and it's about time too. I'd like to see her wed afore I go.'

'Goin' somewhere nice, are you?' Peggy asked with an air of innocence and the old lady grinned mischievously. 'You know what I mean, Peggy Ashley. I thought you would agree with me – she needs a man or she'll be stuck in that shop looking after her father until she's an old maid.'

'Yes, but she needs the right one,' Peggy said. 'I'm not sure she needs a widower with a little girl and memories weighing him down.'

'He's a decent bloke,' Hilda said and frowned. 'There isn't anyone else that I know of and I'd like to see her break out before it's too late.'

'Yes, as long as she doesn't exchange one set of chains for another,' Peggy said. 'I want her to be happy too, Hilda, but I'm not sure Gordon is the one. I invited him this evening, told him Maureen would be here, but he sent a message to say Shirley was a bit feverish and he wouldn't be able to come.'

'Is the girl sickly then?'

'She's as fit as a fiddle, so Anne says; she knew the mother quite well, but both her father and her grandmother fuss over Shirley all the time – they're afraid of losing her to a fever like her mother, I suppose.'

'Understandable,' Hilda said. 'But I see what you're gettin' at, Peggy. Maureen doesn't need a marriage where she comes second all the time.'

'No, that's what I think. Besides…' Peggy shook her head, because it wasn't her business to tell Hilda secrets. If Maureen wanted her gran to know about Rory she would have told her. Not that anything could come of it if he was already married. Divorce was a dirty word round here and Peggy couldn't see Maureen getting involved in anything like that – unless she was desperate.

'Give us a song, Alice!'

Hearing the cries from all round, Peggy smiled as the elderly lady got to her feet a little unsteadily and began to sing her repertoire of songs from the music halls, where she'd learned them as a young girl. First of all she gave them a rousing burst of 'Burlington Bertie', then launched into 'Daisy, Daisy, give me your answer do', followed it with George Formby's 'When I'm Cleaning Windows' and then a rather wobbly attempt at Judy Garland's 'Over the Rainbow', before collapsing to a round of cheers and applause into her chair, and demanding another milk stout before she expired.

Leaving Hilda to sip her sweet sherry, Peggy hurried to supply Alice with her request, and then made the rounds with the last of the mince pies. As usual there wouldn't be much left after everyone had finished. She was a good cook and what's more she enjoyed it. It was a pleasure to give happiness to the people she cared for; her regular customers and neighbours were her friends and Peggy felt pride in the food she put before them and her family and she worked hard to make sure everything was as perfect as she could make it. This wasn't just a gathering of friends, it was like one big extended family, and they all knew each other; there wasn't much that went on in any of the homes in Mulberry Lane that everyone else didn't know about sooner or later.

It was Christmas 1938 and soon they would be into a New Year. Peggy hoped it would be as good as or better than the last one. Rumours of unrest and German activity in the arms race had unsettled her for much of this year. Surely there couldn't be another war just around the corner?

'It's nearly time to wind up now, isn't it?' Laurence asked, standing close to her. 'I've had a long day and so have you, love – and you've got the turkey to cook tomorrow.'

'Yes, I think it's last drinks time,' Peggy said, glancing at the clock. 'I'll just have a word with Maureen and Anne, and then I'll start clearing away.'

'I'll make a start. Some of this lot will move in unless we give them a few hints.'

Peggy smiled and looked round at all the contented faces. She was glad everyone had enjoyed themselves, but Laurence was right; they'd both worked hard all day and she was beginning to grow tired. Once upon a time she could have stayed up all night but she was feeling it; she must be getting older! Shaking her head at the gloomy thoughts, which were not allowed to penetrate at Christmas, she walked over to the table that Anne and Maureen were sharing.

'I just wanted to wish you a Happy Christmas,' Peggy said and took two small parcels from her wide skirt pockets. 'Thanks for your presents, which we'll open tomorrow – and we hope you like these...'

'Oh, you shouldn't, Peggy,' Maureen said. 'It's enough that you give us this party without buying presents.'

'They come with love and a lot of thought,' Peggy said, ignoring the comment. 'Now drink up if you want another one, because Laurence is about to call time on us.'

'Gosh, look at the time. It's nearly midnight,' Maureen said. 'I don't want another drink, thanks, Peggy. I'd better collect Gran and get her home. Dad went an hour ago. He was tired, because he only came out of hospital a few days ago; he told me to stay as long as I wanted, but I didn't realise the time. Goodnight, both of you, and have a lovely day tomorrow.'

'See if you can get Alice home safely too,' Peggy said. 'I think she may have had just a little too much milk stout...' The sound of Alice's cheeky banter with her neighbours seemed to confirm it and Anne went off to see if she could persuade her to go with them.

Maureen kissed Peggy's cheek and then went to winkle

her grandmother out of her chair, smiling indulgently as the old lady protested at being made to go out into the cold night air.

One by one Peggy's neighbours and friends left and then it was just the three of them: Peggy, Laurence and Janet. Pip had helped out earlier with the preparations but then gone off to have fun with his friends. Laurence carted most of the dirty dishes into the kitchen and dumped them in the sink to soak. Thankfully, Nellie had washed up quite a few earlier before Peggy sent her home with her son and daughter, who had come by to collect her and have a drink after visiting friends elsewhere. Nellie hugged Peggy, telling her again how thrilled to bits she was with the lovely plump goose Peggy had given her a voucher for.

'It was the best in the shop,' she'd told Peggy when she collected it that morning. 'You did me proud, lass.'

'I'm glad it was a good one,' Peggy said.

Now she smiled at her family and agreed that the work could wait for the morning.

'We'll all help tomorrow,' her husband said and put his arm about her waist, which was still comparatively slim for a woman who had had two children and enjoyed her food.

Peggy paused as they passed under a bunch of mistletoe and she received her kiss. She smiled up at him in contentment; it had been a wonderful evening. She just hoped it wasn't the last of her Christmas parties...

*

Upstairs in her bedroom, Janet unwrapped the small parcel that Mike had given her earlier that evening, telling her to open it on Christmas Day. Well, it was just Christmas, Janet thought, because her watch told her it was twenty minutes past the hour. She was tired but she knew she wouldn't sleep unless she opened her present from Mike. It was a piece of jewellery, she was almost sure of it, but not the engagement ring she'd half hoped for, because the box was the wrong shape.

Opening the velvet box inside the wrapping paper she saw the bright silver bangle lying on a black bed and took it out with a little cry of pleasure. It was marked sterling silver and embossed with a pattern of vines and leaves, and quite lovely. Her slight disappointment that he hadn't got her a ring melted away as she slipped it on her wrist and held her arm up to admire it.

'Not in bed yet?' her mother said as she put her head round the door. 'Did Mike buy you that? It's lovely...'

'Yes, it is,' Janet said, beaming with pleasure. 'I couldn't wait until the morning and it is Christmas, isn't it?'

'Yes, my darling, it is,' her mother said. 'I think you're a lucky girl. He seems a nice man.'

'I really love him, Mum,' Janet said and skipped over to kiss her mother goodnight. 'I hope you and Dad will like your gifts. Pip and I clubbed together to get you both something nice.'

'We haven't opened them yet,' Peggy replied, smiling at her, 'but having you kids around is all I need, love. Now get some sleep, because you never know what Father Christmas may bring you if you're good.'

Janet laughed as her mother went off. She got into bed still wearing her new bangle. It felt nice on her arm and she didn't want to be parted from it, although she wouldn't wear it for work on the Docks in case it fell off or got damaged.

She slid it up and down her arm, enjoying the feeling that she had Mike's gift here in bed with her; it brought him closer, making her remember all the things he'd said to her about wishing he could wake up in bed with her on Christmas morning. She knew he wanted to make love. He'd been more and more passionate when they were alone of late, his hands slipping up under her jumper to release her bra and caressing her nipples with the balls of his thumbs. The sensation made Janet tingle and press her body against his and it was getting harder to stop him going all the way.

'I want you so much, Jan,' he'd whispered when he'd broken away from her, causing her to gasp with frustration. 'But I'm not going to be daft. We're going to have a decent house and new furniture, and a bit in the bank for when the babies come. I don't want to live the way my folks did when I was small.'

Janet knew Mike had been one of the East End's many kids that went to school with no boots and their clothes patched or torn. His parents had struggled to bring up three children, especially after his father was diagnosed with TB and sent away to an isolation unit for treatment. He'd died there and Mike's mother had simply wasted away over a period of six years, dying when he was twelve. His grandmother had done her best to look after the children but wasn't equal to the task and Mike and his sister Rose were taken into care within a year. His elder brother was sixteen and ran away to join the Navy. He hadn't been heard of since and Mike had no idea whether he was still alive. Rose had gone into service at fifteen and married when she was nineteen; as the youngest and brightest of the three siblings, Mike had used his opportunities at the orphanage to learn all he could so that he was offered an apprenticeship on the ships. He worked as a welder in a shipyard repairing and refurbishing luxury ocean liners, and Janet knew he was highly thought of as a skilled man.

Her future was all mapped out, shining and promising, a future of glowing happiness, she thought as she snuggled into her feather mattress. Mike was all any girl could want and she was lucky that he loved her. She might wish they could be married sooner, but Mike said another year should just do it and surely she could wait until then. She would be nineteen next October and he might get her an engagement ring for her birthday, and then perhaps they could plan a Christmas wedding – or at least early in 1940.

Janet groaned as she buried her face in her pillows. Even next Christmas seemed such a long way off when she was young and passionate about life and wanted to be Mike's wife so very much.

*

Maureen opened her parcels on Christmas morning. Her father had given her four pounds to buy herself a new dress or whatever she wanted, which was the best thing he could have done, because he would have no idea what she would like as a gift. She'd knitted him a nice sweater in grey two-ply, which had taken ages but looked as good as a shop-bought jumper – at least that's what Gran had said when she'd seen her wrapping it.

'He doesn't deserve all you do for him, love,' her grandmother told her. 'He doesn't know how lucky he is.'

Maureen had persuaded her to stay on over Christmas

though she'd been home a couple of times just to check on her things and make sure it wasn't freezing up. Her neighbour had been keeping an eye on the place and banking up the range just enough to keep the pipes from freezing.

'Vera is a good friend,' Gran told Maureen. 'She's got me spare key and if ever I was bad she'd know and be in a like a shot to see what she could do.'

The narrow streets where her gran had lived much of her life were like that, neighbours going in and out of the little back-to-back houses and everyone knowing each other's business, but also looking out for their friends and neighbours. Maureen had often spent time with her grandmother when she was little and she knew just what it was like, the houses often in poor condition with damp patches on the walls and crumbling plaster on the ceilings, but kept as clean as possible by the hardworking women who called them home.

Maureen's grandmother had given her a small gold locket on a fine chain. 'It's not new,' she'd said when she gave it to her on Christmas morning after they got back from Peggy's to find the house in darkness and Henry Jackson in bed. 'But it was given to me by your grandfather when we wed and I want you to have it now. It's always been lucky for me and perhaps it will bring you a bit of luck, love.'

Maureen thanked and kissed her. She'd knitted a pink lacy bed jacket for her grandmother and bought her a pair of fluffy pink slippers and a box of her favourite fruit jellies.

Anne Riley had given Maureen a book of poetry and Peggy had given her a lovely scarf and a pair of silk stockings. She felt a bit guilty as she saw the lovely quality of Peggy's gifts and remembered that she'd made her a pair of red woollen mittens. To receive presents like these after that lovely party, well, it was almost too much, but Peggy wasn't just a friend, she was like a matriarchal figure to them all, always there ready to help anyone in trouble.

Maureen had left the parcel from Gordon Hart until last, but when she opened it she saw that it was a pair of soft leather gloves in dove grey. Maureen tried them on; they were a bit big in the fingers but that didn't matter. She liked them and felt sorry that she hadn't given him anything – but of course, she had sent a bag of sweets for Shirley. Maureen hadn't dreamed that he would buy her a Christmas gift: why should he? They hardly knew each other, but just recently he'd been giving her some warm smiles that showed he liked her.

For a moment she allowed her thoughts to dwell on the night of the church social and the dance she'd had with Rory. For several days she'd half-expected him to come into the shop but he hadn't, nor had he sent her a card for Christmas. Of course he wouldn't, after all this time; she was a fool to have looked for him. The dance had been a moment of impulse, probably regretted as soon as it was over. Rory resented the way she'd dropped him, but he wasn't pining over it. The best thing she could do was forget him.

Chapter 5

Christmas was over and Peggy felt that a cloud hung over them all. Nellie was tearful, because her children had gone to their new jobs and she was having to get used to living alone, and Pip was preoccupied, always with his head in books about aircraft and flying, but worst of all Laurence's mood had got worse recently.

He'd been pleased in the first few days of January 1939, because he'd won another first prize in *The Times'* crossword and this time he'd got two hundred and fifty pounds, but after that he seemed less and less cheerful, and Peggy suspected it was the news in the papers, which seemed to incline more and more to the idea of war.

'You can look after the bar this morning, can't you?' Laurence said, coming in behind her. 'I've got some errands but I should be back to help with the lunchtime trade.'

Peggy wanted to ask how she was supposed to fit in her cooking as well as serve full time in the bar, but she kept quiet, because she didn't want another row and there had been a couple recently.

'All right,' she said but she was annoyed that he hadn't let her know earlier. 'I'll have to ask you to watch those pasties, Nellie,' she said when Laurence went out without bothering to thank her.

'I'll do that for you, love, and I can pop the shepherds' pie you made in when they're done.'

'Thanks, Nellie,' Peggy said and smiled at her as she took off her apron and went through to the bar. Two of the regulars were drinking beer and as she wiped down a couple of tables the door opened behind her. She turned to see two officers in a different uniform to anything she'd seen before; one of them must have been in his fifties and clearly carried a high rank, the other was perhaps ten or fifteen years younger and Peggy thought a captain. He was the one who smiled at her and came towards the bar, asking if he could have two whiskies.

'Yes, of course, sir,' Peggy said and smiled. 'Excuse me, but are you American?'

'Yes, we're over here for a few weeks to talk to… on business,' he said and extended his hand. 'Captain Able Ronoscki, pleased to meet you, and my companion is General Bromwich.' Peggy was impressed; they didn't get many generals round here.

'It's nice to meet you, Captain, and to have our American friends in the bar.'

'We're on a tour of London,' he said. 'My general wanted to see everything while he's here and he's heard a lot about the East End and its people – so when it came on to rain and this place looked so clean and quaint, we thought we'd like to sample the local atmosphere.'

Peggy nodded, not sure she liked hearing the Pig & Whistle called quaint, but at least she'd passed the cleanliness test and that pleased her, because it was a constant fight against the filth of the streets.

'Yes, I'm afraid it's a wet day,' Peggy said, 'but don't believe what people say, it doesn't always rain…'

At that moment Nellie came in bearing a tray of hot pastries and the younger officer wrinkled his nose appreciatively. 'That smells like apple pie to me?'

'Nearly right,' Peggy said and laughed. 'Apple and raisin turnover; I'm serving them with double cream this morning. Can I tempt you to try it – as a goodwill gift?'

'I'll have to take a rain check on that, ma'am,' he replied with a smile. 'We don't have time – but I'll be back, and that's a promise.'

Peggy smiled as she handed him the drinks and his change. She liked him and his warm smile had lifted her spirits, making her feel that perhaps things weren't so bad after all...

*

'Good morning, Maureen,' a voice said as she was tidying the magazines and newspapers. 'Lovely day, isn't it?'

'Yes, almost like spring,' Maureen agreed with Gordon as she turned. 'I know it's only the end of January, but I put some washing on the line earlier and it feels like a spring day.'

'It will change,' he said and chuckled. 'It was freezing last week, remember.'

'I expect the washing will freeze if I leave it out too long.'

'I'll take some Tom Thumb drops for Shirley and a packet of Woodbines,' Gordon said. 'Oh – and I'll have a newspaper too. Did you see the government are talking about doubling the territorials? I shouldn't wonder if they'll bring in conscription before too long.'

'You think there will definitely be a war, then?'

'With the way Germany has been carrying on?' Gordon said, raising his eyebrows. 'The authorities wouldn't be offering us all free air raid shelters if they didn't know it was coming. Haven't you heard the talk about evacuating the school children to the country?'

'Anne Riley was telling me about it,' Maureen sighed. 'She and her headmaster went down to somewhere in Devon. They're part of the committee charged with finding places for the kids. Apparently, they've been offered the use of an old house. The owner lives abroad much of the time and he's said they can take it over for some of the children in the event of a war.'

'That sounds a good idea, keeping children from a certain area together,' Gordon said, 'but I think most will have to go to whoever will take them – unless their mother goes too.'

Maureen could see that he was anxious. 'Are you thinking about Shirley?'

'Yes, she's not quite five and clings to us,' he admitted. 'Ma was sayin' she might go with her if it comes to it. I'm under forty so I'll probably be called up when it happens, even if they go for the younger men first.'

'Oh, Gordon, I'm so sorry,' Maureen said. 'It's a worry for you, because of your daughter.'

'I've spoiled her since we lost her mother, hardly let her out of my sight – and now she cries if I'm not there. She likes Miss Riley though, so if there was a chance of her going to that place she might be all right. She attends the play groups they have at the school now for children of nearly five years; because Anne takes the five and six year olds in class, she also looks after the pre-school kids, who go to learn that school isn't frightening. It's only twice a week, but we thought it was a good idea. Shirley's gran could go to the country too, of course, but... well, she's not as young as she was and she's got a bit of a cough...'

'Nothing seriously wrong, I hope?'

'It isn't consumption, but bronchitis can be very bad in the winter. If I'm away in the Army and anything happens...' He looked upset. 'If her mother had been alive I wouldn't have been so bothered, but you see how it is...'

'Yes, of course I do.' Maureen sympathised with him. 'Leave their address with us, Gordon. We're your friends, Anne, Peggy and me – and we'd look out for her.'

He smiled at her. 'It's good of you to say so, Maureen. Shirley needs a mother but...' He left it open but the look he gave her seemed to be hopeful as if he was expecting something. Maureen didn't know what to say, because she believed they were friends – but the only man she'd ever considered marrying was Rory. 'Well, I dare say we'll think of something.'

'We all look after each other in Mulberry Lane,' Maureen said. 'None of us would see harm come to her, Gordon.'

'You're a lovely girl, Maureen.' His smile was warm now and Maureen felt the colour rise in her cheeks, because she sensed he was seeing her as more than just a friend. 'I'll be in tomorrow...'

Maureen went back to tidying the shelves. Nothing changed much for her and she couldn't see it happening, because even if Gordon had wanted to court her, she couldn't abandon her father – and she would never forget Rory. How could she when she'd loved him so much?

Her grandmother came in just before lunchtime. She'd been down to the market and her basket was filled with bits and pieces.

'That looks heavy,' Maureen said. 'Go through to the kitchen, Gran, and I'll make us a cup of tea.'

'I bought a nice piece of material I thought you'd like. If you do, I'll make a new dress for your birthday.'

'I'm sure I shall,' Maureen said. She followed her grandmother into the kitchen and filled the kettle, placing it on the gas ring to boil. 'I've got some lovely apple tarts that Peggy brought me – I'll put them out for us. If I'm lucky we'll get a few minutes to eat them.'

'I wanted to make you a special dress,' Gran was saying as she unpacked the brown paper parcel, 'and I saw this...' She held up the pretty pale lemon voile and the darker silk rayon that would be used as the petticoat underneath.

'Oh, that is so delicate,' Maureen cried, touching it in delight, 'a lovely summery material.'

Her grandmother started to say something and then cursed as the shop bell went. 'Well, it will be ready for your birthday. Eat your pie, love; I'll answer that,' she said as the door went again.

A few seconds later she was back and shaking her head. 'It was just your father. He has taken some stuff into the stock room. I told him to come and have a cup of tea first, but you know what he is.'

She packed the delicate material back into a parcel and loaded it into her basket as Henry came in. He glared at them both as Maureen got up to pour him a cup of tea.

'Hadn't you better get back to the shop? Anyone could have me till open and the money gone before you'd stir.'

'The girl is due a little break and a cup of tea,' his mother said, giving him a stare equally as hard as that he'd given Maureen. 'Leave her be, Henry. She's not your slave and you'd better remember it or one of these days she'll be leavin' you.'

'Aye, I know she'd go if anyone would have her,' he muttered and took one of the pies. 'You never made this, girl. I suppose that Peggy Ashley's been round here again.'

'Peggy's pastry is much better than mine, and she knows I like apple pies.'

The doorbell went just as her father reached for the last of the treats and Maureen left him munching as she went through to the shop.

'Anne.' She was pleased to see her friend. 'How are you? You look well.'

'I've just got back from the country,' Anne told her. 'We went all over the place looking at buildings to house the kids, but some are too derelict to use. My headmaster thinks it would be better to keep as many of them together as possible. If he can get the go-ahead, we shall be going down with the infants... and our school will be used for other purposes for the duration.'

'The duration?' Maureen caught her breath. 'You're talking about war, aren't you? Gordon Hart was in earlier and he says he'll be called up before long. He thinks the younger men will go first and then the under forties.'

'Yes, that's Mr Miles' opinion too,' Anne said. 'He's in his early forties so he doesn't expect to be called up immediately, but he told me he may volunteer; a lot of men will. Mr Miles wants to make sure the children are settled before then so that he can go with an easy mind. I expect Mr Hart feels the same.'

'Mr Miles sounds a nice person,' Maureen said, because she didn't know Anne's headmaster at all. 'Why does he think of volunteering?'

'He's always been lovely to me.' Anne blushed slightly. 'He only saw the tail end of the last war and has always felt guilty, because his two elder brothers were killed – and so he says he'll volunteer to do his bit. He did his training last time but then the Germans surrendered and he never got to fire a gun in anger.'

'I see...' she said doubtfully.

'It doesn't make sense to me either,' Anne admitted, 'but I've said I'll transfer with the kids if we get permission to move the school.' She looked up at the white-painted shelves. 'I popped in for a box of those Havana cigars for my uncle; I know they're expensive but he likes them and it's his birthday – and I'll have a jar of black and white humbugs please.'

Maureen got the items down from the shelves and wrapped them in brown paper, taking Anne's money. 'Well, good luck with the evacuation then...'

'Yes, I think we may need it.' She was about to leave the shop, then turned. 'Are you coming to the school concert? It's on Saturday afternoon.'

'I'd like to. I'll ask Gran if she'll get Dad's tea.'

Maureen watched as the door closed behind her and went through to the back. If she wasn't mistaken, Anne liked Mr Miles more than a little, which was unfortunate, because he was married. She'd heard someone say that he and his wife had no children despite being married for twelve years, but she'd never met either of them, because they didn't live anywhere near Mulberry Lane. She hoped nothing was going on between them, because it was bound to end in heartbreak for Anne.

About to leave the shop, she saw someone hovering out-side. He glanced in and their eyes met, her heart jolting as she recognised Rory. He realised she'd seen him and hesitated, giving her a half-hearted wave before he turned and walked away. Maureen rushed to the door, jerked it open and called his name.

He turned, walked slowly back to her and looked at her awkwardly. 'Did you want to see me?' she asked.

'I'm in London for a couple of days to visit a few friends, but I wasn't sure whether you'd want to see me. They've given us leave and told us that afterwards we'll be on standby for overseas duty, but they did that before and then it all blew over.'

'Oh, Rory,' Maureen said, a break in her voice, because she'd thought perhaps he'd come to see her. 'Everyone says it's inevitable that we'll be at war before the year is out.'

'It's just a matter of when if you ask me.' Rory shrugged his shoulders. 'The peace at all costs brigade keep sayin' that Hitler doesn't want war with us, but he'll just keep on attacking countries one by one until he gets us all – unless we make a stand, and there's only us to do it.'

'That's what Peggy's husband says.' Maureen felt sick with fear. She didn't know how she would feel if he went to war and was killed, even though they could never be together.

'It won't be long now. Tell your father to get stocked up, Maureen, because once they start attacking our supply ships things will get short here.'

'I've been telling him that for ages, but he hates spending money...'

'Was it really because of him that you broke us up?'

'Yes.' Tears stung her throat and eyes. 'You don't know what he was like after Mum died.'

'I can imagine.' Rory sounded bitter. 'I might not have understood emotional blackmail once but I do now...'

'What do you mean?' she faltered, but he shook his head.

'Nothing that matters. I was wondering if you would have a drink with me this evening – it's my last before I go back down south.'

'I'll tell Dad I'm going round to Peggy's,' Maureen said

without understanding why she was so quick to agree. 'We'll meet there and have a drink if you like?'

'I should like it, even though I don't have the right to ask.'

'It doesn't matter,' Maureen said. 'It isn't as if you've asked for a date. We're just having a drink for old times' sake.'

'Yes.' He smiled oddly. 'I'll be there at seven and I'll wait.'

Maureen nodded and went back into the shop. She closed the door and entered the kitchen. Her father and Gran seemed to be having an argument over something and he looked as if he were losing.

'Who was that then?' he asked, glaring at her.

'Anne Riley. She wanted a box of those special cigars for her uncle's birthday.'

'Why did you go out after her?' His eyes narrowed in suspicion.

'She left her purse on the counter,' Maureen lied. 'I had to call her back.'

She could see he was still suspicious but he didn't say anything more. Maureen's tea was cold so she poured herself another and took a few sips just as the bell went. This time she had quite a little queue of customers and when she finally finished serving them her grandmother came out of the kitchen.

'I'm off home then, love,' she said. 'Your father is coughing a lot. I've told him he should go to the doctor but he refuses to listen. He'll end up a prisoner of his bed and then he'll expect us to wait hand and foot on him, just like his father.'

'Never mind, Gran,' Maureen said and laughed softly. She didn't know why she was feeling so happy because it was ridiculous. Rory only wanted someone to spend a few hours with before he went back to camp. She wondered why his wife hadn't come to London with him, but perhaps she preferred to stay at home... unless Rory had come to London just to see Maureen? Had he hoped to strike up some sort of relationship because of that dance at the Christmas party?

The thought sobered her instantly, because she wasn't the sort of girl to take a man from his wife and children, and yet a tiny seed of happiness flourished inside her because she would see Rory that evening.

*

Peggy served the young soldier with his half pint of bitter and watched him take it to a table in the corner. Somehow she wasn't surprised when she saw Maureen enter a little later and go straight over to sit with him. She'd guessed the girl was still in love with him when she'd seen them dancing at the church social, but she hadn't thought anything would come of it.

Rory had got up and was coming towards her. 'I'd like another half, please, and a port and lemon for Maureen.'

'Yes, of course,' Peggy said. 'What are you doing back in London? How is your wife?'

'Velma's just had a baby so she's not feelin' too good. I've got a bit of business this way so I thought I'd look up some old friends while I was here.'

'Right... does Maureen know about Velma?' Peggy gave him a steely look.

'Yes, of course. What do you think I am?'

Peggy wanted to tell him what she thought of a man who took his former girlfriend out when his wife had just had his kid, but she held her tongue for Maureen's sake.

'You go back and I'll bring the drinks to you. Want anything to eat?'

'We'll tell you when you bring the drinks,' Rory said frostily and returned to the table.

Watching the way Maureen's face lit up, Peggy's heart sank. She was really fond of the girl and this was the way to bring trouble on herself. Married men were no good for girls like her. Yet she couldn't interfere. Maureen was sensible; she would know it wasn't likely to come to anything, but she was still going to be hurt.

'Lost a shilling and found sixpence, have you?' Laurence said cheerfully.

'No, I'm just concerned for her.' Peggy looked at Maureen. 'But you don't need to tell me, it isn't my concern.'

She picked up her tray, collecting glasses as she went and stopping to have a word with Maureen before returning to the bar. Seeing her daughter enter with her boyfriend, she wondered at the look in Janet's eyes and her worries for Maureen were wiped out instantly. What on earth had happened to make Janet look like that?

'Something the matter, love?'

'Mike has just told me he's going to enlist in the spring. He's heard a whisper they're going to start conscription soon and he wants to get in first so he's given two months' notice at his firm and he's going to join the Navy.'

'Why the Navy?' Peggy asked. 'I thought he'd talked about the Army?'

'Yes, he did, but his elder brother Nick came to see him at work this mornin' and told him he should go in the Navy. He reckons it's a good life and Mike was talkin' about him all the way home, how good he looked and the exciting places he'd visited all over the world.'

'Nick hasn't bothered with his family for years. You told me he never sent a penny back to help any of them. It sounds to me as if he's just bragging. Is he stayin' around for a while or what?'

'Mike says it was just a flying visit, but Nick said he's goin' to stay in touch and he made a big impression on Mike – he can't think about anything except joining the Navy. I don't want him to go, Mum.'

'Well, he may change his mind again,' Peggy said, thinking that Mike was a fool. From her memories of the last war, the Germans would target their ships to stop them bringing in supplies of food and other vital goods. Last time it had been gunboats against gunboats, flagships against flagships, but from the stories in the papers about the German U-boats being a threat, Peggy thought they would probably be an even bigger danger this time round. 'If he knows how upset you are he'll wait until he's called up, surely.'

'He wants Dad to let us get married now,' Janet said, looking anxious. 'I've told him Dad won't let me marry until next year at the earliest but Mike thinks he can talk him round.'

Peggy gave her a rueful smile. 'I'll have a word with Laurie but he says you're too young – and with Mike going off to the Navy he's bound to say you must wait...'

'I begged him to wait and see if the war really happens, but he says it will and if he waits he won't get the placement of his choice. I don't want him to go, Mum, but if he's determined – I want to get married first.'

'Well, I'll talk to your father but you know what he's like.' Peggy shot her daughter a sympathetic look and glanced back to where Maureen had been sitting. It was abandoned, the half-empty glasses left on the table.

She wondered where they'd gone, but she had more on her mind now than Maureen's unwise affair with a married man... not that she knew it was an affair. Yet somewhere inside her Peggy felt that he wasn't the man for her friend, even if he hadn't been married. She wasn't sure why, but she didn't much like him.

*

'Won't you just think about it, love?' Peggy begged her husband as she sat in front of her dressing mirror and brushed her hair later that evening. The waves sprang up under her brush as if they had a life of their own. 'I know she's only eighteen, but if he joins the Navy she might lose him...'

'And that's just why I've stuck to my guns,' her husband said. 'She could be a widow before she's hardly a wife and left with a child to care for.'

'But at least she would have had a little bit of happiness.'

'Are you saying we treat her badly? I think she's had everything she wants – and she's still only a child, Peggy. They can easily wait another couple of years before they think of marriage.'

'And what happens if he's killed at sea? Hilda Jackson's younger brother ran away to sea at fifteen and he was killed after a few months... fell from the rigging, broke his neck and died instantly.'

'I doubt that will happen to Mike. He's not likely to be as vulnerable as a fifteen-year-old youth, is he?'

'No, but accidents happen...'

'You're only convincing me that I'm right.'

'Janet really loves him; it's not just a crush for her.'

'I've told him no and I mean no,' Laurence said firmly. 'I'll give my permission when she's nearly twenty and not before.'

'But that's more than a year, and they're in love – what happens if they get too impatient and anticipate their marriage vows?'

'He'd better not or I'll thrash the bugger!'

'Why not let them marry when she's nineteen? I was only eighteen when we married.'

'Janet isn't like you – you were more sensible,' Laurence grunted, his patience at an end. 'Come to bed, Peggy. I'm tired...'

Peggy knew when she was beaten, because once Laurence had made up his mind there was no changing him. He'd been set against Janet getting married before there was any talk of Mike joining the Navy and now he was adamant.

Peggy crawled into bed feeling defeated. She turned on her side and hunched her shoulder when Laurence laid a tentative hand on her. He grunted and rolled the other way, taking her refusal without argument. She didn't know how he could even expect her to make love after he'd been so intractable. Janet was crying in her room even now. Peggy was certain she and Mike must have quarrelled after they left the pub together.

Oh, why did people in high places have to make wars? If there was no talk of war Mike wouldn't have thought of joining up, and perhaps in October, when Janet was nineteen, her father would've given in and let her get married.

She felt a dark cloud settling over her and the ones she loved. Even Maureen was letting herself in for more hurt and pain, and Peggy felt helpless. She didn't want to be at odds with her husband, but if it came to taking sides, she was with her daughter, because when you were young being separated from the man you adored hurt too much. She'd had to endure the separation when Laurence was fighting in the first war – and that was something her daughter was very likely to experience if all the rumours and speculation were true. If war was coming, it was only fair that Janet should have a little time of happiness first.

Chapter 6

Maureen turned over in bed and sighed. She didn't know what she'd expected when she'd gone to meet Rory in the pub, but it wasn't that Rory would spend half the evening telling her about his mates in the Army and asking her what she did with herself when she wasn't working. She'd expected he would try to explain himself, tell her why he'd gone off and got married so suddenly, but he seemed determined to behave as though they were mere acquaintances. Maureen went along with it and wondered why she'd even agreed to come, but then it had all changed and their feelings burst through the polite masks they'd both been wearing.

After leaving Peggy's place they'd walked by the canal, enjoying the fresh air and the pleasure of being together. The sky was light with a nearly full moon and she'd held his arm, feeling as if the years had rolled back and nothing had changed between them, except that he didn't pull her close or try to kiss her, as he would've done when they were courting. She supposed she should be pleased that he behaved as if they were just friends, because it was all they could be.

'What made you decide to make the Army your life?' she'd asked at last, because she couldn't ask the questions she wanted, longed, to know the answers to.

'I needed to get away,' he said simply. 'Things weren't

right for a while and I decided I'd be better off in the Army as a regular.'

'Your – your wife didn't mind?'

'We weren't getting on,' Rory said and sighed. 'I may as well tell you that the reason I married Velma was because she said she was havin' my kid...'

'Your child!' Maureen smothered her gasp of shock. After he'd spent so much time talking about other things this sudden change to personal details made her feel oddly light-headed. 'That's why you got married so soon after... I had no idea.'

'Yes,' he said in a curt tone. 'I was cut up when you dumped me like that, Maureen. I went a bit mad, drinking and women. After I woke up in Velma's bed, she helped me sober up a bit, told me she'd always liked me, and we went out for a while – and then she swore she was pregnant so I married her. It seemed the right thing to do and you didn't want me...'

'Oh Rory, that wasn't true. I've told you...'

'But you didn't tell me then, did you?' he said harshly. 'Anyway, she had a fall a few weeks after the wedding and lost the baby. She was very ill and the doctor told me she was more than five months gone – and that meant it couldn't be mine. I demanded the truth and she told me. She was already pregnant when she took me home when I was drunk. We didn't even sleep together that night, not until a week or so later...'

'I see.' Maureen bit her bottom lip. 'How did you feel about that?'

'I felt I'd been made a fool of for a second time and I went off in a temper – and that's when I joined up. After I cooled down I told Velma. She thought I was going to desert her, but

74

she wasn't fit to work because of how ill she'd been. I told her I'd send her part of my pay, at least the Army does that – and I left her to get on with her life.'

'So you've parted then?' Maureen's insides were tangling themselves into knots.

'Well, it isn't quite like that,' he admitted. 'Some months ago she turned up at barracks and begged me to take her back, said she'd always loved me and like an idiot I agreed. We moved into married quarters and...' Rory hesitated, looking at her uncomfortably. 'She was having another kid and this time it was mine...'

Maureen felt as if he'd punched her in the stomach. Several minutes passed before she could bring herself to ask, 'So why did you ask me to have a drink with you?'

'Because one day in the future I may find myself on the wrong end of a German bullet,' Rory told her. 'After I saw you again before Christmas I couldn't get you out of my head. I'd made myself hate you because I thought you didn't care, but then you told me it was your father's fault and I just wanted to be with you. I didn't intend to tell you any of this but...' He gave a sigh of despair and ran his fingers through his thick hair. 'I wish I hadn't taken her back, Maureen. If I'd thought there was a chance, I would have demanded a divorce but it's too late now.'

'Yes...' Maureen swallowed hard. 'It is much too late...' She felt the tears building inside her and rounded on him, hitting at his chest with her fists in a sudden frenzy of grief. 'Why did you come back at all? Why ask for that dance and why tonight when you knew... you knew it was too late, didn't you? Didn't you?' She collapsed in tears and his arms went about her, just holding her close. She could smell his own special scent, the musk of fresh sweat and his hair oil and just him. He was Rory and she loved him, but at this moment she hated him too.

'I shouldn't have, I know that,' he confessed. 'I suppose it was something inside that drove me to discover why you did it, little Molly...' His tone made the name a caress and she felt the pain sharp and real inside her.

'Rory, don't,' she begged. 'I can't blame you, because I know it was my fault. If I'd been braver – if I'd stood up to my father...'

'Why didn't you tell me the truth? I'd have sorted him. If need be we'd have had him with us, or moved into the flat over the shop. I loved you, Maureen. I loved you so much it broke me inside.'

'I'm sorry, I'm sorry...' She wept and then pulled away from his arms, raising her head as she blinked away the tears. 'What can we do? What are you goin' to do? Tell me, Rory – are you going to stay with her?'

'What choice do I have?' he asked, looking miserable. 'She's only just had my daughter, in January. I can't just walk out on her, and I wouldn't abandon my own kid.'

'What about me? You can't expect that I'll... be your bit on the side,' she ended bitterly.

'No, of course I don't. I never meant anything like that when I came to the shop. I just wanted to explain but it was too difficult and I was walkin' away when you came out to me...'

'Yes, I know,' she said dully. 'Me again – I'm a fool, aren't I?'

'Not in my eyes. I think you're the loveliest girl ever,' Rory told her and for a moment the sincerity rang in his voice. 'But I'm not the sort of bloke who walks out on his wife when she's the mother of his kid – you wouldn't want me to be, would you?'

'No,' she admitted and sighed. 'You wouldn't be the man I love if you could...'

'So,' he said as they stood outside the shop. 'This is goodbye, then?'

'It has to be,' she agreed, meeting his eyes determinedly. Tears trickled down her cheeks. 'Please, don't come here again, Rory. I don't think I could bear it...'

'I'm so sorry,' he murmured softly and her heart broke again. 'I didn't mean to hurt you. I was angry and then... I couldn't help myself...'

'You'd better go, then...'

'Yes...' He stared at her for a moment then, as if he had no will to resist, he reached out and drew her close, kissing her softly on the mouth and then deepening the kiss until it became a hungry raging need that made her knees sag and she fell against him. 'Forgive me...' he whispered and released her, leaving her feeling weak and destroyed as he walked away.

Maureen stood for a moment, trying to recover her composure before she went in. Her father would be up and waiting for her, because it wasn't late. If he saw her like this he would know instantly that something was wrong. She unlocked the door and went in, bolting it behind her before she walked through to the kitchen. A hot milky drink might calm her down a bit, although nothing was going to take away the pain of Rory's confession.

Oh, why had he taken Velma back when she'd so obviously used him? Yet it was still Maureen's fault, because if she'd been stronger he would never have gone off the rails as he had and ended up in bed with the woman who was now his wife.

Maureen put some milk on to boil and then washed her

77

face in cold water. She carried her mug of cocoa upstairs to her bedroom. Her father hadn't been sitting up for her after all, and after a moment or two listening she suspected that he wasn't in the flat. She checked his room and, discovering that his bed was empty, went back down and made sure that the back door wasn't bolted. He would be very angry if he came home and found he couldn't get in, especially if she was sleeping.

Taking her mug with her, Maureen slipped in between the covers and sat up against the pillows to drink her cocoa. She stared into the semi-darkness, realising that nothing had changed. Her life was still as empty as before, with no chance of anything getting better. She might as well accept that she was going to be stuck here for the rest of her life looking after a man who didn't care two hoots whether she was happy or not.

*

'Can't you wait for a while?' Janet asked Mike when they walked to work together the next morning. 'I'm not askin' you to change your mind. I know you want to join the Navy like your brother, but can't you wait for conscription? Mum has promised she'll work on Dad and he might let us get married if you give him time.'

'Not from what he said to me,' Mike told her straight. 'I can see his point of view, Janet, but he hasn't thought about you – about what you want… we want…'

'I can't bear it if you go away now,' she said. 'Dad said you would be exempt from the call up if you're working on the ships. Yours is a protected trade and they will need welders of your experience even more if there's a war.'

'So you expect me to stay at home like a coward just because I can?' Mike said with a look of disgust. 'I do love you, Janet. I want to marry you. I want you bad, you know how much I care... but I have to fight for my country if war comes and if we all stayed at home there would be no one left to fight.'

'But you could be killed...' Janet wailed.

'If I stay I could be killed. My job isn't exactly safe. A lot of men get injured working on the ships, a few die of their injuries – and what do you think it will be like once the war starts? Hitler will bomb the dockyards for sure, and if I'm working there I could die in a raid.'

'If you loved me you wouldn't talk to me like that,' Janet burst out and gave way to noisy tears. 'You said you weren't going for two months. Oh, Mike, please wait for a while – please...'

'I'll wait a bit longer just to please you,' he said, 'but if I do – you must promise that we'll go away for a couple of nights, be together properly.'

'Give me another month or two and we'll go for a week-end,' Janet said. 'I'll think up an excuse for Mum – tell her I'm going to stay with friends.'

'Will she let you go?' he said. 'I was thinking if we just went off and slept together, perhaps your father would be forced to change his mind... especially if something happened.' He touched her face with his fingers. 'I know I should wait but I want you so much, Janet – and it just isn't fair to either of us. If I could, I'd run off with you and marry you, but we can't without either his or your mum's permission. Peggy wouldn't sign for us, would she?'

'If I worked on her she might, but it would mean a terrible row with Dad when he found out and I can't do that to her.'

Janet looked at him shyly. 'No, we'll do what you said...'

'If you were pregnant he'd have to give in.' Mike's eyes lit in a way that made her stomach lurch and any thoughts she might have had about a white wedding fled. Marriage was all she wanted, all she'd ever wanted since she'd met Mike, because she loved him so much. Nothing would make her happier than to be his wife and have his babies.

'He might,' Janet said and hugged his arm. 'Promise me you'll wait just that little bit longer before joining up? I'm so frightened of losing you...'

'I promise,' he said and grinned down at her as they reached the dockyard gates. 'Look, we'll talk about it again tonight. The worst that can happen is you get pregnant and then your parents will have to give in – not that I want it to be like that, but you know I'd marry you if it did, don't you?'

'Yes.' Janet nodded happily.

After their row the previous evening she'd wondered if he really did care about her, but she couldn't doubt it now. She reached up impulsively and kissed his cheek to the accompaniment of some catcalls and jeers from men clocking on to work nearby. Normally they made it a rule not to kiss or show affection when they parted, but this morning Janet didn't care. She felt reckless, because her father was being unfair. He said he was doing it for her own good, but Janet knew she would never be happy unless she was Mike's wife – and whatever it took to force her father's hand she would do it.

Chapter 7

Maureen was tidying the newspapers. She glanced out of the window at what was a miserable day for late April. It was drizzling with rain and she felt down in the dumps, as if there wasn't much to look forward to. Her life had seemed worse since that night with Rory, every day the same, hardly ever going anywhere unless it was the church social or down the pub for a chat with friends.

The Pig & Whistle was really the meeting place for everyone in the lane at night. During the day most people popped in the shop for a word, and when Maureen got a chance she went to see Mrs Tandy and bought an ounce of wool, and sometimes Gran would stand in so that she could go and have her hair done, but otherwise it was the same old routine.

She opened the paper and saw an article about a new film starring Merle Oberon and Lawrence Olivier, *Wuthering Heights*. It looked good and she thought she would ask Anne if she'd like to go to an early evening showing one day.

The door opened, setting the bell jangling, and Tommy Barton entered, eyeing her uncertainly as he jingled some coins in his pocket. His trousers had patches on the knees and looked as if they'd had a row with his shoes, and his hair was so long it was flopping in his eyes.

'Ma says 'ave yer got any damaged tins of corned beef or scraps of ham or bacon?' His cheeks were bright red and she guessed he hated having to ask the question.

Maureen thought for a minute. 'Can you wait a minute, Tommy, while I look in the back room?'

'Yeah, thanks, missus...'

Maureen went through to the store room. She wouldn't have dared to leave some youths of his age alone, but she knew that his mother would thrash him if he pinched from her shop. She looked round for anything damaged but it was all new stock. After a moment's hesitation, Maureen picked up a large size corned beef tin and smashed it down on the floor. It made a satisfying dent in the tin but didn't split it. Smiling, she took it back through to the shop and put it on the counter.

'That one is damaged,' she said. 'I reckon you can have that for a bob if you like.'

'Thanks.' He snatched it up quickly, as if he thought she might change her mind, and took his coins out. 'Have yer got any broken biscuits for the kid?'

Maureen sighed and picked up a packet of perfectly good bourbon creams and put them on the counter. 'One shilling and ninepence altogether.'

'You're a good 'un, Miss Jackson,' he said, counted his pennies carefully and left grinning.

Maureen hoped her father would never notice. He would kill her for throwing his profits away, but it wouldn't hurt him for once and at least the Barton family wouldn't starve today.

It gave her a little secret pleasure to know she'd done a good turn. Maybe her life wasn't all bad after all. She would go down to the pub that evening, and if Anne was there she would ask her if she wanted to see that film.

Peggy entered the kitchen to silence. Nellie hadn't yet arrived for work and she remembered that she'd gone to visit an old friend in the infirmary, because she'd been told the woman was dying.

'It may be my last chance to see her,' Nellie had told her the previous day. 'Irma has the lung disease and it's in the last stages so I want to say goodbye to her.'

'Yes, of course you must,' Peggy agreed instantly. 'Why don't you take the whole day off?'

'I'll come in when I'm back,' Nellie insisted, 'but I shan't be early because I'll need to fancy meself up a bit if I'm goin' visitin.'

'Where's Nellie this morning?' Laurence demanded harshly, bringing Peggy's thoughts back to the present. 'I didn't think she was ever late.'

'She's coming in later after she's visited a friend in hospital.'

'And you didn't bother to tell me. I'm only her employer...'

Peggy sighed, knowing that this had little to do with Nellie taking a few hours off work. She'd pushed him too far in the matter of Janet's engagement and he'd been like a bear with a sore head for the past few weeks. It was May already and the news in the papers seemed to get worse all the time. They were forecasting that Mussolini and Hitler were on the verge of signing a pact and the conscription bill was being brought forward, which meant that men of twenty to twenty-one would soon start to receive their call-up papers. Older men weren't required yet but it was only a matter of time. Laurence was brooding and the trouble over Janet just made things worse.

'I didn't bother you because you were busy and it doesn't

really matter to you if Nellie isn't here for a few hours,' Peggy said.

'It matters because there's too much work for one person.' He glared at her. 'I don't want you being too tired at night.'

He meant too tired to make love, which was another bone of contention between them. Peggy couldn't help herself, but his bad temper and stubbornness over Janet had turned her off. She just didn't feel like falling into a passionate embrace after he'd been grumbling at them all for the past couple of weeks. It was partly her fault for taking Janet's side, but why couldn't he try to see his daughter's point of view? If he'd offered to let them get engaged now and married in a few months she would have been happy, but the way he was carrying on Janet would be lucky to see a wedding ring on her finger before she was twenty-one.

In Peggy's opinion, Laurence was a fool to deny them their happiness and if anything happened to Mike, Janet was going to blame her father. Peggy wanted her family to be the way it always had been, loving and caring for each other – but she was determined not to give in over this.

She cooked breakfast for them both and slid the plates onto the table. Laurence looked at the bacon, egg and tomatoes and pushed it away with a growl.

'I'm not hungry. I'll just have a cup of coffee.'

Peggy snatched the plate up and thrust it on the drainer. She almost threw it in the waste bin but Pip came in from the yard, where he'd been mending a puncture on his bike, and washed his hands under the tap.

'That looks good,' he said, eyeing the cooked breakfast. 'No one want it? I'll have it.'

He picked up two slices of bread from the board, piled the bacon, egg and tomatoes on one and pressed them together, munching with evident enjoyment as he grabbed his schoolbag and left.

'That boy has no manners,' Laurence remarked sourly.

'He'll get indigestion,' Peggy said, 'but I suppose he's late again, no time to sit and eat properly. He reminds me of you when you first came back from the Army; you couldn't sit still for five minutes.'

'Don't remind me,' Laurence muttered. 'I'm going down the church hall this morning. They're havin' a meetin' about measures we'll need to take when the war comes. I think they want volunteers for wardens and suchlike.'

'Laurence...' Peggy's heart quickened with fear. 'It sounds inevitable when you say it like that...'

'Don't you listen to the news or read the papers?' he grunted. 'There's no point in hiding your head in the sand, Peggy. Hitler won't rest until he's conquered Europe and us, so we'll have to make a stand sooner rather than later.'

'If you take a job as a warden you won't get called up, will you?'

'Would it bother you if I was?' Laurence threw her a sulky look and she was reminded of Pip as a little boy. Something tugged at her heart strings and she went over to him, putting her arms about his waist and looking up at him.

'You know it would, Laurie.'

A sigh broke from him and his arms closed about her. 'I had enough last time. I don't want to go, but I'm young enough if they get desperate. I don't want to quarrel with you over Janet, love, but I don't want her to spend the rest of her life as a widow.'

'Just tell her she can get engaged on her nineteenth birthday and married next Christmas. Perhaps that will make her happy.'

'All right, if it's what you want.' He gave in reluctantly. 'If you've got some scones in the oven I could do with one with some butter and jam. I'll get the bar ready and then I'm off down the road.'

Peggy nodded, just relieved he'd come out of his mood at last.

*

'I've got us tickets for a special dance up the West End,' Mike said when he met Janet from work that evening. 'It's on Saturday. I thought we'd have supper afterwards and... find somewhere to stay for the night. You could tell your mum that you'll be late because of the show and she won't sit up for you.'

Janet's tummy did a flying leap and she gave him a nervous smile. Mike had kept his word and he'd put off joining the Navy for a few weeks so she had to keep hers. It wasn't that she didn't want to go to bed with him, she wanted it very much, especially when they'd been kissing and petting heavily, but talking about it like this made her feel apprehensive.

'You haven't changed your mind, have you?' Mike asked, his mouth going tight.

'No, of course not; it sounds lovely,' Janet said and hugged his arm to her. 'I do love you so much, Mike. I want us to be together that way... I love you more than you know.'

'Not as much as I love you,' he murmured, all smiles now. 'I've dreamed about this for months, Janet. I want you so much, my darling. Sometimes I can't sleep for thinkin' of how it will be for us.'

'It will be wonderful,' Janet said, more confidently than she felt. Mike was her first real boyfriend, the first one to

86

kiss her properly and the first one to make her aware of desire. 'I just hope you know what to do, because I don't.'

'We'll muddle through together,' Mike said diplomatically.

Janet suspected it wouldn't be the first time for him, but perhaps that was a good thing. He wouldn't need to practise on her. Although she'd never had any experience of sexual loving herself, she knew it could be both noisy and fun, because her bedroom was next to that of her parents and she'd heard them making love. She supposed they were both still attractive and young-looking, despite being quite old from her viewpoint, and she was glad they were happy, but she wished her father would be more understanding of her. Janet would much rather have been looking forward to her wedding than a secret night in a hotel somewhere.

'Will they let us have a room without luggage?' she asked anxiously and Mike grinned.

'You leave that to me, love. Bring a few things you'll need in your bag to work and I'll book in earlier and leave our case in the room.'

'You've got it all worked out,' she accused him, but with a smile on her lips.

'Yes, clever of me, wasn't it?'

He looked pleased with himself. Janet laughed, more to cover her nerves than anything. He wasn't taking a risk, but she knew only too well how much trouble she would be in if she got caught. That wasn't going to happen! Janet put it out of her mind. She was just going to think about having a lovely time at the dance – and then going to a nice hotel for supper and bed... a little shiver ran down her spine at the thought, but she wasn't sure whether it was fear or anticipation. After all, this was the man she wanted to marry so what could possibly be wrong with anticipating their marriage vows?

'You look lovely in that dress,' Peggy said to Janet when she came down that Saturday evening. 'Green always suits you, love, which is odd because it looks cold on me – but you can wear it.'

'Mike says it reflects the colour of my eyes and yours are bluer than mine.' Janet gave a nervous giggle as her mother leaned forward to embrace her. 'Don't worry if I'm late back, Mum. I've got the key – so don't wait up, will you?'

'No, I shan't do that,' her mother promised. 'I know you'll be quite safe with Mike and you're a sensible girl.'

Janet turned her head away as Pip entered the kitchen covered in bike oil. 'Don't you come near me with those greasy hands...'

'I'll give you a little colour in your cheeks, Sis.' Pip ran at her with outstretched hands and a look of devilment in his eyes. Janet gave a shriek of dismay and dodged away, making her brother laugh. He let her go and went to the sink to wash his hands, but the little diversion had covered the awkward moment.

Mike arrived for her then, looking smart in a navy pin-striped suit and very shiny black shoes. He presented Peggy with a box of chocolates and gave Janet a tiny spray of flowers to pin to her dress. After Peggy had pinned them on for her the couple left hand-in-hand and went running down the road to catch their bus up to the West End. Mike had a sparkle in his eyes as he looked at her and Janet smiled back, feeling like an excited little girl at the treat of an evening at the dance, the nightclub and then...

Thoughts of what would happen later made her stomach churn with nerves, because she wanted it all to be perfect.

Janet had been strictly brought up and she didn't know a lot about sex other than that her mother seemed to enjoy it, and she was nervous of doing or saying something wrong. Mike would still love her afterwards, wouldn't he? He wouldn't think she was cheap for agreeing to spend the night with him?

Janet managed to push her anxious thoughts to the back of her mind. She loved dancing and was looking forward to the dance itself. Nor was she disappointed when Mike produced his tickets and they were passed through to the magnificent ballroom. This was nothing like the Pally where they usually went and she understood then just how much trouble he'd gone to, to make the evening perfect for her, and her nerves fled all at once. Mike loved her and it was going to be wonderful.

As Mike drew her into the throng of happy dancers, Janet let herself relax and enjoy the evening. She felt as if she were melting with bliss as he held her close and they moved over the highly polished floor in time to the soft music. She thought the band was playing a Glenn Miller song and Mike was humming along, obviously recognising it too. He had a good singing voice and she was caught up in a kind of magic that seemed to wrap them both about in a shining bubble.

*

That bubble of happiness seemed to settle around them throughout the dance and the supper afterwards. Janet had never had supper this late in a hotel and it felt decadent and special, almost like a honeymoon – and she realised that Mike had intended it to be this way, so that she felt loved and precious.

The feeling continued as they went up in the lift to their room. Mike unlocked the door and they went in. He pulled her into his arms the minute the door had self-locked after them, holding her close so that she could feel the strength of his body and the bulge of his need. Janet was in no doubt that he wanted her badly and she felt the desire ripple inside her as his lips travelled down her throat and he licked the little hollow at its base. It was a delicate touch, light but very arousing, and the next moment she found herself reaching for his jacket, pushing it back from his shoulders. Mike shrugged out of it and turned her, unzipping her dress and slipping the shoulders down so that it slithered to the floor. Underneath she was wearing a bra and French knickers edged with coffee-coloured lace.

'Beautiful,' Mike said and his hands moved to cover her breasts, kissing the back of her neck and he moaned with need and longing. 'I love you, Janet. I'll love you all my life; I promise there will never be anyone else.'

She knew he meant every word and now there was no fear or apprehension as their clothes were discarded in two heaps on the floor and then they were kissing urgently. Mike swept her up and carried her to the bed, groaning in his urgency, and they fell onto it still kissing and clutching at each other in a frenzy of need.

It felt so good to be naked in his arms. She'd never known the touch of his skin next to hers and it felt warm and silky, hard but smooth as he faced her and whispered sweet words of love, his hands stroking and caressing until she was trembling, beyond thought of anything but him and their mutual need. Her body moved with his, calling out for fulfilment as he entered her with one hard thrust and she cried out at the sudden sharp pain, but he smothered her with kisses and once again she was panting and eager to meet him, to meet thrust for thrust with a sensual reaching of her inner self.

It was swiftly over the first time, because they'd both been in too much hurry, but after some laughter and a flurry of kisses they made love again, and again. In the end Janet couldn't remember how many times Mike had come into her. She just recalled the wonderful state of bliss she'd felt as they lay together afterwards and just held each other, too tired now for more and satiated by their loving.

Janet wasn't naïve and knew full well that she might fall for a child, but, as Mike had reasoned when they discussed making love, it would be very unlucky if she did so her first time and Mike promised to be careful, whatever that meant. Yet during their love-making, Janet hadn't even given it a thought.

She'd slept through the night afterwards, until Mike woke her with a kiss and a cup of coffee.

'What time it is?' she asked sleepily, not really realising where she was at first.

'Six thirty,' he said.

She groaned. 'I want to sleep for hours yet...'

'We need to get you home before your mother realises you didn't come in last night,' Mike said. 'I know, I know. I'd rather stay in bed with you for another two hours, but I'm thinking of you.'

'Yes...' It all came flooding back to her then and Janet felt herself getting warm all over. Last night she'd let herself pretend that it was her honeymoon, just as Mike had planned, but now she was faced with reality. She felt a faint flickering of apprehension as she recalled their passionate loving, but even if she had fallen for a baby, Mike wanted to marry her, so that was all right. A sneaking thought reminded her that if she did happen to get pregnant her father would have to let her get married. 'I'd better get washed.'

'I had a shower,' he said. 'It's quick and easy and wakes you up. You can use the shower cap and then it won't mess up your hair.'

Janet went through into the little bathroom that adjoined their room. She'd never been anywhere like this in her life; it was so posh and really did feel like a honeymoon hotel. The bathroom was sparkling clean. There were marble tiles on the floor and walls and the taps were chrome and shiny; white fluffy towels hung from a warmed towel rail and on the shelf above the bath there were tiny bottles of bath salts, shampoo and little soaps in paper with the hotel's name on them. Janet decided to slip a couple into her bag to take home, to remind her of such a lovely night. There had been nothing sordid or dirty about any of it and to her surprise she didn't feel any of that either; she'd thought she might, but instead she just felt happy. In her heart and mind, she truly belonged to him and felt as if they were married and she was sure he felt the same.

It was only when they parted outside the pub that the truth of what she'd done hit her. If anyone saw her arriving at this hour and mentioned it, her father would go mad. She just had to hope that because it was Sunday everyone was still in bed.

Letting herself in the back door, Janet held her breath as she listened. She couldn't hear any movement in the kitchen and knew that any other morning both her parents would already be getting things ready for work. As it was Sunday they wouldn't open until eleven and would close from one to six in the evening, and then stay open until nine at night. The laws on licensing were quite strict, but Janet's parents made their own regulations and restricted the hours on Sundays to the minimum. However, she could hear nothing and crept up to her room, where she quietly took off her dress and threw it over a chair, slipping into bed and closing her eyes.

Janet feared the door would fly open and her avenging parents would storm in and demand to know where she'd been until this hour, but no one appeared and within minutes she'd fallen asleep.

Chapter 8

Peggy lay listening to the sounds of Laurence's breathing. He was sound asleep. Saturday was always a late night and this was his one chance of a lie-in. She heard the sound of Janet's soft footsteps coming upstairs, of her bedroom door opening and closing, but she didn't jump out of bed to accuse her daughter of staying out all night. The resulting argument would've woken the house and the last thing Peggy wanted was for her husband to discover what Janet had done. He'd been angry enough when Mike asked if they could get married, and Peggy knew she'd made things worse by trying to change his mind.

Laurence had finally agreed to think about letting them get engaged on Janet's next birthday, but if he knew she hadn't come home until this time in the morning he would be furious. There would be no chance of it happening then. No, Peggy would wait until she got a chance to talk to Janet alone so that she could ask why she'd stayed out all night. She could only pray that the girl hadn't done something stupid.

Peggy was almost ready to dish up the lunch that day when the chance came. Laurence was gently persuading the last of his customers it was time to go home, when Janet entered the kitchen wearing a flared skirt and a short-sleeved pink jumper.

Peggy turned to look at her as she got the cloth out and spread it over the table. 'And where did you get to last night, miss?' she asked severely and saw the flush creep up her daughter's neck. If that wasn't a guilty look, she wasn't born, Peggy thought and felt sick. 'I hope you haven't been stupid, Janet?'

'It isn't stupid to love someone enough to want to be with them all night, is it? Mike is going to join up soon. If he waits any longer he's afraid he'll get his call-up papers and then he won't get a choice where he goes.' The government had begun to conscript men of twenty to twenty-one years of age in April, because they had to be prepared if a war should break out; Mike was twenty-three and hadn't got his papers yet but he would soon enough.

'That is no excuse for staying out all night. Don't pretend you came in before morning, because your bed was untouched when I went to the bathroom at five o'clock.'

Janet held her head proudly. 'If I've done something you don't approve of, it's Dad's fault. I love Mike more than anything in the whole world – and I wanted him to know how much so I stayed up all night with him.'

'Is that all you did?' Peggy looked at her hard but Janet wouldn't answer. She didn't really need her to, because she instinctively sensed what her daughter had done. There was a new air about her this morning, as though she thought she knew what life was all about. Of course she didn't; there was a hell of a lot more to it than passion and sex, but Janet couldn't know because she was too young and at the moment she thought being in love was all that mattered. She would learn when children came along and she had to face the reality of all that marriage entailed.

'If your father knew you were out all night he would

forbid you to go out with Mike ever again.'

'You won't tell him.' Janet was suddenly all defiance. 'He can't stop me seeing Mike when I can – I should run away and find somewhere to live near his base and we'd be together, even if I have to wait until I'm twenty-one to marry.'

'That's a nice way to speak to your mother,' Peggy said. 'What have I ever done to deserve that, Janet? Have I hit you or shouted at you or made you go without anything I could afford to give you?'

'No, you've always been good to us,' Janet said and looked ashamed. 'I never meant to be rude to you, Mum...' She slumped down on the old sofa and put her hands to her face. 'I love him and he's going away soon. I read in the paper that war is inevitable. They're making plans to evacuate the school kids. Mike says we'll be in as much danger in London as he will at sea... but I'm afraid, Mum. I'm afraid he'll be killed and I'll never be his wife.'

'I know.' Peggy left the gravy to simmer and went to sit next to her, putting an arm about her shoulders. 'I've tried, love. I've pleaded and argued until I'm out of breath but to no avail. Your dad won't budge. Short of all-out war, I don't think there's any more I can do.'

Janet gave a shaky laugh. 'I don't want you and Dad to fight over it, but surely he can understand how we feel? How would he like it if it was him and you?'

'He wouldn't and nor would I, but he joined the Army at nineteen, and we didn't marry until he came home on a month's leave when he was twenty-one. He'd been out at the front for well over a year and a half by then, before that he was training down south somewhere and got a few short leaves, but all we had when he went overseas were letters. He'd been wounded a couple of times when they finally shipped him home for a rest. They used to stand them down for a while, treat minor wounds at field hospitals, and then send them back up the line. There was no such thing as a visit home then, unless you had what they called a Blighty, a wound bad enough to send you back home.'

'It must have been terrible, Mum.' Janet looked at her curiously because her parents never talked about the last war.

'It was, especially for the poor devils out there.' Peggy drew a deep breath. 'The war was nearly over by the time Laurie was fit to fight again, but it was months before the men were allowed to go home and live their own lives, and your father had to go back out there. I heard him crying the night before he left; it took something out of him, Janet. I wasn't quite nineteen when we married, but my folks didn't care as long as he could earn a decent living and keep me and any children we had, and we were lucky enough to get the pub.'

'Why can't Dad be like that?'

'I suppose you're still his little girl and he can't bear the idea that you'll leave home and belong somewhere else. It's silly – but I can't force him to change his mind.'

'I know.' Janet brushed away her tears. 'I'll get on with setting the table and then I'll dish up the vegetables. You'd better watch that gravy, Mum, or it will burn...'

Peggy sprang to her feet and rushed to the pan. She had a heavy heart as she watched her daughter move about the kitchen. Janet wasn't a bad girl and she could only hope that nothing went wrong because of what she'd done the previous night.

*

'Did you get away with it?' Mike asked the next day. He kissed Janet's cheek, looking at her pale face. 'Did your father catch you creeping in?'

'No, but Mum knows. She'd seen the empty bed when she went to the bathroom. I told her we stopped up all night, but I'm not sure she believed me.'

'Well, maybe she'll persuade your father to let us get married before I leave.'

'She's already tried everything she knows,' Janet said mournfully. 'Mum is on our side, Mike – but Dad still thinks I'm a little girl.'

'He's selfish and wants to keep you at home for himself,' Mike said with a spurt of anger. 'I asked him properly. We could have run off to Scotland and married over the anvil.'

'I don't think it works like that these days, does it?'

Mike shrugged. 'It's probably too late now anyway. I saw the postie delivering an official-looking letter this morning just after I left the house. It's more than likely my papers – which means I'll have to be quick or I won't get a choice where they put me.'

'What do you mean?'

'I'm giving my final notice this morning and at lunchtime I'm going to sign up,' Mike told her grimly. 'If I've already signed before I get the letter they can't force me into the Army.'

'Oh, Mike. I thought you'd be here another week at least...'

'I'm sorry, Janet. You know it's important to me where I serve.'

'Yes, I do,' she said, a catch in her voice. 'I know you'll have to go soon now they've started to conscript men but you're doing an important job... they might not make you join.' Janet looked at him hopefully, but she saw the determination in his eyes.

'It might not be my papers,' Mike said and for a moment she thought he was wavering, 'but we know war is looming, Janet. It's been threatening for a while but the government has been trying to avoid it. I don't want to stay at home if the rest of them are out there fighting. We'll all have to go soon – your dad too.'

'He's forty-three, forty-four in August – surely too old,' Janet said, feeling a flicker of fear as the reality of war came closer. 'I know there's been a lot of talk but I thought it would all just fade away like it did last year.'

'Unfortunately, I doubt that,' Mike said. 'Your father isn't too old to do his bit. He's sure to be called up eventually, even if it's only a safe job knocking raw recruits into shape.'

'My mother will never manage the pub on her own,' Janet said. 'I might have to give up my job and help her.'

'I was hoping you might get a job somewhere near my base, wherever that turns out to be. I'll be at sea most of the time, but I'll be home for leave and if you're nearby we could see more of each other.'

'Dad would go berserk if I said I was leavin' home to be near you.'

Mike scowled. 'Your father wants it all his own way, Janet. One of these days you'll have to make a choice between us.'

Janet thought he was being unfair, but she didn't protest. She wanted to be with Mike as much as she could, but leaving her home and going to Portsmouth, or wherever Mike's home port was, would be a big step. Even if they were married she would prefer to live near her mum so that she could pop in and see her, perhaps give her a hand with the pub sometimes. Mike had never talked about going away until his elder brother turned up out of the blue and Janet wished he'd stayed away but kept her thoughts to herself, because the last thing she wanted was to provoke a quarrel with Mike.

*

'Your father's joined the civil defence,' Peggy announced when Janet walked in that evening. 'They're making plans for how to keep the country going once the war starts. We've all got to have blackout curtains it seems, and they'll be giving us free air raid shelters and lists of stuff we need to keep safe. I've got to have a stirrup pump upstairs and more than one down here just in case there's an incendiary bomb.'

'What's that when it's at home?' Janet asked and helped herself to one of her mother's cheese scones. 'This is still warm. You must always be cooking, Mum.'

'When I'm not serving in the bar or cleaning. Thank goodness for Nellie. She did the toilets and the bedrooms out today.'

'If Dad is off to meetings about civil defence, how will you manage in the bar?'

'I was hoping you would help me for a few hours this evening, Janet?'

'Mike Rowan is coming round, but he can sit and talk to me while he has a drink.'

'He can clear tables if he likes,' Peggy said with a wicked look. 'I shan't keep you longer than I need, love. It depends how long your father is at his meeting.'

'I can't see what they have to talk about,' Janet protested as she sat down to eat her portion of hotpot.

'According to your father they have an awful lot to plan.

There will be so many restrictions, Janet. I expect we'll find it hard to get all the beer we need; it may even be rationed.'

Janet sighed. 'Mike signed up today. They told him it will be about two months or so before he gets his orders so it should be the end of the summer before he goes.'

'That's good,' her mother said. 'You'll have a bit more time together – and there may not be a war in the end.'

'Mike says it's certain. He wants me to find work near where he's stationed, Mum. I told him Dad wouldn't let me and he said one day I'll have to choose.'

'Your father has every right to forbid you from leaving home until you're twenty-one,' Peggy said severely. 'Besides, I'd hoped you would live near me when you get married.'

'Mike says we could have more time together...'

'And what about all the times when he's away at sea and you're left at home on your own? How you will feel then, Janet?'

'I shouldn't like it much,' Janet admitted and sighed. 'It isn't easy having a relationship, is it, Mum?'

Peggy offered a sympathetic look. 'Not easy at all, my love. I know you want to be with Mike when he's on leave, but you have to think of yourself – and your family – and you'll miss your friends.'

'I wish Mike hadn't joined the Navy. All I wanted was to get married and live round the corner near you and Pip – and Dad. I thought it was all settled, nice and easy, but now everything has changed, and it's all because of that rotten Hitler. If he hadn't made all this trouble everywhere, Mike would never have thought of leaving the shipyard.'

'You're not the only one who thinks like that,' her mother sighed. 'I'm terrified your father will be called up, even if it's only office work – and what am I going to do then? I'll need help here, Janet, especially in the evenings. I'd hoped you might be around to give me a hand sometimes.'

Janet nodded; she felt as if she were being torn in two and didn't know what she wanted. A part of her was ready to follow Mike wherever he went, but the other side of her, the bit that wasn't so brave, was thinking about not seeing her family and friends, and all the lonely hours when Mike was away.

Chapter 9

'It's a lovely day, ain't it?' Maureen's customer said brightly as she bounced into the shop wearing a pretty dress of yellow and white spotted cotton. 'I think it's summer at last.'

'Yes, Mrs Adams, lovely,' Maureen agreed, though the late July sunshine had no power to banish the clouds that had hung over her these past few months. 'You look happy?'

'Yes, I am,' the young woman said. 'My Reg has just been told he's in a reserved job and he's promised me he won't join up unless they make him, and...' She paused for effect, the joy bubbling out of her. 'I'm expecting my first.'

'How lovely for you,' Maureen said. 'Congratulations, I'm very pleased for you.'

'My Reg is over the moon.' The young woman couldn't contain herself. 'He wants a boy but I don't mind; a little girl is lovely to dress up and they don't 'ave to go away and fight.'

Maureen nodded, serving her with the cheese, butter, bacon and tinned goods she'd asked for. Her father came into the shop as the door closed behind the young woman.

'What was she so pleased about?' he asked.

'She's having a baby and her husband has been told he's in a reserved job so he won't be getting any call-up papers.'

'Should be ashamed of himself,' he grumbled. 'Well, I've made up my mind. I'm going to do my bit.'

'What do you mean?' Maureen was startled. 'You won't be called up, Dad. Fifty-one is too old, besides, you've got a bad chest.'

'I'm not in my dotage yet, but I wasn't thinking of joining the regular army. I'm going to sign on with the civil defence lot like Laurence Ashley. All the local businessmen are doing it.'

Maureen nodded, because every other man that came in was either preparing to join the forces or the civil defences. Peggy had told her that Laurence was out most nights, delivering leaflets or sitting on committees. Once the war started properly he was going to be an air-raid warden, but he wasn't yet sure of his duties. Peggy was hoping it would be sufficient to stop him being called up.

The shop door opened and a girl wearing a flared grey skirt and a short-sleeved white blouse entered.

'It's nice to see you, Janet. Have you got the day off work?'

'Yes. Mike is leaving for his posting this afternoon. His orders came yesterday morning. I'm going to the station with him later so I took the day off. Mum is busy and asked me to do some shopping for her first.'

'You'll miss Mike when he goes.'

Janet nodded glumly. 'If we were married we could live in married quarters in Portsmouth. He says he'll be based there while he's training, though afterwards he might move to Southampton or Liverpool, because the Navy send you all over... but he'll come home on leave when he can.'

'Oh...' Maureen was at a loss as how to answer. 'I heard your dad said you were too young to get married. I'm sorry, Janet. I know it's awful when you're parted from someone you love.'

It was agony and Maureen knew only too well what the girl was suffering. There wasn't a day that passed when she didn't hope for a letter from Rory or look up when the doorbell went in the hope of seeing his tall figure in the doorway.

Janet looked miserable as she paid for her shopping and left. Maureen felt for her and was angry with Laurence Ashley for refusing to listen to his daughter's pleas. Peggy had told her all about it over coffee in the back kitchen, but Maureen hadn't realised how distressed Janet was until she saw her that morning.

It was almost August now and looking at the newspaper headlines, Maureen sometimes felt that war had already started. Since the conscription of men of twenty and twenty-one years of age had been brought in at the end of April, it wasn't unusual to see young soldiers in their uniforms on the streets, because men of all ages were signing up. But the reports of IRA bombs going off in post boxes all over the country and a dreadful accident involving a submarine, when seventy-one men died during routine training, made for dire reading. As did the Pact of Steel between Italy and Germany and pictures of Mussolini's men doing their version of the goosestep; the way that Jews were being treated in Germany and Hitler's menacing threats towards Poland made things look worse by the day.

All this posturing and the threats the Prime Minister was issuing to Germany seemed to make the war a matter of time rather than something that might never happen. It was clear the government was preparing for it when they urged farmers to plough up pasture land to grow more crops, because the threat to British shipping in war was unthinkable.

Maureen's father believed it to be serious, because he'd taken out some of his savings and their stock room was packed from floor to ceiling with tinned goods, sacks of dried fruit and bags of sugar. He'd also bought things like packets of needles and pins, cottons and knicker elastic as well as boot laces.

'They're the sort of things that got short last time,' he'd told Maureen when she smiled over the extra boxes. 'You'll see, girl. In a few months you'll have people begging for a bit of knicker elastic.'

Maureen was glad he'd stocked up on things that their customers were always asking for. Some of them were already buying extra, just a tin of fruit or a pound of sugar more than normal. Some richer folk had tried to buy huge quantities of sugar and caused uproar, because hoarding by the public was frowned on even though it wasn't actually illegal yet. After all Britain wasn't at war and nothing was rationed, though everyone knew it would happen once the hostilities started. There were going to be a lot of restrictions and new requirements according to Peggy, and Maureen groaned inwardly as she imagined all the extra paperwork it would make.

She pushed the small irritations to the back of her mind as the door of the shop opened and Gordon Hart entered. He bought his cigarettes, a jar of strawberry jam and some sweets for Shirley and paid for them, but instead of leaving he stood looking at her in silence for a moment.

'Something you've forgotten?'

'No...' He was still hesitant, then, 'My mother is taking Shirley down to Essex to stay with some relatives of hers on a farm. Everyone is talking about the kids being evacuated and she wants to see how they get on. If they like it, they will probably live there until afterwards... when I get back...'

'Oh, Gordon, have you received your papers?' She wrinkled her brow. 'Surely the conscription bill was for men of twenty and twenty-one only?'

'Yes, that's true, but I've been warned that they're going

to put a bill through parliament to take older men, gradually at first, but we'll all be in once it starts, believe me – so I thought I might as well go in now. I'll get a better choice of what I want to do.' He looked at her a bit sheepishly. 'You might think that's foolish?'

'No, because if you wait it will all happen in a rush...' She hesitated, then, 'What will you do with your house while you're away?' Gordon was in the fortunate position of owning his own home, a small terraced house in Crispin Street.

'I've got a bit of time, but I'm thinking of letting it to a bloke I used to know years ago. He's been working away but now he's been transferred to London. Geoff is in a protected trade. He won't be called up and he wants to bring his family up to town for a few years. They'll go home when things get back to normal and I'll have my house back.'

'Are you sure that's a good idea?'

'Well, I don't know what else to do. If my wife... but it's either let or leave it empty, because I don't want Shirley in London.'

Maureen nodded. 'When do you leave?'

'I don't report for two months, so I might take a few days off and go down and see them when Shirley's had a chance to settle – but it seems my trade of carpentry is needed in the Army, and since my mother looks after my daughter they say I would be called up in time.' He jingled the coins in his pocket awkwardly. 'I should've spoken weeks ago. I was wondering if we could have a drink at Peggy's... talk about the future, Maureen.'

'I'm not sure what you mean, talk about the future?'

'I know I couldn't expect you to marry me just like that,' he said. 'But Shirley needs a mother and I thought perhaps...'

He left the idea trailing and Maureen was stunned.

'This is a bit sudden, Gordon,' she managed.

'I know – ridiculous,' he admitted. 'I've been thinking about it for a long time, but I couldn't bring myself to ask you out... it wasn't that I didn't want to, but it seemed disloyal to *her* memory...'

'Yes, I do understand,' Maureen said, her sense of amusement rescuing what might have been a tragedy. It was funny in a way. Gordon seemed to think it was just a case of his making up his mind. Perhaps he saw her as an old maid who would snatch eagerly at any offer?

She could see one of her regulars about to enter the shop and thought swiftly. 'I will meet you this evening, Gordon, because we can't talk about this now. I'm sure we can find some way of easing your concerns about Shirley.'

Gordon nodded and went off as the next customer entered the shop.

Maureen wanted to laugh but knew if she started she might end up in tears. Did she come over as a desperate old maid? The brutal truth was that she was unlikely to get married and have children of her own... unless she accepted Gordon's half-hearted offer. He wanted a mother for his daughter, but had the thought of love or what Maureen needed ever crossed his mind?

*

Maureen's father raised no objection to her going out that night, because he was off to a meeting as soon as he'd eaten his dinner. She did tell him she was going to meet a friend, but she doubted he was listening, and if he did he assumed it was Anne Riley or Peggy.

Maureen dressed in her second-best summer frock, but she didn't wear the lovely new one that Gran had made for her birthday. She'd turned twenty-four this year and apart from a few cards and presents, it had passed without incident. Her father had given her three pounds, but hadn't bothered with a card. A few customers, including Mrs Hart, had left one in the shop for her. Mrs Hart had signed it from her, Shirley and Gordon, but Maureen doubted he'd known much about it, because he'd come into the shop on the day and hadn't mentioned it or wished her happy birthday.

Maureen saw Gordon waiting for her at a table in the corner when she arrived. He had a half pint of bitter in front of him and what looked like an orange juice.

'I wasn't sure what you wanted,' he explained. 'I bought you a gin and orange, but you can have whatever you like.'

'That's lovely,' Maureen said and sipped it. 'Yes, thank you. I don't much like gin with tonic but I don't mind it with orange.'

Gordon pushed a little parcel across the table. 'I got these for you when Ma told me it was your birthday a few weeks ago. Sorry, I didn't know and she didn't tell me she'd signed a card from all of us. I'd have got you one myself, if I'd realised.'

'You didn't have to,' Maureen said but opened the little parcel and discovered a pretty pair of silver clip-on earrings in the shape of a rosebud. 'These are lovely, Gordon, thank you.'

'I think a lot of you, Maureen,' Gordon said. 'I've wanted to ask you out and get to know you for ages. You've always got a nice smile and you're a generous, lovely woman. I just waited a bit too long...'

'It isn't all that long since you lost your wife. You felt it was too soon. I do understand, Gordon. Besides, I've had my father to think about. You know what his health is like.'

'Yes, I've thought of all that,' he said, his colour heightened. 'It wouldn't be easy, but we could all live together – not in your flat but my house has four bedrooms. My grandfather left it to me, but my mother has the right to live there for her lifetime if she wants, but we could all fit in there. If you felt you could... well, marry me, I needn't let it to anyone...'

'Oh, Gordon, I do like you a lot,' Maureen said. 'I know you need a mother for Shirley and I do understand how you feel – but I want a husband who loves me for myself... someone I love.'

'I knew you would say that and I don't blame you, Maureen. I've made a right mess of things. If I'd done it the right way, asked you out and made a fuss of you...'

'My answer would've been the same. You see, I've been in love and I would never take less,' she said. 'I'm sorry, sorrier than you realise – because the man I love can't marry me. Marriage to you would give me a better life than I have...'

'Then why not marry me?' Gordon pleaded. 'I wouldn't ask much of you, just look after the home and Shirley. I wouldn't even touch you if you didn't want it.'

He was digging a hole to bury himself and didn't realise it, because had he loved her, she might have considered it. 'I'm sorry – but I'm not turning my back on you, Gordon. Give me Shirley's address in the country and I'll keep in touch with her. I shan't interfere while your mother is able to care for her but... if ever she couldn't... well, I'll take her in and look after her until you return.'

Maureen made the offer without considering the consequences, because she felt sorry for him, but she couldn't have seen the child of someone she knew sent away to an orphanage. Children deserved love and a home, and from what Gran had told her those places were awful, little better than prisons for the poor kids who had to live there. Maureen wasn't sure it was entirely true these days, because the only evidence her grandmother had belonged to her own childhood. Yet she felt in a close knit community like theirs, her friends would think it only right to do what they could for a child in need.

Gordon looked at her in silence and then smiled. 'You would really do that for her – for us?'

'Yes, I give you my promise,' Maureen said, because she felt closer to him than ever before. 'I will stand in as her mother and guardian until you come home.'

'And if I shouldn't?'

'Then I should adopt her – if the authorities would allow it.'

Gordon nodded. 'I reckon I could do that legally before I leave,' he said. 'If I give you her guardianship in my absence, and until she is of age, they wouldn't be able to object to you having her.'

'Well, I'd be happy to do that,' Maureen said, 'but I think you should bring her round to tea on Sundays until she goes to the country with her grandmother. She needs to get to know me and where she has to come if her gran can't look after her – but it will probably never happen.'

'I know.' Gordon looked relieved. 'I wish I'd talked to you months ago, Maureen. You're a sensible woman.'

Maureen watched as he went to the bar for more drinks. She'd made a huge undertaking, because if both Gordon and his mother died she would have to bring up his daughter alone. Her father would create merry hell if she ever had to make good her promise, but she hadn't been able to resist the look of appeal in Gordon's eyes – and she couldn't bring herself to marry him. The memory of Rory's kiss was too fresh in her mind to settle for less.

Chapter 10

Peggy was polishing the mahogany bar, enjoying the way the old wood shone like silk so that she could almost see her face in it. The little brass rails that held the bottles securely on the shelves were gleaming and Peggy smiled at her industry. She was singing to herself when the door opened and Alice Carter walked in.

'Sorry, Alice, we're not open for half an hour. I must've left the door unlocked when I finished cleaning the glass panel.'

'That's all right, Peggy love,' Alice chirped. 'I ain't come fer a drink, not that I couldn't do wiv a drop of port and lemon – but I'm round collectin' fer the church jumble sale.' She winked at Peggy. 'Got ter get a good word in with 'im upstairs, ain't we?'

Alice's humour was irrepressible. She was always the life and soul of the party on a Saturday night in the pub, and always ready to laugh at life no matter what it threw at her.

'Well, I've just about finished here,' Peggy said. 'Let me put the lock on the door, Alice, and we'll go upstairs and see what I've got in the wardrobe.'

'Righto, Peggy, me darlin'.' Alice followed her, grinning at Nellie as they met on the stairs. 'All right then, Nel. You've got a good job 'ere, gal. I wouldn't mind a few stints behind that bar meself.'

'You'd drink all the profits when Peggy's back was turned,' Nellie said and Alice cackled with laughter, not in the least offended by her old friend's remark. 'Are yer comin' to the church do on Friday night then, Nellie?'

'Well, I might pop in if Peggy doesn't need me,' Nellie said. 'What are yer after now, yer old scrounger?'

'Just anythin' Peggy doesn't want fer the jumble.'

'Right, well, yer can walk 'ome wiv me when yer done. I've got some stuff yer can 'ave – mind you, I don't want ter see yer wearing it unless yer buy it at the jumble.'

'As if I would,' Alice said indignantly but winked at Peggy behind her back. 'Ole Nel and me go back a long way... we was mates back in the last war. Worked down the munitions fer a while, us did, afore she was married.' She gave a sigh as they reached the top of the stairs. 'Them's steep ole apples and pears, Peggy love, and I ain't as young as I used ter be.'

'It's the heat,' Peggy said and smiled as she led the way into one of the spare bedrooms. 'It's really hot again today. I know it's August but we don't often get it quite this hot.'

'You're right about that,' Alice agreed, looking round with interest. 'Nice room, but it ain't yours, is it?'

'No, this used to be a guest room,' Peggy told her and opened a large deal wardrobe that had been there when Laurence took over the pub, along with several other large pieces of old furniture. 'This is some of my mum's stuff – and a few bits of Percy's too. I couldn't throw them out after he died so I shoved them in here – but I've been meaning to get rid of them.'

Alice gave a chortle of delight as she pulled a moth-eaten fox fur out of the wardrobe and draped it round her neck. 'Yer ma looked a treat in this, love. I remember she 'ad it when she were wed. Yer father bought it out of the pawnbroker's fer 'er as a weddin' gift... couldn't afford new, o'course, but she were as proud as punch of it.'

'Yes, I asked her once why she didn't throw it out, but she said it reminded her of the good old days.'

'They were good an' all,' Alice said. 'We 'ad less money than we've got now but we didn't care 'cos we was all in the same boat, see.'

'Well, you can have anything you like from here,' Peggy said. 'It's probably a good time to clear this stuff out, Alice. People won't be able to buy much soon if we have a war like the last one. Percy told me how bad it got... we used to sit and talk about the old times when he was ill...' Tears stung her eyes and she was surprised as Alice flung her arms about her and hugged her. 'This stuff makes me weepy – best if it goes...'

'I'll take as much as I can now and come back in the mornin' fer the rest,' Alice said. 'Yer the best, Peggy Ashley. Do yer know that? We none of us say much but if there was a popularity contest round 'ere yer'd win by a mile. There's a king and queen sits on the throne, but Peggy's our own Queenie round 'ere.'

Peggy laughed and hugged her back. 'Flattery will get you everywhere, Alice. Why don't you keep Mum's fur for yourself? It's too far gone to fetch much at the church jumble sale.'

'Gawd bless yer, love,' Alice said and gave her a wet smack of a kiss on the cheek. 'I'd like to 'ave yer ma's bit of fur and I shan't say no. But I'll give the rest to the church, 'cos they do a bit o'good round 'ere and I've got a feelin' we'll be needin' 'em soon enough.'

'Yes, I dare say we shall,' Peggy agreed. 'And I'll pop into the church sale in the afternoon after we shut. Every little helps, as the old woman said as she widdled in the sea... as Ma used to say.'

Alice whooped with delight and started to caper about the bedroom floor with the fox fur draped over her shoulders, singing 'Knees Up Mother Brown'. Peggy started laughing. She laughed and laughed, until she cried, but they were healing tears.

'Thank God for you, Alice Carter,' she said and dried her eyes. 'Come down to the bar when you've got what you want and I'll pour you a milk stout on the house.'

*

Maureen saw Peggy leaving as she arrived at the church jumble sale the following week. She laughed as she saw her carrying a large china elephant.

'What are you goin' to do with that then, Peggy?'

'Stick it in the guest room until someone comes askin' for stuff for the next jumble sale,' Peggy said and smiled. 'I bought a few raffle tickets and then saw this and it made me smile – so I bought it. As Nellie says, it's all for a good cause.'

'Alice said you gave her some things for the sale?'

'Just some of Mum's stuff and Percy's. I kept Mum's pearl earrings and her bead purse she had when she was sixteen – and Percy's silver watch and chain, but I thought other people could do with the clothes.'

'Alice asked us too. I gave her some of Mum's hats, but I'd already given a lot of things away.'

'Come round and have a drink when you can, Maureen. I've got to get back now – but I'd love to have a catch up.'

'Yes, I will,' Maureen promised.

Peggy nodded and they parted, Maureen stopping to talk

with various people as she made her way into the church hall where the sale was going on. It was busy, because nothing on sale was offered at more than a shilling or two, which meant there were lots of bargains to be had, and hard-up mums were busy hunting for toys for their kids and clothes that they could make over, either for themselves or their children.

It was rare for Maureen to get away from the shop in opening hours, but her gran had stepped in and was holding the fort. Maureen didn't think she would find anything much she wanted for herself, but she might discover a book or an old record for her gramophone if she was lucky – and if not she would spend money at the cake stall and buy raffle tickets. Like Peggy, she wanted to support the church, because without them some of the people here might go hungry when the money ran out mid-week, as it often did in the poorer families. The people of the East End might not be as poor as they had been half a century ago, but there were still kids running about with holes in their shoes and trousers that had been patched.

As if to prove her thoughts, a young boy cannoned into her. He looked up at her, his face dirty and covered with spots. He was thin and his clothes looked as if they were held together by a wing and a prayer, and Maureen smiled as he offered a cheeky grin.

'Got a halfpenny ter spare, missus?'

'Yes, I have,' Maureen said and took three pennies from her skirt pocket. 'Have a penny lick, Jimmy Brown – and next time you've got nothing to do, you can clean my shop windows for sixpence.'

'Cor…' He looked at the pennies in his hand, drew himself up and gave her a smart salute. 'Yer all right, missus. I'll be round next Saturday mornin'.

Maureen nodded and watched as he ran off. He was a good kid and it wasn't the first time she'd slipped him a penny, because she knew that his father was an invalid after an accident at the Docks and his mother didn't have time to look out for him, because she worked as a char woman in several offices, cleaning all night and looking after her husband all day.

At least Maureen had always had plenty to eat and someone to care about her when she was a child, even if life wasn't all she could wish for now she was grown up.

Chapter 11

'What's all this for then?' Maureen's father asked as he walked into the parlour and saw that she had laid the table with the best white cloth and was setting it out with her mother's special rose-pattern china plates. 'Who's coming to tea?'

'Mrs Hart, Shirley and her father, and Gran,' Maureen said. 'I've made a strawberry blancmange and some fairy cakes, as well as a jam sponge; we're also having pink salmon and cucumber and cress sandwiches – and I'll open a tin of fruit cocktail to go with it.'

'Humph,' Henry Jackson said with a sour look. 'I don't hold with that pap. Good thing I shan't be home. I'm going to visit someone.'

Maureen sighed with relief, but didn't let it show. 'Anyone I know?'

'None of your business,' her father muttered. 'Make sure you've got the list ready for the wholesaler tomorrow. If you're going to be usin' me stock entertainin', I'm soon goin' to run out.'

Maureen made no comment. She'd paid for the extras out of the small personal allowance her father gave her but he wouldn't care about that; he just enjoyed grumbling at her, because he thought she had no choice but to stay here and work for him. It was true she had no other training, but Maureen didn't think she would have much difficulty in finding work these days. There were adverts for women workers everywhere now that a lot of the men were joining up. Besides, she knew that Gordon would be glad to put a ring on her finger and that would give her independence, but for the moment she was content to carry on as she was, because at the back of her mind there was always the hope that by some miracle Rory would be free to come to her.

Gran was the first to arrive. She'd brought a paper bag full of ripe gooseberries she'd picked from the allotment of a friend of hers for Shirley. 'She won't want them after this lot,' she said when she saw the table. 'Is it someone's birthday?'

'No, of course not,' Maureen laughed. 'I wanted to give her a treat – so that she likes coming here, Gran. I promised Gordon that I would look out for her if anything were to happen to her grandmother while he's away. He was going to bring her last week but she had a nasty cold, but she's better now and I'm looking forward to meeting her properly.'

'Shirley is a nice enough child but a bit spoiled since her mother died,' Gran said. 'I think her father and grandmother give her whatever she wants, and that's not good for her, but it's nothing to do with me.'

Maureen didn't answer immediately. Gran's words made her a little nervous, because Shirley didn't really know her and she might not take to her, which could make things awkward.

When Gordon arrived a few minutes later with his daughter and mother, Shirley's face was a bit red, as if she'd had a tantrum on the way there, but she said hello when she was told and sat down at the table like a good girl. However, she shook her head at the salmon sandwiches and pulled a face at the cucumber and cress, making a grab for a fairy cake.

'Bread and butter first,' her grandmother told her. 'Put the cake down until later, Shirley, and have a nice salmon sandwich.' She pushed the plate at her and the child reluctantly took one.

'Don't like it... tastes nasty,' Shirley said, spitting her first bite out on the pretty little china plate. 'I want bread and jam.'

'You naughty girl,' Mrs Hart said, looking pink in the face. 'Auntie Maureen has gone to a lot of trouble to get this tea for you.'

'It's all right, she can have some bread and jam if she prefers,' Maureen said swiftly. 'What kind would you like, Shirley – plum or strawberry?'

'Strawberry,' the child said sulkily. 'I like strawberry best.'

Maureen went to the dresser and took down a pot of jam, spooning some of it into a dish and putting it on the table while she buttered two slices of fresh bread. Shirley stared at the jam and bread and butter, clearly waiting for someone to spread it on for her. Maureen hesitated, because surely the girl was old enough to spread it for herself or at least try. Mrs Hart gave the girl a cross look but spread the jam thickly and placed the bread before Shirley. She ate one slice and then pushed it away and grabbed at the fairy cake again.

'Would you like some of the strawberry blancmange, Shirley?' Maureen asked when they'd all finished their sandwiches, and received a blank stare in response. 'It's this pink stuff and there's some fruit cocktail to go with it, and a little fresh cream.'

'Don't like fruit,' Shirley said sullenly.

'Well, I do,' her father said. 'I'd love some blancmange

and fruit cocktail; it was always my favourite at the church party when I was a kid.'

Maureen filled a small dish and passed it to him, having served both Gran and Mrs Hart first. Shirley immediately pulled at her father's arm and wanted to try both the fruit and the blancmange. She ate it with evident enjoyment and wanted more, but her father pulled his dish away.

'Perhaps Maureen will give you some for yourself if you ask nicely, Shirley.'

For a moment the child looked mutinous, clearly unused to not getting her own way, but something in her father's manner must have warned her, because she turned large innocent eyes on Maureen and asked sweetly if she could please have some. Maureen smiled and gave her a dish of blancmange and fruit.

Shirley finished all the blancmange and most of the fruit. Maureen asked if anyone wanted a slice of jam sponge and the adults all said just a tiny piece because they were full after such a lovely meal; she served them all a thin slice and gave Shirley hers without asking. The child crumbled a corner of it and ate it and then took a couple of bites. She accepted a glass of orange squash, but after one mouthful asked her grandmother if she could get down from the table.

'Not yet, Shirley,' her father said, looking annoyed. 'Just wait until everyone else is finished.'

Shirley scowled and kicked at the table legs, impatient now that she'd finished her food.

'Sit still, Shirley, there's a good girl,' Gordon said.

'I want to go home,' the child said and glared across the table at Maureen, as if accusing her of being the reason she was having to be polite. It was obvious that her grandmother spoiled her and let her do much as she liked, because she kept tugging at the woman's sleeve and asking her if she could go out to play.

'You're not at home now,' Mrs Hart said, looking harassed. 'Just be quiet for a while, Shirley. We want to enjoy our tea and talk.'

'Want to go home, want to go home.' Shirley chanted the phrase over and over and suddenly Gordon's patience broke and he turned and slapped her bare arm hard. Her face went white and then red and she screwed up her face and burst into tears.

'Now look what you've done,' Mrs Hart said. 'There, there, my love. Your daddy didn't mean it. You're tired, that's what it is. I told him you were still poorly but he insisted we come.'

She looked apologetically at Maureen. 'It was a lovely tea and we've enjoyed ourselves, but Shirley is tired. I'd better take her home. No, you don't have to come with us, Gordon. Goodbye, Hilda, Maureen – and we both thank you for the tea.'

She picked up her jacket and Shirley's wool cardigan and taking the child by the hand went out into the hall. Maureen followed down the stairs to let them out of the front door, because the yard was locked up. Mrs Hart apologised again, but was already fussing over Shirley as she led her away.

Gran was pouring another cup of tea for her and Gordon. They'd moved from the tea table to the comfortable chairs and he stood up as Maureen entered the room and apologised for his daughter's appalling manners.

'It's the first time she's been out to tea like this,' he said. 'She probably felt nervous and didn't know what to say or do. I'm sorry she made such a fuss, Maureen.'

'It wasn't your fault. Shirley doesn't know me very well,

Gordon. I expect she's used to doing things differently at home.'

'I seldom eat with them, because she's ready for bed when I get in. I'll have a talk with her, make sure she knows how to behave before she comes again.' He looked uncomfortable. 'That's if you'll put up with her again...'

'Of course I will,' Maureen said. 'Perhaps next time I won't set the best china and cloth. I'll just have a simple tea and let her get down when she's had what she wants.'

'No, she ought to learn some manners,' her father said. 'My mother indulges her because it is easier, but I'll make sure she knows what to do before she goes to tea anywhere else.'

Maureen couldn't argue with that, because she knew he was embarrassed by his daughter's behaviour. Clearly he hadn't been aware how much she was being indulged by her grandmother. He took his leave about twenty minutes later, apologising again and thanking her for a lovely tea.

'It was my pleasure,' she assured him. 'I'm only sorry that Shirley didn't enjoy herself more.'

'She enjoyed the blancmange and fruit very much. I've never seen her eat as much as she did today,' he said. 'It is my fault she's been allowed to be so naughty. I hadn't realised what was going on, Maureen. I'll have a word with my mother at home.'

'Perhaps she finds it easier to let Shirley go out and play. It can't be easy looking after a young child at her age.'

'I know you're right,' Gordon said. 'I should have done something before now instead of letting things drift.' He aimed a quick peck at Maureen's cheek before leaving.

Gran shook her head at Maureen when she discovered her with her arms up to the elbows in hot water, washing the plates and dishes.

'If that's what the child is allowed to do at home, you'll have a terrible time with her if you ever have to take over, Maureen. I don't think you know what you've let yourself in for, my girl.'

'I didn't expect quite so much hostility,' Maureen said, 'but she's not a bad girl, Gran. Mrs Hart has spoiled her, but I dare say her father will sort that out now he realises what's been going on.'

'If it isn't already too late for that? Shirley has been indulged so much that she will resent anyone who applies the reins, Maureen – and if that's you, expect storms.'

'It may never happen,' Maureen said, though the doubt had taken seed in her mind and she wondered if she'd taken on more than she could manage. To foster anyone's child would have been difficult, but when the child was spoiled and already hostile it would be a thankless task.

Chapter 12

Janet looked at her diary and felt a cold shiver trickle down the back of her neck. She was a few days late, and she was always regular. Did it mean that she was pregnant? Had she fallen when Mike came home on an unexpected thirty-six hour leave at the beginning of August? She must have done, because she'd had a period after he went off to Portsmouth so it must have happened during his leave. Her mother hadn't fallen for several years after her marriage and Janet hadn't really thought she would. Fear made Janet cold all over, because she could just imagine what her father would say if she had to tell him. Mike would come home as soon as he got leave and marry her, but it was going to cause such awful rows in the house.

Tears stung her eyes as she thought of the last time she'd seen Mike at the railway station. She'd kissed him but she hadn't clung because he'd told her firmly that he didn't want tears.

'I'll be back again on leave soon, until we put to sea anyway,' he'd told her and he held her back and looked into her face. Janet had been fighting her emotion and Mike looked grim.

Janet supposed the wonder was that she hadn't fallen for a child earlier, because Mike hadn't been content with that one night in the hotel, but she'd believed they'd got away with it; although they'd made love in the park lots of times and once he'd smuggled her into his lodgings when his landlady was out. She'd felt so uncomfortable and hadn't enjoyed that at all. At least in the park she could be just one of many other courting couples, who took advantage of the darkness to indulge their passion. That last time, the ground was hard, but it had been dry and Mike had placed his overcoat for her to lie on, yet it wasn't like the first time. That had seemed right and beautiful, but the other times... Well, if Janet were truthful, it felt a bit sordid. Janet hoped that Mike would get more leave soon, especially if she was pregnant. That wasn't the sort of thing that she could tell him when he phoned her at home, and she didn't want to write it in a letter. Maybe, she was worrying for no good reason. A few days late was nothing, after all, but the niggling doubt remained at the back of her mind and she couldn't quite get rid of it. She just wished Mike was here so she could tell him.

*

Peggy had noticed that her daughter was looking pale and un-happy, but she dismissed it as being the result of Mike going off to Portsmouth for his training. It was a pity they couldn't have been married first, and then she could have gone down with him until he went to sea. Peggy didn't want her only daughter living too far away, but Janet could have met her husband at his base port for his leaves and come home to her in between.

It was hopeless to expect Laurence to change his mind. Recently, his mood had worsened and it was months since they'd made love. Peggy wasn't sure why, except that he was always a bit reserved and she'd given up trying to cuddle up and bring him round.

After years of a satisfactory marriage a rift had come between them and Peggy was unhappy with it, but she couldn't bring herself to be the one that did the making up. She might have upset him because she'd taken Janet's side, but Laurence was nursing a grudge of some kind that had nothing to do with their daughter. She thought he was restless, bored with their marriage.

'That was a big sigh,' Nellie said. 'Anything wrong, Peggy?'

'Not really.' Peggy forced a smile. 'I think everyone is in the same boat, Nellie. We're all under a cloud, just waiting for it to happen. In a way it will be a relief when it does.'

'Your Janet won't think that,' Nellie said. 'My Peter wrote me a long letter this week. He loves it in the Army. He's training hard and says he's exhausted when he falls into bed, but he thinks it's necessary so they have a chance to survive when they are sent overseas to fight.'

Peggy shuddered inwardly. Nellie was being remarkably cheerful considering that her daughter was also training for the WRNS. She was going to work as a probationary nurse and would be based at Portsmouth where she would be helping to look after wounded servicemen.

'You must miss your Amy?'

'I think I miss Pete more,' Nellie said. 'Amy is a good girl, but Pete – well, there's something special about a woman's son, isn't there?'

'Yes, you're right,' Peggy agreed. She would never let it show, but Pip always had been her favourite. Perhaps because of that, she'd deliberately spoiled Janet. 'Thank goodness Pip is too young to join up yet.'

'They wouldn't take him at the moment,' Nellie said, 'but

you wait until they get desperate; they won't inquire too deeply then, mark my words. A lot of lads joined when they were still under seventeen the last time round – and the poor little devils were killed before they knew what hit them.'

'There were quite a few like that,' Peggy replied, 'but they won't take them too soon this time, I'm sure.'

Nellie looked unconvinced but didn't argue. 'I'll 'ave more time to spare now,' she said. 'I can do a few extra hours if you need me, Peggy.'

'Well, I can always do with some help with the washing up in the evenings,' Peggy said, 'especially now that Laurence is off to meetings, three or four nights a week. I don't know what they're up to but they seem to do a lot of talking and make an awful lot of lists.'

'They're like a bunch of excited kids.' Nellie dismissed the businessmen and councillors with a little snort. 'Still, I suppose with the government puttin' out another directive every other day someone has to make sense of 'em. I reckon we'll soon need a permit to go to the lavvy!' She went into a cackle of laughter and Peggy smiled with her.

'Janet?' Peggy looked up as her daughter entered the kitchen. 'What are you doing home this early?'

'We've got a problem at work,' Janet said. 'There was an explosion up the road. At first they thought it might be one of those IRA bombs that have been going off all over the place, but someone said it was a gas leak. Anyway, there's no gas so they sent us home and closed up for the day.'

'You can give me a hand with the cooking,' her mother said. 'Unless you've got something else you want to do?'

'No, not really,' Janet said. 'I've been thinking, I could do part-time work, Mum, and give you a hand here – if you wanted?'

Peggy looked at her intently. Something was wrong and she suspected it was more than Mike going off to his training.

'We'll see what your father has to say,' she promised. 'Oh, I nearly forgot – there's a letter on the sideboard upstairs. I think it's from Mike.'

'Thanks!' Janet's face lit up as she turned towards the stairs.

'It's a pity that girl couldn't get married,' Nellie said. 'I remember what it was like when we were young – and it's hard on her that he may be away for years.'

'Yes.' Peggy kneaded the dough harder. Sometimes, she wished this dough was Laurence so that she could knock a bit of sense into his head.

*

Janet read the letter twice, holding it to her lips and smiling as she nursed the lovely feeling inside. Mike was coming home in a week's time. He'd got lots to tell her and he'd bought a matching wedding and engagement ring set that he thought she would like.

I saw it in a shop and couldn't resist. Your father can stop us getting married but he will surely let us be en-gaged, Janet. I want to think of you as waiting for me when I come home from sea. I haven't actually been out of port yet, but they say we'll do that after our leave. I can't wait and I'm really glad I joined the Navy, Jan. It's a wonderful life for a man and I've realised what I was missing. When we are married, I'll get a place for us to live. You'll soon make friends here, because everyone helps each other and the wives and girlfriends all go out together when their men are away.

I miss you all the time and I love you. I think about you when I'm in bed and I hope you're thinking of me too. I'll be with you the first week of September. Until then, be true to me. Your loving Mike.

It would be a month since she'd seen Mike by then, Janet thought as she put his letter with the others in her special place. She'd been due for her period three weeks ago and was sure she was pregnant, though she hadn't seen a doctor. When she told Mike he would insist on speaking to her father; she wouldn't have to face him alone and then they could buy a special licence and get married. Her dad wasn't going to like it, she knew, but he surely wouldn't refuse her when he understood the truth.

Feeling much better, she went downstairs and told her mother that Mike was coming back in a few days' time.

'That's lovely, darling,' Peggy said and smiled at her. 'You can put these cheese scones in the oven for me – and then come through and help me in the bar. Your father says he's rushed off his feet. There are a whole lot of soldiers in and they're all hungry.'

Chapter 13

Peggy listened to the news broadcast with Laurence, Nellie and Pip. It had come eventually on Sunday 3 September 1939. At last the Prime Minister had sent an ultimatum to Germany and there had been no answer, which meant that the country was now at war. The king had made a stirring speech to his people, which was a big thing for a shy man with little pleasure in public speaking to do, but his grateful people knew nothing of what it had cost him to make that speech. All they knew was that at long last the uncertainty was over.

A hush descended as those that survived the last war remembered and felt sick with apprehension, and those that had no idea of what was coming thought it was vaguely exciting. Men had been joining up for months in anticipation of war, but now the recruiting stations would be overrun by eager young men wanting to serve their king and country.

'It looks as if my Pete will be in the thick of it then,' Nellie said and gripped her mug of tea until her knuckles turned white. 'Amy should be all right working in the hospital, but your Janet's boyfriend will catch it in the Navy. The poor girl will wish she'd married him.'

Laurence looked at her but said nothing. Peggy saw that a little nerve flicked at his temple and his nostrils were pinched as he struggled to control whatever he was feeling.

'I'd better open up,' he said. 'We'll have plenty of customers in later.'

'Sorry, love, I didn't think,' Nellie said after he'd gone. 'It was me mouth working without me brain.'

'You only spoke the truth,' Peggy said. 'Mike is due to come next week for a visit. I just hope they don't cancel all leave, because she would be so upset.'

'They usually give them leave before they pack them off,' Nellie said. 'He's only just started his training.'

'Yes,' Peggy agreed. 'Let's have a sit down and a cup of tea before we start, shall we?'

Peggy bent to put a batch of scones in the oven just as they heard a strange wailing sound. Pip had gone out to the yard to work on his bike, but he came rushing in, his face white and shocked.

'It's the siren,' he said. 'Should we go down to the cellar, Mum?'

Peggy stared at him indecisively. 'It won't be a bomb yet,' she said, crossing her fingers behind her back. 'It's much too soon for anything like that. Mr Chamberlain has always said the Germans don't want to fight us...'

'Don't you believe it,' Pip said. 'Our history master says they're spoiling for a fight, because they haven't forgiven us for humiliating them last time.'

'It's all right, listen,' Nellie said. 'That's the all clear, Pip. It was just a false alarm. I expect they were testing it out to make sure it works.'

Peggy shivered suddenly. She felt as if a sliver of ice had run down her spine and the cold spread all over her. Her eyes closed and she visualised what might have happened had a bomb been dropped near her home.

'I think we ought to move some stuff into the cellar just

in case,' she said, pulling herself together. 'We'll take some chairs, a little table and a mattress and some bedding down for a start. I bought a little paraffin stove for use there; it will keep the things aired if we put it on now and then, and we can boil a kettle if we have to stay down there for a while.'

'I'm lucky, I'm only a few yards from the Underground,' Nellie said. 'I've got my bag packed and every night I'll be making a flask of something hot to take with me. I reckon I shan't want for company, girl.'

'I think you're wise to be prepared,' Peggy said. 'It would be too far for us to make a dash; besides, Laurence wouldn't abandon the pub or his customers. The cellars are big enough to hold several of us – they extend quite a way, and once we start to use up the stock they will be nearly empty.'

'Dad has been stocking up for months,' Pip said, 'but I reckon the beer will run out first – if we can't buy more.'

'You're sure to get some,' Nellie said. 'All the pubs will get something, but beer will be scarce and whisky will be a thing of the past.'

'Not for Dad, at least not for a couple of years,' Pip said and then coloured. 'He told me to keep quiet about it, but he's got the back cellar full floor to ceiling with wine and whisky and things.'

Peggy frowned. 'He told me not to go in there because it wasn't safe – and he keeps the key.'

'I think he didn't want you to know about it – he only told me, because if anything happens to him someone ought to know...'

Why was Laurence keeping things from her, Peggy wondered. She had no idea where the extra money had come from and it stung that he hadn't told her – as if he didn't trust her. What had she done to deserve that? As far as Peggy knew there was no reason her husband should hide things from her.

Just where Laurence had got the money to buy that sort of stock in that quantity? Laurence had told his son to keep quiet and he hadn't breathed a word to her, which made Peggy sense that something wasn't quite right about it. Over the years, Laurence had been offered cheap goods, but because he knew they had to be off the back of a lorry, he'd always refused. Had he broken his habit of a lifetime?

She made up her mind to ask him about it sometime, but she wouldn't say anything in front of Nellie or Pip; this was between her and Laurence.

*

'Certainly you can have a few days off to see your boyfriend,' Janet's supervisor said the day after war was declared. 'We were thinking of increasing your hours now, Miss Ashley, but we'll talk more about that when you return after your little holiday.'

'We're not going away anywhere,' Janet said, 'at least I doubt it, but once he goes back to sea he may be away for months at a time so I wanted to make the most of the few days he has home.'

'Yes, of course. Well, run along now – and good luck.'

Janet wondered why Miss Brown had wished her good luck. She couldn't know that Janet was pregnant; it didn't show and she hadn't been sick or even felt ill as yet. Perhaps that came later. She hadn't been to the doctor to confirm her fears, but she was never late as a rule and that made her pretty sure she was carrying Mike's baby.

Janet didn't sleep much that night. She was longing to see

Mike again and ninety per cent sure that he would be pleased that she was pregnant so that her father would be forced to let them marry. Yet her stomach was knotting and she kept waking in fright every time she dozed off for a few minutes. What would her father do or say when they told him?

Janet was up early the next morning but her father was already up lighting the range in the kitchen. On lovely summer mornings it often made the kitchen unbearably stuffy and so her mother worked with the back door open to let the heat out and give them some fresh air. The door was what was often called a stable door, because you could swing the top half back while leaving the bottom locked. Turning his head, her father gave her an odd look.

'You're up early this morning. What's wrong?'

'Mike is coming home today,' she said. 'I've got a few days off to be with him, because he'll be going to sea once he returns to base.'

'Finished his training, has he?' he said gruffly. 'Well, a few months at sea will make a man of him, that's for certain.' He hesitated, seeming as if he wanted to say something more and then Janet's mother walked in and he turned away to finish what he'd been doing. 'Put the kettle on, Janet. It's just about hot enough now.'

Janet did as he asked, wondering what he might have said had her mother not come in when she did, but it was probably nothing important. In a way she was glad he hadn't tried to make it up between them, because that would only have made things worse when Mike told him that they had to get married quickly.

Even her mother was going to be shocked and angry. At least Janet was luckier than most girls that got themselves into her predicament, because some of the men didn't want to marry them even though they'd sweet-talked them into getting their way.

'What are you going to do with yourself until Mike comes?' Peggy asked as Janet busied herself with the tea tray. 'You can help me with the cooking if you like. Nellie is making up the beds in the guest rooms, because we've got two new people coming for a couple of days.'

'Of course I'll help out,' Janet said. 'What do you want me to do?'

'You can get breakfast for you and your dad,' her mother said. 'I'm going to make steak and kidney pudding for lunch and a big cheese and onion tart and some pasties for this evening. I want to get ahead, because I'll also be cooking a fish pie this evening for us and the guests – and I thought a nice treacle tart for afters.'

'I love your treacle tart,' Janet agreed as she bustled about making breakfast. 'Poached egg on toast all right for you, Dad? I think I'll just have toast and marmalade.'

She looked in the cupboard for the marmalade and picked up the tin of golden syrup, shaking it because it was clearly nearly empty. After looking for another, she told her mother that there was none left.

'You won't get a treacle tart out of this, Mum,' she said and showed her the empty tin.

'Oh, what a nuisance,' her mother said and frowned. 'I remember now, I used it up last week. I meant to buy some more when I was in Maureen's yesterday. Oh well, you can pop and get some when you've had your breakfast, Janet.'

'I'll wash up and do a few jobs first, because you'll be busy with the other stuff for a start, won't you?'

Peggy agreed she would and Janet smiled at her mother. She made her a slice of toast and marmalade and her mother ate it as she started to peel potatoes and scrape carrots. The smell of chopped onions was strong and Janet felt a bit queasy. She had no sooner finished her toast when she experienced an urgent desire to be sick and left the table abruptly, running upstairs to bend over the toilet. The bitter vomit spewed out of her and she wiped her mouth on the back of her hand, looking at her pale face in the mirror as she realised that this was the start of her morning sickness. Rinsing her mouth with cold water, she splashed her face and towelled it dry, then she went down the hall and into her bedroom. She combed her hair and applied a smear of lipstick.

'Are you all right, Janet lovey?' Nellie looked at her anxiously as Janet emerged into the hall. 'Only, I was cleaning next door and couldn't help hearing you in the toilet...'

'I just felt a bit sick,' Janet explained. 'Mum was peeling onions and I suddenly felt awful.'

'Onions always took me that way, too,' Nellie said and her eyes were sad. 'Peggy doesn't know yet, does she?'

Janet considered pretending she didn't understand, but knew that wouldn't fool Nellie for a minute. Her wise old eyes were not condemning but compassionate, and Janet recognised that here was someone she could confide in.

'Mike is coming home today. He will marry me, Nellie, because he loves me – but Dad is going to be furious. It's his fault, because we might have been married, but I know I shouldn't have done it...'

'None of us are perfect, lovey,' Nellie said. 'You're not the first girl to be caught out and you won't be the last – but at least your young man wants to marry you.'

'Yes...' Janet's eyes stung because Nellie's kindness made her feel tearful. 'You won't tell Mum, will you?'

''Course not, lovey,' Nellie said. 'I'm surprised she hasn't noticed but I dare say she didn't want to.'

'I don't show yet.'

'It's just something in the eyes,' Nellie said. 'Don't look so worried, lovey. Nothing is that bad and your dad will get over it.'

Janet wished she felt as sanguine about her father getting over the shock of his daughter's disgrace as Nellie did. She knew only too well that he would never forgive her. He might have to accept it and allow them to marry, but he would never forgive her for letting him down.

Sighing, Janet picked up her cardigan and went downstairs to the kitchen. Her mother looked at her oddly, but her father had finished his toast and gone through to the bar to start polishing glasses.

'Here's a list of what I need,' Peggy said and gave her a purse and the small piece of paper. 'Maureen should have everything, but if not you'll have to go to the shop in Bell Lane.'

'Yes, all right,' Janet said. 'You've asked for three tins of golden syrup, is that right?'

'Treacle tart is easy to make and popular with the customers,' Peggy said. 'I'll want Bird's custard powder too. I can use the other make, but I like Bird's best so be sure to ask Maureen for it.'

'Yes, and if she hasn't got it I'll try the other shop you mentioned.'

'Are you all right, Janet?' Her mother's eyes were anxious. 'What made you run off like that just now?'

'I wanted to go to the toilet,' Janet said, because it wasn't a complete lie; she had headed straight for the toilet.

'I hope you're not getting a tummy upset. You used to

have them as a child but you haven't had one for ages.'

'Perhaps I ate something at work that wasn't quite right,' Janet said vaguely. 'I'll get off and do the shopping now then, Mum. I don't want to miss Mike when he gets here.'

'Do you think he would like to stay here? We've still got one room free.'

'I'll ask him,' Janet said awkwardly. She picked up her shopping basket and left before her mother could say anything more.

*

Maureen had all the items on her mother's shopping list. She ticked them off one by one and added the price against them so that Peggy could see what she'd been charged.

'It's lucky I stocked up on golden syrup the other month,' she told Janet as she packed the basket for her. 'Dad said yesterday that they hadn't got any at the wholesalers. They told him they hope to have it in again next week, but they've had a run on it. People are beginning to realise that it comes in handy for sweetening if you've run out of sugar. We're down to our last dozen tins now but perhaps we'll get some more next time Dad goes to the wholesaler.'

'Mum uses it a lot,' Janet said. 'She would be upset if she couldn't get it – so put another three tins by for her when you get some more in, won't you?'

'Yes, of course, if I can,' Maureen said. 'We're not actually short of anything yet, because we've been increasing our stock for months, but some things are getting low at the wholesaler. They would only let Dad have six tins of pink salmon yesterday – and the war has hardly started.'

Janet nodded and smiled politely, but she wasn't much

interested in Maureen's problems. If things got short people would have to buy something different, she supposed; it wasn't everyone who could afford tins of salmon anyway. A lot of folk made do with pilchards or sardines, though the very thought of them made Janet queasy. However, she didn't feel as if she was going to vomit again; it seemed to have been just the onions that made her run for the toilet.

Janet didn't hurry home. The sun was warm on her face and she was enjoying the rare feeling of freedom. She knew there were jobs she could do for her mother at home, but she could do them when she was ready and for a few minutes it was good just to know she didn't actually have to work for some days.

Once she was married and in a home of her own she could please herself what she did with her time. As long as the house was clean, Mike's clothes washed, and food on the table, she would be her own mistress. What a lovely thought that was… Janet revelled in the anticipation of being Mike's wife. They wouldn't have long together before he had to leave, of course, but at least she would be his wife and she couldn't wait to get that ring on her finger.

Mike was sitting in the kitchen drinking coffee and eating a scone with butter when she got back. His kitbag stood behind the door and he was wearing the uniform of a sailor. He stood up as she entered and she flew into his arms.

'Jan darling,' he said and embraced her. 'I've been think-ing of this for days.'

'I've got something I need to tell you urgently,' Janet whis-pered in his ear as he held her.

Mike turned his head and looked into her eyes. Janet half-nodded her head, but realised he didn't know what she meant. She sighed, feeling impatient to be alone with him, feeling relieved when her mother said, 'Can I rely on you to take the pie out of the oven in ten minutes, Janet?'

'Of course you can, Mum.'

She sat down as her mother picked up two plates of cheese scones and took them through into the bar.

'What's wrong, Jan?' Mike asked.

'I'm pregnant,' she said. 'We have to get married by special licence, Mike – and Dad is going to hit the roof.'

'Serves him right,' Mike said harshly. 'He could easily have let us get married before this. He was just being a dog in the manger, wanting to keep his little girl for himself.'

'You make him sound awful,' Janet said doubtfully. 'He has every right to say no, Mike – but I hope he won't.'

'Oh, he'll be threatening me with a shotgun now,' Mike said and grinned. 'Besides, if he said no we would just take the train to Gretna Green and get married there. I've got the rings and the form your parents have to sign just in case; I told you in my letter I was going to ask again, didn't I?'

'Yes.' Janet smiled, feeling better than she had for weeks. Perhaps at the back of her mind there had been a tiny doubt, but it had vanished now. Mike was here and he still loved her – and now she wouldn't have to tell her parents alone, although it was still going to be dreadful...

*

'We didn't mean it to happen this way,' Mike said, his face white but proud as he looked Janet's father in the eyes. 'If you'd let us get engaged and married this Christmas as we asked it wouldn't have...'

Even in her dreams Janet hadn't thought it would be this

awful. The look in her mother's eyes and the blind fury on her father's face was terrible to see.

'You little bastard,' Laurence yelled in fury. 'How dare you tell me it's my fault that you've shamed my daughter?'

'I love Janet and I want to marry her. I've got the rings and the consent forms and I'll get the special licence as soon as...'

Before Mike could finish what he had to say, Janet's father struck him a heavy blow in the face. It landed on his chin and sent him reeling. Mike hadn't seen it coming and it took him a moment to recover. She saw his fists tighten and knew that he was considering hitting her father, but she caught at his arm in anguish.

'No, Mike, please don't; fighting won't solve anything.'

'You shouldn't have done that, Laurence,' Peggy cut in before either of the men could do or say anything further. 'I know he has behaved badly to our daughter, but we have to think of her future now. Mike says he wants to marry her and I think that is the best thing for her. You must see we can't do anything else.'

For a moment Laurence stared at Janet with loathing, and then he inclined his head. 'You can give her permission if you wish, but I'm having nothing to do with any of it. As far as I'm concerned I want her and him out of my house within the hour and you are never to speak of her to me again.'

'Laurence, you can't throw her out! Where would she go? She doesn't have any money and she's having a child – your grandchild.'

'It's no kin of mine,' Laurence said. 'If you're so concerned give her some of your money, but I want nothing to do with her.'

He strode out of the kitchen, slamming the door behind

him. Janet watched her mother's face and her heart wrenched with regret as she saw the pain she'd caused her.

'We'll go now, Mum,' she said. 'I'll pack a case and you can bring me the rest once we've found somewhere to stay. I've got a little bit saved.'

Mike had wiped the blood from his nose. He'd been recovering from the blow, but now he said, 'We'll be all right, Mrs Ashley. All we need is your signature on a form and then we can get married by special licence. I shall go and get it later today.'

Peggy nodded and went to the kitchen dresser, taking down the square tin on top. She took ten one pound notes from it and pushed them into her daughter's hand.

'Take it to please me,' she said. 'I know you've got a bit but you'll have a lot of expenses. I always thought you would be near me and I'd be able to help – that your father would give you a hundred or two when you got married...'

'I've got money saved,' Mike said. 'But take the money your mum is giving you, Jan, to please her. I'm sorry this had to happen, Mrs Ashley, but your husband was wrong to refuse us even some hope.'

'Yes, he was wrong,' Peggy agreed but her eyes didn't smile as she looked at him. 'But you're wrong too, Mike – and Janet knows what she's done. I'm not sure Laurence will ever forgive you, Jan. I'll do the best I can but not yet. It will take time and I daren't even try until he's calmed down.'

'Don't quarrel with Dad over me,' Janet said. 'I'll be all right as long as we can get married. Please, Mum.'

'Give me the form and I'll sign it,' she said wearily and Mike took it from his kitbag and handed her a fountain pen. Peggy signed her name and returned it. 'Take care of my daughter. I don't want her hurt more than she is already.'

'Mum, I'm so sorry,' Janet said and hugged her. She broke away and dashed upstairs, beginning to throw things into a suitcase.

When she got back down to the kitchen her mother was alone and Mike was waiting in the yard for her. Janet could see that her mother's face was wet with tears.

'Don't cry, Mum, I'll be all right,' she said.

'I'm not sure I shall.'

'Please don't say that. I feel bad enough already.'

'Yes, I know you do,' her mother said. 'I knew something was wrong. I should have guessed. If you'd told me, we might have found a way... but it's too late now.'

'Why is Dad so against me getting married? What has Mike done to make him hate him so much?'

'Nothing – except take his little girl away from him,' she said and looked sad. 'It might have happened whoever you wanted to marry – but if you were older he would have seen sense. Now...' She shook her head and looked hopeless and Janet's heart sank.

'I don't want him to take it out on you, Mum.'

Her mother's eyes were bleak. 'We haven't been right for a while now, love. It started months ago, but got worse when I tried to persuade him that he should let you at least get engaged, but it isn't just you and Mike...' She sighed. 'Don't let it spoil things for you two. Be happy together – and keep in touch. I'd like to see you whenever you can manage it – and the baby, of course, when it comes, even if I have to meet you somewhere else. I shall miss seeing you all the time...'

'Oh, Mum, I do love you,' Janet said, hugged her again and ran outside to Mike.

'It will be all right, love,' he said and hugged her. 'I promise you there's nothing to worry about. I've got a bit put by and I'll arrange it so they pay some of my money to you each month. You can come down to Portsmouth and I'll be able to see you until I go to sea. It's what we've wanted, so cheer up.'

'I was thinking of Mum.' Janet forced herself to smile. 'I know you will look after me, Mike. I love you and I want to be your wife.'

She just wished it hadn't had to be like this, her family ripped apart by quarrels and her mum looking as if she had lost everything.

'It's going to be fun,' Mike said enthusiastically. 'I can't wait to show off my lovely wife to the other blokes. They won't half be envious.'

Janet laughed, but inside she felt as if she were being torn in two. She hated it that her father despised her and it hurt because she'd caused her mother pain, but there was nothing she could do. Her ties with the past had been cut; she had to make a life with Mike now and put this upset behind her.

Chapter 14

Peggy got up to start working, preparing the cheese and onion tarts and the Cornish pasties she'd planned. The guests had moved into their rooms and she must provide an evening meal for them as well as food in the bar for the regulars. She had no heart for the work, because in a few hours her family had been ripped apart and she felt as if her world had ended, but of course life had to go on. At least Janet could get married to her sailor and she'd probably live quite happily somewhere miles away, and Peggy would hardly ever see her daughter but Janet would surely keep in touch by letter.

It was the only bright thread in all this, Peggy thought, and tried to be happy for Janet, because the girl was very much in love. However, her own life seemed to be hopeless. Laurence was like a stranger. She hardly knew the man who had stared at her in hatred as he told her he no longer had a daughter. Clearly, he blamed her, Peggy, for what had happened, though she couldn't see why. If anyone was to blame for the situation other than the young couple, it was Laurence for refusing even to allow them to become engaged. Janet had behaved badly, because she'd known how her father would react, but she was young and in love.

Peggy sighed. Had she once been as much in love as her daughter was now? The years of her marriage had seemed good for a long time, although even before they'd fallen out over Mike and Janet, Peggy had noticed that things were not quite the same. She'd put it down to getting older and the distractions of business. Both she and Laurence worked hard, but they had been happy surely... and yet this past year, since around the time her stepfather died, it had seemed as if a shadow hung over them. And since the quarrel over Janet things had got so much worse. Before she'd just put his moods down to tiredness or a bad temper, but now she was realising that all this had been there beneath the surface for a while, waiting to bubble over. It had taken a big quarrel to bring it all out and she wondered if there was anything she could do to make things better, but decided it was impossible as things stood.

Nothing would change the way things were. After such a rift there was no going back, and Peggy couldn't see her husband ever embracing his daughter and her family. It was a bleak prospect and one she could hardly bear to contemplate, but she had to keep going. There was Pip to think of and her other responsibilities. She didn't know if she still cared for Laurence, but the pub was her life and she couldn't even start to think what she'd do if she left.

She took the hot pastries through to the bar and placed them in the glass cabinet on the counter, where the customers could see them. She left other dishes on the kitchen table to cool for later and went upstairs to lay the dining table for supper. While there were guests in the house she must be the cheerful landlady and carry on as if nothing had happened, but in her heart she knew that nothing would ever be the same again. Her life had changed and no matter what she did she couldn't get back that old feeling of content.

'Oh, Peggy, I'm so sorry,' Maureen said as they sat in her back room having a cup of tea the next morning. 'It must have been awful for all of you. Poor Janet. I'd noticed she wasn't looking well for the past few weeks, but I didn't dream it was anything like that. I suppose you can't blame Laurence for being angry. He was so very proud of her, wasn't he?'

'Yes, I expect that's it,' Peggy agreed and sipped her tea. 'I was upset too, but I wouldn't have thrown her out. I don't know where she is or what they did after they left me. I doubt if I shall be asked to the wedding – and I probably couldn't go if I was.'

'You must if Janet lets you know where and when,' Maureen said and touched her hand in sympathy. 'I know Laurence is angry, but she's your daughter, Peggy. You would be so upset if you didn't go, you know you would.'

'Yes, I expect I should,' Peggy admitted and smiled. 'I'm glad I've told you, Maureen. I know it won't go any further and I just had to tell someone. Nellie knows, of course, but she'd guessed about Janet being with child. I wish I had, because if I'd known I might have managed things better. Laurence was so shocked and angry. He knocked Mike down, and I'm sure Mike was ready to have a go at him, but Janet begged him not to.'

'Well, she wouldn't want them fighting over her, would she?' Maureen sighed. 'I do hate rows. It always makes things so uncomfortable.'

'Yes, and you have enough to put up with. I didn't ask you how you got on with Shirley the other week. Was she a right little madam?'

'Yes, just a bit,' Maureen confessed. 'Gordon got cross and smacked her and her grandmother took her home, but that was just what she wanted. I was hoping she would like coming here and get used to me, but there was no pleasing her, I'm afraid.'

'Oh well, perhaps Gordon will think better of making you her guardian if Mrs Hart should become ill or worse.'

'I don't think so. He asked if I was still willing to have her round to tea and I said yes. He needs to know that she will be all right if anything happens to him. I think he's terrified they might put Shirley in an orphanage if his mother died and he was away or dead.'

'Well, I suppose they might, if you don't agree to have her,' Peggy said. 'Because legally none of us could do anything to stop it, unless he does make you her guardian. We look after our own, but once the kids' welfare lot get involved they take over. But won't you find her a tie – if the worst should happen?'

'My father may kick up, but Gran says we can both go to her if we want, and I think Dad would realise that it was better to have both of us than let me leave.'

'What about your wishes, Maureen? You're not thinking of marrying Gordon Hart?'

'No. I like him and he has asked, but I said I wouldn't. I promised to help over Shirley, because I don't like the idea that she might get shoved off in an orphanage somewhere and I know that's what is upsetting him.'

'You'll want to marry one day, love. What happens then?'

'I can't see it happening,' Maureen said. 'I think you know about Rory – but he's married, Peggy. If I can't have him, I don't want anyone. I don't want to be tied to a man I don't love. I've had enough of that, always having to consult someone else's wishes and tip-toeing around when he's in a bad mood, believe me.'

'Yes, I know what you mean. Sometimes I think women are absolute fools. We fall for all that love and marriage stuff and then, when they've got us where they want us, they act as if we're slaves with no feelings.' Peggy spoke angrily and then went red, feeling hot all over. 'No, I don't mean it, Maureen, don't look so stricken. I'm just down in the dumps because of Janet. I suppose I still care for Laurence.'

'Of course you do. Some days I feel fit to murder my father, but then when he's ill I worry about him until the doctor comes.'

'Your father is lucky to have such a caring daughter. Not many would have done what you did, love.'

'Sometimes I wish I hadn't,' Maureen admitted and decided to change the subject. 'Anne came in earlier today. She's taking the last of their children down to Devon this week. They've got the building they were after and it's being turned into a sort of boarding school. She says the bedrooms are all big enough to take at least three kids so they will get all the children that want to be evacuated. Some parents have put their foot down and are refusing to let them go, although Anne says they may have to in the end.'

'I think it's all right if the mother wants to take her kids down herself,' Peggy said thoughtfully. 'I suppose if your husband is away it's just as well to evacuate with your family – but I shouldn't want to live surrounded by fields and cows.'

Maureen laughed, looking younger and prettier, Peggy thought. 'There are villages and smaller towns, Peggy. It's just safer there than here in London – at least that's what everyone says.'

'I still don't want to go.'

'You can't leave the pub anyway,' Maureen said. 'It's like me and Dad and the shop. If we just ran away now we should lose everything. We couldn't afford to just throw it all away.'

'Everything would grind to a halt if we all went,' Peggy agreed. 'It's just the kids really; they're our future and they ought to be protected – but I'm not sure I should have wanted to send my two if they were younger.'

'Oh, do let's talk about something else,' Maureen said. 'Let me know if you hear from Janet. I should like to see her wed, and to give her a present.'

'I'll pop round and tell you as soon as I hear something,' Peggy promised and finished her tea. 'I'd better get on. Laurence said he had a meeting this evening so it looks as if I shall be coping on my own, unless Pip gives me a hand in the bar.'

'I wish I could help,' Maureen said. 'I don't see why I shouldn't come after I close the shop, just for an hour or two. Would that help?'

'Of course it would,' Peggy said and smiled. 'You're a real brick, Maureen. I only wish there was something I could do for you.'

'Just keep coming round for a chat,' Maureen laughed. 'I'll see you later then. It will make a real change for me.'

*

Maureen was collecting dirty glasses that evening when the telephone rang and Peggy was nearest so she answered it. She heard deep breathing and then Janet's slightly nervous voice.

'Is that you, Mum?'

'Janet? Oh, thank God! Are you all right?'

'Yes, of course.' Janet's voice went up a tone. 'We've found a room and we've got a special licence. We're getting married at three o'clock on Friday – can you get away?'

'I'll make sure I do, just tell me where,' Peggy promised. 'I'll bring a case with more of your things, love.'

'Good. I was afraid you wouldn't come.'

'I thought you might not ask, but Maureen said you were sure to – oh, she'd like to come too if she can?'

'Of course, I'd like to see her,' Janet said. 'Is Dad there?'

'No, he went to a meeting earlier and he still isn't back. Did you want to speak to him?'

'No! I just wanted to be sure you weren't getting black looks.'

Peggy heard the pips go and frowned. 'Put some more money in, love.'

'Haven't got any more change; we'll see you on Friday at the Register Office in Bow Road...'

The phone was abruptly cut off and Peggy cursed. It was just like Janet to phone without enough change, but at least she knew when and where her daughter was getting married.

'Was that Janet?' Maureen asked, returning with her loaded tray. 'It was a bit quick, wasn't it?'

'Her money ran out and she hadn't got any more change,' Peggy said and smiled wryly. 'Can you get away on Friday afternoon? We'll need to leave soon after two in the afternoon to get there in plenty of time.'

'I'll ask Gran to stand in for me.' Maureen's face lit up with pleasure. 'I'm so glad, Peggy. It will be nice for you and I'd like to see her married – what shall I give her as a present?'

'They haven't got much, but I suppose money is as useful

as anything. I should think they'll be in furnished rooms for a start, probably some kind of married quarters if they're lucky.'

'Well, don't look so sad,' Maureen said. 'Janet is happy and that's what matters, isn't it?'

'Yes, of course it is,' Peggy said and put on a smile as she went off to serve a customer with a pint of best bitter. Maureen was right. It could have been worse. At least Janet had shown willing to keep in touch, and for the moment it was the most she could hope for.

*

Everyone was ready to go in when Peggy and Maureen arrived. The Register Office looked a bit pokey from outside and Peggy's heart sank, because her daughter should be getting married in white at a local church. However, inside it looked much better; the mahogany fittings had a shine to them and there was an overwhelming scent of lilies from the large vase of them on the table in front of which the registrar stood in order to carry out the brief ceremony. He was a white-haired man dressed in a formal black suit, but his eyes smiled.

Janet was wearing her best pale blue dress, which had a full skirt and a little boxy jacket that covered her waist; it hid any signs of her pregnancy if there were any to see yet. She'd bought a little pillbox hat in white with lots of veiling, which she'd perched on the back of her head, and she carried a small posy of white rosebuds. Mike looked smart in a navy blue suit, his shoes polished to within an inch of their life and both of them looked really happy as after a brief ceremony they were pronounced man and wife.

As they emerged into the autumn sunshine, Maureen and Peggy threw some confetti over them, and Mike's witness, a lanky, sandy-haired young man, who had worked with him at the shipyard before he left for the Navy, took a few photos on a box camera. He was introduced as Tony, and they learned later that he was the son of Italian parents who were the owners of a restaurant. A few other people had gathered and Peggy and Maureen were introduced to Mike's sister and a few friends of the couple.

A little girl gave them something tied up in blue ribbons and Maureen gave Janet a lucky horseshoe made of silver-faced cardboard tied with blue ribbons, and an envelope.

'I wasn't sure what to get so I thought money would be useful for your new home,' she said, looking shy. Janet kissed her and thanked her. Mike kissed her too and Maureen blushed bright pink.

'I've packed a few things in your suitcase from me,' Peggy told her daughter. 'Pip sends his love but he has some special lectures at school and couldn't get away. I hope you will both be very happy, darling – and you will write often, won't you?'

'Yes, of course,' Janet promised and hugged her. 'You're coming to have a drink with us, aren't you? Mike has arranged a few sandwiches and a sponge cake...'

Peggy's throat caught with regret. If things had been different Janet would have worn a special white dress and she would have closed the pub to put on a splendid reception for them. The thought that she would never have that opportunity made her eyes sting with tears and she was glad she'd taken extra money from the savings tin to give Janet and Mike; it still wasn't what she'd planned, but they would have fifty pounds to help them get started and it wasn't every young couple that had that much.

'Of course we're coming, aren't we, Maureen?'

'Yes,' Maureen agreed happily. 'Gran is holding the fort and thoroughly enjoying herself. I'm in no hurry to get back.'

So they all packed into the taxi that Mike had hailed, Janet sitting on Mike's lap so that they could all squeeze inside. They arrived at what was obviously a small restaurant in Stepney; it was a short distance from the London Hospital, but Peggy had never been there to eat. As they approached the door opened and they were welcomed inside by a rather rotund Italian lady. She had smiles all over her face as she welcomed the wedding party and took them through to her dining room.

'We're staying here,' Janet whispered in her mother's ear. 'Tony told Mike that Mrs Rossini had a room we could have for a few days. She's been really kind.'

Peggy could see their hostess was a kind woman and generous. She'd put flowers around the large room and set the tables with bright red cloths. The plates were sparkling clean and the bowls of delicious salads had a distinctly Italian look and flavour. Cold meats, pasta and chunks of fresh bread and butter were on offer, as well as a fresh fruit salad with vanilla ice-cream that her husband had made fresh that morning. In pride of place was a three-tier sponge filled with jam and fresh cream and with a thin white icing on top. She'd certainly done them proud at short notice, and the crisp sparkling white wine offered on arrival was lovely. As the guests started to arrive, a mixture of the couple's friends and Mike's family, about twelve in all, the small room began to fill and there was a buzz of laughter and congratulations.

'Here's to your happiness, my love,' Peggy said, blinking because she regretted that Janet's father and brother weren't there. 'You too, Mike. I wish you a long and happy life together.'

'Thank you, Peggy,' he said and kissed her cheek. 'We appreciate your coming to the wedding.'

It was nearly five when Maureen and Peggy left to go home. Peggy knew it wouldn't leave her much time to get ready for the evening opening. She'd cooked as much food as she could earlier and left it ready on the table, but some of it had been sold during the morning, and unless she cooked a few extra scones they would probably run short.

She and Maureen parted company after they left the tram and Peggy walked as quickly as she could, but it was a quarter to six when she finally entered the kitchen. Laurence gave her a slaying look, because she hadn't made any secret of where she was going. She'd had a faint hope he might come too, but of course he had ignored all mention of his daughter or her wedding.

'Have you eaten, Pip?' she asked.

'We cooked some eggs and bacon,' her son said cheerfully. 'Was it all right, Mum?'

'Yes, lovely,' she said and shook her head, mouthing the word 'later' at him. Pip coloured and shot an apprehensive look at his father, but didn't say another word.

Peggy tied an apron on over her dress and got the mixing bowl out. Laurence had gone through to the bar and could be heard clinking glasses.

'Why won't Dad talk about Janet?' Pip asked. 'What has she done that is so wicked?'

'You know that she and Mike are having a baby, but they're married now so it's all right – but your father can't forgive her for letting him down.'

'Is that all? I thought it must be something much worse.

Jan told me Dad wouldn't let her get married, and I guessed the rest. She was upset when Dad told her she'd got to wait for years,' Pip said, frowning. 'Why didn't he say yes, Mum? Lots of girls are getting married young because the war has come. Couldn't Dad see what might happen?'

'He wouldn't let himself,' Peggy said. 'He thought Janet was his little girl and he didn't want her to grow up and get married. It was a great pity, because we missed having a lovely white wedding and a reception here.'

'I still don't see why he won't speak to her. I'd have come with you if I could, but I couldn't miss school. I care about Jan, even if Dad doesn't.' Pip came to her and put his arms about her. 'Poor old Mum. You're the best cook anywhere and you would have loved to give her a wonderful do – and it's a rotten shame you didn't get to see her married in white.'

Peggy's eyes misted because her son was so understanding and kind. She kissed the side of his head and smiled. 'It was a nice reception anyway; Mrs Rossini made it lovely for them – and Janet wore a white hat and looked very pretty.'

'Not the same though, is it?' He gave her a hug. 'Never mind, Mum. You've still got me. And maybe Dad will come round once he's got over his temper.'

Chapter 15

'Every time that damned siren goes off it gives me the shivers,' Peggy complained to her husband as she was preparing for bed one evening. 'They've done it twice today; there hasn't been a raid so why frighten us all?'

'We shan't always have false alarms, Peggy. One of these days you will be glad of the extinguishers I told you to buy. Fires can be put out if you act quickly, and the cellars are safe enough. I think they would take even a direct hit, although then there wouldn't be much left of the rest of it – but all we can do is follow the rules and hope we're lucky.'

Peggy shivered even though it was a warm night. 'We've put our lives into this place and we could end up with nothing, no business and no home.'

'We could always start again somewhere else.' Laurence hesitated, then, 'I've got a bit put by. It isn't a fortune, but it would be enough to set up again if we had to.'

'How did you manage that? We do well, but most of it goes back into stock – at least I thought it did...'

His eyes avoided hers. 'I had a bit of a win on the horses, Peggy. I don't often gamble, but a customer gave me a tip and I put a hundred quid on it at odds of twenty to one – and it romped home. I decided it was meant to be and tucked it away as a nest egg.'

'You didn't tell me?'

'I thought you would be angry, because you hate gambling – and if I'd lost it you would've been furious.'

'Gambling can be addictive and lead to trouble.'

'Well, it was just the once and I got lucky. It's safe in the post office bank and the book is in both our names, so if anything happens to me – or to the pub – you'll have something.'

Peggy felt cold inside. 'Please don't say things like that, Laurie.'

He half-smiled as he met her eyes. 'You haven't called me that for ages,' he said, then, 'I didn't want to fall out with you, love.'

'I know,' she admitted and went to him, putting her arms about his waist and looking up into his face. 'I'm sorry if you think I let you down.'

'You did what any mother would do,' he said. 'I'm not saying I forgive her, Peggy, because I can't. I thought the world of that girl and she let me down.'

'I know...' Peggy looked up and he bent his head, kissing her softly. 'Can we be friends again?'

'I love you,' he said but looked serious. 'I just wish we could turn the clock back and things would be different.'

Peggy was puzzled, because she'd thought he would want to make love now that they'd made up their quarrel, but he walked away and reached for a dark overcoat and his tin hat.

'Are you going out at this hour?'

'We're at war,' he replied. 'I'm on fire watch at the munitions factory. We've all got to take our turn now. It means you'll have even more to do when I'm on early watch, but I'm taking the midnight to six watch tonight.'

'When will you sleep?' Peggy asked doubtfully.

'I'll have a lie-in after I've done the fires in the morning,' he said and his expression hardened. 'If I don't do this, they'll find some excuse to call me back to the Army.'

'Surely not? They've got thousands of younger men they can call on first.'

'And one battle could cost the lives of thousands of them,' Laurence said grimly. 'It won't be too long before they ask for older men – and then they will make it compulsory.'

'You did your bit last time.' Peggy remembered what it was like when he'd had to leave for the Front the first time. It had broken her heart. Suddenly, she regretted all the anger between them. 'I love you, Laurie.'

'Do you?' He smiled oddly. 'I thought you'd forgotten about us – you love Pip and Janet, and you've got lots of friends. I thought I came a long way down the list.'

His words cut her and she couldn't find the right ones to answer him. Peggy sat on the edge of the bed and wept after he'd left. She felt empty and hopeless, as if the bottom had fallen out of her world. Laurence couldn't mean that, surely? He'd spoken as if it was over; as if he'd accepted that there was nothing much left of the marriage and the love they'd thought would last forever.

Laurence seemed to have shut right off from her. He'd kept a big win on the horses a secret from her, and the store of spirits in the cellar that Pip had mentioned, so what more was there that Laurence wasn't telling her? Or was she imagining things now? The trouble was that once the cracks started you could never be certain of anything.

*

Over the next few weeks, Peggy like most people was on the alert, thinking that they were going to be bombed every time the siren went, but as time passed and the all clear was called without an attack she began to relax. Perhaps it would all blow over after all. Poland had fallen and now the Germans had turned their attention to France, Hitler's forces were too busy to bother with England and the people he'd tried and failed to woo over to his side.

Janet telephoned one morning in late October.

'I'm frightened, Mum,' she confessed. 'I don't know what I'll do if anything happens to Mike. I don't know many people down here yet. My landlady is all right, but she wouldn't look after me if anything happened.'

'This is still your home,' Peggy told her. 'Try not to worry, love. Nothing much is happening yet. We have the siren most days but they're only false alarms.'

'Don't you read the newspapers, Mum? Ships on the Atlantic run are already being torpedoed and sunk, merchant ships and their escorts.'

'Is Mike on that run?'

'I don't know. He wasn't told much, just that they were going to sea for training purposes. For the first couple of weeks he came back to me most nights, but he's gone now and he told me it would be a while before he was home.'

'Well, it's his job,' Peggy said, 'but I'm sure lots of ships are getting through perfectly safely. You've got to think positively – for the baby's sake, if not your own.'

'I am trying to,' Janet said, 'but it's lonely when he's away.'

'I wish I could tell you to come home for a visit, but you know your father... but if you're really miserable I'm sure you could stay with Nellie for a while.'

'I can't come home in case Mike returns unexpectedly,'

Janet said and gave a little laugh. 'It's all right, Mum. I'm just feeling down in the dumps at the moment. I'll be all right tomorrow.'

'You've got to try and make friends there,' Peggy advised. 'Are you doing a little job? I should've thought you could work for a while.'

'Mike didn't want me to work, but I'm thinking of looking for something. I might get a few hours in a pub or a restaurant.'

'Why not try a shop or an office? You don't need to do menial work.'

'I'll do anything for a bit of company,' Janet said. 'We're all right for money, though. I get half Mike's pay when he's away.'

'Good.' Peggy sighed. 'It's never easy when you're first married. You'll get used to it, love.'

She stared into space as Janet rang off. It would've been so much easier if her daughter was living round the corner, so that she could visit and Janet could come to her when she was anxious, but there was nothing she could do to help at this distance. Peggy was sympathetic, but Janet had made her choice and must put up with the loneliness that came with living in the way she had chosen. Just as Peggy had to put up with the emptiness of her own life, because even though her husband was still with her, for all the love or closeness between them she might as well have been on her own. Laurence no longer put his arms about her and kissed her neck when she was standing in her petticoat, and in bed he simply turned over and went to sleep, even if he was there, which he wasn't a lot of the time. When he wasn't working in the bar, he was at a meeting or on fire watch. Peggy had asked why it was necessary when they hadn't had one bomb attack, but he merely sighed and looked at her as if she were stupid for not understanding.

Since the declaration of war everything was changing; they were bombarded with leaflets and new rules, as not only did every house have to have a stirrup pump and blackout curtains but the government were urging people to paint the edges of their windows black to prevent even a chink of light showing. Mr Churchill was back as First Lord of the Admiralty and had caused a buzz of excitement in his party. Just this month, the battleship *Royal Oak* had been sunk by a German torpedo in her home base of Scapa Flow. And thousands of troops had been sent to France.

Perhaps Peggy shouldn't be surprised that Laurence was too busy to make love to her. Yet war didn't explain this barrier between them. Was it her fault, or had Laurence simply got bored with his life?

Chapter 16

'I thought you were in the country,' Maureen said as Anne entered the shop that chilly autumn morning. 'Your last letter said you were enjoying it there.'

'Yes, I was but Mrs Miles has taken over my job and I've been sent back to London. This is the first chance I've had to come round – though I saw Peggy last night. The school is being requisitioned as a military depot of some kind and I've been asked to help sort out our things for storing until after the war – and then I have work as a supply teacher. I'm hoping to be based in London, because quite a few older children chose to remain with their parents and they still need teachers.'

'Your class will miss you, Anne.'

'Yes...' Anne sighed and looked a bit misty-eyed. 'But at the moment I have to go where I'm needed. Not all the children evacuated with us; some went with their parents to stay with relatives, and a lot of the second and third-year kids were sent on the train and ended up with strangers.'

'That was what Gordon Hart was afraid of, which is why his mother took Shirley down to stay with people she knows for a while. I never thought I would miss the boys playing football in the street, shouting and making lots of noise, but I do.'

'Yes, it feels odd to me too. I'm used to teaching the little ones but I've just been told I may be coaching secondary modern boys who are working for important exams next year. Some of them may leave school sooner than planned and go into the Army.'

'I suppose most of the young lads will sign up as soon as they are old enough,' Maureen sighed.

'Yes, I expect so – but it's worrying for their mothers.'

'Very much so; I know Peggy is terrified that her son will go the minute he's eighteen,' Maureen said. 'He had important exams this year, I know.'

'Laurence will stop him if he can, but once he's eighteen there's nothing he can do; besides, he'll be called up once he's old enough.'

'Is that everything?' Maureen asked as she put the half pound of loose tea into a thick bag and placed it with the other goods on the counter. 'These come to seven and sixpence.'

'Yes, that's all I need for me,' Anne said. 'I have my lunch at school – and I eat with the others in the canteen at night.'

'Canteen – is that at your school?'

'Oh no, I've joined the WVS and I've just started work in a canteen four nights a week. It's set up in what used to be an empty warehouse. It's not much of a place, even though it's been brightened up a bit. We've hung a few flags up and put some pictures of film stars on the walls; they've got a kitchen of sorts out the back; for the men it's basic tables and chairs, and a few comfortable armchairs. Someone brought a gramophone in and we've got some records of Vera Lynn and a few oldies we can play for the men. We let them smoke and don't rush them out when they've eaten so it serves its purpose.' Anne hesitated, then, 'I was going to ask if you wanted to join us, Maureen. We look after servicemen and give them a meal, and we fix them up with an address for cheap lodgings if they're on leave and don't know London – all that sort of thing. It's just for a start, until things get going. I've done a first aid class and once war starts properly, we volunteers will help wherever we're needed.'

'It sounds like a good idea,' Maureen said thoughtfully. 'Once, I would've said it wasn't possible for me to come, but my father has joined the civil defence service and I'm usually alone at night. I couldn't start until after I close the shop.'

'That doesn't matter.' Anne looked pleased. 'I'll give you the address of the hall where we meet and you can come any time up until ten at night. We're glad of any help, and it isn't just serving tea and cake – but I'll show you when you get there.'

'Yes, please do,' Maureen said and slipped the piece of lined paper into her pocket. 'I'll try and get there this evening.'

She was smiling as Anne left and another customer entered. It would make a pleasant change serving in the canteen. She would meet some young men for a change...

*

That evening Maureen divided her time between washing up and making corned beef sandwiches. The only time she saw anyone but Mabel, another volunteer, was when she went through to the canteen proper to load a tray with more dirty dishes.

'I'm sorry you got stuck with all the chores this evening,' Anne said as they walked home together. 'Two of our volunteers didn't turn up so Mabel was short-handed. It won't always be like that; I'll see you get your chance serving the men.'

'I didn't mind. I spoke to one or two of them when I was

clearing the tables. They all look so young, Anne. I'm sure some of them aren't eighteen.'

'They certainly look younger,' Anne agreed. 'Perhaps we're getting older, Maureen. A couple of spinsters...'

Maureen looked at her because she sensed that beneath the self-mockery was a little bitterness. 'Is anything wrong, Anne?'

'No, not really.' Anne sighed. 'I thought someone cared for me. I might as well be honest: he is married but he swore he loved me and would leave her... but now she's with him in the country and I'm here in London, and I know he'll never divorce her as he promised.'

'Oh, Anne, I'm so sorry,' Maureen said. 'I had no idea.'

'I couldn't talk about it... after all I had no right to expect anything. Besides, I wasn't sure how you would feel about me seeing a married man. Peggy doesn't condemn me but she's older.'

'I would never condemn you, Anne. Surely you know I wouldn't? Anyway, I know how it feels – no, I really do, love. Rory is married and his wife has had a baby. He says he's always loved me, and I had my chance to marry him years ago, but I couldn't leave Dad after Mum died... and Rory didn't understand. We quarrelled and he went off – now it's too late.'

'Oh, Maureen, that's even worse,' Anne said. 'I don't think Harry ever really loved me, though I think I was in love – but it's over now. I've seen him for what he really is and that's a coward. His wife threatened that she would get him sacked if he left her... and when the Army turned him down, he seemed to cave in to her demands.'

'If he had any guts he'd stand up to her.' Maureen felt angry for her friend.

'It would mean throwing away all he's worked for,' Anne said and smiled oddly. 'I can't see Harry doing that for me – and I don't want him to. I'd feel guilty. I'll get used to being an old maid.'

'Oh, don't,' Maureen begged. 'You're still young enough to find love.'

'So are you, but I can't see you making a change,' Anne said with a little challenge in her eyes.

'I've done something by coming to the canteen,' Maureen said. 'I couldn't just walk off and leave Dad, because he is a sick man – even though he puts some of it on, but I'm going to get out more. I might as well, because he's out a lot of the time at meetings.' Maureen laughed. 'He wears a tin hat four nights a week and goes round looking for a chink of light through someone's curtains and then he knocks on their door and reminds them there's a blackout and they're breaking the law.'

'My uncle calls them "little Hitlers",' Anne said and laughed.

'Yes, I think Dad enjoys his authority,' Maureen agreed and smiled. 'I'd better leave you here. This is my bus stop.'

'I'm just round the corner. I heard this afternoon that I'm being transferred to a school outside London next week, but you won't stop helping out at the canteen, will you?'

Maureen saw her bus coming and stepped forward to flag it down, but she shook her head and mouthed the word 'no' as she got on board, waving as the bus drew off from the kerb. She was sorry Anne wouldn't be around for a while but she'd quite enjoyed herself that evening, even though she had been on kitchen duty most of the time.

*

'It sounds like a good thing to do,' Peggy said when Maureen told her about her work at the canteen a week or so later. 'I knew Anne had been working with the WVS but she told me she thought she would be transferred somewhere else for a while.'

'I don't think she really wanted to go,' Maureen said, 'but she doesn't have much choice.'

'I wish I could do something to help the war effort,' Peggy said, 'but it takes me all my time to keep the pub going. I've told Laurence I need help and he finally said I could get a girl part time if I could find one willing to work for what he's willing to pay.'

'It's a pity Janet isn't in London,' Maureen said and then wished she hadn't as she saw Peggy's stricken look. 'I'm sorry. I know you must miss her a lot.'

'I do, of course – and she's miserable when he's away, but Mike was home on leave last time she rang. She sounded happy then, because he'd been put on short trips for the moment. Of course even our own seas aren't safe now. Laurence said the Germans have dropped mines in the North Sea, and I think Mike is one of the escorts for the minesweeper. I think it's disgusting what's happening. Hitler says he wants to make peace with Britain and France and then he goes and does something like that.'

'I saw in the paper about the damage the U-boats are doing,' Maureen said. 'What does your husband think about it all, Peggy?'

'He doesn't talk about his opinions much,' she sighed. 'All he has to say these days concerns the pub or his war work.'

'I know they're calling up thousands of men. Do you think Laurence will get his papers?'

'I'm not sure. He told me once it was bound to happen

once the volunteers ran out, but I'm hoping he's too old.'

Maureen nodded, understanding how Peggy felt. Rory would probably be in the thick of any fighting the British troops were involved in, whether that was in Norway or France. He hadn't been in touch with her since the evening they'd kissed, but that didn't mean he was ever out of her thoughts. She worried if he was all right and wondered if she would be told if he became injured. Probably not, as she wasn't a relative, and that thought hurt. Rory could already be dead and she wouldn't know.

*

'You're new here, aren't you?' The young soldier caught hold of Maureen's wrist for a moment as she cleared his table. 'You remind me of someone, but I can't think who it is.'

Maureen smiled and removed herself from his grasp. 'I don't think we've ever met, Sergeant.'

'I've seen your face, at least I think it was you – but you looked younger. One of the men had your picture up on his locker.'

'Surely not,' Maureen said but her heart jumped. Rory did have a picture of her taken four years previously. He'd taken it on a summer's day in the park. 'What was his name?'

'I've forgotten, but it will come to me,' the sergeant said. 'So you haven't got a sweetheart then?'

'No, I haven't,' Maureen said, because Rory wasn't hers. 'I don't have time for courting. When I'm not here I'm looking after my father and the shop.'

'I'm Jim Cotton,' the sergeant said and offered his hand. 'My father had a small haberdasher's shop in a country town, but he died last year; my mother died when I was a kid and

I was an only child – so we were close until he went. What sort of shop does your father run?'

'I'm sorry about your loss.' Maureen paused, then, 'Dad's shop is a grocery business. We sell a bit of everything. People come for their food, tins and sugar and tea mostly, and at night the men come in to buy cigarettes and sweets for the kids or a box of chocolates for a treat for their wives.'

'Whereabouts are you?' he asked.

Maureen hesitated, and then gave him the location. 'It's made things difficult for passing trade now, because several things can't be replaced. We've got plenty of sweets, because we stocked up on them, but it won't be long before we have to ask for coupons for sugar.'

'I'm only surprised they haven't done it already.'

'They are letting us have a decent Christmas this year, because it will get much worse as time goes on. Dad hasn't had to bother with rationing yet at the wholesaler, but they say it can't be far off.'

'My father said it was difficult last time – it wasn't just the coupons; the shops were running out of everything but the basics.'

'I've had a leaflet to say they'll issue margarine coupons and they will be used for all sorts of things, but if there's nothing to buy the coupons will be useless.'

'It's a funny old world,' Jim Cotton said. 'Well, I'll see you around then, miss – someone said your name was Maureen?'

'Yes, it is,' she agreed as he put on his cap, got up and left. Maureen stared after him. He seemed nice, but he wasn't Rory and there was no point in getting to know him, because her father would just cause trouble and she couldn't be bothered to go through all that for nothing.

However, she was serving in the shop the next morning

when Jim entered. He bought a newspaper, some cigarettes and a packet of black and white mints.

'I don't suppose you'd come to the flicks with me this evening?' he asked. 'I've got tonight free and then they're shipping me out again.'

'Oh...' Maureen hesitated and was lost. 'I don't see why not, it's just for one night.'

'That's all,' Jim agreed and grinned at her. 'You're a pretty girl, Maureen. I'd like someone to write to when I'm away, if you could be bothered...'

'All right,' she said and smiled. 'Just as friends, though.'

'Yeah, just as friends,' Jim said and went to the door. 'I'll be waiting at the end of the road at half seven.'

Maureen agreed. Her father wouldn't think much of it if he discovered she was going out with a man she'd only met twice, but she didn't have to tell him and Jim was only in London for one more night.

*

Maureen smiled at herself in the mirror the next morning. She'd had a really nice time at the cinema the previous evening. Jim had bought her a quarter-pound box of Fry's milk chocolates, which they'd eaten as the films progressed. During the interval, he'd fetched an ice cream tub for them and afterwards, as they walked to her home after leaving the tram, he'd bought a twist of chips and they'd shared them.

'I had a lovely evening,' Maureen said when they stopped at the end of her street. 'Thank you, Jim. It was good of you to take me.'

'My pleasure, Maureen. I wish we'd had more time to-gether...' He offered his hand to shake hers. Maureen shook hands but then reached up to kiss his cheek. 'I'll be thinking about you, and I hope we'll meet again one day.'

'Yes, I shall hope to see you home safe,' she said. 'Let's pray it won't be long before it's all over.'

'Our boys are doing their best,' he said and for a moment she saw fear in his eyes. 'But the Germans are more prepared than we are. I reckon when they make their mind up to do it they'll just walk over us and keep on coming.'

'Oh no, surely not,' Maureen said, alarmed. 'My friend Peggy's husband says the Germans are fighting on too many fronts and they'll stretch themselves too far.'

'Don't you believe it.' Jim looked solemn. 'They've been building up to this for years and they don't intend to get beaten this time. But don't you worry, Maureen love. I reckon the boys in blue will defend this little island of ours, even if the Army can't.'

Maureen watched as he turned and walked away, feeling an icy tingle at the back of her neck. There was something about him as he strolled off, an air of defeat almost, as if he thought he wouldn't be coming back.

Chapter 17

In November Hitler had narrowly escaped being killed in a bomb blast, which German intelligence was blaming on British agents. While knowing nothing of the truth, Peggy thought it a pity it hadn't succeeded. Perhaps if Hitler had left at his usual time instead of going early he would be dead and the world might have drawn back from disaster. In December, the Germans had scuttled the pride of their fleet when she was trapped by British warships, but nothing much seemed to change. Except that in London the theatres reopened after closing in the initial blackout; it seemed that people had decided it was best just to live and get on with it.

Peggy looked in her housekeeping pot and realised there wasn't much left over to pay for her Christmas party this year. She could rustle up some food for her guests and a few drinks, but unless Laurence was willing to contribute she wouldn't be able to provide the free drinks she'd lavished on her guests in previous years.

'Have you thought about Christmas?' she asked him that evening before they opened the bar. 'It's only a couple of weeks now and I haven't got much put by for drinks this year.'

'Well, you might have to give it a miss then,' Laurence said. 'You know the brewery told me I would be getting less of everything next year. We can't afford to just give our stock away, Peggy. I'll let you have a bottle of sherry and two dozen bottles of mild ale at cost and that's it.'

Peggy turned away, biting her lip. He knew how much she looked forward to the Christmas party, but unless she could get more drinks it would hardly be worth having. She didn't argue with Laurence, because the atmosphere had been a little better between them of late, and she knew there was no changing his mind once it was set.

It was Maureen who gave Peggy the idea when she went in for her shopping the next morning. She was looking through a pile of magazines, which she'd put together in a folder, and on the cover she'd pasted a picture of sunshine, wine and fruit in Spain. The people were drinking from glasses and in the bowl shown there were oranges and lemons as well as other fruits.

'Is there an article to go with the picture?' she asked Maureen, and was given the magazine to look for herself. The writer of the article had given her readers a recipe for a drink made of fruit juices and wine mixed with sugar. It said that a small amount of brandy could be added if wished but was not necessary.

'Are you thinking of trying it out?' Maureen asked as Peggy scribbled notes in the little book she kept for her shopping list.

'It would be cheaper to make than straight drinks of whisky and sherry – for the Christmas party. Laurence can't spare much this year and I spent a lot helping Janet get married, so I thought a couple of bottles of wine that I use in cooking sometimes, some orange juice, a few slices of lemon and sugar mixed together, might make a decent substitute.'

'What a good idea,' Maureen said. 'I think the ladies will enjoy it – and if the men want something different they can go and buy their own beer at the bar. It's the company I come for, Peggy – and Gran is the same.'

'I think that's what I'll do,' Peggy said and smiled. 'You'll come, won't you? Anne sent me a card and said she'll be staying with her uncle but will pop in and see me on Christmas Eve so perhaps she'll stay for the party.'

'Did she say how she was getting on in her new job?'

'No, just that she would be home...' Peggy broke off as a youth entered the shop and put some envelopes on the counter. 'A letter from someone in the forces?'

Maureen blushed as she scooped it into her apron pocket. 'I met him at the canteen. He took me to the flicks and asked me to write to him. It's just friends, Peggy.'

'Well, it's nice for you to have a pen friend.' Peggy was surprised that Maureen had been out with a young man she hardly knew, and even more surprised that she was writing him letters, even if it was just as a friend. 'What does your father think about it?'

'I haven't told him,' Maureen admitted. 'I don't see why he needs to know. He's out most nights, and he knows I go to the canteen, but he can't grumble, because it's war work.'

'Yes,' Peggy said and sighed. 'Laurence says we do our bit in our own way – we get quite a few soldiers in most nights. Some of them are little more than babes, Maureen. I shudder when I think Pip will be old enough to enlist in a year or so's time.'

'I read in the paper that some Canadians were coming over to fight with our troops,' Maureen said. 'It's nice to know the Commonwealth is standing with us, isn't it?'

'Yes, I heard that too,' Peggy agreed. 'We had an American in the other evening. He said he'd come to join the British Army, because his parents were Polish Jews and they had

177

family in Poland they hadn't heard of for months. He says the Nazis are evil and they have to be stopped.'

'Well, I agree with that,' Maureen said. 'I expect most of us would. You can borrow that magazine if you want, Peggy.'

'I've copied down all I need,' Peggy said. 'I'll see you at the end of the week.'

Peggy felt more cheerful than she had for a while as she left. Sometimes Laurence made her feel as if she wanted to scream at him. Didn't he know what he was throwing away? Yet he appeared to think everything was all her fault and acted as if he were the injured party.

At the end of Mulberry Lane, she paused to have a few words with Alice Carter and her neighbour Sally Brown, who had been to the market and wanted to gossip, getting thoroughly cold and eager to hurry inside by the kitchen fire. Nellie was washing some bar towels by hand and wringing them out, before taking them out to the yard to dry. They'd probably freeze before long and she'd end up thawing them out over the range at night.

'You've been gone a long time,' Laurence said abruptly as he entered the kitchen carrying a sheaf of official-looking papers.

'I was talking to Maureen about Christmas, and then I met Alice. I've got an idea to make the drinks go further...'

'Damn your party,' Laurence said and his mouth was white-edged with temper. 'What do you think of that?' He thrust the papers under her nose and Peggy stared at them as her heart began to beat wildly. 'I shall be lucky if I'm here to see it this year – not that that will bother you.'

'Oh, Laurence, no,' Peggy said and stared at the papers. 'What do they say? When do...'

'I have to see someone tomorrow afternoon. I'm to have

a medical and if I pass it they want me for special training purposes.'

'Training... you won't have to fight then?' She looked at him with a glimmer of hope.

'I'm not sure what it means. I have to take the medical and if I'm accepted they have important work for a man of my experience.'

'What do they mean?'

Laurence shook his head. 'I'm damned if I know. I fought on the Somme – but, as I told you years ago, I spent some time as a German prisoner, before I managed to escape and make my way back through the lines. I picked up a bit of the language, but I've forgotten it. I can't see where I'll be much help, unless they shove me in the lines with the rest of the poor devils. Cannon fodder, that's what we were last time and that's what we'll be this time.'

Peggy's heart was pounding and she felt sick. Laurence had always said they might decide to call him up because of his experiences in the last war, but she'd never believed it until now.

'Perhaps they won't pass you fit enough,' she said, but his look poured scorn on that idea. 'Surely there's plenty of younger men.'

'They sent nearly two hundred thousand to France a couple of months back, and we'll be fighting all over the show once it really gets going, Peggy. I'm going to have to go and there's an end of it.'

She nodded, but her throat was tight with tears. The rift between them had grown slowly over the months, but she'd hoped they might make it up, perhaps at Christmas. Now it looked as if he would leave with nothing resolved between them.

'I'm sorry,' she said, feeling helpless. 'I don't want you to leave – and I shall care if you're not here. I know things haven't been right…' She broke off as Nellie came back into the kitchen, blowing on her hands and complaining of the raw day. Laurence shook his head and went through into the bar.

Nellie became aware of an awkward silence and looked at her. 'Did I walk in on something, Peggy?'

'Laurence has been called to a medical. He's got to attend tomorrow and, if he passes it, he'll be going for some sort of training.' Her throat was tight with fear. 'He said it would come, but I've been praying he was wrong.'

'I'm sorry about that, love,' Nellie said and sat down heavily at the table. 'Wasn't it enough that he did his bit in the first one? It took him ages to get over it after the last war.'

Peggy nodded, too upset to answer. Instead, she went to put the kettle on, making them both a cup of hot Bovril and buttering a plain scone.

After a few minutes the gloom lifted and she told Nellie what she was planning for her party. Peggy knew it wouldn't feel the same as other years, especially if Laurence had gone off to goodness knows where to train with all the other men who would be asked to sacrifice their lives for their country. Yet she was determined to carry on if she could, because otherwise it was letting them win – those faceless beings that decreed a man's lot in life; you had to fight against the Fates or they just ground you into the mud.

As she cooked the vegetable soup and a minced beef and onion pasty for lunch, Peggy thought about her life.

She would try once more to make it up with Laurence before he was sent away, Peggy decided. She didn't want this rift to widen and become bitter – and, if anything were to happen... it didn't bear thinking about!

Picking up the cold dishes she'd prepared earlier, she took them through to the bar and placed them on show. Hot food was brought through to the bar from the kitchen only when it was ordered to keep it fresher.

'Good mornin', ma'am,' an American voice greeted her as she turned to serve the man who had approached the bar. 'Mr Ashley was just tellin' me what a good cook you are. I don't suppose you've made an apple pie this mornin'? I sure do favour apple pie the way my mom makes it.'

'No, I'm afraid I didn't make apple pie today,' Peggy apologised. 'I've made mince and onion pasties, cheese scones, treacle tart with custard – and vegetable soup with fresh bread.'

'I'd like fine to have a bowl of the soup with bread – and maybe try a piece of your treacle tart after.'

'Yes, of course, sir,' Peggy said, trying to recall if she'd seen him before. He might have been in once but she couldn't be sure it was the same man. 'I'll bring it over to your table.'

She'd noted where the American officer was sitting and went over to wipe the table, then disappeared into the kitchen to reappear with a tray with a pretty cloth. A blue and white bowl of tasty soup, some chunks of fresh bread with a tiny pat of butter, and a knife and spoon filled her tray.

'I'll bring the tart when you've eaten your soup,' she said. 'Are you serving with the British forces, Captain?'

'I'm an American serviceman here on liaison duties with my general,' he said. 'Talks with your Mr Churchill I reckon, ma'am, but I'm not allowed to say any more than that.'

'Well, it isn't my business to ask.' Peggy smiled at him.

She'd thought he was very young when he'd spoken to her earlier about his mother's apple pie, but now she noticed the crinkle lines at the corners of his eyes. He looked as if he'd spent quite a lot of his time outdoors looking into the sun, but although handsome, he was older than she'd thought before – probably mid-thirties, which was still younger than Peggy. 'Enjoy your soup.'

Laurence was busy at the bar. Peggy went to help him pull pints and serve orange squash to the women. Noticing the American seemed to have finished his soup, she went to fetch his tart, pouring the thick custard into a little jug so that he could use as much or as little as he wanted. Most of her customers smothered the tart in custard, but she thought this one might be a little more discerning. He looked up as she brought the dessert and smiled.

'That's the best food I've had in a British diner since we got here. That treacle tart looks good, very sweet. My mom would tell you that her boy has a sweet tooth – her grand-folks came from the East End, ma'am. She told me to be sure to look up my aunt and cousins, but I haven't been able to find them. The last she heard they lived in Frying Pan Alley... but no one has heard of them.'

'I know most people in the area. What were they called?'

'Morrison, that's Mom's grandfather's name.'

'No, it doesn't ring a bell. I'll ask around, though, see if anyone knows where the family went.'

'That's extremely kind of you, ma'am. I had an aunt but no one seems to remember.' He smiled as he looked at his tart. 'I'm really looking forward to this.'

'I hope you enjoy it,' Peggy said and left him to his food. Returning the dirty dishes to the kitchen, she hurried back as Laurence called for her. Peggy was kept busy for the next hour or so and didn't notice the American paying his bill until Laurence showed her the half-crown he'd left.

'The tip is for you, Peggy. He certainly enjoyed that treacle tart – said he'd be back tomorrow and hoped that apple pie was on the menu.'

'I'm glad he enjoyed the food. We'll need to bring more customers in for the food if the beer is short.'

Peggy returned to serving the customers. When they were packing up, she saw that Laurence had left the half-crown behind the bar next to the till. Peggy picked it up and put it in the party pot. It would go towards her drinks fund for Christmas.

Laurence came into the kitchen as she was dishing up their meal. He sat down at the table and began to eat in silence. Peggy sat opposite. She'd saved a mince pasty each for them and finished cooking it just before they closed so that it wasn't dry or overdone.

'That American said he hadn't tasted food this good since he came here,' Laurence said. 'I told him we might have difficulty in obtaining some of the stuff we need when the rationing came in. He said he might be able to help, if he's still around.'

'I expect we'll get extra coupons because we serve food in the bar,' Peggy said. 'I've got to look into that, but if not I'll have to find new recipes somehow.'

'You were speaking about a new idea for Christmas.' He looked at her oddly. 'I think I said something foul to you, Peggy. I apologise for whatever it was. I was in such a mood I don't really know what I did say.'

'You said damn my Christmas party, but I understand, Laurence. I know you must dread having to report back to the Army after all these years.'

'It took me years to get over what they did to us last time,' he said. 'I'm not sure I can take it all over again...'

'Oh, Laurence, no, you mustn't!' Instinctively, she got up and went round to him, bending to put an arm about his shoulders. She felt a slight tremor run through him and remembered the nights when he'd lain with the covers pulled up to his throat, shivering and shaking in bed after one of his nightmares. It was years since he'd had one of those, but she hadn't forgotten.

'Peggy,' he said in a cracked voice. 'I'm not a coward, but I've never forgotten the hell of those trenches; your feet rotting in wet boots all the time, lice crawling all over you, and rats gnawing at anything that didn't knock them away. I woke up once and found one of the damn great blighters chewing at my ankle. If I hadn't knocked it off it would have taken a chunk out of my flesh.'

Peggy shuddered. 'I've heard about them eating the dead soldiers, but I didn't realise they attacked living ones too.'

'If they get too hungry they'll have a go at you, but normally they run if you shout or chuck something at them.' He smiled wryly. 'I just hope our chaps don't get bogged down in those bloody trenches for months this time.'

'It probably won't be the same,' Peggy comforted him. 'Anyway, you don't know what they want yet. It might not be as bad as you think.'

'No, it may not,' he agreed and gave her a rare smile. 'Worrying about it won't change anything, Peggy.' His hand grasped her wrist as she would've moved away. 'Can you forgive me for the way I've been?'

Peggy didn't hesitate, bending to kiss his cheek and smile. 'I'm sorry too. Let's be friends again, Laurie?'

'I was hoping we might be more than friends...?' The look

in his eyes made her heart catch, because it was so long since he'd given her one of his special looks and she wanted to cry.

*

They made love that night for the first time in months. It was good but not quite the same, at least not for Peggy. Something inside refused to respond the way it always had, though she did her best not to let him see it wasn't as good for her. He seemed happy, and when he had to leave in the early hours for his shift on fire duty, he was whistling cheerfully as he went down the stairs.

Peggy listened to the door closing behind him. Her lashes were wet and spiky but she wouldn't give way to foolish tears. At her age she shouldn't expect fireworks, but that warm glow of satisfaction she'd always felt was missing. If she'd let herself she might have felt a bit used, but she resolutely blocked such thoughts out. At least Laurence was in a cheerful mood, and that was better, because she couldn't have stood it if he'd had to go away with their quarrel unresolved.

After lying restless for a couple of hours, Peggy got up and went down to make a cup of tea. Laurence had banked the fires before they went to bed and she made the kitchen range up again so that it would be warm when she was ready to start cooking. Laurence wouldn't be back much before nine and she wanted to get ahead for the day. She'd decided that she would make an apple pie and she'd order a pot of cream from the milkman, though it was unlikely that he would have any to spare.

Chapter 18

Janet hunted for a shilling for the gas meter. She hated this system of having to put money in the meter every time she needed to cook or light the fire in the little room. In fact, she hated everything about this place, but she hadn't told anyone, certainly not Mike who thought they'd been lucky to find two decent rooms.

'You've got a nice little sitting room with a gas ring to heat a saucepan or kettle for tea. Mrs Johnson will cook you a dinner and you can make something for yourself in the middle of the day. Besides, there are plenty of little cafés where you can go.'

Janet hadn't minded where they lodged when Mike was there most of the time. For the first week or two he'd been home every evening and he'd even had a Sunday off to show her the sights. She'd thought it was fun, feeling grown up and happy to be a young wife, newly married and so much in love – but it was weeks since she'd seen Mike now and she seldom bothered to go further than the shop on the corner to buy a few groceries.

Mrs Johnson's cooking was all right if you weren't used to Peggy's food, which was so much tastier. Janet found her meat puddings stodgy and the rabbit stew her landlady ladled out at least once a week turned her stomach. Her morning sickness had eased, but the greasy stew made her feel full after a couple of mouthfuls and she'd sent it back uneaten last time, which annoyed Mrs Johnson.

'We can't afford to waste good food, Janet,' she'd scolded. 'There are plenty of people out there who would give anything for a plate of my rabbit stew.'

'I'm sorry, it's just me,' Janet told her. 'I would prefer just a tomato and cheese sandwich...'

'Some people don't know when they're well off,' the woman had scolded and looked at her askance. 'You're pregnant, of course. When I took you in, Mrs Rowan, I didn't expect you to be with child this soon. I'm not sure I can put up with a young baby in the house.'

'Are you saying you want me to move out?' Janet felt a surge of panic, because Mike had told her most of the rooms available were far worse, and he thought they had no hope of finding a house of their own, unless he could wangle married quarters for them, and he hadn't managed anything before he was told he was being sent to sea with his ship.

'Now, I didn't say that, but we shall have to see,' Mrs Johnson said. 'I'm not one to put a young woman out on the streets – but I can't have you here for the birth. You'll have to go to the hospital – unless your mother will look after you.'

'She might come down,' Janet said, though she knew it was unlikely, but it was the only thing she could think of to put her landlady off.

'Well, I should think your husband would prefer you to have a nice little house of your own. He told me this was only temporary when you came here that day. I should start looking round if I were you.'

And all because she'd had the temerity to tell the woman she couldn't eat her rotten rabbit stew! Janet gave up searching for a shilling and fetched her coat. She would go to the café and have toast and soup and a pot of tea. It was somewhere to sit for a few hours, and if she had to sit staring at these four walls for much longer she would go mad.

Walking past shops that were decorated for Christmas, but without all the fancy lights they'd had on in previous years, Janet felt the sting of tears. Her mother would be preparing for her Christmas party and it would be the first time she would miss it.

Janet missed her home and her mother desperately sometimes. When she finished knitting a little coat or a bonnet, she put it aside in tissue paper and wished that she could show it to Peggy. Oh, why had Mike decided he wanted to be in the Navy after all those years working in the shipyards? Janet wished his brother had never come home again, bragging about all the places he'd been to and all the things he'd done, because Mike might have stayed in the shipyards then and she would still be in London.

She felt the sting of tears on her cheeks, and not looking where she was going, was taken by surprise when she bumped into someone. Glancing up, she saw a man of around thirtyish; because he was wearing thick, horn-rimmed glasses, a raincoat and a trilby hat pulled low over his brow, she could only just see that he was clean-shaven and attractive.

'I'm so sorry,' he said, catching her arm to steady her. 'Forgive me, ma'am. I wasn't looking where I was going.'

'Nor was I,' Janet replied and laughed. 'It wasn't your fault. I was miles away.'

'Did I tread on your foot?'

'No, not at all,' Janet said. 'Please don't give it another thought. I'm just upset because I had a few words with my landlady.'

'Oh dear, that is unfortunate.' He smiled wryly. He tipped his hat to her and she caught a glance of reddish-brown hair, and he was suddenly far more attractive. 'I'm Ryan Hendricks. I'm just here on a flying visit, but I know what landladies can be. My job takes me all over the country and my wife says she thinks I'm a stranger when I go home.'

'I'm Janet Rowan. My husband brought me here when we got married, but he's been at sea for weeks now and it gets lonely. My family is in London...' Janet wasn't sure why she was telling this man anything, but his manner seemed to invite it. 'Forgive me; you must want to get on.'

'As a matter of fact I have two hours to kill before my next appointment,' he said. 'I was just looking for a nice tearoom to sit in for a while.'

'There's a good one in the next street. I plan to have tea and toast – it's something to do for a few hours. I shall spend the evening knitting. I'm having a child, you see...' She laughed in embarrassment. 'Oh dear, as if you wanted to hear my life story.'

'Well, why not?' he said with a gentle smile. 'If you won't think me too familiar – why don't we have tea at this nice place you mentioned and keep each other company for a while?'

'Oh, yes, I should like that,' Janet said and let him take her arm. 'If you can bear it?'

'I shall enjoy having tea with a pretty young woman. My wife is beautiful, you know, and I have two wonderful children. May I bore you by telling you all about them and showing you their pictures?'

'Yes, please,' Janet said. She was warming to this stranger. 'I should like that very much.'

'I dare say you will wish me to Jericho before we're done,'

he said and she could hear the laughter in his voice. 'There never were such bright or enchanting children as my Mary and Jonathan, Mrs Rowan. All my friends tell me I am besotted, but I assure you I am right.'

Janet was eager to hear more and she felt really happy as they were shown to their table and her companion ordered tea, buttered toast with honey and a plate of cakes. She wanted to protest at his extravagance but somehow she didn't, because she knew he wouldn't allow her to pay her share. Now that they were in the light she could see that he was as well-dressed as she'd thought from the start, obviously from the middle classes, and with his hat removed, he was extremely good-looking in a gentle, intelligent way. Of course he didn't have Mike's rugged good looks, but he wasn't a blue-collar worker. Janet judged him to be someone who worked in business or an office, perhaps inspection work for the War Office. It was the most likely explanation for his having to travel all over, because otherwise he would probably have been in the forces.

They spent more than an hour over their tea, talking, looking at the photos he kept in his wallet and thoroughly enjoying the interlude. When he took money out to pay for their meal, his wallet was bulging with notes. An important man, travelling all over the country and lonely, he missed his family and talked about them most of the time, though he also listened when Janet told him about Mike, and somehow about falling out with her father, too.

'You must try to make it up with him,' he'd told her with a gentle smile. 'I dare say he's sorry now – and Christmas is a time for forgiveness. You should write if you can't get back, but if your husband isn't going to be home, you should visit.

It might be too late before you realise and then you would never forgive yourself.'

'I don't think my father is as understanding or forgiving as you are.'

'Oh, I'm not always forgiving. I fell out with my brother when I was younger. We quarrelled and he went roaring off on his motorbike and I never saw him again. They told us he skidded on a patch of oil, mounted the pavement and crashed into a lamppost. Jack died in hospital an hour after they got him there.'

'I am so very sorry,' Janet said and impulsively placed her hand over his on the table.

'So was I,' he said and patted her hand before removing his. 'That's why I never let a quarrel go cold on me. So remember and make the effort. After all, your child will need his grandparents.'

'Yes, he – or she – will need them one day,' Janet said. 'Thank you, Ryan. You have no idea how much this brief interlude has meant to me today. It was so kind of you to take pity on me.'

'You've paid for it by listening to a lonely man talk,' he said and smiled. 'It was lovely to meet you, Janet, but now I have to leave. We must both get on with our lives.'

'Yes, of course,' Janet said. She rose when he did and he helped her on with her coat. Outside in the chilly evening air, they parted company. Janet felt a pang of regret as they shook hands. Of course they could never have been anything but friends, but she was sorry that they would never see each other again. It was the sensible way, of course, and Ryan hadn't offered her the chance of another meeting or given her an address. He was happily married and so was she. It would be foolish to think that because they were both feeling lonely anything more was necessary; they had helped each other to pass a couple of hours on a winter's afternoon.

Returning to her cold little room, but with some shillings in her pocket after buying an evening newspaper, Janet felt a pang of regret. At least Ryan's wife knew that he would be returning to her when his business trip was over. Janet lived in fear that Mike wouldn't come back to her, but in that she was wrong…

*

Janet finished writing her Christmas cards. She had to post them that morning or they wouldn't arrive by the day and she didn't want Christmas to pass without sending her parents something. She'd purchased two pretty lace hankies and a scarf for her mother, and these were wrapped in tissue and then in brown paper. Janet intended to post the little parcel when she posted the cards to her parents, her brother, Maureen and a few more friends, not forgetting Nellie. She'd bought a packet of chocolate ginger for Nellie, because she'd remembered that her mother's helper was partial to it.

Going out of the front door, Janet walked to the shop on the corner and posted her gifts. Her brother had a postal order, because she had no idea what he liked and usually gave him something he'd mentioned he wanted, but Pip had only sent her a postcard once saying he hoped she was happy and this year she didn't want to send a bulky gift that he wouldn't use when money would do just as well.

Janet had bought Mike a lovely wool scarf and a bottle of whisky, but she wasn't sure when he would get them, because he'd told her not to try sending him gifts when he was away.

'It isn't like being in the Army,' he'd said. 'Keep presents for when I come home and we'll celebrate then, love.'

Janet had received a few cards from home. Her mother must have given Maureen her address and one or two other friends. She'd stuck them on the mantel but made no other attempt to decorate for Christmas; there didn't seem much point when she would be alone, though she might buy a small sponge cake or something of the sort. She found herself thinking wistfully of her mother's party and regretting the bitter scene with her father.

She hurried in out of the cold, glad that she'd made sure of some change for the gas fire, but as she reached her room she saw that the door was open and Mrs Johnson was standing on the threshold speaking to someone. Had she shown someone else round her rooms? Janet was about to demand an explanation when Mrs Johnson saw her and smiled.

'Well, who's the lucky one then? Here's your husband back for Christmas.'

'Mike...' Janet rushed past her into the room and straight into Mike's open arms. He embraced her, kissing her face over and over until there wasn't a spot of it that hadn't been thoroughly caressed. 'Oh, Mike. I've missed you so much...'

Somehow the door had closed behind their landlady and they were alone. Janet looked at her beloved husband, drinking in every feature as if she would never have enough of him.

'I've missed you, too, darling,' Mike said and hugged her again. 'I've got nearly a week, Janet, and I think we should go to a hotel somewhere. Mrs J's cooking is all right, but I'd rather have my Christmas dinner somewhere else.'

'So would I,' Janet said ruefully. 'We might end up with her awful rabbit stew.'

Mike looked at her seriously. 'I know this isn't perfect, Jan. I never intended we should live here for long. I've been told there's a small cottage close to the base we could have. It belongs to the captain's wife and she rents it out, but her last tenant let her down. When I told the first mate I was looking for a proper home for my family he mentioned it – and the captain is going to speak to his wife.'

'Oh, Mike, that would be wonderful,' Janet said and smiled happily. 'When shall we know?'

'They're going to her parents for Christmas so I may be back on board,' Mike said, 'but Mrs Jamieson will probably come and see you after Christmas. The cottage is furnished so you won't have to bother about much – though you will need sheets and things. I'll make sure you've got some money and if everything goes well you can move in while I'm away.'

'Yes, all right,' Janet said. She didn't want to think about him going away again, because he'd only just got back and it was Christmas. 'When shall we be able to see it?'

'Well, you'll have to look on your own for a start,' Mike said. 'I'm sure the captain and his wife will want to make the most of his time off, same as us – but I've been told it's decent, and it has to be better than two rooms, doesn't it?'

'Yes, of course,' Janet laughed. 'Oh, what a lovely surprise this is, Mike. Christmas in a hotel and then our own home...'

'I've got you a present, too. I bought it in port when we docked to pick up fresh supplies. For a while there I didn't think we were going to get home with it, but our luck held.'

'Was it awful?' Janet asked and felt coldness at the back of her neck.

'Pretty bad,' he said, looking grim. 'One of the vessels we were escorting caught it amidships and sank. We picked up the men in the water, but those below in the engine room...'

Janet felt like weeping. She could imagine the scene when the merchant vessel was torpedoed and the men crammed into the tight quarters of the engine room were trapped by the in-rushing sea and the utter chaos that must have ensued.

'I'm so sorry,' she whispered, tears burning behind her eyes, but she knew better than to let them fall.

'Come on, grab a few things and let's go,' Mike said, refusing to give into the emotions he'd held inside. 'It's Christmas, I'm home and we're going to have some fun.'

Chapter 19

'They've told me I shan't hear anything for definite until after Christmas,' Laurence said, 'but the doctor seemed to think I was in pretty good condition so I imagine I shall be assigned next year. So we'd best make the most of this Christmas, Peggy. I know you like your party so go ahead and ask people. I'll give you a few bottles.'

'I shan't need much,' Peggy told him with a smile of relief. This was the man she'd loved for years. 'Beer for the men and a bottle of sherry and one of whisky, if you like, but I've tried that wine and fruit drink I told you about and it's good. I'm going to be serving that with some savoury pastries and apple pie and mince pies. I shan't be making an iced cake this year, not for the party and not for us either. Some icing on the mince pies will be enough to make it special.'

'I'll chip in if you're short,' he said. 'You may not be able to do it at all next year, Peggy.'

'No, I'll stick to what I've planned. We're not the only ones cutting back this year, Laurence. It will get much worse as the shortages become more noticeable. I'm going to try out several new savoury flans and tarts. With things the way they're going I shall need to adapt if I'm to keep the bar food going so I might as well make a start. If it's offered free they will try it and maybe they'll like it.'

'Well, the offer's there,' Laurence said and went through to the bar whistling. He seemed relieved to know that he wouldn't have to leave before Christmas, but his medical had gone well and so had the interviews he'd had a few days later, so they had to assume he would be called up to this training programme after the festivities. However, it seemed that he wouldn't be joining a fighting unit just yet. Whatever they had in mind for him, it was not immediate shipment to a combat regiment.

Peggy had sent her daughter a small parcel a few days previously, clothes for the baby, a pretty maternity dress she'd made for Janet to wear as her pregnancy advanced, and some money by registered post. She was aware Mike's money provided for all they needed, but sometimes it was good to have a bit of your own tucked away.

Peggy knew that her daughter wouldn't come home unless she absolutely had to; Janet was as stubborn as Laurence, and neither would like giving in. Laurence had softened a little since they'd made love once or twice, and Peggy thought he might have forgiven his daughter in his heart even if he wasn't willing to say so.

She was just preparing to make a cup of tea for her and Nellie when the postie came. 'Cards and a little gift by the looks of it,' he said as Peggy opened the back door to him. 'Postmark is Portsmouth – that'll be from your daughter and her husband, I should think. There's one here for your lad as well. Lovely girl, your Janet; she wouldn't forget you at Christmas.'

Peggy smiled and exchanged pleasantries. Sometimes his habit of telling her who her post was from was annoying. However, he'd been delivering the letters for years and seemed to think it was his right to comment.

'Here, have a hot mince pie, Reg,' she offered him the plate.

'Thanks, Peggy,' he grinned as he helped himself and walked off munching, clearly pleased with the offering.

'You've got a lot of cards in the bar,' Nellie said and pulled up a chair for her mid-morning break. 'I've had one from my daughter but Pete's hasn't arrived yet.'

Nellie's son had been sent to France with others earlier that month and she'd been waiting for a letter ever since. Peggy felt sympathy for her, but she wasn't the only mother who waited with bated breath for the post these days.

Peggy opened her cards and put them on the top shelf of the dresser. She put the small soft parcel to one side to open on Christmas Day, a pang of regret that for the first time ever she wouldn't be with Janet when she opened her gifts.

'Missing her, I expect?' Nellie said and Peggy let out a sigh.

'Yes, it won't seem the same without them, will it?'

'No, but at least you've still got Pip and Mr Ashley.'

'You know you're welcome to come to us for Christmas Day, Nellie.'

'I'll go and visit my sister Agnes. She's on her own as well, but she's used to it. She mostly comes to us – but this year I'll be going there.'

Peggy nodded. 'Well, we're having the party as usual. Maureen and her grandmother are coming, and Anne, and you, of course, and all the regulars. Some faces will be missing, but we'll do the best we can.'

Nellie nodded. 'Before I forget, you need some washing soda and the tea is getting down the caddy.'

'Thanks for reminding me. I'll pop to the market and then go to Maureen's on the way back...'

Maureen was stacking tins on the shelves behind the counter when Peggy entered. She turned with a smile of greeting, getting down from the steps she was using and indicating a pile of cards and letters on the counter.

'I've been so busy all morning. I opened some of my post but the rest is just lying there. Dad managed to get some extra tins of fruit, salmon, Spam and corned beef this week. Not individual tins of corned beef, the large ones to slice, so that is a bonus.'

'I'll have some of the corned beef if you can spare it. Men like it with pickle if they come in at lunchtime, and I like a nice corned beef hash myself.'

'Yes, so do I if the potato is nicely browned on top,' Maureen agreed. 'I got a card from your Janet. She enclosed a note, says she's getting on well, but isn't keen on her landlady's cooking. She's been spoiled, Peggy.'

Maureen picked up a card and opened it, her cheeks going pink as she read the message inside.

'Card from someone special?' Peggy asked.

'It's from a friend, but not a special friend,' Maureen said. 'Jim is in the Army. I may have told you, we went out once.'

'Yes, to the pictures I think,' Peggy smiled. 'He's still writing then.'

'Yes.' Maureen hesitated, then, 'He says he's sent me a gift. I can't imagine why he did that.'

'He obviously likes you.'

'Yes, but...' Maureen shook her head. 'He knows it is just friends. I mean, I sent him some cigarettes and sweets, but that didn't cost me much.'

'I expect he just wants to give you a little something in

return. He's grateful that you write and send a small parcel now and then.'

'Well, everyone tells me how much it pleases them, at the canteen. The men say it means the world when you're away from home, just a letter and a parcel. They like homemade cakes and things, but I think they would be stale by the time they got them.'

'Biscuits would keep best, if you pack them in greaseproof and a flat tin, or a fruit cake, but dried fruit isn't easy to get hold of now, as you know,' Peggy said. 'It takes a bit more thought these days, but I know Nellie made some ginger snaps and also some coconut ones to send her son.'

'Any chance of Janet coming home for Christmas?' Maureen asked.

'I shouldn't think so. Laurence may be going away next year, so I might ask her to come then if she'd like to.'

'Yes, you'll miss him when he does,' Maureen said and gathered her post under the counter. She was just assembling Peggy's order when the shop bell rang and a youth came in. His uniform declared that he worked for the post office and he was carrying a telegram.

'Telegram for Miss Maureen Jackson?'

'Yes, that's me,' she said, feeling shocked. 'But I don't know who would be sending this to me.'

'Sorry, missus, it's one of them,' the boy said and threw her a pitying glance before leaving.

'What did he mean?' Maureen asked and opened the envelope, extracting the single sheet of buff-coloured paper inside. 'Oh, my goodness... how awful...' She handed the paper to Peggy who read it aloud.

'This is to inform you that Sergeant Jim Cotton has been killed in action. Letter to follow.'

'Poor, poor man,' Maureen whispered, tears springing to her eyes.

'That's a horrid thing to get so near Christmas,' Peggy said, noticing that Maureen had gone white. 'He must have named you as the person he wanted contacted in the event of his death.'

'But why? I hardly knew him...' Maureen felt numbed, her hands shaking. It wasn't as if she were in love with the friendly soldier, but she'd liked him and she enjoyed getting his letters – and she'd only just opened his Christmas card. 'The poor, poor man... he couldn't have had anyone else... or he would have named them instead of me.'

'No one he cared about anyway,' Peggy said. 'I'm sorry, Maureen. Are you all right, love?'

'Yes. It was a shock, and I'm sorry it happened – but I feel more upset that I was his closest friend. It makes me feel guilty that I didn't feel more for him.'

'You were a friend and that's all he asked you to be,' Peggy said and paid for her goods. 'Try not to dwell on it too much, Maureen. Now don't forget my party. You won't let it stop you coming, will you, love? I know it's sad that this young man has died, but we all have to go on and it wouldn't be the same without you.'

'Definitely not,' Maureen assured her. 'You're right, I know, and we do have to carry on, because otherwise the enemy would win.'

'That's the spirit,' Peggy smiled, picked up her basket and left.

*

Maureen went back to stacking her shelves, but she felt

extremely shaken, close to tears. She felt guilty, not just because she hadn't realised what her letters meant to Jim, but also because of the surge of relief that had gone through her when she read the telegram and realised it wasn't about Rory. It was awful of her to be thankful that it wasn't the man she loved, and that had made her feel terrible, because of course she was sad for Jim.

She was just thinking of making herself a cup of tea when the shop door opened and a woman came in. She was wearing a thick coat that hardly covered her bulging stomach, the evidence that her pregnancy was well advanced. She looked pale and her face was a little bloated, as if the child-bearing was causing her trouble, and at first Maureen didn't know her. It was only when she addressed her by name that she realised it was Velma – Rory's wife.

'You don't know me, do you, Maureen?'

'It's Velma, isn't it?' Maureen felt a bit sick. She'd managed to push the thought of Rory's wife out of her head, but seeing her looking unwell brought the reality to her with a shock. She had no right to even think about Rory, and it was this woman who would be notified if anything happened to him, not her. 'Are you back in London now, then?'

'I just came home until the baby is born, sometime in March next year I think,' Velma said. 'You did know I married Rory – didn't you?' There was a hint of gloating in the woman's face now.

'Yes, I knew,' Maureen agreed and looked at her bump. 'What are you hoping for this time?'

'What do yer mean, this time?' Velma glared at her.

Maureen blinked. 'I heard you had a child earlier this year... a little girl.' Rory had told her that his wife had a daughter in January 1939 and it was only December now;

if Velma's baby was due in March, she'd fallen again only months after giving birth. Yet Maureen had believed Rory had been shipped out with his unit soon after the birth of his first child...

'Oh, that.' Velma shrugged. 'Yeah, well, it got sick and died a few weeks after Rory was shipped off to Belgium.'

Maureen could scarcely believe her. How could she talk about her dead child so callously? Rory had only stayed with her because of the child; he must have been devastated.

'Trouble is, I fell for another too quick,' Velma said. 'Bloody men – they're all the same, never think about us as long as they get what they want.'

Maureen felt sick. To stop herself being rude, she changed the subject. 'Your mother will be glad to have you home for a while.'

'I cramp her style with her men friends,' Velma said bitterly, 'but my landlady wouldn't let me have the kid there so I came home; I'll find somewhere for us once I'm over the birth. I'm just too bloody tired to go traipsing round the streets looking for the moment.'

Maureen didn't comment. She'd heard rumours that Velma's mother liked the men, but her husband had died years ago so there was no reason why she shouldn't go out with men if she wished.

'You're not married then?' Velma stared pointedly at Maureen's left hand.

'No, I'm not married.' She took a deep breath and then, defensively, 'As it happens the soldier I was writing to has just been killed over there in France.'

'Oh, sorry, ducks.' Velma looked genuinely contrite. 'Didn't know you were courting.'

'Well, it was just friends,' Maureen said. 'It won't be

anything more now though...' For some ridiculous reason she felt her eyes getting wet and had to brush the tears away.

'Didn't mean to upset you,' Velma said. 'I just came in for a packet of fags and some mints.'

'Are the cigarettes for you?' Maureen asked. 'Won't they upset the baby?'

'Nah, shouldn't think so,' Velma said. 'To be honest, I don't care if they do. I can't manage without me fags. You need somethin' to keep you goin' these days. What wiv him bein' away and me havin' to come back here...'

Maureen served her with the items she'd asked for and took the money. Velma hesitated for a while, then, 'Me ma said she saw you havin' a drink with Rory when he was on leave. Did he tell you anythin' about me – us?'

'No, I only saw him for a few minutes,' Maureen lied. 'He was just talking about the Army... what he thought about the war.' She looked at Velma but couldn't quite meet her eyes.

'I thought that was all it was, old friends havin' a chat,' Velma said. 'He wouldn't leave me. I told me ma that but she thought he used to be sweet on you and might be regretting what he did.'

'I'm sure he doesn't,' Maureen said, because she had no right to think or say anything else. 'I hope everything goes all right for you and the baby, Velma.'

'Yeah, thanks. I'm sorry about your bloke,' Velma said and scooped up her purchases before leaving.

Maureen stared after her. She was such a fool, a fool to think that there could ever be anything between her and Rory. He was married and his wife was having another baby.

She sighed as her shop bell went again, but thankfully this time it was her grandmother.

'Time you had a break by the looks of you,' Gran said

cheerfully. 'What happened – did the cat die?'

'I had a telegram about Jim – the soldier I was writing to. He's been killed, Gran, and he named me as his next of kin because they notified me. I don't think he'd got anyone else because he hardly knew me but he asked me to write so I did.'

'Poor lad,' her grandmother said. 'Go and make a cup of tea, girl, and sit down for a bit. I can mind the shop.'

'Thank you, I will,' Maureen said. She'd had two shocks that morning and she was still reeling from the first, though in a way seeing Velma had been more difficult. 'I'll bring one for you in a few minutes.'

'Just take it easy for a while; you're as white as a ghost,' Gran said. 'Even if he was just a pen pal to you, this soldier was a human being and it's never nice getting news like that.'

*

Peggy smiled as she saw Maureen come in with her grandmother. She was glad the sad news about Jim Cotton hadn't stopped her friend coming to the Christmas party, because they none of them knew what was coming next. So far they'd got off pretty lightly here in London. The Germans had dropped a few bombs on Shetland and some mines in the Thames Estuary, but apart from explosions caused by the IRA all they'd had to put up with was lots of regulations, a rise in the price of petrol and some restrictions; the rationing proper was due to start in the following January.

Watching as her friends enjoyed the food and drinks she'd provided, Peggy felt her eyes moisten because her daughter wasn't one of them. She'd telephoned earlier to wish them all a Happy Christmas and tell Peggy that Mike was home.

Well, at least Janet was happy. Peggy blinked away her tears as she prepared to take the mince pies round again. The fruit and wine drink she'd made was going well and Alice was singing her repertoire at the top of her voice. It looked like being another party to remember and at least Laurie and Pip were here. Her son was now seventeen and never stopped talking about joining the RAF the minute he could. She was thankful she would have him home for another year at least.

'All right, Peggy?' Mrs Tandy came up to her. 'I wanted to tell you I got some more of that pink wool you wanted – I've put twenty ounces by as you said, and you can buy it as you want.'

'Thanks, love,' Peggy said and offered her a mince pie. 'I didn't know if you'd be able to match it.'

'I've got shelves full out the back, because I'd been stocking up,' Mrs Tandy said, 'but that pink you bought was the last so we were lucky.'

Peggy nodded, because she'd picked it out especially for making things for Janet's baby, if it was a girl – and if not she would make her daughter a cardigan instead.

Somehow, she would go down there when the baby was due. She wasn't going to miss out on seeing her grandchild. She smiled at the thought and turned as Laurence came up to her.

'Happy?' he asked and she nodded.

Happiness was a fleeting thing, and you had to make the best of it while you could, because they none of them knew what the New Year would bring.

Chapter 20

Christmas at the hotel had been wonderful, so much happier than Janet had expected when she hadn't known if Mike would be home. The day after Boxing Day, Mike took her to see the cottage he hoped would be theirs once he'd arranged it with his commanding officer. Set by the road, but with pasture to the rear, it was a little isolated, but Janet had had enough of living in digs. They couldn't go in, of course, but they walked round the small garden, which was mostly rose bushes, a tiny lawn and a few straggling perennials at the front, and a well-dug vegetable patch at the back. Peering through the windows, Janet saw a pleasant sitting room with an oak dresser and a set of bentwood furniture piled with lots of chintz cushions, some small tables and chairs. The kitchen had a deep stone sink and wooden draining boards, also a painted wood dresser, a pine table and four chairs.

'What do you think, love?' Mike asked.

'It's lovely,' Janet said and hardly dared to breathe. 'If only they will let us have it. I could grow my own stuff in the garden and cook the sort of things Mum cooks.'

Mike hugged her to him, bending his head to kiss her tenderly on the mouth. 'I love you so much, Jan. I know you'll be happier here – but it's not near any other houses. What about when the baby comes? Will it be too isolated for you?'

'I shall go into hospital to have the baby, and there's a red phone box just up the road. Besides, it's not far to those houses we saw from the bus, and the bus stop is only a few yards away. I'll make friends, you'll see...'

'I'm sure you will in time,' he agreed and kissed her again. 'The CO's wife may know of a little job that would suit you. I'm sure it's the best way to make friends, Jan.'

'I inquired about a job in a café where I go sometimes,' Janet told him. 'Julie said one of her staff is leaving this month so she might give me a few hours on the till, because I'm too big to do anything else. I'll ask her if there are any voluntary groups I could join near here.' She was filled with confidence because he was with her. 'And you'll have a home to come to when you're on leave.'

'If you're sure it isn't too isolated?' Mike looked a bit doubtful as they joined hands and walked across to wait for the bus. 'I suppose it's only a few minutes to the town or the Docks on the bus, so it's good for both of us.'

'I just hope we get it now that we've seen it and liked it,' Janet said, smiling as the bus came round the corner. 'There, that's a good omen, regular buses. I've seen two go by while we were looking round.'

'I'll pay the hotel bill and then we can go back to the rooms and start packing. I can ring this evening and maybe we'll know if we're going to get the key.'

*

Janet could hardly believe it when Mike returned with the good news. The cottage was theirs but they couldn't pick up the key for another week, which meant that Janet would have to move in on her own. It would've been nicer if somehow they could have got the key before Mike had to re-join his ship. However, he helped her pack their things into cases and bags, and they went shopping to buy a few small things, although, as Mike said, it would be better to buy bulkier stuff after the move.

When the time came for him to leave Janet felt the familiar ache in her chest. She'd been lucky to have him home for Christmas, but now he was returning to duty and she guessed that it was going to be the longer run this time, though Mike couldn't give her any details.

'You can contact this number at the base if anything happens but it will be months before I'm back this trip, Jan. You'll just have to get used to being alone. Make sure you see your doctor and get them to book you in for the confinement with the midwives at the hospital.'

'I'm going to ask Mum if she'll come down for a few days nearer the time,' Janet said. 'I don't know if she will be able to leave the pub, because she said she thought Dad might be called up soon... but she might.'

'There isn't anyone else you could ask to stay nearer the time, is there?'

'No.' Janet shook her head. 'I haven't got any close friends. Maureen is always busy, just like Mum. No, I'll manage, Mike, you'll see.' Janet didn't want him to worry about her. 'If I get anxious I could always catch the train to London...'

'Yes, I suppose so, though would your father have you?'

'I think Nellie might,' Janet said and smiled brightly. 'I'm going to be fine, Mike – just forget about me and look after yourself.'

'I could never forget you, darling,' Mike said and drew her close once more. 'I sometimes regret joining up when I think of you alone, Jan – but the call-up would've come in time.'

'Yes, of course,' Janet said, but in her heart she wished he was back safe in his job at the Docks. She wasn't going to tell him how she really felt. Nothing must spoil this last precious night together.

As she lay in his arms, held close to his naked body, Janet felt the quiver of desire and the need to be one with him. They'd made love over and over again during this holiday, Mike treating her with great care but loving the reason for the need to be gentle. He caressed her bump and kissed it, telling her again and again how much he loved both her and the child she carried.

'One day when all this is over, we'll have more children and perhaps we'll buy a house of our own somewhere nice, but for the moment I shall be happier thinking of you at the cottage than where you were.'

'It hasn't been brilliant here,' Janet said, 'but at least it was clean and decent, and a lot of places are much worse.'

When Mike finally slept beside her, Janet lay awake and her cheeks were wet, because she could hardly bear to think of the days and weeks when he would be away at sea and in danger.

'Let him come back to me,' she prayed and then finally she slept.

*

Mrs Jamieson sent a letter to Janet arranging to meet her at her lodgings early in January 1940.

I can pick up your belongings and take you straight out to the cottage in my car. I've arranged for it to be cleaned and a fire to be lit in the range, which I'm told can be tricky. I shall look forward to meeting you and will be there at ten thirty on Tuesday morning.

Janet immediately took to the friendly, attractive blonde-haired woman who pulled up in a small Morris car and greeted her with an effusive handshake.

'I am delighted to meet you, Mrs Rowan,' she said. 'My husband told me about your husband. He thinks a lot of Mike and when I heard you were having your first baby I was delighted. I hope we shall become friends and I shall enjoy babysitting now and then if you need anyone.'

'It's lovely to meet you, Mrs Jamieson. Mike took me to have a look at the cottage and we peeped in the windows. I can't wait to have my own home.'

'I'm glad to get a good tenant,' she said. 'Please do call me Rosemary. I have two children, both boys in their teens and away at boarding school. I miss them terribly and I'm always joining things to keep me occupied while they're away. At holiday times we cook and play together, but it gets lonely when my husband is also away.'

'Yes, it's lovely when they're home,' Janet agreed. 'I shouldn't mind joining a club or a group – one that helps with the war effort if possible.'

'I can help you there.' Rosemary beamed approval at her. 'If you need a few hours' paid work I can arrange that too when baby is here – they want young women to serve teas at the canteen for the ratings, but I have several good causes and if you're not careful I'll enrol you in them all.'

Janet felt as if a shadow had lifted from her. Julie at the café had told her she could help out two mornings a week when she was able, and if she did a couple of mornings at the canteen and joined Rosemary's groups she would have far less time to sit and mope. Money wasn't really a big issue, as Mike's pay covered all she really needed, but the extra would buy things for their home.

'I don't mind what I do,' she said, warming to her bright and enthusiastic companion. 'Just tell me where to go and when.'

'I'll do better than that,' Rosemary said. 'I can pick you up two evenings a week. One evening we knit socks and scarves for the Army, and on another we sort donated clothes, which we then volunteer to wash and iron; the best are given to children's charities or those in need and the rags are sold to fund other good causes. On Sunday afternoons we have tea in the church hall for all the elderly folk – and we make cakes and sausage rolls or whatever we can find to take along. Once a month we hold an event to raise money for our servicemen, and when we have enough we give a social evening for them.'

'It sounds as if you're busy all the time,' Janet said, impressed.

'There are other things I do to help the vicar and his wife with their functions, but if you let me I'll bore you to death.'

'I'm not in the least bored,' Janet said. 'Meeting you was just what I needed. I've made one friend since I came down here, but I couldn't take anyone back to the rooms – and I didn't feel settled. Now I could ask my brother to come and stay or my mother, if she has the time.'

'What does your mother do?'

'She helps my father run a pub, does all the cooking and serves in the bar too. Mum is a really good cook, and I think I've picked some of it up from her – but I'll be asking for some of her recipes now.'

'Oh good, I like swapping recipes,' Rosemary said. She

drew the car to a halt in the lane at the front of the cottage. 'Now let's transport you inside and put the kettle on. Then we can make a pot of tea and really get to know each other.'

*

Janet was aching all over by the time she fell into bed that night. Even though Rosemary had had the cottage cleaned for her, it seemed that she still had a lot to do before she felt ready to settle down. She'd unpacked her clothes and Mike's, hanging them in the wardrobe side by side. Her books and personal bits and pieces were arranged where they looked nice, and she put the pans she'd bought new on the dresser in the kitchen. There were some cooking utensils and some crockery, but Janet was glad she'd bought a set of yellow cups, plates and dishes, because they really brightened things up and made her feel it was her home.

Mike had bought a second-hand wind-up gramophone from a junk shop, and a small collection of records, including some Glenn Miller songs. When Rosemary left, about two hours after they arrived, Janet put the music on so that it didn't feel too silent or lonely. She needed a wireless, because she would want to hear the news and the programmes she'd liked at home. She'd seen one in a second-hand shop in town and thought she would go in and ask the price another day, but for the moment she had too much to do to feel isolated or lonely. Rosemary had arranged to pick her up and take her to the canteen to meet people the next day; in the evening it was the knitting circle and Janet was intending to join the other women. She'd learned to knit as a child and would enjoy making socks with a group of friends, and now that she had her own home she could start making more baby clothes too.

'Once you get to know us, you'll always have someone calling in for coffee or inviting you out,' Rosemary said cheerfully before she left.

Janet wasn't sure she wanted to be that busy, but she smiled and agreed. She'd been lonely at the lodgings but already the cottage was beginning to feel like home. Before she finally tumbled into bed, Janet had written a long letter to her mother, which she would post the next morning at the post box down the road next to the telephone kiosk.

For the first time since she'd left her home in London, Janet began to feel as if she might be able to settle down and make a proper life for her and Mike in this place.

*

Peggy recognised the writing and opened the letter as soon as it arrived. She was on her own in the kitchen and sat down in the comfortable chair by the range to read what her daughter had to say. Immediately, she knew that Janet was feeling much better. The tone of her writing was more cheerful and she sounded happy for the first time in ages, instead of scared and worried.

Giving a little prayer of thanks, Peggy slipped the letter into her apron pocket as Laurence walked in from the bar. As she saw his face the feeling of pleasure evaporated and she felt sickness in her throat.

'Has it come then?' she asked and drew a sharp breath as he nodded. 'When do you leave?'

'Tomorrow on the early train. I'm allowed to tell you that I'm going to be training in Scotland.'

'Oh, Laurie.' Peggy was on her feet and across the floor to him. She put her arms about him. 'I'm sorry. I shall miss you, but you're the one who has to put up with it all...'

'I'd hoped I'd done my bit last time,' Laurence said and frowned. 'I've been setting things in order, Peggy. If anything happens to me, you'll find my will and everything you need in the desk upstairs. You can read it if you want. It leaves a few pounds to Pip and the rest is for you.'

'What about Janet? She's still your daughter.'

'I was angry when I made it, but once I've gone you can give her something if you want... I haven't time to change it now.'

'Oh, Laurie.' Peggy felt tears sting her eyes. 'I know she let you down, but surely you're not still angry with her?'

'I'm just hurt, and disappointed in her. I wanted more for my daughter,' he said. 'If she needs you when the child comes – well, you should get someone in here and go to her or tell her to come here for the birth.'

'Thank you for that,' Peggy said as the hurt twisted inside her. She'd never got back to where they'd been before the quarrel and still regretted it. 'But I pray nothing does happen, Laurie. Perhaps you won't have to fight.'

'Maybe I shan't,' he said and smiled oddly. 'But I wanted everything proper. You've got a good stock in the cellars, as Pip knows – but you'll need to keep badgering the brewery for beer. We can't stock up on that and I'm afraid we might not get our full share if I'm not here to bully them.'

'Leave it to me,' Peggy soothed. 'I'll make sure we get what we're entitled to, believe me.'

'I dare say I'm worrying for nothing,' he sighed. 'I suppose there isn't a cup of coffee going – and one of your scones? I've been spoiled, Peggy, and I'm going to miss my home comforts once I leave.'

'Sit down and I'll take over the bar,' Peggy said, pouring

him a cup of her fragrant coffee and pushing a plate of warm scones, butter and her own strawberry jam in front of him. 'I'm not sure how much longer we shall be able to buy real coffee. Maureen let me have extra last week, but she said their stock is low and her father could only get that bottled stuff from the wholesaler.'

'That's all right if you make it with hot milk,' Laurence said. 'I know it won't be easy for you here, Peggy. You'll have to take on more staff to help you. It's a pity Janet went away. You'd have been happier with her working here.'

'Oh, I'll find someone,' Peggy said. 'I've a couple of ideas.'

'Well, I shan't be able to help you,' Laurence said. 'I shall think of you wrestling with the fires in the mornings, love.'

'You concentrate on looking after yourself,' Peggy said and went through to the bar, because she could feel the sting of tears and didn't want to upset him more by seeing her cry.

The first person to enter was one of their regulars, a travelling salesman who called every few weeks. He sold office supplies to several factories in the East End, but although no older than Laurence, Mr Hillier had one leg shorter than the other and needed a special boot to walk. He had a pronounced limp which was more noticeable these days, almost as if he were making the most of his disability so that he wouldn't be thought a coward, because he wasn't in uniform.

'Half of bitter and a pasty please, Mrs Ashley,' he said and sat down at his favourite table in the window.

Peggy had just served him when three more customers entered the pub. She was kept busy for some minutes serving both drinks and food, and then, the American serviceman she'd served before Christmas walked in.

'I'd like coffee if I may, ma'am,' he said. 'And is that apple pie I can see in your glass counter?'

'Yes.' Peggy smiled. 'I'm afraid I can only offer you custard with it, sir. I don't have cream today.'

'Your custard will be fine,' he told her and then placed a thick paper bag on the counter. 'I promised your husband I'd see what I could do, ma'am.'

Peggy peeped inside and smiled more broadly as she saw two bags of fresh ground coffee; it was an American brand and unknown to her, but very welcome just the same.

'How thoughtful,' she said. 'What do I owe you for this, sir?'

'It's a gift from the USA to our British friends,' he said and grinned broadly. 'Just call me Able, ma'am. I'm goin' home tomorrow and I like to keep my word when I can – and if that apple pie is as good as it looks I'll take back fond memories of my visit.'

'I'm sorry you're leaving,' Peggy said. 'And the apple pie is my gift to you, Able.'

She cut him a large slice and put a generous measure of custard into the jug so that he could help himself, but an influx of young women from the munitions factory put paid to any more talk and Peggy was serving flat out until Laurence came in to relieve her.

Returning to the kitchen with her precious bags of ground coffee, Peggy went back to baking. She put two trays of pasties and a large cottage pie in the oven and then sat down to read her daughter's letter again.

Now that Laurence had relented, she could write to Janet and tell her to come home for the birth of her child.

Chapter 21

Janet pressed a hand to her back as she felt the ache getting worse. It was March 1940 and she was so large and ungainly that it was an effort to do anything; her time had to be very close and sometimes now she felt very frightened. Rosemary called most days and had coffee with her, and she had her to Sunday lunch most weeks now that Janet had given up work.

'You have to think of me as family for the moment, Jan,' she'd told her. 'If you start getting violent pains ring the ambulance and then me. I'll be here first and make sure they look after you.'

What sort of pain did Rosemary mean? Janet wondered about it, because this ache was nasty and it was making her restless. She'd cleaned the kitchen and tidied the front room but she couldn't sit still. Ought she to telephone for the ambulance or just ring her friend?

Unable to bear the pain combined with the loneliness of the house, Janet picked up her jacket and her purse and walked out of the cottage. The phone box was just a few yards up the road. Janet dialled Rosemary's number but her friend wasn't there. Frustrated, Janet hesitated and then dialled her mother's number in London. This time the phone was answered immediately.

'Hi, Pip speaking, can I help you?'

'Pip? It's Jan,' she said. 'Is Mum there?'

'Jan, are you all right?' her brother said. 'I haven't talked to you for ages, how are you getting on? I want to come and stay for a few days – can I?'

'Yes, if you can put up with me looking like a swollen whale,' Janet laughed shakily. 'When do you want to come? Only I think I might be having the baby very soon...'

'Good grief! You're not having it now, are you?'

'I thought I might be,' Janet said, 'but the pain has eased off now. Can I talk to Mum?'

'Sorry, she's out,' he said. 'Why don't you come home to have the baby, Jan? Mum said she'd told you that you could.'

'Yes, she did, but I thought Dad might not like it. Besides, I thought I'd got another couple of weeks...'

'Dad isn't here.'

Janet heard the pips going. 'I'll have to ring off now, Pip, or I shan't have change if I need to phone.'

'You should have it put in...' Pip began but the phone cut off suddenly mid-sentence.

Turning away from the kiosk, Janet walked slowly home. She was feeling miserable and then she saw Rosemary's car draw up and began to smile.

'I was just phoning you or trying to,' she called as her friend got out and walked towards her. Seeing Rosemary's expression, Janet felt suddenly cold all over. Something was wrong. She stood still, the sense of foreboding growing as she saw both pain and sympathy in Rosemary's eyes. 'What's happened? What's wrong?'

'We'll go in and sit down,' Rosemary said. 'I could do with some coffee – and a drop of something stronger too...'

Janet unlocked the door and led the way inside. She had the kettle ready and moved it onto the heat, then she brought the tray to the table and fetched a small bottle of whisky, and then she sat down, waiting. Her body felt icy cold and she was numbed, her mind refusing to accept what she knew Rosemary was going to tell her.

'I hate to be the bearer of bad news,' Rosemary began, 'especially as you're so close to having the baby – but they told me first and it took me a while to find the courage to come...'

'It's Mike, isn't it?'

'It's all of them,' Rosemary said and swallowed hard. 'The ship was hit three days ago and it was lost. There were some survivors but... it doesn't seem that either Mike or – or John is amongst them...'

Janet wasn't sure who was making that awful screaming noise, whether it was her or Rosemary. She put her hands to her ears trying to block it out, but it just went on and on, a terrible wailing that hardly sounded human. Rosemary moved swiftly and slapped her just once across the face. The screaming stopped and for a moment she was stunned into silence, then as Rosemary spoke the tears started to trickle down her cheeks.

'I'm so sorry, Jan,' she whispered and Janet could see that she was crying too. 'I know how much it hurts but hysterics won't help you or the baby. You have to think about your baby, just as I have to think of my children. I can't go to pieces because they've lost their father and they mustn't lose their mother, too.'

Janet stared at her, angry at first that she could be so calm. Didn't she care? And then she saw beneath the mask to the abject misery Rosemary was trying to conceal.

'Oh, Rosemary,' she said brokenly, 'what are we going to do?'

'I'm not sure,' her friend said in a voice that wobbled on the verge of breaking. 'I think we either accept it and weep our hearts out, or we refuse to believe they've gone and just get on with things.'

'Do you think – could they have survived somehow despite not being on the lists?' Somehow it was easier talking about a shared burden, because it helped to feel that she was not alone.

'It is possible...' Rosemary hesitated, seeming unsure of whether to go on or not. 'There were German battleships in the vicinity even though it was a submarine that took our ship out...'

'You think it possible that they could have been picked up by a German ship?'

'It's a chance in a million. The other chance is that one of the surviving merchant ships might have picked them up.'

'Wouldn't they have reported this once they docked?'

'Unless it was one of the French ships,' Rosemary said, looking thoughtful. 'Apparently, it wasn't just British ships in convoy this time. There was a French vessel and a Norwegian merchant ship. They sailed with the convoy until the attack but lost contact in the ensuing chaos. They think the Norwegian ship tried to send a message, something about breaking off to make her own way, but it wasn't clear and they lost contact before they could get more details...'

Janet felt a little calmer. Talking about the possibilities made it seem unreal. She could picture the dark night, fog making it difficult to see as far as the next ship in the convoy, and then an explosion, fire lighting the sky and smoke and the chaos that would've ensued, and she shivered as she thought of the men struggling in the water or caught below decks as the ship went down – and yet because it was all the stuff of nightmares it didn't seem possible that it could be the end of Mike or Rosemary's husband.

'Perhaps they're together,' she said. 'On board the Norwegian ship...'

'I wish I could believe it,' Rosemary said and the look in her eyes was almost pleading, as if she were the one begging for comfort now. 'It would be all right if they were prisoners of war.'

'The Norwegian ship was trying to send a message, it could have been about the men they'd picked up – and it could be our husbands, Rosemary.'

'Yes, my dear, it could,' the older woman said, but Janet knew she was struggling to believe it.

Janet's next words surprised even her. 'I don't believe Mike is dead,' she said and even as she spoke them she felt they were true. 'I think he's on board that ship or one of the others that haven't made contact.'

'Oh, Janet.' Rosemary's eyes pricked with tears. She sat looking at Janet hopelessly. 'My dear girl... I just pray that you're right.'

'I'll put the kettle on again,' Janet said and got up. As she did so the pain shot through her and made her gasp and bend over, clutching at her stomach in agony. 'I think the baby is coming. I thought it might be earlier but...' She felt a stinging sensation between her thighs and then the wetness as her waters broke. 'I think it's coming soon, Rosemary.'

'Hang on until we get you upstairs and on the bed,' Rosemary said, suddenly practical and alert. 'This is something I can cope with, Jan. I did nursing before I was married, you know. It was ages ago and I'm a bit rusty, but I remember the basics. I'll get you breathing properly and then nip over and telephone my doctor.'

'I wish all my patients were as obliging as you,' the midwife said as she finished washing the little girl, wrapped her in soft towels and placed her in Janet's arms. 'Mostly, I get called out hours too soon and have to go off and come back before baby is born – but this little darling came along with no trouble at all.'

'Is that how it seemed to you?' Janet asked ruefully and Rosemary laughed. 'I was in labour for nine hours before my first and six with my second,' she told Janet ruefully. 'You made a proper job of it in just less than two hours – that's good going, love.'

'It was bad enough, and I think I'd had rumblings all day,' Janet replied, but she knew she'd been lucky, especially when she looked down into the sweet face of her baby. 'She's gorgeous, isn't she?'

'Beautiful,' Rosemary said with a little touch of envy in her voice. 'I always wanted a daughter. I wouldn't part with my boys, but I'd hoped for a girl…' There was a little break in her voice and Janet knew she was thinking that perhaps it was too late now.

'You're not too old to have a girl,' Janet said, because the birth of her daughter had somehow made her stronger. She refused to accept that Mike had been lost to the sea. Something inside her would've known if he were dead. If he was alive he would get back to her and their child when he could – even if she had to wait until the war was over. 'I'd like a boy for Mike next time.'

The look of pity in Rosemary's eyes nearly overcame her, but Janet looked down at the pink mouth of her little girl and refused to let grief overwhelm her. Her love was keeping

Mike alive for both their sakes. It was wrong that this child would have to grow up without ever knowing her father and Janet wasn't going to let that happen. If she refused to accept Mike was lost, he was still alive and would be thinking of her and his child.

'What are you going to call her?' the midwife asked as she finished clearing up the debris of birth. 'Had you decided on a name?'

'Margaret Lauren Rowan,' Janet said. 'If she'd been a boy we were going to call him Mark Laurence Rowan...' Her throat caught with sudden emotion, because they'd argued over the second name. Mike hadn't wanted to call his son after the man who had refused to let them get married properly from her home, but Janet had held out stubbornly. Her father might relent one day and want to see his grandchild.

'She'll probably be called Maggie,' the midwife said. 'Still, it's a good name – my granny's name, actually.' She took the child from Janet's arms, placing her in her cot. 'Will you be able to cope here alone, Mrs Rowan? I'll pop in later to make sure you can manage to feed her, but you need to sleep for a while.'

'Janet won't be alone,' Rosemary said. 'I'm going to stay for a few days, until she's feeling better, and I'm sure her mother will come down soon for a while...'

'Mum has the pub to run. I doubt she can spare the time – that's why I intended to go into the maternity home for the birth.'

'Well, Maggie was in too much of a rush,' the midwife said, 'but I expect your mum will come down to see her grandchild, even if it's only for a day.'

*

It was evening when she woke to the sound of her baby crying. Rosemary entered with a tray of tea and biscuits. She set them on the chest of drawers, bent to pick Maggie up and carry her to the bed.

'She's hungry, Jan, can you try and feed her now? You were exhausted and you've slept for a while. I nearly prepared a bottle, but Mrs Robinson said I should wake you because baby needs her feed.'

Janet looked down at her baby and saw how red in the face she looked. 'Someone should have woken me sooner. Poor little mite.' She pulled her nightgown down and held Maggie to her breast, helping her to find the nipple, but a little to Janet's surprise, she didn't need much encouragement and latched on lustily. 'Oh, it feels strange...'

'Yes, doesn't it?' Rosemary laughed. 'It's a bit shocking at first to feel that tug, but it's nice too – isn't it?'

'Yes, she's so lovely.' Janet ran a finger over the soft down on Maggie's head. 'She hasn't got much hair yet.'

'Some do, some don't,' Rosemary said and smiled. 'Give her a little break now, Jan, and then try her on the other side or it may start to get a bit sore.'

Maggie whimpered a bit as the nipple popped out of her mouth and then burped. Jan rubbed her back and moved her into the other arm, giving her a moment before letting her latch on to the other side. Maggie sucked heartily for a little while and then stopped, her eyes closing.

'Do you think she's had enough?' Janet was anxious.

'I expect she knows what she wants for now,' Rosemary said. 'My eldest always wanted more than I could give so we had to supplement his feed with a bottle after a couple of weeks, but my youngest was far less greedy. I worried because he didn't put on as much weight, but it seems to be his nature. He still eats fussily and the doctor tells me he'll always be lean, while the eldest may struggle with his weight one day... if he gives up sport.'

'Have you been in touch with them?'

'No, they're happy at school. I shan't tell them about the... ship until the holidays; there's no point until we hear more.' Rosemary turned away for a moment. 'I rang your mother and told her you'd had Maggie. She's coming down in a couple of days and will stay for a while.'

'How can she manage that?'

'She said someone named Anne was between jobs at the moment and had volunteered to look after things in the pub until she gets back.'

'Oh...' Janet nodded and handed Maggie to her. 'I think she needs changing. I'm sorry to put this on you.'

Rosemary shook her head, smiling as she took the baby. 'Oh dear, that smells ominous, little one. I'd better get you changed and clean as soon as possible.'

'This is so kind,' Janet said, watching as Rosemary expertly changed and cleansed the child's bottom. 'I should've been in trouble without you.'

'And I needed you,' her friend said. 'I need this, Janet. I can just about keep it at bay while I'm needed here, but when I go home...'

'Yes, I know.' Janet blinked hard. 'I'm not going to give in, Rosemary. Mike is alive. I know he is – and you have to believe...'

Rosemary restored the now clean baby to her cot and touched her forehead gently. 'New life is always so welcome. I'm glad you can believe, my dear, but you see I know... I know my John has gone.'

Chapter 22

Maureen smiled as she saw the soldier enter the shop. He looked smart in his uniform and she thought he seemed much fitter and happier than when she'd last seen him.

'Hello, Gordon,' she said. 'How are you getting on in the Army – and how is Shirley?'

'I'm going down to see her tomorrow,' he said and gave her an oddly shy look. 'I've got ten days leave and I wondered if you might come with me, just for the day.'

'Well, it is Sunday, and I don't have anything in particular to do,' Maureen said. It was the second week of March and although the weather wasn't really much like spring it would be nice to go on a trip to the country.

'Would we go on the train?'

'I've borrowed a car from a mate,' Gordon said. 'I thought we could pack a nice picnic and take Shirley off for a few hours somewhere before we come back.'

'Yes, I'd like to come – and you can leave the picnic to me,' Maureen said. 'I've got some eggs and I'll make egg and cress sandwiches, fairy cakes and jam tarts. Nothing posh or fancy. We can take a flask of tea if you like and a bottle of lemonade.'

'I've got a little picnic stove so we can make fresh tea, if we have the ingredients, and I'll take a bottle of water.'

'I should think that will be lovely,' Maureen said. 'It's just a bit of luck that I had a box of fresh eggs delivered today. They're getting scarce these days, at least in London, though your mum can probably buy them in the country. A lot of country folk have their own hens.'

'Yes, I'm sure they have,' Gordon said, looking pleased. 'Now, can you make me up a big bag of Shirley's favourite sweets please?'

*

'Why you want a day in the country is beyond me,' Maureen's father grumbled as she bustled about packing the picnic basket. She'd fried his breakfast and made him a pot of tea, but he resented being hurried. 'I should've thought you had plenty of jobs to get on with here. What with your good works and your days out, you're neglecting me and the business, Maureen.'

'No, I don't think so, Dad,' she replied, biting back the angry retort she might have made. 'I haven't had a day out for years, and I never do housework on Sundays. Mum wouldn't have liked it.'

He went on grumbling, but Maureen resolutely ignored him. She'd discovered that the best thing was just to go ahead and do whatever she wanted and put up with his moaning. Otherwise, he'd have her sitting here doing nothing but look after him and his shop for the rest of her life.

She was downstairs with her basket of food several minutes early, and decided to pop one of the new comics in her basket for Shirley. Gordon had spent enough on sweets for her, using his personal coupons to please his daughter's sweet tooth.

'Sorry I'm a bit late,' Gordon said when he drew up outside the shop and got out to open the door and put her things in the back. 'The stupid thing had a fit and wouldn't start, but fortunately a friend managed to get it going for me. I know we could've caught the train, but it wouldn't be the same, would it?'

Maureen agreed it wouldn't. She got into the front seat with him and smiled, feeling a thrill of excitement as they moved off. After being cooped up at the shop most days, it was a real treat to be taken on a trip like this into the Essex countryside. Gordon Hart's mother hadn't wanted to go too far from London and had chosen a nice little village a few miles from Braintree. Maureen hadn't heard of Finchingfield, but Gordon's mother had a cousin there. They were farmers and lived just outside the village, but it was to the village that they were headed.

Gordon wanted to spend as much of the day with his daughter as he could so they started out at seven o'clock. Because it was a Sunday the roads were much quieter, and although they passed a few private cars, buses and the noisy trams as they left London, once on the open road there was very little traffic.

'I suppose it's harder to get petrol these days,' Maureen said, remarking the quiet roads and looking out of her window with interest. 'It's like everything else now; they either ration it as they did food in January, or you can't buy it anyway.'

'Petrol will be tightly rationed soon,' he agreed. 'That's why I thought we'd have this treat while I can get enough. I've filled up and I've got a five-gallon can in the back, so it should be enough to get us there and back. I'd hate to run out when we're havin' a nice day out.'

'That would be a catastrophe,' Maureen agreed. Her father had kicked up enough fuss about her going out for a day. She couldn't imagine what he might say if she didn't get back until the early hours of Monday morning.

However, Gordon seemed to have it all under control and she sat back, relaxing and determined to enjoy herself.

*

Maureen had been a little concerned that Shirley might play up again, but she was relieved to discover that the child seemed pleased to see her and took it for granted that she'd come with her father. She ran to hug him, breaking free of her grandmother's hold and then, when Maureen bent down, allowed herself to be kissed.

'Daddy!' she cried and clung to his hand as if she would never let it go. 'Come and see the ducks. Grandma said I can feed them – can I, can I, Daddy?'

'If there's anything left over from our picnic?' He looked at Maureen, as if asking permission.

'I've packed lots of things,' Maureen told the child. 'There are egg sandwiches, chicken paste and jam. Also fairy cakes and jam tarts – I think there might be a little bit left over for the ducks.'

'All my favourites,' Shirley said and looked at her a little oddly. ''Cept for strawberry blancmange. I do like that, Maureen, but Gran says I only have it when I come to tea with you. Can I come again?'

'One day,' Maureen promised vaguely. 'Perhaps your daddy will bring you next time he comes home.' She looked at Gordon and he smiled, then he bent down to swoop Shirley up in his arms.

'Let's go and look at the pond,' he said and strode off towards the rather picturesque pond, on which ducks were swimming.

It was such a peaceful scene, a truly charming setting for what looked like being a happy day. Set amongst winding lanes that led down past green fields and white-washed cottages, the village with its beautiful Norman church and its Georgian cottages was picture perfect. Gordon fell in love with it, as Maureen had instantly, and it seemed pointless going anywhere else when they had such a wonderful spot for their picnic. So instead of using the car, they explored the village and its surrounding lanes and then settled by the pond to play games with Shirley and eat their picnic, sharing the crusts with the ducks that squabbled excitedly over them.

Everyone was happy, laughing and talking, enjoying the unexpected break in the clouds, giving them surprisingly warm sunshine. Here in this timeless place it seemed impossible that a war was happening somewhere out there. It was a world away and for a while Maureen forgot that she had a shop to run, a father who never stopped grumbling at her, and a broken heart.

*

It was past five when they took Mrs Hart and Shirley back to the farm. Maureen was introduced to their cousins and asked to have a cup of tea and a slice of home-baked fatless sponge with strawberry preserve before leaving; and when it was time to go, she was presented with her own basket filled with good things from the farm: homemade soft white cheese, a slab of real farm butter, some eggs and a crisp lettuce, as well as some garden radishes, a brace of pheasants, and a pot of blackberry preserves.

'This is very kind of you, Mrs Hunter,' Maureen said, feeling oddly shy. 'Are you sure you can spare all this?'

'Oh, we don't go short on the farm,' the farmer's wife said, beaming. 'We know you townsfolk don't get much really fresh, and we're grateful to you for your interest in little Shirley here.'

Maureen's cheeks flushed, because she'd only agreed to take an interest in Shirley because her father seemed so upset over the prospect of leaving her, though from what she'd seen the child was fine here and would be perfectly well looked after if anything happened to her father and grandmother. However, when Maureen asked for the bathroom and Mrs Hunter took her upstairs, she stopped to chat for a moment.

'I'm glad to have met you, Maureen,' she said. 'I'm fond of the child in my own way, but I couldn't look after her if anything happened to my cousin. This is a working farm and with most of the men going off to the war I've more than enough work to do without the care of a young girl – and she's a spoiled young madam. There were tantrums when she first came here, I can tell you. I had to take my hairbrush to her. She soon learned not to turn up her nose at good food then. I can't abide waste – and even a child should do her chores before she goes off to play, don't you agree?'

Maureen mumbled something, because she didn't want to disagree with her hostess, who had been generous, and she could see that there was no place for a disobedient and spoiled child on this farm.

When she and Gordon took their leave Shirley wept and clung to her father until she was told sharply not to be a baby by Mrs Hunter. Seeing the look of apprehension in the child's eyes, Maureen bent down to her.

'You remember where I live, Shirley?' she asked in soft

voice and Gordon's daughter nodded. 'Well, I've got a little bed there that has your name on it. If ever you need me, send me a postcard and I'll come and take you back with me – do you understand?'

A little smile trembled on the girl's mouth and Maureen saw the sparkle of tears in her eyes. She clung to Maureen's hand for a moment, and then said, 'Promise…?'

'Yes, I promise,' Maureen said. 'I'll send you a packet of postcards with stamps on, and one day I'll come and visit again.'

Shirley clung to her hand for a moment more and then stood back with her grandmother to let them go. Gordon looked at her as he started the car.

'I didn't think it would be so hard to leave her.'

'She's all you have to remind you of your wife.'

'No, that's not it. Sometimes, I can hardly recall Jenny's face now. It's Shirley, because she's so vulnerable and I don't think she's really happy there. Did you notice anything?'

'I expect it's still strange after being in town.'

'Shirley likes the farm animals, she told me so – but there's something she doesn't like there, but she wouldn't say what.'

'Shirley is all right with your mother, Gordon. You can't do anything else but leave her there.'

'No…' He sighed. 'I hadn't planned on spending the rest of my leave there, but I might pop down again in a couple of days. She was too subdued for my liking.'

Maureen could have told him that his daughter was experiencing strict discipline for the first time in her life, but if she did that it would simply make him more uneasy. She didn't think Mrs Hunter was unnecessarily cruel, she just believed in the old maxims that children should do as they were told and not argue.

'I think that's a good idea,' she said at last, 'but your mother won't let anything bad happen to her.'

'No...' Gordon looked thoughtful. 'I suppose not.'

*

It was when they were about halfway home that the engine of Gordon's borrowed car suddenly spluttered and died. He cursed softly and pulled over to a lay-by, got out and opened the bonnet. After a few minutes of watching him stare help-lessly into the engine, Maureen went to stand beside him.

'What do you think is wrong? We haven't run out of petrol?'

'No, I made sure of that... I think it's probably something simple, but I'm not a mechanic. I saw a garage about a mile or so back. Sit in the car, Maureen, and I'll walk back and see if there's anyone about.'

'Why don't you just lock the car and I'll walk with you? I'd rather we stayed together. It's a bit isolated here.'

'Yes, perhaps you're right,' Gordon said. 'The car is safe enough. We'll see if the garage owner will come out tonight, though he may not be willing.' He glanced at his watch. 'I'm not sure where the nearest railway station is or if there are any trains running on Sunday night.'

'We can ask at the garage,' Maureen said. 'Come on, it's not far if we walk briskly.'

'You're a brick, Maureen. Most girls would be screaming their heads off at me by now.'

'You didn't make it break down,' she said and put her arm through his. 'Best foot forward, Private Hart.'

*

Maureen was right; it didn't take long to reach the garage, but when they got there it was in darkness, and so was the cottage next to it. Gordon rang the doorbell but there was no answer. He glanced at his watch again and shook his head.

'We're not going to get anything done tonight, Maureen.'

'No...' She hesitated, then, 'We can either look for somewhere to stay the night – I think we passed an inn that does bed and breakfast just a few hundred yards up the road – or we can sit in the car and try to sleep.'

'Let's see if we can get you a room for the night and I'll stay with the car.'

'All right,' she said reluctantly. 'That may be for the best, Gordon. If the inn has a phone I can give my father a ring and let him know what happened.'

They trudged back to the inn in silence. Maureen knew her father was going to hit the roof when she told him she wouldn't be home, and Gordon was obviously anxious about his friend's car.

The landlord was friendly and sympathetic. He said that they wouldn't have found anyone at the garage, because the owner was away for the weekend, but he knew someone who would come to the car in the morning. He had a spare room for Maureen and offered Gordon the loan of a blanket.

'You can return it tomorrow when you come to pick up your young lady and arrange about the car, sir. I do a good breakfast if I say it myself and you'll be ready for it by the morning.'

Maureen thanked him. She asked if she could use his phone and tried ringing her father, but there was no answer. His wife then took her up to her room and promised a pot of tea and then left her alone to make herself as comfortable as she could. Apart from the anxiety of knowing her father would be furious when she got home, Maureen was surprised at how calm she felt. It was after all a little adventure and she didn't get many of those.

Maureen had a wash in the tiny basin and then sat on the bed to drink her tea. She thought of Gordon sleeping in the back of the car and hoped the flask of tea Mrs Hunter had made up for them was still warm. He would be very uncomfortable, but she supposed he might have to face far worse when he was fighting the enemy.

Curling up in what was an extremely soft feather bed, Maureen fell asleep quickly. She was tired after a long day in the country air and slept until she was woken by someone knocking at her door the next morning.

'Breakfast is being served for the next hour, Miss Jackson.'

'Thank you; I'll come down soon.'

*

Maureen was just sitting down to breakfast in the dining room when Gordon joined her. He was smiling and told her that the car had already been repaired. He'd had a wash in the hotel and paid their bill, and as soon as they'd both eaten they could be on their way.

'What was wrong?' Maureen asked.

'Something needed cleaning, spark plugs and another piece,' Gordon said with a shrug. 'If I'd known I could've done it; still, no real harm – I managed all right and you look as if you slept well.'

'I did,' Maureen said and smiled at him. 'How long will it take us to get home now?'

'An hour or so.' He frowned. 'I forgot about your father. Will he be very angry?'

'Yes, I expect so,' Maureen said. 'Don't look so upset, Gordon. It wasn't your fault and I had a lovely day yesterday. I think Shirley trusts me more now – and that has to be a good thing, doesn't it?'

'Yes, it does.' He looked at her shyly. 'I still wish you would marry me, Maureen. I'm not a rich man, but whatever I have would be for you.'

She smiled and shook her head, because she knew he liked her a lot, and it would suit him if she said yes to becoming his wife, but he wasn't in love with her. At least, she'd never seen any sign of it and she thought she would know if his feelings were stronger than mere friendship.

'I'm sorry, but I'm not in love with you. You're a friend, Gordon, and I like you, but I don't love you – and I don't think you're in love with me.' She smiled as he would've protested. 'You might be fond of me, Gordon, but that's not real love – and you know it.' She saw the little nod he gave and knew she was right. Gordon wanted a mother for Shirley and he thought he could trust her – but that wasn't for her.

'Oh well, if you change your mind…'

Maureen shook her head. She liked Gordon but she was in love with Rory, even if she knew the whole thing was impossible.

*

Maureen was feeling apprehensive as she let herself into the shop. It was past eight and the newspapers were waiting for her to sort out. She put her basket in the kitchen, unloaded the goods Mrs Hunter had given her and went through to the shop. After opening up, she started to go through the papers she'd found in the passage. They were tied up with string and it was unusual for her father not to have taken them in first thing.

She didn't turn her head as someone entered the shop, thinking it was her father and waiting for the axe to fall, but when the voice spoke she turned in surprise.

'Peggy, this is early for you, isn't it?'

'I was worried about you,' Peggy said in a choked voice. Her eyes were red, as if she'd been crying. 'When they told me the house was in darkness and they couldn't make you hear I thought something must have happened to you as well...'

'What do you mean?' Maureen asked. 'Has something happened to my father?'

'That's one of the reasons I came round,' Peggy told her. 'Henry came to the pub last night. He was looking for you, said he wasn't feeling too good and thought you might be with me.'

'Gordon took me down to a village in Essex to visit his daughter. On the way home the car broke down and I stayed overnight at an inn; he slept in the car to guard it. I've just got in.'

'Then you don't know – your father was taken bad last night. He's in the infirmary, Maureen. I let your grandmother know and I thought she would've come round to see you.'

'No, I haven't seen her yet.' Maureen frowned. 'I feel guilty for taking a day off...'

'Don't be daft, love,' Peggy said, but the look in her eyes told Maureen she was very emotional. 'Well, I'll have to get back. We're all at sixes and sevens today. Of course, you don't know our news; Janet's had a little girl.'

'That's a bit early, isn't it?' Maureen smiled. 'Not that it matters – as long as they're both all right?'

'Yes, Janet and the baby are fine,' Peggy assured her but then she swayed and put a hand to her face. 'Janet had a terrible shock, Maureen. It's what brought the baby on early... she's been told Mike's ship was hit and he's missing.'

'Oh Peggy, no,' Maureen said, understanding why her friend looked so pale and tired. She couldn't have slept all night. 'She must be so upset – you all are. I'm so very sorry.'

'I'm going down as soon as I can arrange things here. I can't wait to see them... I can't do much but I need to be with Janet...'

'Of course you do, love. If I can help with anything while you're away...'

'Anne is going to look after the pub, but she could probably do with a hand in the evenings.'

'Yes, I'll do what I can,' Maureen promised.

'You've got enough to do with your father and the shop.' Peggy gave a choking sob. 'It never rains but it pours. Well, I'd better get back. Nellie is holding the fort.'

'I've got something for you,' Maureen said and dashed through to the kitchen. She brought the brace of pheasants back and offered them to Peggy. 'I was given these and I wouldn't turn them down, but I don't want them and Dad certainly won't – so you might be able to use them in the pub.'

'Of course I can,' Peggy said. 'These will be lovely, Maureen. You must let me pay for them.'

'No, just take them,' Maureen said. 'You've given me enough.'

'Well, if there's anything I can do while your father is ill...'

'Thanks.' Maureen watched as she left. 'And thanks for coming round. Take care of them, Peggy, tell Janet to come home...'

Maureen felt the sting of tears. Why did everything have to be so horrid? She was worried about her father, of course she was, but her heart grieved for Peggy and Janet, and Mike. Janet was so young and she'd gone off with her husband to make a new life – and now it was all in tatters. She'd had such a short time of happiness, and yet she had Mike's child.

Maureen thought she would give anything if she could hold Rory's baby in her arms, and her throat tightened with tears, because it was never going to happen.

Chapter 23

'Peggy told me she would have to close the pub for a few days so I offered to take over while she was away and I'm enjoying myself,' Anne informed Maureen when she popped in to buy some sugar, golden syrup and a few other items Peggy had told her were needed. 'I'm just making simple things for the bar – sandwiches, scones and rhubarb crumble with custard. I'm not as good a cook as Peggy, but I can manage pastry and scones.'

'It's so lucky you were here and not on one of your supply jobs,' Maureen said, weighing up the sugar into strong blue bags and folding the tops over expertly to keep it safe. 'Otherwise she might have had to close for a while.'

'She was desperate to go,' Anne said. 'Why did it have to happen, Maureen? This wicked war! Laurence away somewhere and Peggy has no idea how to contact him, and now Mike is... missing...'

'Perhaps he got picked up,' Maureen suggested. 'I know it sounds dire but people do get fished out of the sea days later and are still alive. I remember something in the paper once.'

'But there was a battle going on. If he was trapped below deck...'

'Oh, don't!' Maureen begged. 'I can't bear to think of it –

what Janet must feel I don't know. She was so much in love when they got married.'

'And with a new baby too... Peggy wasn't expecting it to happen for at least a week or two.'

'At least Janet has something of him,' Maureen said and her eyes stung with tears. 'I'm so sorry but it upsets me. I cried half the night after Peggy told me the news.'

'Yes, I must admit I shed a few tears, though I've hardly met Mike – but I feel for Janet and Peggy.'

'Won't they mind you taking time off from your teaching?' Maureen changed the subject to stop herself bursting into tears again.

'I'm not sure what I want to do,' Anne replied. 'The jobs are not always around now; they want me to relocate to the country for the duration, but I feel I want to stay here in London.'

'The papers keep warning us we're bound to be bombed soon.' Maureen frowned, because 1939 had been almost like a phoney war in some ways. 'Wouldn't you be better off in the country if it happens?'

'I feel as if I should be doing something more useful – something that helps the war effort.'

'You could re-join the WVS with me if you like,' Maureen suggested. 'We're busier now than we were when I joined and I've been taking a first aid course, because you never know when it might come in useful. We were helping out at a football ground in January and the crowd surged forward when the barriers were opened; a couple of elderly men fell and needed resuscitation before they were taken to hospital.'

'Yes, I could do that, but I thought I might join the ambulance service,' Anne said. 'I learned to drive last year; I should need to take advanced lessons to drive an ambulance, but it's either that or the auxiliary fire service, I think.'

'Oh, that's marvellous,' Maureen said. 'It would be lovely having you back in London again, Anne. We've missed you.'

'I've missed all of you,' Anne admitted. 'I think I shall apply for the ambulance service first as a driver, but if they don't want me I'll try the fire brigade. I know they need women volunteers because someone was telling me the other day.'

'They will be in the thick of it if we get bombed, but I sometimes feel it's all a lot of hot air the government puts out to stop us moaning about the shortages.' Maureen pulled a face. 'Sometimes, I think it's all a daft dream.'

'Oh no, I'm sure it will happen. Hitler has been too busy elsewhere, but just you wait. He'll get around to us and when he does we'll wish we only had the shortages to moan about.'

'What we all need is something to make us smile... a good old film like Charlie Chaplin's.'

Anne laughed. 'I was talking to Alice Carter this morning. She told me she got arrested last night for causing a fight.'

'Alice – you mean our Alice from across the road?' The elderly woman was one of them and Maureen couldn't imagine her in trouble with the law. 'Why?'

'She'd had a few apparently, and this other woman was saying that Hitler would walk right over us, and Alice wasn't having it. Apparently, she said she'd personally give Hitler a bloody nose if he set one foot in London – and when she was laughed at she gave the other woman a smack on the nose. A copper walked into it as they were fighting and asked what the trouble was and Alice knocked his helmet off...'

'Oh dear,' Maureen said and they both laughed. 'Still, they didn't keep her in the cells for long.'

'No, apparently she's a bit of a favourite with the local

bobbies and they let her go. Seems they all felt the way she does. One of them told her he believed she would do it and winked at her as he gave her a cup of tea and a biscuit. She said he was a bit of all right and if she were twenty years younger she'd show him a thing or two.'

'That's Alice all over.' Maureen giggled at the idea of Alice in her flowery pinny, her hair in its usual pins and a hairnet, and a young good-looking policeman having a passionate kiss. 'She's right though. I think we'd all fight rather than let them take over.'

'My uncle keeps a loaded shotgun by his bed and another in the hall inside the long case clock; he vows that he'll kill as many as he can before they get him.'

'I pray it never happens…'

'Me too,' Anne said. 'I'm not paranoid the way Uncle Henry is, but I have to admit he's not the only one living in fear of an invasion.'

'No, though my father doesn't think they'll get that close.'

'Let's hope he's right.'

'Well, good luck with running the pub while Peggy is away.'

'Thanks, I'll need it!'

Anne picked up her basket to leave as another customer entered. Maureen was sorry to see her friend go, especially as the new customer was one of her more awkward ones.

*

'It was very good of you to give up your time to look after Janet, Mrs Jamieson. I came as soon as I could but it took a few days to arrange and I'm not sure what she would've done if you hadn't been here. I hoped she might come home 'for the birth, but I think it took us all by surprise.'

'Yes, Janet didn't expect to give birth just yet, but you never can tell with the first, can you?'

'No, you can't,' Peggy agreed, hesitated, and then, 'I'm sorry to hear your sad news...'

'Well, we don't know for sure, do we?' Rosemary said brightly, though Peggy suspected the cheerful manner was assumed for her sake. 'I'd better go home, but I'll pop in to see how Janet is – and if you should need me, please don't hesitate to ring.'

'I'm sure you have plenty to do at home...'

'No, I really don't,' Rosemary said and left abruptly.

Peggy would have thought her rude under other circumstances, but the poor woman was clearly struggling with her grief. She felt a pang of fear as she wondered how she would react if Laurence was reported missing but then realised that it was different in her case. It would be awful of course, but something had changed since Laurence had been so intractable over Janet's marriage. The cracks had really started about the time of Percy's death but after she'd taken her daughter's side, Laurie's moods had become more frequent. Peggy knew in her heart that they'd been drifting apart for a long time but she wasn't sure why.

She pushed the thoughts to the back of her mind as she carried the tray of tea upstairs to Janet's room. Her daughter was lying with her eyes closed but opened them as she deposited the tray on the chest by the bed. Maggie's cot was beside her, and Peggy bent over it, her heart gladdened by the sight of the child's sweet face. She was sleeping and Peggy resisted the urge to pick her up and cuddle her.

'Has Rosemary gone home?'

'Yes, just this moment.'

'She was dreading it. She's convinced that Captain Jamieson is dead, because she says he wouldn't have left the ship while there was a chance of getting his men out alive.'

'I could see she was holding it all inside. It must have been awful for her, having to tell you, Jan – and then the baby arriving so suddenly. She hasn't had time to grieve.'

'I think it was what she needed, to keep busy. We could share it, you see, Mum, share the burden, but she doesn't believe there's a chance they're alive and I do. I don't feel Mike is dead and I think I would if he'd been killed. He may have been picked up in the fog and smoke by a Norwegian merchant ship or... a German ship.' Janet held back a sob. 'There is a chance, isn't there, Mum?'

'Yes, my darling,' Peggy said. 'Of course there's always a chance, but you mustn't count on it too much, because... well, if he doesn't come back it will be so much worse.'

'I can't give up on him yet,' Janet said. 'I just can't, Mum.'

'I'm not going to tell you that you must,' Peggy said and handed her a cup of tea. 'I'd like you to come back to London with me for a while, but that's up to you.'

'What if Mike comes home and finds the cottage empty?'

'You can leave your address with Mrs Jamieson and she'll let you know – and I'm sure there will be an official letter soon one way or the other, love. I can't leave the pub for longer than a week, and I don't think you should be alone here until you're over things.'

'I don't know.' Janet sipped the tea. 'I miss you so much, Mum, but I know Rosemary needs a friend and she's been so good to me. I'd like to come and stay for a while, but I'm making a life here – besides, what would Dad say? He threw me out...'

'He's sorry now,' Peggy said, although she wasn't sure if

Laurence had really forgiven his daughter. 'Anyway, he isn't at home. I haven't seen him for weeks.'

'Can I have a little time to think about it?'

'Of course; it will always be your home and you can come whenever you need to,' Peggy said. 'I just want to look after you, my love.'

'I know and I'm glad you came down, but I can't help feeling it would be like deserting Mike if I abandoned the cottage...' Janet sighed. 'I'm so tired. Do you mind if I sleep for a while?'

'Of course not, it's to be expected; after all you've just had a baby.'

Peggy went out and left her daughter to rest, feeling a bit upset. She'd gone to a lot of trouble to get here only to find that Mrs Jamieson was in control of the situation. She and Janet had been getting on perfectly well and Peggy felt left out of it. Rosemary had taken herself off, but she'd sensed her reluctance and Janet had seemed disappointed that her friend had gone, concerned for her, as if she'd been looking after her rather than the other way round. It made Peggy feel shut out, as if the bond that had always existed between mother and daughter was not important to Janet now.

She'd moved on with her life, found new friends and become independent, and was probably blaming her parents because she hadn't had longer with Mike – and that was Laurence's fault. Peggy felt hurt and angry – angry with her husband for causing the rift rather than Janet. Pushing the upsetting thoughts from her mind, she got started on washing the baby's nappies. Janet hadn't meant to upset her. Yet somehow Peggy knew that if her daughter had remained in London they would have been closer – she would have been present at the birth of her first grandchild and would have seen Janet's joy as the babe was placed in her arms.

You just didn't replace memories like that.

*

In the end Peggy stayed for five days. Janet was getting out of bed by then and Rosemary had sent her char woman to clean the house for her, visiting twice a day regularly, and bringing special food she'd cooked herself. Other ladies started to call, also bearing gifts for the child and for Janet, members of the knitting group she'd joined; cheerful, kind generous women who seemed to think Janet was theirs.

At the end of the fifth day Janet told her that she thought she was well enough to manage without her help.

'It was good of you to come down, Mum,' Janet said and kissed her cheek. 'I do miss you and I've enjoyed seeing you – and thanks for looking after us both, but I don't feel like leaving here just yet. I should feel as if I were giving up on Mike... deserting him.'

Peggy's cheeks were wet with tears because they'd received official confirmation of the ship's loss and the information that Mike was one of the missing crewmen. Many of them had been saved but seventy-five had been lost without trace. The official letter did not hold out much hope that Mike or his captain had been saved, because their names were not on any list of men recovered from the sea that fateful night. It seemed pretty clear that Janet's husband had died along with Captain Jamieson, but Janet was being very brave, refusing to accept it and insisting that she knew he was alive.

'It's your choice to stay here, but if it becomes too much or you change your mind, your room is waiting for you, love.'

'Yes, I know, Mum.' Janet gave her a quick hug. 'I'll visit soon, I promise – but I'm not ready yet. Can you understand and… not be hurt? I'm not shutting you out; I just need to be here for a bit.'

'Yes, I understand,' Peggy said and she did, and yet she was hurt; she did feel shut out and she needed her daughter to come home. She wanted the fun and excitement of seeing her grandchild grow up, the sharing and love she'd always hoped for, but at the moment Janet's emotions were too centred on her child and Mike to spare more than a fleeting thought for her mother. 'I just wanted you to know that I'm there if you need me.'

Chapter 24

Maureen read the letter from Gordon and smiled. He hoped to get leave again soon, because for the moment he was stationed in England, and was looking forward to seeing her and his daughter. It was his intention to fetch Shirley up to London for a few days so they could all go out to the pictures and the zoo.

> Shirley told me you'd sent her parcels and letters, and a card on her birthday. She really likes you, Maureen, and is looking forward to coming to tea again soon...

Maureen folded the letter and slipped it into her pocket as her father came into the kitchen. Although he'd left hospital with a warning to slow down a little, he'd ignored the doctor's advice, just as he ignored his daughter's pleas to take more care of himself. He was looking a bit grey in the face and coughing. His cough was getting worse, despite the fact that the weather was beautiful now.

The papers were filled with stories of the terrible disaster that was Dunkirk; so many brave men had been forced to retreat before the German onslaught to become trapped on the beaches across the Channel. What occurred then would never be forgotten, because other brave men had taken their little boats to sea and joined the naval and fishing fleets to rescue those trapped men. Although many had died on those beaches, thousands had been snatched to safety, which meant that Britain still had an army: broken and bleeding, but ready to lick their wounds and go back into the fray. The individual acts of valour and the shared grief and joy at the way their people had stood up to be counted had lifted people and given them hope, even though things looked blacker now than since the start of the war, but Mr Churchill, who was now Prime Minister, had told them all that there were better things to come and they should never think of surrender.

Maureen's father refused to talk to her about the war, telling her that she wouldn't understand what was going on and should stick to what she did best, which was looking after the shop and gossiping.

'You should go to the doctor with that cough, Dad,' she told him as she took his supper from the oven and put it on the table. 'I'm afraid it's Spam fritters, mash and cabbage again...'

'I don't want it,' he said and pushed the plate away. 'You can get me a cup of tea, girl, and fill a flask. You can make me a sandwich if you like – cheese and onion, something with a bit of taste.'

Maureen removed the plate from in front of him. She felt like throwing the food into the bin but decided against it; she'd noticed a stray cat hanging about the yard and how thin it looked. Not many people had food to spare for a cat these days, in fact a lot of people had followed the government guidelines and had their pets put down at the start of the war. She would put the food out for the animal; it was better than wasting it.

She made up the flask of tea and a packet of sandwiches

in greaseproof paper and put them on the table. Her father pushed back his chair and scooped them up, leaving without a word. His temper wasn't improving and Maureen felt angry that he was behaving so badly towards her, but short of packing a case and leaving she didn't think there was much she could do.

She fetched her jacket and purse and left the flat, going down to the back door and out through the yard. It was a lovely night, the sky clear and the air still, though the heat of the day had made the drains smell a bit and she wrinkled her nose. Reaching the canteen where she helped with anything that was asked of her, Maureen discovered it was a hive of activity. Baskets, hampers and boxes were being taken out and loaded into one of their vans.

'What is happening?' she asked one of the girls she often met there.

'Oh, I'm glad you've arrived,' Susie said and looked relieved. 'We've been told there is a shipment of wounded men coming into Liverpool Street station this evening. We want volunteers to go down there and meet them, give them tea and sandwiches if they want or sympathy if not. I imagine there will be loads of ambulances coming and going so we need to be in position ahead of time – you'll go, won't you?'

'Yes, I'll go,' Maureen said, though her stomach lurched at the thought. She'd served men with empty sleeves and scarred faces at the canteen but seeing the badly wounded arrive was different. 'Who is stopping here to look after the canteen?'

'Some of the girls couldn't face the thought of seeing the men arrive so they're staying here. I'll be coming with you – give me a hand with this trolley. We'll need it when we get to the station, and the van is so crammed I hardly know where we'll sit ourselves.'

It took a bit of ingenuity to pack the boxes round the trolleys and sort everything out. Maureen was lodged between a rather large woman named Betty and Susie on the front seat. Betty smelled of stale perspiration and Susie was wearing a very strong cheap scent, so by the time they arrived at the station she was taking shallow breaths and glad to be allowed out.

After the suffocating atmosphere inside the van, the smells of the Victorian station were rather fresher and she worked eagerly to help set up the various stalls with disposable cups as well as the thick mugs they served tea in at the canteen. The station was vast with ironwork arches and glass overhead, and a bewildering number of platforms, some of which had to be reached by crossing an ironwork bridge. A newspaper stand and an old woman selling flowers stood near the entrance and just outside a coster with a fruit and vegetable barrow was just packing up for the night. Sparrows perched above them, twittering and flying up as somewhere a train blew its whistle and a guard blew his. As the trains came in the smell of oily engines became stronger and the noise of the wheels screeching against the rails made her cringe.

Their stalls ready on the platform where they'd been told to expect the military train to arrive, the women waited anxiously, not really knowing what to expect. Sandwiches were packed in greaseproof and labelled, though Maureen wondered how many of the wounded would really fancy cheese or paste sandwiches, but the tea, water and orange squash would probably be very welcome.

Maureen saw men and women of the ambulance service arrive, and realised the train must be imminent. Her heart quickened and she felt her palms start to sweat as it drew to a halt at the platform. Some of the windows were down and faces were staring out; they were pale and strained, and, as the doors opened and the first men got down, she could see they were the walking wounded with bandages around their heads or arms in a sling; a couple of them were blind and shuffled behind one of their friends, hands on shoulders, trusting in the leader to take them forward.

Maureen started pouring tea and taking it to those who looked as if they might appreciate it; most of the men smiled and accepted gratefully, and some of them paused at the stalls and picked up packets of sandwiches, slipping them into the pockets of greatcoats, as though they thought they might be needed later. Others just ignored the proffered tea and walked by with a blank stare. Then the men and women of the ambulance service took over, leading away the worst of the men able to walk; others went onto the train and began to carry stretchers from it. At first they just brought them off the train and placed them down on the platform. Maureen's breath caught as she saw the more serious injuries, burned faces and men with one or both legs missing… just lying there, moaning softly in pain or crying. She took cups of water and offered them to those that looked as if they were capable of drinking a few sips, but a lot of them lay with their eyes shut and in such fearful pain that she didn't dare to ask. One man caught at her skirt as she passed and she looked down at him.

'Would you like water or tea?'

'You ain't got a fag, love?'

'Yes, I have.' Maureen felt in her jacket pocket. She'd brought a packet of Players with her, because men often asked for them at the canteen and she gave them freely; her father would have a fit if he knew where his stock was going, but she paid the cost price herself and didn't see why she shouldn't liberate the odd cigarette or bar of chocolate. She lit it and put it in the soldier's mouth for him, noticing that both his arms were covered by bloody bandages that looked as if they hid the remains of mutilated hands, and his head was swathed in bandages. He took a puff of the cigarette and she hid her shock as he winked at her.

'Courtesy of bloody faulty explosives, this lot,' he told her. 'Went off before it should, see.'

'Do you want another draw?' she asked and he nodded.

'Stick it in the side of me mouth and I'll manage, love. Thanks for botherin'.'

Maureen swallowed hard because she wanted to cry. She left him puffing at the cigarette, seeming to manage better than she would've imagined, and walked on down the line. Her throat tightened with pity again and again as she saw the horrific injuries the men had suffered. One or two asked for cigarettes and some for water, but all too many just stared blankly up at her and didn't seem to understand what she said.

Some of them looked as if they were close to death, and she wondered that any of them could survive the injuries and still live. Some were clearly drugged and out of it; they were the lucky ones, and it was the faces of those who were so obviously suffering that hurt the most.

Gradually, most of the stretchers were carried away, and then she saw the soldier bending over one of his comrades. The man on the stretcher was calling out, begging for help, and his comrade was trying to comfort him but without success. One of the doctors went up to them and opened his bag, taking out a syringe and plunging it into the man's thigh, which was open to the air, red and suppurating with puss. His screams stopped immediately and he was carried off. The soldier who had tried to help stood up and turned towards Maureen and she felt a shock of recognition.

'Rory...' She started towards him, stopping as she saw the dressing covering one half of his face. He'd been wounded too, and she thought it might be burns, because she could see reddened skin at the edge of the bandages. 'Rory, can I help you?'

'Maureen...' For a moment she thought he was glad to see her and then he put out a hand as if to ward her off. 'What the hell are you doing here?'

'I'm with the Women's Voluntary Service. We're offering tea, water and food – if you need anything.'

'No thanks. I have to go. I need to know where they've taken him.'

'Rory...' Maureen stared after him as he brushed past her and followed the men carrying his colleague away. 'Rory, please...'

Maureen wasn't sure what she was asking, but he didn't hear her. She saw him disappear into the crowd of men waiting for transport, either by ambulance or by truck. Rory got into one of the ambulances and was driven away. Maureen went back to her colleagues. The platform was almost clear now and normal travellers had been allowed on.

'That's it then,' Susie said. 'I think that all went very well. We can pack up now and get back to the canteen.'

'I'll help you pack this stuff,' Maureen said, 'but I'll make my own way home, I think. I need some air...'

'Yes, it was rather ghastly,' Susie said. 'Well, we've done our bit and that's all we can do; the poor devils are in the hands of the medics and God now.'

'Yes...' Maureen bit back the tears that sprang to her eyes. What she'd seen had brought home the reality of war in a way that she hadn't really understood before. These men had suffered things she would never experience in her life and yet they survived; it made her life seem so safe and so useless. 'Goodnight, Susie... Betty...'

She walked away from the station, gulping down the cool night air, feeling a bit shaky and sick. It wasn't just the terrible wounds; it was the hopelessness in their eyes... in Rory's face, what she'd been able to see of it. He hadn't wanted to talk to her, but could she blame him? After what he'd seen and experienced, he must feel so bitter and angry. Feeling the sting of tears, she walked and walked, going past the various bus stops, because she didn't want to go back to her empty flat and her meaningless life... and then she thought of Peggy. She would go to the pub. Peggy was always there, always the same, and in times like these they needed to stick together.

*

In the morning Maureen found it a struggle to open the shop as usual; she had never resented the day-to-day chores as much as she did now. How could her father grumble the way he did when he was safe at home while young men died and suffered for him? She wanted to rage and scream, to cry out her hurt and pain – and her loneliness, but she didn't. She just painted a smile on and served the customers as if nothing had changed, but it had... oh yes, it had changed so much. Rory was hurt badly and she couldn't rest until she knew how he was getting on.

Which hospital would he have been taken to? As soon as the first rush of customers was over, Maureen found a telephone directory and began to ring the hospitals in London. After trying six or seven she realised that it was an impossible task. She needed to ask someone who would know.

She telephoned Susie at home and was relieved when she answered. Susie worked at the WVS at nights and often helped out at various shelters during the day.

'Do you know where they took the soldiers last evening?' she asked.

'I expect they went to various hospitals in London and perhaps some were taken out of London, to a military hospital – why?'

'I just wanted to ask after someone.'

'They won't tell you unless you're a relative. I tried a couple of times, but they say they can't give out privileged information.'

'Oh, I see. So he might have been at one of the hospitals I rang...'

'I'm sorry I can't help, but it's best not to get involved.'

'Yes, thanks,' Maureen said and replaced the receiver just as her father walked in.

'I hope you're not wastin' my money, girl.'

Maureen glared at him. For two pins she would have walked out but knew she couldn't just leave – just as she hadn't left when Rory had asked her.

'Now you're here you can look after the shop for an hour,' she said and picked up her purse. 'Don't look like that, Dad. I'm entitled to a dinner hour and I'm takin' it now.'

'Where are you goin'?'

'That's my business,' she said and walked out.

Maureen didn't look back. She needed to know how Rory was and there was only one person that could tell her.

*

'So you've heard,' Velma said as she opened the door of the terraced house. The lane was run-down, most of the houses derelict and the gutters choked with filth that the remaining occupants threw out. At that moment, Velma looked as if she belonged there. She was wearing a stained dress and her hair was greasy and hung lankly about her pale face. Maureen could hear a baby screaming in the house, which probably accounted for how tired and washed-out Velma looked. 'I might have known you'd hear it on the grapevine.'

'I saw Rory arrive with other wounded soldiers last night. I wondered if you knew where he'd been taken and how he was?'

'You'd better come in,' Velma said and stood back to allow her to enter the small dark hall that stank of yesterday's cabbage and what Maureen suspected was dirty nappies waiting to be washed.

'Who the bleedin' 'ell is that?' a woman asked, coming into the hall. Her hair was bleached blonde and rolled up in wire curlers, her mouth smeared with red lipstick and she wore a dirty pink dress. 'Oh, it's 'er, is it? What does she want?'

'She's askin' after Rory.'

'Yeah, I bet she is – well, tell 'er and get rid of 'er. He's no bloody good to yer now, Velma. You was a fool to marry 'im when he wanted 'er in the first place.'

'Shut yer mouth, yer old bag,' Velma said, sounding nearly as coarse as her mother, which shocked Maureen, because Velma had always spoken better than that. 'When I want yer advice I'll ask.'

'Tell 'er to clear orf and you can go too and take that bleedin' brat as well...'

'You'd better go,' Velma said and shook her head. 'She's

hardly ever civil these days and she's been drinking some rot-gut stuff she gets from somewhere. Rory is in the London, but he doesn't want visitors. They told me not to bother coming because he wouldn't see me.'

'Thanks for telling me,' Maureen said, glad to leave. 'Did they say what happened?'

'He was caught in an explosion of some sort and had burns to his face. One eye was damaged so he may be blind in it, but they're not sure – he won't be going back to the Front for a while, that's certain...' Velma looked back at her mother who had shuffled into the kitchen. 'She won't have him here and he wouldn't come. We had married quarters but I don't know what will happen now – or if we'll stay in London.'

'You won't let him down, will you?'

'What, run orf because he's going to look ugly now?' Velma thought for a moment. 'I think I'd rather put up with a scarred face than her bleedin' tongue. I was thinkin' of moving out soon as I feel able – so I'll look for a place for us and move in. If he wants to come he can or he can bugger orf if he likes.'

Maureen swallowed the angry retort that flew to her lips. Velma was a cold-hearted bitch but there was no point in quarrelling with her.

'As long as he has somewhere to go when he leaves hospital...'

'You've got plenty of room, haven't you?'

'We've got a spare room, but it's not my property,' Maureen said. 'I'll help him to find somewhere if he needs help. You can tell him when you do see him.'

'I shan't be visitin'. He knows where I am if he wants me. You go if you're interested.'

'They wouldn't let me, I'm not a relative.'

'Tell them you're his wife,' Velma said. 'They won't know any different and I ain't goin'.'

'All right, perhaps I shall,' Maureen said and saw a flash of jealousy in Velma's eyes as she turned to leave. Despite the harsh words, Velma still didn't want Maureen to have him.

She was seething with anger as she walked home. If only she'd had the right to fetch Rory from hospital and take him home so that she could look after him. If he were her husband her father would have had no choice but to accept him if he wanted her to continue looking after his shop, but he would put his foot down if she suggested it now.

*

Maureen fretted over what Velma had told her for the rest of the day, and even when she went to the canteen that evening, she couldn't get that filthy hovel and the stench of it out of her nostrils. Rory couldn't go there when they discharged him from hospital. She made up her mind she would visit the next day and talk to him, whether he liked it or not, but she wouldn't get away with making her father stand in for her so she sent a message to her gran and told her what she was planning to do.

'I understand how you feel, love,' Gran told her when she visited her at the shop that morning, 'but if you brought him here your dad would hit the roof.'

'I have to offer him something, some hope,' Maureen said. 'I love him, Gran, I always have. I should've married him when Mum died. I let myself be blackmailed then, but I'm not going to give in over this.'

'You could bring him to me,' Gran suggested. 'I wouldn't

mind having a young man to make a fuss of for a while – he wouldn't stay once he was better anyway.'

Maureen looked at her dubiously. 'Wouldn't it be a lot for you to do, looking after him?'

'You couldn't manage the shop and do all the rest. Be sensible, Maureen. Visit your young man, tell him he can come to me until he feels able to look out for himself – and make sure he knows how you feel about him. I don't know the family well, because they live in Thrawl Street and I don't often visit that way, but by the sound of that wife of his and her mother, he must feel as if he has nothing to live for.'

Maureen had been thinking the same thing and she fretted about it until she left for the visiting hour. She didn't want Rory to die because there was nothing to live for, and Gran was right, she couldn't really take care of him properly, but her gran would.

The ward nurse showed her where Rory's bed was at the far end of the ward. Apparently, he was one of the least seriously injured and didn't need to be under constant supervision like some of the men. Maureen's heart twisted with pity as she saw them lying pale and still, many of them with their eyes shut as if to block out the unbearable pain and suffering.

'He said he didn't want visitors but it would do him good to see you, Mrs Mackness.'

Maureen's cheeks went hot, because she felt awful about lying to the pleasant, helpful nurse, but she knew it was the only way. She nodded, but didn't answer, pausing for a moment before she moved the curtains slightly and went in. Rory was lying propped up against the pillows. The heavy bandaging had gone and she could quite clearly see the puckering and red blisters on one half of his face. His left eye was covered by a white patch, but his right was closed and she thought for a moment he was asleep, until he spoke.

'Maureen, what are you doing here?'

'Rory, how are you?' she asked breathlessly. 'I had to know how you were...' She didn't ask how he knew her, because she understood that he'd sensed her, probably smelled her perfume.

'How did you know I was injured?'

'I saw you at the station, don't you remember? You spoke to me but you were worried about your friend.'

'He didn't make it,' Rory said flatly. 'I came here with him but he died that night.'

'That's a shame,' Maureen said. 'Was he a good friend?'

'Yes.' Rory looked straight at her. 'How did you get in? It's a wonder they let you...'

'They think I'm your wife. Velma said she wasn't feeling up to coming and suggested I lie to the nurses.'

'She would – and don't pretend. She doesn't want to come and can you blame her? Take a good look, Maureen. I must be a mess.'

'Your cheek looks sore and painful,' she said. 'What does it matter if you're not as pretty as you used to be? I want you to come to us when you leave here – not to the flat, to Gran's. She told me she would be happy to have you until you're ready to leave.'

'I'm sorry to disappoint her then, because I shan't be coming.'

'Why not? You can't go to Velma's – her mother doesn't want you or her either...'

'I'd rather jump off Tower Bridge,' he said and smiled

lopsidedly. 'I think I'm going on to another hospital some-where – one that deals with burns. Thank your gran for her offer, though, and I mean that, Maureen.'

'Well, if you have to go to another hospital...' she said and felt a wave of disappointment. 'I thought perhaps we could see each other sometimes...'

'What good would that do?' he asked and there was a note of bitterness in his voice. 'I'm still married and I've been told I have a child. If the Army don't need me any more I'll have to find work of some kind – and somewhere to live.'

'Oh, Rory, I only wanted to help. I thought perhaps you might still care, after you were here last year.'

'Wanting isn't getting,' he said bitterly. 'I might wish I'd never married Velma, never given her a child, but I did and...' He stopped and moved his shoulders. 'I'm stuck with it, Molly love, and I'm not going to abandon my child... I don't want her to be dragged up by Velma and her mother.'

'No, of course not.' Maureen wanted to cry. She wanted to tell him that he was never out of her thoughts and that she would have his child and care for them both, but she couldn't. Rory felt that she'd made her choice when her mother died; she'd chosen her father and of course she had, and she couldn't blame him for resenting it. 'I brought you some of the mints you like. Do you want me to come again?'

'What I want doesn't come into it. I don't think you should come again, but that doesn't mean I don't want it.'

Maureen nodded. A sudden impulse made her bend and softly press her lips to his and her fingertips caressed his poor burned cheek, but her touch made him wince and she felt ridiculous and pulled away, leaving the cubicle without another look at him. She thought she heard him moan and say her name, but she didn't go back inside. It had been the wrong thing to do – she shouldn't have come and she shouldn't have kissed him or begged him to love her and to forgive her. Of course she hadn't in so many words, but it had been there in the air between them, and she'd wanted so badly for him to agree and say he would stay with Gran. She was hurting as she walked away, and the tears trickled down her cheeks, because all this time she'd been dreaming that one day Rory would walk into the shop and claim her and it would somehow be all right, and it wouldn't and couldn't be, because she'd chosen her life and she was trapped in the prison of her own making.

Chapter 25

The Germans were pounding British airfields day after day, and a German plane had been brought down over London. Peggy looked at the newspaper headlines; it was *The Times* and Laurence had always liked it because of the intricate crossword they printed. She thought of how he'd once won a prize of two hundred and fifty pounds as well as several smaller ones, but Peggy couldn't do them and there were other papers she preferred. She hadn't cancelled it when her husband left for his training, but she'd had only a couple of brief letters since then, and he'd told her that he was busy and wouldn't be home for ages. He'd also told her not to worry, because he liked what he was doing and it wasn't dangerous. His last message had been brief:

I've been lucky, Peggy old thing. They aren't sending me off as cannon fodder this time. I've got a job I really enjoy, but that's all I can tell you. I've put in for leave at Christmas, but I can't be sure I shall get it so don't count on it. Shall you have a party this year? I should if you can manage something...

Peggy frowned because Christmas was still months off

and it was obvious that Laurence wasn't considering coming home before then. She wondered what the job could be. He'd said he couldn't tell her anything about it but it must be something important – something he was good at, because otherwise they wouldn't have bothered calling him up. So far they hadn't asked for men over forty to join the fighting forces, but Laurence would be forty-five that August and yet they'd called him in for special duties. After the bloodbath in France and the retreat to the beaches of Dunkirk earlier in the year, which had somehow become a victory thanks to the way the men of England had turned out in their little boats to get the soldiers home, the Army must need all the volunteers they could get, and Peggy was certain any men who were fit enough would be called to help soon enough.

So what was Laurence doing that was so important he couldn't come home before Christmas – and why hadn't he written more often?

She folded *The Times* and took it into the kitchen. The only thing it was good for now in her opinion was lighting fires. She would cancel it next time she went to the newsagents. Peggy could pick up a paper at Maureen's whenever she felt like it; she didn't need the paper delivered.

'Mum.' Pip's voice made her turn in surprise. She looked at her tall, handsome son with pleasure. He reminded her of his father when Laurence was young, but there was something of her in him too – but he was cleverer than either of them. Laurence might be good at cryptic clues, but Pip was brilliant at maths and sciences, as well as practical stuff. 'I've got to tell you...'

Peggy's heart caught, because the look in his eyes told her. She'd known ever since his seventeenth birthday that she had a year at most, but she'd hoped the RAF would turn him down, tell him to come back in a couple of years – by which time the war might have been over.

'What is it, love?'

'You knew I went to see them... the recruiting office for RAF personnel.' Peggy nodded, her heart sinking. 'Well, they're glad to get me. I'm just the sort they're looking for and they've told me that now I've finished my school exams this year, I can take their entrance exam, and, if I pass, start my pilot's training after Christmas. I'll be eighteen by then. Otherwise, I'd have to try for something like ground staff or gunner or something, but I want to be a flier.'

She had a few more months before they took him from her. Peggy was so overcome with relief that she couldn't stop the tears rolling down her cheeks even as she smiled and went to hug him.

'That's wonderful, darling,' she said, because she knew how much he wanted it. 'Your father expects to get leave at Christmas. I'll write and let him know and it will be nice for us all to be together again.'

'Will Jan be here?' Pip asked. 'I've rung her and asked if I can go down this weekend and she said yes. She's had the phone put on now, because she said she needs it in case Maggie is unwell. I really want to see my niece and Jan too. It seems ages since I last saw her, but I've been swotting for my school exams; you know the RAF won't consider me if I fail, at least, not as a pilot – and it's a long way down there. Besides, Jan told me not to go for a while after Mike...'

'I asked her to come back to London after it happened.' Peggy choked because she didn't want to say the words.

'After Mike's ship went down,' Pip finished for her. 'That was rotten luck, because she's in limbo – doesn't know if he's coming back but won't give up hope. Can I ask her to come for Christmas, Mum? Please?'

'Yes, you ask her,' Peggy said. 'Your father has got over his disappointment now and he's sorry they quarrelled – but they were both at fault.'

'Dad was stupid over her getting pregnant. It's happening to lots of girls now. Anyone could make that mistake and it wasn't just her, you know. Mike had a hand in it.'

'You haven't got someone in trouble?' Peggy said, alarmed, and Pip gave a shout of delight.

'Mum, I've been swotting for exams, and reading up on the RAF, when would I have the time? Besides, I want to see a bit of life before I tie myself down.' He put an arm about her shoulders and squeezed. 'Come on, Mum, it won't be so bad. I'll probably be stationed somewhere near London and I'll always be popping in with a kitbag full of dirty washing.'

'Good,' Peggy said and laughed. He was as tall as his father now and she liked his smile, because it was young and confident with none of the disillusionment that life handed out.

'I've got a free evening tonight,' Pip said. 'Why don't I give you a hand in the bar? Let Anne have the night off for a change. If she isn't working for the school, she's driving ambulances or serving drinks.'

'I'm sure she would be grateful,' Peggy said. 'I've got to finish my cooking and then write to your father. I shan't write to Janet. You can ask her yourself.'

'Do you know where Dad is now?'

'No, I write to a central address and they send it on, but his letters have a Scottish postmark so he may be there, but his work seems to be hush hush so that might be a red herring.'

'Talking of red herrings, can I have *The Times* if you've finished with it please? I like to do the hard crossword; the easy ones are too simple but the hard one is fun.'

Peggy smiled and handed him the newspaper. In some ways he was just like his father and yet in others... somehow, she trusted Pip far more than she trusted his father these days. It wasn't fair of her to suspect Laurence of having an affair, but there was something missing in his letters, something that told her there was more than one reason why he had chosen to delay his visit home.

She frowned and hastily put the doubts to the back of her mind as she heard the siren. These days it wasn't something to be ignored because the battle for Britain was well and truly engaged in the skies.

*

Laurence frowned over the cryptic code he was working on. The message had come from one of their top agents in France and seemed to be of vital importance, and yet his gut feeling was that something was false here. Had the agent and his codes fallen into enemy hands?

Laurence had been sure he was being sent back to the Front because of his knowledge of explosives and his experience in a German prisoner of war camp the last time round. He'd learned a smattering of German while he was there during the first war, but he hadn't stayed long enough as a prisoner to become proficient, because he and five others had killed their guards and escaped the morning they were due to be transported to a more secure camp in Germany. He'd spent a while wandering around the devastated villages and towns of Belgium until he found his way back to his own lines and reported for duty. For a while they'd half-suspected him of deserting, but all five of them had stuck to their story and in the end they'd been believed, and praised for bringing back useful information. Laurence had received a medal for his bravery in risking his life to get back to his own side.

He'd been sure he was going to be asked to return to France as an explosives expert and imagined his training would be on the new weapons available now, but although they'd said they might take advantage of his knowledge to help train recruits in time, what they wanted most was his skill in deciphering cryptic codes, and creating new ones.

At first he'd been given easy messages to decipher, which he did in record time and then sat chewing his pencil while the rest of the class laboured over theirs. His tutors soon caught on that he was even better than they'd thought, and he was asked to invent a new code that would be virtually unbreakable. The first three took his tutor two days each to break so Laurence gritted his teeth, determined not to let Major Harris walk all over him. He'd laboured over his cryptic code for a week, working long into the night and then when he was satisfied, taken it to the major.

After another week had passed, Major Harris summoned him to his office and offered him a glass of whisky and told him he couldn't break it. He asked Laurence to give him a few clues, which he did, and then his tutor solved it in two days, but he hadn't been able to do it without the clues.

'You're damned good, Ashley,' he said when they next met. 'I knew you had to be when you beat me to the first prize on that crossword in *The Times*, but I didn't expect you to be quite this good.' He offered his cigarettes and Laurence accepted one and a light. 'You've signed the Secrets Act, haven't you?'

'Yes, sir. I know it's vitally important not to talk about what you do here.'

'Good show,' Major Harris said. 'We're in constant touch with wireless operators in Belgium and France, and we've actually got a few in Austria and one or two in Germany. It's very dangerous for them and we have to keep changing the frequency as well as the codes, because the Germans are good at breaking them and we lose too many agents – but I don't think they could break the one you just came up with, unless they knew the obscure book you used.'

'It's not to be found on every library shelf, but my son loves obscure books about ancient civilisations and I often buy them for him. The book I used is a little-known translation from the Greek and I haven't given it to him yet – it just occurred to me that there are only half a dozen known copies left because it was a small print run. It would be secure as long as it didn't fall into the hands of the enemy.'

'Of course. Once they have the agent they normally get the codes and we get all kinds of weird messages, but we have other safeguards and usually we'll find a small mistake, something we know our agent wouldn't have used. What we want you to do is to decode for us, to learn the various codes and how to know when something is different – and we are always needing new codes.'

Laurence had been delighted. He was getting paid generously to do something he did for amusement at home, and he liked his surroundings, his companions and the idea that he was important to these people. They treated him with respect; he had a decent room, the food was good – and there was Marie. She was half French, half English, and she was a wireless operator; she was also ten years younger than Peggy and very lovely – and she was attracted to Laurence.

As yet they'd only been out for drinks and a meal, but they played cards or darts at the local pub and had a laugh and a sing song round the piano with the others who worked for the code breakers, but Laurence knew in the way all men do that she was ready to make love with him if he asked. She teased him in her funny little way, so French despite her English mother and upbringing, saying things to him that only a French girl would say...

Laurence gave an exclamation of glee and circled the word in the message he'd deciphered. The agent who was supposed to have sent this in was English and male, but this phrase was one that Marie often used when she was laughing at him. Agent Marco wouldn't say that in a million years – unless he was being forced to send the message and wanted them to know it was false.

Smiling, he took the paper to Major Harris and showed him the words. 'As you suspected this isn't Marco sending freely. He would never have called an operative his poor little one.'

'Perfectly right,' Major Harris said. 'His operator suspected it wasn't his usual touch and I felt something was wrong, but couldn't put my finger on it. Yes, you're right, he'd hardly call Sandra little, would he?'

'At five foot eleven in her stockings and twelve stone, I doubt it.'

'It was the best he could do to tell us he'd been coerced into sending that message. Hell and damnation! I didn't want it to be true. Marco is one of our best at picking up the new codes.'

'Is there anything we can do to get him out?'

'I doubt it. He has back-up over there. If they could do anything they would. No, we'll have to wait and try to set up again in a few weeks.'

'I could go in and try to reach him.'

'No, Ashley. I appreciate the offer. You're not trained for it – and we need you here. No, we do have someone, but we shan't send her just yet. One of the group might make contact soon. If not we'll have to send her in.'

Laurence accepted the refusal. He wasn't sure why he'd offered. The last thing he'd wanted when they sent for him was to go out there, but he'd been caught by the excitement of it all and he admired the men and women who did go out there to live under false names, living every moment on the knife edge, but Harris was right. He would need months of training, and as Marie was always telling him, his French wasn't good enough.

A smile touched his lips as he thought of his date with Marie that evening. Was it so very wrong of him to think about making love to her? He was married to Peggy, and he still cared for her in his way – but she didn't excite him the way Marie did, and she loved her children more than him.

Their marriage had become stale, after all the years of working and living together. Laurence had been aware that he was bored and needing excitement for a while before he came here. He'd been angry that she was fond of Percy, when the old sod had been quite the lothario when he was younger. Didn't his wife know he'd never been faithful to her mother? He wasn't sure that Peggy cared about their marriage any longer. Besides, she would never need to know...

Chapter 26

'You will come home at Christmas and bring Maggie to stay for a while, a few weeks at least,' Pip said. 'Mum is lonely and she misses you – and she hates not seeing the baby.'

'I'm not sure, that's ages yet,' Janet said. She was sorry he had to go after the awful raid on the naval base they'd had the previous night. At one time the noise had been horrendous; with planes screaming overhead and the sound of bombs dropping over the dock area and the ack-ack of their guns popping back at them. She wasn't sure how she would've felt alone there with Maggie. 'I'll come up some time, but I'm a bit worried about the bombing, Pip. You've had several raids lately in London and I don't want to risk Maggie.'

'She'd be as safe with us in the cellar as she was here last night.'

'They go for the base and factories more than an isolated house. Besides, Mike might manage to get home for Christmas.'

Pip looked at her sadly. 'If he'd been picked up by the Norwegian ship you would surely have heard by now, Jan. It's halfway through September and it was months ago that you were told he was missing.'

'Yes, I think he must be a prisoner of the Germans,' Janet agreed. 'We should have heard if he'd been picked up by another vessel, even a fishing boat. Mike would have got in touch if he could.'

'Well then,' he persisted, putting an arm about her shoulders. 'Mike would understand. He'd telephone you as soon as he could – and the Germans are bombing ports and coastal towns almost as much as London. Come on, Jan, they went right over us last night. You're closer to the danger here than we are at home – and so far we've mostly got away with it in our lane.'

'All right, you twisted my arm,' Janet said. 'I think Rosemary will probably go home for Christmas and I should be on my own a lot – so yes, I'd like to come for a week or so, but I don't want to give up my home yet.'

'I know,' Pip said, 'but it will make sense to you once you know for sure. I don't think you really wanted to come down here at the beginning, did you?'

'I hated it in lodgings, but I've made the cottage a home for us, and I do enjoy living in it. Rosemary is my best friend here, but I've made others.'

'You had lots of friends in London.'

'That was before I got married.' Janet glanced at the kitchen clock as it struck the hour. 'You'd better get going or you'll lose your train – and you don't want to miss those exams tomorrow. If you don't get them the RAF might ask you to sit them again.'

'I think they need all the recruits they can get more than ever now, Jan. I know some chaps from the class above mine at school and they're already flying missions almost round the clock. They need all of us if we're to stop them bombing our ports and cities. This is only the start and I'm sure it will get much worse.'

'Poor old Mum,' Janet sighed. 'She's lost us all now – or

she will soon. Me first, then Dad, and you after Christmas. Don't worry, Pip, I'll go home to see her as often as I can manage it.'

'She wouldn't tell you herself, but she feels abandoned. I don't know what Dad is doing, why he can't visit more often.'

'You don't think there's someone else?'

'Another woman?' Pip was astounded. 'I can't believe he would do that to her – to us...'

'No, of course he wouldn't. I just wondered if that might be why they haven't been getting on as well... but it's my fault. What I did – Mum fought for me and he was so angry. If he leaves her I'll blame myself.'

'Don't be daft. If he does such a bloody awful thing I'll know who to blame – and that's him. All Mum has ever done is work hard to make a living and do whatever he wants – and it was OK between them in bed, as well, because I heard them before he went away.'

'Things change.' Janet frowned. 'Dad, us, and the pub are Mum's life – I don't know what she'd do without it all.'

'Well, she won't do without me,' Pip said. 'She's a good mother and I'll never let her down.'

'You might not be able to help it when you start flying...' The words were in Janet's mind but she stopped them leaving her mouth. Pip was here, he was her brother and she loved him. She couldn't think of losing him too.

Instead she hugged him, told him to be good and sent him on his way with a basket of garden produce for her mother.

There were times, especially in the middle of the night, when Janet felt lonely. At those times she missed her mother and once or twice she'd come close to throwing some stuff in a suitcase and going home – but if she did that it would be letting Mike down, admitting that he wasn't coming back, and she wasn't ready to give up yet. Rosemary was grieving, but she put a brave face on things and got on with her life, organising all the fund-raising days and the sewing circle as before, but deep down it wasn't the same for either of them, and once or twice her friend had spoken of her home in Devon. Janet hadn't been brave enough to ask her the question, but she was afraid Rosemary might decide to leave her home here and return to her house in Devon.

Would Rosemary continue to rent out the cottage if she left or would she want to sell it? Janet would hate going back to lodgings, but even if she did want to go home, would her father allow her to stay? It was all right for Pip to encourage her, but Janet remembered all too clearly the way her father had told her he didn't want to see her again. Her mother thought he'd relented, but if she gave up the cottage where could she go other than home? For the first time Janet faced the future without her husband; she had a child to bring up alone and it wouldn't be easy even with her mother's help.

*

Janet was restless after Pip left. She dressed Maggie in a pretty coat and bonnet she'd made, over leggings of fine white wool, and put her in the pushchair with a thin blanket over her. It was September but still mild and fine, though the wind could be chilly and she was very careful not to let her beloved child catch a chill. Maggie was so precious. Rosemary often told her she would spoil the child, but Janet couldn't let her cry. She picked her up and carried her around if she cried, and she'd made a sling so that she could keep Maggie close to her chest while she did small things like making tea or dusting.

Maggie was looking up at her with big innocent eyes

as she took her out to the bus stop. The conductor got off the bus as soon as it stopped, helping her to load the little pushchair and settle herself before asking for her fare.

'How old is she now, Mrs Rowan?' he asked.

'She was born in March.' Janet smiled at him. He was a regular on this route and he'd been polite and helpful ever since she'd started using the bus often. He wasn't old, no more than late thirties, but he had one leg shorter than the other and had to wear a built-up shoe, which was why he was working on the buses rather than joining up. 'Thank you for asking, Fred. How is your mother?'

'She's quite well now she's over that cold she had, thank you,' he said and looked pleased that she'd remembered. 'They caught it on the Docks last night. Did you hear them go over?'

'My brother was staying with me. He woke me when it started and we sheltered under the stairs, but it didn't last long...'

'Fortunately, only one ship was anchored in port, but that was damaged – and the naval installations took a pounding.'

'What about the town?'

'They ignored us this time,' he replied and handed her her ticket. 'I think they were after the harbour area and shot off back home once our boys got after them. They say we got two of the bastards and they ditched in the sea... oh, excuse me, Mrs Rowan, I didn't mean to swear at you, but it makes me so frustrated when I can't do much to help.'

'You do your bit,' Janet smiled, because she knew he was on fire watch at one of the local factories several nights a week.

Fred went to assist an elderly woman get onto the bus and Janet looked on approvingly. She would miss things like that if she went home. In London the buses were always filled to bursting, but here there was plenty of room except sometimes on market days, and life was lived at a slower pace.

She got off in town and went shopping. There were queues everywhere and if you wanted anything in particular it could take hours, but Janet joined the shorter queues and bought bread, butter, margarine, flour, some tinned corned beef and a tin of pilchards in tomato sauce. She didn't need much for one. Maggie was still on the bottle and not ready for proper foods, though Janet sometimes dipped her finger in honey and let her taste it. Maggie smacked her lips then; she liked honey and she'd liked the taste of stewed apples mashed into a puree but she was too young to start on solids yet.

Janet had grown vegetables in her garden over the summer. She'd bottled gooseberries and raspberries and plums and liked making fruit pies. She ate fresh salads and cooked fruit for most meals with a little cheese or fish if she could buy what she fancied. People grumbled about how little meat you could buy these days, but Janet thought she could quite happily have become a vegetarian, and of course she never went without eggs, because Rosemary had her own chickens and there were always enough for her own use and her special friends. She'd suggested that Janet should have a couple of hens and a rooster herself, but so far she hadn't got round to it.

'Janet – Janet Rowan, is it you?'

The man's voice interrupted the flow of Janet's thoughts. She turned round and stared at him for a moment and then she smiled as she remembered the day just before the previous Christmas when she'd been feeling so lonely and he'd taken her for tea.

'Ryan... Mr Hendricks,' she said and felt pleasure in seeing him again. 'How are you – and your family?'

'All very well, thank you,' he said. He glanced down at the little pushchair where Maggie was fast asleep, her pink mouth pursed in what might have been a smile. 'And is this your baby?'

'Yes, this is Maggie; she's a bit over six months,' Janet said and bent down to touch Maggie's face with loving fingers. 'And still at the stage where she sleeps a lot of the time.'

'That won't last,' he said and made a rueful face. 'Are you settling in now? I remember that you were feeling a bit lonely when we met – your husband was away, of course...'

'He... he came home for Christmas,' Janet said. It would be impossible to tell him that Mike was missing. She didn't want to say it, because he was smiling and she didn't want to see pity in those warm eyes.

'Ah yes, that was lovely for you, but he must be away so much,' he said and the sympathy was there anyway. Janet felt the tears prick her eyes. She fought to hold them back but they fell relentlessly, trickling down her cheeks and she couldn't stop them. 'What did I say...?' He took hold of her arm, guiding her towards a small black car parked at the side of the road and opened the front passenger door. 'Please get in, Janet, and I'll hand you Maggie and see to the pushchair.'

Janet felt helpless. She hadn't cried like this once since Rosemary broke the news. She felt the sobbing take her over as he put Maggie on her lap, fitted the pushchair in the boot of the car and then got in beside her. He handed her a large spotlessly white handkerchief, which she accepted gratefully and tried to pull herself together, but for some reason the tears didn't stop as he drove away from the busy shopping area.

Ryan didn't speak for several minutes as Janet wept into

his handkerchief. Maggie woke up and let out a wail of distress and that made her pause.

'Oh, what a fool I am,' she said as she pressed wet cheeks to Maggie's soft ones and tried to hush her. 'I'm so sorry. What must you think of me?'

'I'm taking you to a nice pub I know. They will make us a pot of tea – and a drop of something stronger if you wish for it?'

'I'll be all right in a minute. I don't know why I cried,' Janet said and took a deep breath. She cradled Maggie in her arms and succeeded in soothing her. 'I hadn't cried like that not since... I screamed then and sobbed and got angry, but after that... I just wouldn't believe it. I still don't. He'll come back, I know he will...'

'Missing?' Ryan turned his head to look at her as he drew the car to a halt in front of the ancient inn. Situated away from the busy port and town, it looked peaceful and normal, its ivy-adorned red-brick walls mellowed to rose by time, and the small mullioned windows winking in the sunshine beneath the overhanging thatched roof. Janet was glad he'd brought her here rather than taking her to Julie's café or to her home.

'Yes. His ship was sunk and quite a few of the crew were rescued, but Mike and Captain Jamieson were both missing, believed... Rosemary thinks her husband is dead, but I don't. Honestly, I think Mike was picked up, perhaps by a German ship. He may be a prisoner but I believe he is alive – which makes it all the more stupid of me to break down and cry.'

'I don't think you're stupid,' Ryan said and leaned across to kiss her cheek softly. 'I think you're brave and beautiful and you deserve to be right – you just keep on believing in him, Janet. If you feel he is alive, he probably is.'

'Thank you,' she said and smiled through the tears. 'You're so very kind – and we hardly know each other.'

'I think we know each other well enough to be called acquaintances,' Ryan said and grinned. 'If we keep meeting like this we'll graduate to friends in a year or two.'

Janet laughed. It was ridiculous how much better she felt for having let go, but it was strange that she hadn't cried when her mother fussed over her or when Pip looked at her so sadly – or even when she saw despair in Rosemary's eyes. Ryan was a kind of friend, she supposed, though it was only chance that had brought them together.

'Come on and have that tea then,' he said, 'and if you're ready I'll take you home afterwards.'

*

She'd told Ryan that her mother wanted her to go back to London to live. He'd asked about the pub, where it was and how her parents were managing with the shortages.

'I think my father stocked up well before it started,' Janet said. 'Mum is managing with help from friends at the moment, because my father was called up for some special training. I've no idea what, because it isn't fighting – at least we don't think so.'

'Oh, they have all sorts of stuff going on these days,' Ryan said. 'I get a lot of funny looks because I don't wear a uniform, but I am working for my country, Janet.'

'Of course you are. You shouldn't worry what people think; after all if everyone went over there we would have no one left to do the important stuff here.'

'They tell me what I do is important but I sometimes feel that I'd like to take a gun and start shooting the enemy,' Ryan said. 'I'm not going to. I'd make a very bad soldier and I have a job that has to be done – but when I see houses bombed and people frightened and crying... or worse still dead in the wreck of their house...'

'It must be terrible to lose everything,' Janet said. 'I can't imagine how they feel...' She broke off as they heard the roar of planes overhead and everyone jumped up and went to the windows to look out. 'Not again. I thought it was bad enough last night.'

Some people had run from the room out into the gardens and were looking upwards, pointing at a dog fight in the sky above them. Janet watched from the window as the German bomber was hounded by a pair of Spitfires and she saw a stream of smoke coming from its tail.

'They've got it – they've hit it. I think it's heading towards the harbour, hoping to ditch in the sea.'

'I doubt the pilot will make it,' Ryan said, stretching his neck to follow the course of the plane. 'His crew should bail out if they can, because that thing is coming down before...' The sound of droning got less and less and most people sat down again, though some had hurried away as if to get home and make sure their house was safe.

'I'll take you home in the car.' Ryan spoke just as they heard the huge explosion. Janet felt the room shake and knew the plane must have hit something. She hoped it wasn't the school or the hospital. 'Let's go.'

Ryan led the way, Janet carrying her baby in her arms. Maggie had slept most of the time but now she was whimpering, ready for a bottle when she got home.

They could see a pall of smoke coming from somewhere towards the naval base and Janet shivered suddenly as the fear gripped her. Surely it couldn't be... and yet she knew it was near her home. Not the cottage – it wasn't possible…

'What is it?' Ryan asked, looking at her pale face.

'That's near where I live,' Janet said, her throat tight. 'It must be very close to my cottage…'

'Perhaps I should get you a room here while I investigate?'

'No, I have to go home. I need to know. It's probably the houses just down the road from me.'

'Yes, much more likely,' Ryan said to comfort her, but the coldness was spreading through her as she directed him and the closer they got to her home, the thicker the smoke and the louder the sounds of the sirens and the noise of the fire itself, increasing until they had to halt because the police had barriers up and all traffic had been stopped.

'I'll take a look and come back and tell you,' Ryan told her as he parked the car. Janet wanted to protest but Maggie was crying now and she had to rock her to soothe her. The baby was hungry and upset, as if she too sensed that her world was turning upside down.

Janet could see where the fire was and she knew it must be bad. Whoever or whatever was under that wouldn't survive. She had a sick feeling in her stomach and was just about to get out and fight her way through the cars and people to look for herself when she saw Ryan coming back and a woman was walking with him – it was Rosemary.

She got out of the car just as her friend ran at her. Rosemary was crying and she clutched at her desperately. 'You're all right. You're alive, both of you – I thought you must be in there. I thought you were dead…'

'Is it the cottage?' Janet felt faint and ill as she saw the answer in Rosemary's eyes.

'It's demolished and burning like a furnace. They say the crew must have been trapped in the plane because they didn't bail out. The firemen are trying to get to them, but no one can be alive, Janet. I'm so thankful you were out...'

'I should've been back by now but I met a friend. Ryan took me for tea and we sat talking.' Janet was shaken to the core. Had she not gone with Ryan, she would have been making coffee and preparing Maggie's bottle, and the plane would have fallen on them...

'I'm so sorry,' Ryan said. 'What can I do to help? You'll need somewhere to stay... food for the baby... clothes...'

'It's all right,' Rosemary said and smiled at him. 'You saved her life by taking her out to tea. I'll look after them now.'

'Ryan Hendricks,' he said and offered his hand. 'I am mostly awfully sorry, Mrs...?'

'Jamieson,' Rosemary said. 'I wish we'd met in different circumstances, but if you could turn your car and take us to my home we'd be very grateful.'

'Yes, of course,' he agreed and glanced at Janet. 'I don't think they will save anything, Janet. I shall be glad to assist you with money... anything that I can do at all...'

'Thank you, but it's all right,' she said, feeling numbed and unable to take in what they were saying. 'Most of the stuff belonged to Rosemary. I'll stay with her for a day or so and then I'll go home.'

Chapter 27

'Are you sure you want to go back to London?' Rosemary asked the following week. Janet had managed to purchase a few bits for Maggie and a couple of second-hand dresses from the market for herself. Rosemary had given her some new underclothes, toiletries, also a pair of grey suede shoes and a bag to carry her things in. She'd offered suits and dresses from her own wardrobe, money and a home, but Janet had refused to take more than she'd been forced to accept at the start.

'Mum insisted I come as soon as I felt up to travelling. I can have my old room and there's a small one for Maggie, and I've still got some clothes and other things there. It will give me a start – and I've got my savings. The post office is sending a new book to the pub; they were really kind and helpful and allowed me to draw five pounds even though my book was lost in the fire.'

'People are kind when something like this happens,' Rosemary said, because several friends had turned up with gifts for Maggie: soft toys and a shawl, little coats and leggings, bonnets and bootees they'd sat up all night to knit. 'The Navy will send Mike's money to you until…'

'Until they decide he's officially dead, and then I get a small pension,' Janet said and swallowed hard. 'Yes, I know, Rosemary. I can live and work with Mum. I'm not too worried about the money side... but I'm going to miss you and the cottage. I'm so sorry about your beautiful cottage.'

'Yes, I'm sorry too...' Rosemary hesitated. 'I was thinking that I might go home to Devon at Christmas and if the boys are happy there I shall probably sell this house – not just yet but in a year or so. I still own the land the cottage stood on but I doubt anyone would buy at the moment.'

Janet nodded, feeling a lump in her throat. If Rosemary was thinking of cutting all ties with the base, she might have had to move even if her home hadn't been demolished by the crashed German bomber.

'I would've kept the cottage while you needed it,' Rosemary said as if reading her thoughts. 'But London is your real home, Janet. I don't think you would want to stay here forever if Mike doesn't come home.'

'Perhaps not.' Janet shook her head. It all sounded so final. She hadn't wanted to admit that Mike probably wasn't coming home, that she was a widow and her husband was dead. 'I would rather have stayed there but...' She shrugged. What was there to say now it had happened? Everyone said it was a chance in a million – that a plane shot down as it flew over the town should crash on a small cottage alone at the edge of a field, and so close to gaining its objective, which was to ditch in the sea. If the pilot had made it he might have saved the life of his crew and himself, but he couldn't quite manage it and perhaps he'd thought he could come down in the field but her home had got in the way.

She could only thank God that she and Maggie hadn't been in the middle of the inferno that resulted. If she hadn't met Ryan and started crying she would have finished her shopping and caught the bus home two hours sooner and then... it would all be over.

Janet blinked hard. She was alive and she still had her beautiful Maggie. Her mother was eager to have her home and was already planning special things for Maggie's first Christmas, and Rosemary was promising to write and to come to see her in London when she had the time.

'You'd better go then – that sounds like the taxi.'

'Thank you for everything,' Janet said and kissed her cheek. Rosemary picked up her bags and Janet wheeled Maggie outside. She stared in surprise as she saw not the taxi Rosemary had said she'd ordered, but Ryan's car. He was getting out, smiling at her as he took her bags and put them in the boot and then turned to stow the pushchair. 'How did you arrange this?'

Rosemary looked smug. 'He asked me to ring him, because he's going to London and he wanted to see you got there safely – Ryan Hendricks is a lovely man, Janet. I'm sure he's only being a good friend...'

'Yes, of course. He adores his beautiful wife and his children,' Janet said and kissed her again. 'I'll keep in touch.' She turned to Ryan as he opened the door for her to get in. 'This is so good of you.'

'I wanted to take you home, Janet,' Ryan said. 'After what happened, it is the least I can do. You've had a rough time, my dear. Let me help where I can, please?'

'Yes, thank you,' Janet said and waved to Rosemary as he put the car into gear and glided away. 'This is so much nicer than the train.'

'Nice for me too,' he said and glanced at her. 'I like you, Janet Rowan. I didn't forget you while I was elsewhere and I shan't forget you now. I'll be keeping an eye on you in future so don't be surprised if I turn up from time to time.'

Janet felt warmed by the kindness he'd shown her. She

knew it was just the thoughtful gesture of a generous man who adored his family, and she didn't want it to be anything else. She loved Mike and one day... one day he would come back to her, but that didn't stop her having a friend.

*

'Oh, Janet, my love.' Peggy put her arms about her, drawing her into a loving embrace. 'I'm so glad you've come home, you and Maggie. I was afraid you might choose to stay with Mrs Jamieson.'

'Rosemary offered me a home with her. I think she's lonely and I think she'll go back to Devon soon. She and Captain Jamieson have a family home there and the house in Portsmouth was just for a few years; they always intended to retire back to Devon...' Janet kissed her mother's cheek. 'I didn't want Mike to think I'd deserted him, but he'll know I had no choice now, won't he?'

'Yes, of course he will,' Peggy said and looked at her sadly. Janet was refusing to accept that Mike was gone and it was just storing up misery for the future, but she hadn't the heart to force her to face facts. 'Well, I've got you home now and I'm glad. You can help me here and that will give you plenty of time to look after Maggie – and to go out with friends sometimes.'

'I'm not sure I want to go anywhere much, Mum. I had friends in Portsmouth, but we were all getting together for a reason, making things to send out to the troops or to sell for money for them.'

'I'm sure you can find something similar here, love.'

'Yes, I expect so,' Janet said but didn't sound enthusiastic.

'It was so nice of Mr Hendricks to bring you home, Janet.'

'Yes, it was kind,' Janet agreed. 'We stopped for a lovely meal on the way back. Ryan is very generous, Mum. He asked me if I was all right for money and promised to help in any way he could. I asked him if there was any way of discovering if Mike was a prisoner of war and he promised to do what he could.'

'Oh... well, perhaps he might be able to discover something. It would be better to know one way or the other, Janet.'

'Yes, I know.' Janet smiled at her. 'I know everyone thinks I'm foolish to keep saying that Mike is alive, but I can feel it inside. I really can – and I don't want to let go of that, because then he might die.'

Peggy turned away quickly because her eyes filled with tears. She found it difficult not to break down in front of her daughter, because the hope in Janet's eyes was soul-destroying when you knew how unlikely it was that Mike had been picked up. The men lucky enough to be fished out of the water after the sinking of the destroyer were all back home, either in hospital or on leave until they were deemed fit to return to their duty.

She saw the brewery's wagon draw into the back yard and felt the tension drain out of her as she said, 'Ah, here is our delivery of beer. I wonder how much we'll get this time. I've been badgering them to give us more so let's hope they've decided to cooperate.'

Peggy went out into the yard to watch as the barrels of beer were unloaded and carried down to the cellar. It took half an hour for the consignment to be delivered, checked and signed for and when she returned to the kitchen, Janet was busy cooking an apple pie. Peggy smiled as she saw her daughter's concentration. Marriage had been good for Janet; she'd grown up and learned to do things for herself. Who knew, perhaps her instincts concerning her husband's survival were truer than anyone gave credit for.

*

The large box from one of the most prestigious shops in the West End was delivered a few days later. The man parked the distinctive green and gold van in the back yard and came to inquire if Mrs Janet Rowan lived there before he carried the big cardboard box in and set it on the floor for them.

'Will you sign here please, madam?'

Janet stared at the box with the unmistakable labels and frowned. 'I didn't order anything from Harrods.'

'It is a gift,' the man said. 'It says so on my list. One of your friends has sent you a present, madam.'

Janet hesitated and then signed his form and he departed. Peggy watched as Janet snipped the string binding the box and then rolled it up and twisted it in a knot. 'It must have come from Mrs Jamieson,' Peggy suggested as Janet still hesitated to open it. 'No one we know has the money to send something like this from that store.'

'Rosemary knew I didn't want money or gifts,' Janet said and lifted the flaps of the box. She gave an exclamation, though Peggy wasn't sure if it was from pleasure or annoyance, as she began to lift out layer after layer of lovely things. Baby clothes, a beautiful basinet complete with all the creams, powders and cotton pads needed to keep Maggie clean and sweet; a pile of good-quality napkins in best terry, soft towels, little nightgowns, dresses, knitted coats, pretty bonnets, a silver teething ring with a coral drop, a set of tableware for a child's first solid meals, a lovely little bath, and right at the bottom wonderful satin covers for a cot and pram. 'Oh no, he shouldn't have spent all this money...'

Janet was looking at the beautiful things that filled their table and spread out to the floor and chairs around them. She found the card inside.

'I should've made them take it back... I can't accept all this stuff...'

'Of course you can,' Peggy said firmly. 'You lost everything in that fire and if Mr Hendricks wants to give you this... well, he must think a lot of you, Janet.'

'He is a friend,' Janet admitted, meeting her mother's gaze. 'We've only met a few times but it was as if... as if we'd always known each other.'

'Is he in love with you?'

'No, I'm sure he isn't,' Janet said. 'He adores his wife and children. He told me that from the beginning – and I was pregnant. It's just friendship, Mum – but I didn't expect or want all this.'

'Well, I dare say he has plenty of money and just rang up and placed an order and left it to the store. He would be upset and offended if you sent it all back, Janet, and to be honest you're lucky to get it. Most stores have very little to show these days.'

'I'm not sure I could,' Janet said, fingering some of the delicate lace on the tiny dresses. 'I just feel a bit over-whelmed, that's all.'

'You must thank him,' Peggy said and Janet nodded and then stared at her.

'I don't know his address, Mum. I never thought to ask – besides, what would his wife think if I rang him and wanted to thank him for a present like this?'

'Probably the worst,' Peggy said wryly. 'As long as you're sure he won't expect anything in return?'

'Mum! Ryan isn't like that. You don't know him.'

'Nor do you,' Peggy pointed out. 'If you send it back now it looks rude, so I think you will have to keep it. Your father wouldn't have let you open the box, but I have to admit I was curious.'

'Yes.' Janet laughed. 'It isn't often something like this happens, is it?'

'At least it made you laugh,' Peggy said. 'Just take it and be grateful, Janet. If it really was meant to be a gift of friendship, you probably won't see him again.'

Janet nodded, automatically clearing away the packing, which she'd just let fall to the floor. She didn't want Ryan to fall in love with her. She wanted Mike to come home and never leave her again, but she was beginning to accept that it might never happen.

Chapter 28

Maureen looked up as the shop door opened and a woman entered. Velma looked very different from the woman she'd last seen some months ago in that horrid little terraced house, her hair brushed in a new style and recently cut, bright red lipstick and matching nail polish and a lilac tweed suit with a pink jumper underneath and a pink felt hat perched at an angle on her head.

'Velma?' Maureen's nerve ends tingled. 'You look so much better.' She waited, fearing the worst, but as Velma hesitated, she asked, 'How is Rory? Did he go to the special hospital?'

'I had a message to say he was going away for treatment,' Velma said and her eyes glinted. 'I suppose you've been visiting him all this time?'

'I just went the once, but he didn't want me to visit again.'

'Well, it doesn't matter now,' Velma said, her voice harsh. 'The brat died and I'm off. I've had a better offer, see, and I came to tell you that you can have Rory. He's no use to me anymore. He'll be half-blind and scarred – and I want a bloke with money who can give me a good time. Terry is a businessman, see. He's got a few quid to spend and he's told me the war will make him rich. He ain't much in bed, but he bought me a new wardrobe and paid for me hair – and he's taking me to Birmingham with him in his car. He's got a posh Daimler and we're going to a big hotel. It's the high life for me in future.'

Maureen stared at her, hardly believing her ears. Had Velma just told her that her baby was dead... Rory's child? Now she was going on about all the money her new man was spending on her.

'What about Rory? Have you told him the baby died?'

'Why should he care?' Velma hesitated, then, 'Anyway, the brat wasn't his; I never told 'im I was avin' it, nor that his brat died. Why do yer think I never went to the hospital? If he'd seen me he would've known but by the time he got home fer good he'd never 'ave known the difference.'

'How could you...?' Maureen knew how much Rory had wanted his child to have a decent life; Velma had allowed two young babies to die. What kind of a woman did that? 'How did the baby die this time?'

'She got a tummy infection and then she caught a chill; the doctor said it might 'ave been pneumonia. I reckon the old bitch put her in damp clothes, because she just kept spewing over them and messing herself.' Velma shrugged. 'It's better this way. Rory won't be much good at earning a living now – and I didn't want the brat.'

Maureen felt the tears sting. She couldn't bear to think of the neglect and misery that tiny baby had endured in its short life – a mother who couldn't be bothered with looking after her and a grandmother who just wanted her gone.

'You cold-hearted bitch,' Maureen said, unable to keep it inside another moment. 'You ought to be birched. That poor little girl – and Rory did want his child. You knew that – you intended to lie to him, let him think this baby was his daughter...'

'What of it?' Velma's eyes snapped at Maureen. 'Well, I've

told you so you know he's yours if you want him.'

'He's still your husband.'

Velma laughed bitterly. 'Not so as you'd notice. Besides, he ain't. I was still married to another man when I married him. We had a quick marriage when I was sixteen and working up West, 'cos I thought I was in the club and I was scared, but it was all a mistake. He was a rotter and he took everything I had and left me. Men are all rubbish and this time I'm going to get all I can.'

Maureen stared after her as she left the shop, banging the door behind her. How much of that could she believe, and how many lies had just tripped off Velma's tongue? Yet, if Rory had been still serving in France for another year or two, he might never have guessed that he'd been deceived again.

Her anger against Velma intensified. Yet she knew that there was nothing she could do to stop her hurting Rory like this... and perhaps somewhere at the back of her mind a tiny spark of hope sprang to life. Yet as swiftly as it came, it died – Rory hadn't wanted her to visit. He was bitter and angry and the fact that his wife had left him couldn't matter.

Maureen blinked hard as a customer entered the shop. It was no use getting upset because there was nothing she could do about any of it.

*

Peggy heard the siren go just as she brought a plate of caramelised onion and crisp crushed-potato and herb tarts through to the bar. The smell from them was tantalising and made her feel hungry, but she had two hours before she could call last orders and now she had to make sure her customers were safe.

She rang the brass hand bell she kept in the bar to grab everyone's attention. 'If you prefer to get to a shelter, you'd best leave now, but anyone who wants can come down to the cellar with us. Bring your drinks and I'll bring some food. We'll have a little party and bugger Hitler.'

A rousing cheer met her invitation and most of her regulars grabbed their drinks and trooped through the opening in the bar. Nellie picked up the coffee jug and what was left of a fatless jam sponge and someone put the lock on the door as the only two customers to leave shot off in a hurry. Janet came down the stairs with her baby in her arms as the last of the customers scrambled down the steps to the ancient cellar.

Peggy smiled, because all her customers were friends, either from Mulberry Lane itself, or round the corner in Artillery Lane or Gun Street.

'Come on, Alice,' she said to the elderly woman wearing a grey net over her hair and clutching her glass of stout as if her life depended on it. 'Come and sit here, love, in this chair. I've got the stove going and you'll be lovely and warm, and there's a fresh cooked tart and another stout for you. This is my treat and we'll have a sing song just to show we don't care.'

'I'll sing fer yer,' Alice said and put her glass down on a wooden crate. 'See no one don't pinch me drink, Peggy love.' She gave her throaty, twenty-ciggies-a-day laugh, pulled up her dress to show the long knickers that reached almost to her knees and began to caper about the cellar.

'It was like this,' she said, adopting a pose which she fondly imagined made her look like a heroine of the music hall. 'We was movin' 'ouse, see. So we packs all our stuff in the van and there weren't no room for little ole me...' She drew her audience in with a doleful face and dabbed at her eyes, and there were cries of '*Poor ole Alice...*' Alice dropped her head and pretended to sigh. 'So...' She suddenly launched into, 'My ole man said follow the van, and don't dilly dally on the way...' Her voice, which was strong and tuneful despite her advanced years, belted out the popular music hall song. 'Off went the van with me ole man in it and I followed on wiv me ole cock linnet. But I dillied and I dallied... dallied and dillied...' Every time she said the word dallied, Alice made a little gesture with her hand as though drinking from a glass, which made her audience laugh. 'I dillied and dallied... all day through... now I've lost me way and I don't know where to roam. I dallied and dillied and dillied and dallied... and I can't find my way 'ome.' Alice bobbed and lifted her skirt to show her ample backside in the silky pink bloomers. 'And that's for Mr bloody 'itler.' She farted loudly.

A rousing cheer and laughter greeted her cheeky gesture and a chorus of voices joined in the chorus as she belted out more verses. Alice's words were not always strictly accurate, but she knew the gist of a lot of the music hall songs, especially those sung by the ever-popular Marie Lloyd, and they were soon all joining in lustily with her so that even the sounds of bombs dropping quite close did not stop them having a good sing song.

'That one wasn't far away,' Nellie said to Peggy and looked at her in dismay as the felt the ground shake and a little bit of cement floated down from the ceiling.

'I think it might have been a couple of streets off,' Peggy said and then jumped as another loud bang was clearly much closer. For a moment there was silence as everyone held their breath but then Alice started singing again.

'If you were the only girl in the world and I was the only

boy… nothing else would matter in this world today…' For a moment hers was the only voice but then a couple of others joined in and white faces and scared eyes looked at each other, some friends holding hands and leaning in closer.

The next bomb was further away and the sounds gradually died off so that they could hear only the faint ack-ack of the guns as the men of the civil defence tried to shoot the bombers down as they turned for home.

'They must 'ave heard your singin', Alice, and it scared 'em so much they high-tailed it back 'ome…'

'Yer cheeky monkey,' Alice said and gave her neighbour and lifelong friend Jim a cuff round his ear. 'Yer can buy me another stout or I'll sing all night long and yer'll never get a wink of sleep again.'

'That's told yer,' someone said and there was general laughter as Peggy renewed their drinks and they settled down to wait for the all clear.

*

'How is Janet settling in then?' Maureen asked when Peggy visited the next morning. 'She's had a rotten time, Peggy. If there's anything I can do to help her – make a few clothes for Maggie perhaps?'

'Janet has all she needs for Maggie,' Peggy said. 'A friend of hers sent her a lot of nice things so she doesn't need to worry for a while. I've still got Pip's pram. It's a bit shabby but I'm having it polished and done up a bit at the shop and it should be nice when they've finished it. She hadn't bought a pram yet and was using a little fold-up thing, which she had with her when she was out.'

'Thank God she was out,' Maureen said. 'It's bad enough losing your home and your things, but if she'd been there...'

'A lot of people are losing all they have in the raids now,' Peggy said. 'It was a bad down the Docks last night and a couple of houses over Bishopsgate way caught it. Nellie said the ruins were smouldering when she went past earlier this morning, and the fire crew was still trying to make it safe. From what I hear, a house in Gun Street had a lucky escape; the bomb went off in the garden and shattered all the windows, but it's still standin'.'

'Gran and me heard the bombs last night when Dad was out. We went down in the cellar, but the only damage here was a cracked window in the back kitchen.' Maureen sighed deeply. 'Ask Janet to bring Maggie round and come for tea. I'd love to see her.'

Peggy gave her a sharp look. 'Is something wrong – more than the usual with your dad?'

'Yes, though it's nothing to do with me,' Maureen said. 'Rory's wife told me their baby died and she's cleared off to Birmingham with a rich businessman.' Maureen hesitated, then, 'She told me this last baby wasn't even Rory's. She's lost two babies to neglect now.'

'Women like her should be locked up,' Peggy said and Maureen agreed.

'Do you think Rory knew she'd been with someone else while he was away?'

'He's well rid of her if you ask me,' Peggy said. 'Velma's mother came in the pub last week trying to pick men up. Even the older ones wouldn't look at her and told her to clear off. In the end I gave her five bob and told her to go away.'

'She'll be back for more money,' Maureen said as she

filled Peggy's basket. She shivered as the door opened and a cold blast of air followed her grandmother inside. 'You look frozen, Gran. There's a good fire in the kitchen – go on in and put the kettle on.'

'Don't mind if I do.' Gran smiled at her. 'You look smart, Peggy. Is that a new coat?'

'Well, new to me,' Peggy said. 'I bought it down Petticoat Lane, off the nearly new stall. I don't buy much second-hand as a rule, because most of it is worn out before you get it, but I liked the look of this. I took it to the cleaners and it has come up a treat.'

'I wouldn't mind a new coat,' Gran said. 'I'll put the kettle on then, Maureen.'

Maureen nodded, finished totalling Peggy's list and gave her the change from a pound note.

'If you get any golden syrup in this week don't forget me,' Peggy said. 'It's something I use all the time.'

'It's getting to be like gold dust,' Maureen said. 'But I'll put two tins under the counter for you if we get some in. I wish Dad would let me go to the wholesaler, because Mr Stewart is inclined to let me have more than he does my father, but he won't accept that. He thinks I pay too much.'

'Men,' Peggy said and shrugged. 'They're all the same.'

She laughed as she picked up her basket just as the postman brought a handful of letters in for Maureen, stopping to exchange a word or two with him.

'Did you have anything for me today, Reg?'

'I left you a couple of letters and a parcel,' he replied. He showed her his heavy bag. 'I think people have got nothing better to do than make work for the poor postie these days. My shoulder is killing me.'

Peggy shot Maureen a look that made her want to laugh

but she hid it as he deposited her letters on the counter and left. Most of them were bills or directives from the various government departments, including another ominously thick one from the Ministry of Food. No doubt there were more rules and regulations on the way. At the bottom of the pile was a handwritten letter for her father, and as she picked it up, Maureen caught the smell of heavy perfume. She frowned, because the idea that her father was getting a letter from a woman was strange. She slipped it into her apron pocket to take upstairs for him later.

Gran came through with a mug of hot tea for her. 'Busy today?'

'On and off,' Maureen said. 'We get all the usual trade, those that registered with us for the rationing, but not so much passing trade as we used to. We're still making a profit, but I'm not sure how long we shall continue to if things don't improve.'

'Well, you can't get half the stuff these days,' Gran said. 'Some shops have more under the counter than on their shelves, I reckon.'

'You don't mean that?' Maureen looked at her anxiously. 'Where do they get it from, that's what I'd like to know?'

'A little man at the back door late at night, I expect. Most of it is black market, has to be – or off the back of a lorry, which is the same thing.'

'How can people make money like that when there's a war on? We're all in it together and everyone should get their fair share.'

'They will stamp on the culprits hard if they catch them,' Gran said. 'Did you get any letters today, love? I saw you put one in your pocket.'

'It's for Dad but personal.' Maureen took it out and

offered it to her grandmother. 'Smell that.'

'Violets, I think.' Gran wrinkled her nose. 'Horrible when it's so strong. She must have sprinkled the stuff all over.' She frowned as she looked at the writing. 'What is my son up to now? I hope he isn't going daft in his old age. A woman like this isn't good news, Maureen.'

'Why shouldn't he have a friend?' Maureen said. Her mother had been dead for some years, and yet it hurt in a way that he could think of another woman.

'I wouldn't say anything to him marrying a decent woman; she could take some of the load from your shoulders,' Gran said. 'But I bet you ten bob to a farthing that this one is anything but decent.'

'Oh, Gran.' Maureen burst into laughter and then gave her grandmother a hug. It didn't matter how down she felt, Gran would always pick her up. 'I'm so glad I've got you.'

'Just you remember I'm on your side. You can always come to my house if you need somewhere to go,' Gran said darkly and Maureen felt coldness at her nape. She could guess what Gran was hinting at. If her father did have someone, and if he actually married her, Maureen might find herself being squeezed out. In a way she would've been glad to leave, but she wasn't sure what she would do with her life if she no longer had the shop to run. Shaking her head, she handed her grandmother the empty mug and turned to her next customer, but long after she'd served the woman, the thought lingered. Maureen had always supposed that one day the shop would come to her, but she saw now that there was a distinct possibility it might not.

Well, she could make her own life, she supposed, but she'd given up her chance of happiness for her father and she felt a bit resentful when she saw the look on his face when he scooped up the letter that evening. He was pleased with it, inhaling the perfume and smiling as he took it off to read. Gran might be right, Maureen thought. Perhaps she should start to think about what she might do if her life changed.

Anne had joined the ambulance service and was dividing her time between her job and helping Peggy in the pub. Maureen supposed she might join one of the women's services, though she wasn't sure which. The sight of the terribly injured men had aroused her pity when she'd witnessed their arrival at the station. Perhaps she could train as an auxiliary or even as a nurse... nursing was a career she could follow after the war.

Maureen sighed, because her life could've been so very different. She knew that if Rory had been her husband she wouldn't have let him put up a wall of bitterness between them. He'd been hurt by the war, enduring and witnessing so much that no one should be forced to see – but if he was hers she would hold him in her arms and let him weep until the bitterness was all gone and then she would kiss him and make him want to live again.

*

'She's really beautiful,' Maureen said when Janet put her child into her arms. 'Yes, you are, darling, beautiful.' Maureen bent to kiss Maggie's forehead, breathing in the fresh clean smell of her skin and the powder Janet had used on her. 'What lovely clothes she has. Peggy said someone had given you some lovely things – she looks a proper treat.'

'Yes, she does,' Janet said, a faint flush in her cheeks. 'People have been so very kind to me since I lost everything...

I got lots of little things when she was born from Rosemary and her friends, but we've been thoroughly spoiled this time, haven't we, Maggie?'

'It must have been awful to see your home burning.'

'I didn't see much because Ryan made me sit in the car and wouldn't let me see when the plane was on fire and the cottage was blazing. I feel so sorry for the men on board. I know they were German but it's a horrid way to die, isn't it?'

'Yes, if they knew much about it, but there were explosions when it hit. I should think they were killed instantly; the papers seemed to imagine it happened that way, didn't they?'

'I think the pilot was still alive for a while,' Janet said and then shook her head. 'I don't want to think about any of it – I'm just glad I wasn't there.'

'Thank goodness you weren't. Peggy said you'd been out for tea with someone?'

'Ryan took me. I was upset over something and...' She shook her head at Maureen. 'Don't imagine it is a love affair, it isn't. Ryan is in love with his wife and kids.'

'You're not over Mike yet, are you?'

'You're the only one who seems to understand that,' Janet said. 'Even Mum seems to think I ought to accept he's gone – but I can't. I don't want to...'

Maureen touched her hand in sympathy. 'Of course you don't, love. You loved him and you want him back. I know how you feel.'

'Do you?' Janet looked at her and then smiled. 'Mum said there was someone you should've married. Do you still care about him?'

'Yes, I do,' Maureen admitted. 'I think I always shall.' She looked down at the sleeping child in her arms. 'I'd give anything to have his baby – just someone of my own to love and care for.'

'I'm sorry if I upset you,' Janet said, but Maureen smiled and gave her back her baby.

'No, of course you didn't. Sometimes I feel a bit sorry for myself, but I'll get over it.'

Chapter 29

The dark cloud that had been hanging over Maureen deepened when her father announced that evening that he was bringing Violet Briggs to tea on Sunday so that they could meet.

'I've known Violet since I was in short trousers,' he announced after supper. 'She was married for nine years and she's a widow – lost her husband to a nasty illness, just like I lost your mother. I want you to be nice to her, Maureen, and make a good spread – like you did when you had that child here.'

'Yes, if that's what you want,' Maureen said warily. 'I've got some tinned stuff in the cupboard that I put away so I shan't need to raid the stock.'

'That's just as well, because there are a whole lot of new regulations coming in,' her father said. 'We've got to account for every damned thing we sell now and there will be fines if they catch us selling goods we didn't buy from the wholesalers.'

'I read all that stuff too, Dad. It can't make any difference to us, surely? We only sell what we get from our regular suppliers, don't we?'

'Well, I get a few bits and pieces elsewhere now...'

'Oh, Dad, you haven't been buying black market stuff?'

'I wouldn't pay their prices; they're downright robbers,' he said wrathfully, 'but I've bought a few bits from a mate of mine. Those big tins of corned beef and some other tinned stuff.'

Didn't her father know how dangerous it was to sell stock that had been stolen from somewhere else? He could lose his business if they closed him down, and he might end up serving a prison sentence.

'It's a bit risky, isn't it?'

'I'll be the judge of that, besides, you've sold it all and the empty tins have gone in the rubbish. You just keep serving in the shop and leave the rest to me, Maureen.'

'I don't want to go to prison – and I would rather you didn't either.'

'So just keep your nose out of things and then you can plead ignorance,' he said and pushed his chair back. 'So I've told you then. Violet has wanted to tell you for months but I'm thinking of gettin' wed again so you'll have to know. Just make sure you get her a decent tea and be nice to her – or you'll hear from me afterwards.'

'Are you going to see her now?'

'It's none of your business where I go, but as a matter of fact I'm on duty tonight. You've had too much of your own way since your mother died, but now you'll have to move over, because Violet will be mistress here.'

Maureen didn't reply, because she couldn't. She was so angry that she wanted to shout and scream at him, but it wouldn't have done any good. She was tempted to pack her bags and walk out, let him get on with running the shop himself. Gran would take her in, but she wasn't going to walk out just like that. Her father had never paid her proper wages; he said she had her living and he'd always paid for her clothes, though he'd only given her a few shillings a week recently. In the morning she'd tell him she wanted two pounds a week and if he refused, then she would take everything that had belonged to her mother and leave.

*

'You'll get no more than ten bob same as usual,' Maureen's father said when she confronted him the next morning. 'You're my daughter and you'll do as you're told.'

'Not any more,' Maureen said and glared at him. 'I've had enough of your bad temper and your meanness. I stayed after Mum died, because I thought you needed me – well, you don't need me now, and your wife won't want me here. I'll run the shop until she's ready to take over, same as I always have, but I want two pounds a week, as well as my keep. The money is for me so that I have something when I leave here.'

Her father glared back at her and she saw his fists clench, as if he itched to strike her. 'You'll be the ruin of me, girl!'

'No, you'll ruin yourself,' Maureen replied calmly. 'I could do better at the wholesaler without resorting to pinched stuff. When I leave I'm taking Mum's silver candlesticks and her tea set, because she gave them to me – and her other bits and pieces, too. Don't think you can give them to Violet, because you can't; they're mine and I shall make sure they go with me.'

'You're a wicked girl to speak to your old father so cruelly.'

'No, Dad, I'm not. I've stood behind this counter and broken my heart because of you, but when you bring another woman in here, I leave. I've nothing against Violet, but I'm telling you – I won't live here and work for nothing for the rest of my life and then see it all go to her.'

'Well, you won't get a penny,' he said, a vindictive note in his voice. 'You can take your two pounds, but you'll not get another penny from me.'

Maureen turned away as he slammed out of the shop, leaving her with tears burning she couldn't shed, because the hurt went too deep for tears. He'd never loved her mother and he didn't care for her – he'd just used her because he needed someone to get his meals, keep the house clean and serve in the shop. Well, he'd find out the difference when Violet realised how much work there was to do and how little to be got from it. Maureen did the books for her father and knew the profits were smaller than before the war. Violet probably thought she was marrying a rich man, but she would be disappointed when she learned the truth.

Maureen took two pound notes from the till and slipped them in her pocket. Her father might change his mind when he got back and empty the till out, leaving her with only some coppers for change.

That evening he didn't come home for his supper and she assumed he was sulking. Feeling angry because of their quarrel, she packed a suitcase with some of her clothes and the silver and pretty pieces of china her mother had left her, and her jewellery; it wasn't worth a fortune, but every piece meant something to Maureen and she wasn't going to let her father's new wife get her hands on any of it. She carried it round to her grandmother's and took it up to the little bedroom that Gran said she could use.

'Come to me when you're ready, love,' Gran said. 'And try not to let it upset you. You said it yourself, the business is failing and the property doesn't belong to Henry. If his woman thinks she's gettin' her hands on that she's wrong.'

'I thought Grandfather left him the business?' Maureen

was puzzled because she'd been doing her father's books for years.

'He did, the goodwill and the stock,' Gran said, 'but the house and shop aren't Henry's; they're mine.'

'I've never seen an entry for rent in the accounts.' Maureen looked at her curiously, because all this was news to her. Her father always spoke of everything as his, but perhaps he took it for granted that it would be when Gran died, especially as she hadn't charged him any rent. 'Why haven't you charged us anything?'

'Because I don't choose to, or at least nothing you'd notice,' Gran said, a little smile on her mouth. 'The property belongs to me, Maureen. It was left to me by my grandfather and I rented it to your grandfather and then to your father, but it's a peppercorn rent of a shilling a year and I make sure he gives it to me, and there's a proper agreement signed and sealed by a lawyer. Why do you think Henry bothers to listen to me? I've used my influence for you, my love, but I don't make a song and dance about it, because he's my son, and money never bothered me. I just wanted you all to be happy, but Henry knows that I could put him out at the end of his lease, and that's next March. It was your mother's home and yours. I allowed it to go on after she died, because I thought it would all come to you – it will be yours when I die, as will everything I've got. I don't have much money, but the property is yours, Maureen. So if Violet Briggs thinks she's going to be rich one day, she will be disappointed.'

'Oh, Gran.' Maureen burst out laughing. 'You've made me feel so much better. He's been such a mean old devil. I've hardly had a penny to spend for years, apart from the few pounds Mum left me – and what you've given me.'

'Perhaps I should've charged the old skinflint rent,' Gran

said, 'but he was my son and I never thought of the shop as being meant to make me money, just as a means of helping my husband start up in business and then Henry wanted to carry it on so I agreed the same terms – but if I'd known how he would treat that lovely girl he married, and you...' She shook her head. 'The property isn't worth a lot of money, Maureen. I suppose it might make five hundred pounds if someone wanted it badly enough – but at the moment you couldn't sell easily, because a bomb could fall on it tomorrow and you wouldn't get a penny in insurance because they won't pay out. I've tried everywhere but they all say the same; they don't insure against malicious damage by an enemy during wartime.'

'You would lose your property if we were bombed?'

'I'd still own the land and if I had the money I could rebuild.' Gran shrugged. 'As long as you were all right I wouldn't give a damn – but I'm glad I didn't give in and sign it over to Henry, because I want you to have something, my love.'

'It belongs to you, Gran. You should sell it and use the money to look after yourself. I'm young and I can find a job – somewhere they actually pay me to work.'

'It's a pity you didn't walk out on him when you had the chance years ago,' her grandmother said, but looked thoughtful. 'You wouldn't mind if I did sell then? Only I did have an offer once but I thought it was your home...'

'I stayed because he was ill, Gran – but if I'd had my choice I would've married and gone with Rory. He only moved away because we broke up.'

'I wish you'd told me how much this man meant to you, love. You never let on he'd asked you to marry him, or that your father was putting pressure on you to stay. I would've looked after your father, Maureen. I know him for what he is but he's still my son. So if you have another chance, you go, regardless of what happens next.'

'You won't tell her... Violet... you won't tell her he isn't rich?'

'If she's fool enough to believe it, let her,' Gran said and gave a cackle of laughter. 'No, I'll not stand in his way, but next year, when the lease is up, I'll likely think a bit more about what I want to do.'

'I think I'm going to sign up as an auxiliary nurse when I leave,' Maureen told her. 'I might train to be a nurse if I get on all right – but I know they want beginners, people to do all the dirty jobs and running around after the nurses.'

'And will you like that?' Gran looked at her oddly. 'Your father was right in one regard; you've been free in many ways these past years. I know he's a bad-tempered devil but you were more or less your own boss in the shop.'

'I expect it will be hard at first,' Maureen said. 'I'm going to ask if I can work in London, at one of the hospitals here. I'd like to live with you for a while, Gran – if you can put up with me?'

'You know I will,' Gran said. 'It will be a delight for me to have you, my love, but I want what's best for you. Are you sure you don't want to stick it out at the shop? I can sort him out for you if you want?'

'No, I've decided to leave,' Maureen said, her head lifting determinedly. 'I wouldn't have left him alone, but if he has a new wife he doesn't need me.'

'Nor want you around, I imagine. I suppose I ought to tell you that he didn't want to marry your mother; he got her pregnant with you and his father forced him to do the decent thing. I liked Doris very much. We got on well and they met when she came to do some sewing for me, so I blamed myself for what happened – but Henry didn't want to marry her. He had his eye on the daughter of a rich man. That was one time when I was proud of my husband. He did what was right and he told Henry that if he didn't marry her he would cut him off without a penny. It wouldn't have suited Henry to fend for himself, so he did what he was told – but he made her pay for it, over and over again.' Gran shook her head. 'In those days girls got married or went away to have the child and it was adopted, and I wasn't prepared to see that happen. I'd never have known what had happened to you.'

'Oh, Gran.' Maureen's throat was tight with emotion. She'd wondered so many times why her father didn't love her, and why he hadn't loved her mother. Now she understood and it made things so simple; it was time to move on with her life. 'I'm so glad I've got you.'

'Never forget that I love you.' Gran squeezed her hand. 'You put a spread on for her like Henry told you. Make her feel welcome and then you can walk out with an easy heart.'

'Yes, I can,' Maureen said. 'I've brought away all the things I really minded about her having, so she's welcome to the rest. I'll bring my clothes on Sunday morning and then I'll be ready.'

*

Violet was a large plump woman with pale bleached hair set in rigid waves, and blue eyes. She wore make-up and dressed smartly in a good frock that had been cut superbly, and she had drenched herself in her favourite perfume, but in every other regard she was entirely different to what Maureen had imagined. She smiled at her warmly, exclaimed in delight as

315

she saw the spread Maureen had put on for her and kissed her cheek.

'What a kind girl you are,' she said. 'I told Henry I didn't want a fuss, just to meet you – because I didn't think it right us seeing each other all this time and you knowing nothing about it.' She looked coyly at him. 'Especially now we're getting married...'

'Yes, that will be nice for both of you,' Maureen said. 'You'll be able to keep each other company.'

Violet looked a little disconcerted and the warm smile slipped a little, but soon recovered. 'What a generous girl you are to welcome me – and to accept that there will be a new mistress here.' Her eyes swept round the room, lingering on the few pieces of nice china as if looking for something more. 'You have a nice little place here, Henry, but my bits will make it more comfy – more a home.'

Maureen's father glared at her, because he'd noticed the gaps where her mother's precious bits had gone. Ignoring his look, she smiled at Violet.

'How soon will you be married? I hope it won't be long, because I have to report for duty in two weeks' time.'

'What are you talking about?' her father demanded.

'Oh, didn't I tell you?' Maureen put on an innocent air. 'I've signed up as what they used to call a VAD – but I'm called a nursing auxiliary now apparently, and I shall be reporting for duty. So I shall be out of your way, Violet.'

Violet stared at her, suspicion in her eyes. 'Well, I'm sure I never intended to turn you out of your home, dear. Though it might be for the best, of course.'

'What about the shop?' Maureen's father demanded. 'What am I supposed to do when you leave?'

'I expect you and Violet can manage between you.'

'Oh no, dear,' Violet said. 'Henry wouldn't expect it. I've got my little business, you see – I fit ladies' corsets and make a nice living from it, I can tell you. I shan't have time to take care of my business and his.'

'Oh well, Dad can run that easily himself,' Maureen said and smiled sweetly. 'You've always said I didn't do much, Dad, so it shouldn't make a lot of difference.'

Her father held his tongue, though she could see it cost him. He would have something to say when they were alone, but he wasn't going to say it in front of Violet.

'Well, that's settled then,' Violet said. 'I'm sure we'll manage quite well without Maureen – and you can always get a young lad in to help if you need him.'

'Would you like another cup of tea, Violet?' Maureen offered. 'No? What about you, Dad?'

'No, I do not want more tea.'

'Then I'll clear the table and wash up – no, Violet, you sit there. Today you are my guest and I wouldn't dream of letting you help.' Violet hadn't offered but Maureen could see that her father had begun to take in the implications of his daughter leaving. Violet wasn't the sort of woman who would have time to bake; it would take her all her time to clean and look after her corsetry business. She might even decide to employ a woman to help out with the cleaning...

A wicked smile played over Maureen's lips as she went through to the kitchen. She didn't think Henry Jackson would be quite so pleased with himself in a few months from now. If she'd been vindictive she might have taken pleasure in the knowledge that her father was either going to have to work himself or pay for help, but because she'd always been a caring girl she felt a bit sorry for him, and for Violet. He was all sweetness and light to her at the moment, but when he found out just how much he'd relied on Maureen, his temper was bound to fray.

*

Peggy shuddered as she read the news about the tragedy in Liverpool, where a bomb had killed more than a hundred and fifty people in an air raid shelter. It seemed as if there was something every few days; constant raids on London, the Balham Tube disaster in October and then the terrible blitz of Coventry when their beautiful cathedral had been destroyed; almost simultaneous raids in Birmingham, Manchester and now this latest. Would it never end? Was Hitler determined to destroy the whole country?

She put the newspaper into the basket for lighting fires, and went through to the bar to open up. Every night when the siren went, Peggy expected it would be their turn, but so far they'd been lucky and the worst the pub had suffered was a few broken glasses and a cracked window. Even if they'd had a hole in the roof, like the Co-op round the corner, they would've patched it up and carried on. Life had to continue no matter what Hitler did, and the people of Mulberry Lane would be in for their beer regardless of the latest catastrophe. Peggy wasn't the only one to be sickened by all the death and wanton destruction; the whole country was under attack. Even the thought of Christmas celebrations was hardly enough to lift the gloom.

*

'Well, good for you,' Peggy said when Maureen confided her news when she popped in on her way to the WVS canteen.

'It's about time you had a life of your own – but you could've had a job with me, Maureen. Anne is busy again. She's got two days a week teaching as well as her voluntary ambulance work so she doesn't have much time to help me. Of course Janet is here now, so she helps in the bar in the evenings, and when Maggie is asleep, but she's been crying a lot these past two days.'

'I hope it's nothing serious?'

Peggy smiled fondly. 'No, just a little tummy ache, nothing to worry about – but if the nursing doesn't work out, remember me next time.'

'I'm hoping it will work,' Maureen told her. 'If I do well I'll apply to train as a nurse and then I'll have a job when the war is over.'

'Surely you'll get married one of these days? Velma told you she wasn't ever married to Rory so why shouldn't you get what you've always wanted?'

'Rory didn't want me to visit him at the London, and he went off to have treatment somewhere. I don't even know where he is...'

'We could probably find out,' Peggy said. 'Janet's friend Ryan works for the government and seems to know a lot of things. He's trying to find out more about what happened when Mike's ship went down. I'm sure it would be easy for him to discover where Rory went for treatment.'

'I think I should wait for Rory to get in touch,' Maureen said. 'I've signed up now and I don't want to let them down. The nurses are rushed off their feet.'

'You'll find the work a lot different,' Peggy warned, 'but if it's what you want to do...' She shrugged, and Maureen knew her friend thought she was mad to have taken on a commitment like that when for the first time in her life she

319

was free to do as she pleased, but Peggy hadn't seen those soldiers arrive at the station. She hadn't seen them crying with pain, or the hopelessness in their eyes. Maureen wasn't a nurse and she might never be good enough to become one, but she could help those hard-working women who were, by doing the dirty repetitive jobs that were a big part of nursing.

Maureen was thoughtful as she entered the canteen later on. She'd enjoyed coming here, but this was her last evening. She knew that once she started work at the hospital she wouldn't have time to come here four evenings a week. As yet she wasn't even sure that she would be in London. She'd been told she could be asked to go anywhere.

'We try to keep people as near to their homes as we can,' they'd said at the recruitment centre, 'but even if we sent you to a London hospital for a start, you could be moved.'

Maureen didn't particularly want to leave Gran alone for weeks on end, but otherwise she wasn't bothered where she went. It was an adventure just to be out of the shop and she'd moved in with her grandmother as soon as Violet left that Sunday evening. Her father had shouted at her, calling her disgusting names and saying that she was a conniving bitch just like her mother. She'd given him a look that left him temporarily silent, picked up the suitcase she'd packed earlier and left.

Maureen was enjoying her freedom. One morning, she'd taken a bus up to the West End and walked round the shops, looking at the sights and watching people walking in the park, their coats pulled up round their necks, with hats and scarves to keep out the bitter chill. All the important buildings had piles of sandbags outside the doors and everywhere the windows were taped in case of a bomb blast. Some shops had started to build their Christmas displays, though fancy goods were in short supply and even British-made goods were scarce. There were trenches in the park, in case there was an attack, and several large notices pointing the way to the nearest shelter in the event of an air raid. Maureen saw some signs of damage, buildings that had been hit and a few gaps where a building had burned to the ground, though nowhere near as many as in the East End. Until she'd walked out on her father, Maureen hadn't been aware of just how much damage had been done everywhere, because although she'd read newspaper reports and heard the noise of the raids as they happened, she hardly ever went further than Peggy's pub, the market, or the canteen and it had shocked her to see that in some places whole rows of houses had disappeared, gone for ever, sometimes taking the people who had lived there with them.

She thought about what her gran had said about the property not being insured for destruction by enemy bombs. It was all her grandmother had except for a few pounds in the bank, and if that went up in flames it would leave her nothing. Gran ought to have sold it ages ago and put the money by for her own use, but she hadn't because it was Maureen's home. Well, it wasn't any more and she hoped Gran would be sensible and take what she could for it.

Chapter 30

'There's someone here to see you, love,' Peggy called upstairs that morning in early December. 'It's Ryan, so make yourself decent.'

Janet smiled, because what did Mum think she was going to do – walk down to the kitchen in her petticoat? 'Coming,' she called back and gave a quick glance in the mirror. Her hair was tidy and she was wearing a pale pink lipstick but no other make-up.

Her stomach tightened with nerves as she went down to the bar, because she knew that Ryan wouldn't have called on them unless he had something important to say. He'd phoned a couple of times during the weeks since she'd returned home, but if he'd come to see her he must have some news. Janet's nails curled into her palms as she wondered what he'd discovered – would he tell her that there was proof of Mike's death?

She walked into the kitchen and saw him standing by the window looking out into the yard. Something told her that he had news and that it wasn't good, and as he turned to look at her, Janet saw the grave expression on his face.

'I came as soon as I got the confirmation,' he said and moved towards her to take her hands, holding them tightly. 'It's good news and bad I'm afraid.'

'What do you mean?' Janet asked, her voice trembling. 'Please tell me. Nothing is worse than not knowing.'

'Mike was picked up by the Norwegian vessel,' Ryan said. 'The reason you haven't heard is because he's been very ill, Jan. I'm so sorry, my dear. Mike had a nasty blow to the head and he swallowed some of the oil in the water. For weeks no one knew who he was because he couldn't tell them. He was in a fever and they weren't sure if he would live, but then he regained consciousness and they say he is slowly recovering from his injuries but... Mike doesn't know who he is. He has no memory of anything before he woke up in a Norwegian hospital.'

'Mike has no memory of anything?' Janet stared at him in shock. 'He doesn't remember me?'

'No, I'm sorry, I'm afraid that is the case. He was brought back to England two weeks ago and is convalescing in a specialist hospital in the country. I've written the address for you to write to here. One of the men already there for burns treatment recognised him, and that's how we discovered where he is...'

'Oh, thank God,' Janet said and sat down abruptly on the lumpy sofa. 'He's alive and that's all that matters, isn't it?'

'The doctors aren't sure whether he will recover his memory,' Ryan went on, looking at her sadly. 'And his lungs may be affected by the oil he ingested. It won't be easy for either of you, but they've said you can visit him in the New Year.'

'Not before then? Why?' Janet was suddenly afraid. 'What else aren't you telling me?'

'He has burns to his hands particularly but also to other parts of his body – legs, back, although he isn't as badly burned as some of the other men. The doctors want to do a couple of small ops before you visit and they've asked that you wait.'

'It's a bit unfair of them to ask that of me,' Janet said; her chest felt as if the pain might crush it and she could only just stop the tears falling. 'It's nearly a year since I've seen my husband and months since I was told he was probably dead...'

'Yes, I know, my dearest girl.' Ryan moved towards her, touching her cheek gently with his fingertips and looking at her as if he wanted to do much more. 'You've had a baby alone and you've lost your home and now this. But you will need to be brave for a little longer please. Mike needs time to come to terms with his loss of memory and the fact that he has a wife and baby. He is still in pain and rather unwell. They hope he will be feeling a little better in a month or two.'

'And if he isn't? How long do I have to go on waiting?'

'They can't force you to wait, Jan, but for Mike's sake – and your own – it would be best.'

Janet was on the verge of dissolving into tears but something stopped her. She sensed that if she did, Ryan would take her in his arms to comfort her and that would be wrong for all of them – for her and Mike and for Ryan and his family. Janet was very aware that there was something stronger than friendship between them, and it wasn't sensible or possible to let it grow into a love affair. She had to be sensible – besides, he was right. Janet wanted to rush to Mike's bedside, but that wouldn't be a good idea, for several reasons. She had to get used to the idea that he'd forgotten her, forgotten how much they were in love, and how much he'd wanted her, and Mike needed to let his body and mind heal.

'Yes...' She blinked and smiled through the hovering tears. 'I know you're right, Ryan. I can't thank you enough for what you've done for me. It might have been months before they let me know if you hadn't made it your business to find out.'

'I wanted to make things right for you, Jan,' Ryan said. He hesitated, then, 'I shan't visit again unless you need me.' Taking a small white card from his pocket he wrote an extension number on the back. 'Please do not give this to anyone else. You may telephone me at this office. If I'm out of town my assistant will get a message to me. I shall still be there if you need me, Jan, but I don't think I should visit... do you?'

There was something in his voice, a look in his eyes that seemed to beg her to contradict him, but she knew that Ryan had made the right decision. If they continued to meet this feeling between them would become too strong and then people would be hurt: Ryan's wife and children, whom he loved so much, and Mike... if Mike ever remembered that he had loved her.

'You've done so much for me,' she said and her voice cracked with emotion, because she didn't want to send him away, but knew she must for all their sakes. 'I shall only ring if I'm desperate.'

'And if I come to you before that, you will know that I couldn't stay away.'

Ryan turned and left her standing there alone in the kitchen. Jan was fighting her tears when her mother walked in, looking at her anxiously.

'Is there news?' she asked tentatively.

'Mike is alive but has burns to various parts of his body – and he's forgotten me, Mum. He doesn't even know his own name...'

'Oh, Janet, love,' Peggy said and looked sad. 'That's awful

for you – but wonderful that he is alive. Where is he?'

'Ryan left his address on the table,' Janet said. 'I can write to Mike care of the hospital but they don't want me to visit until after Christmas.'

'The time will soon pass.' Her mother tried to comfort her. 'Your father phoned just now, while I was in the bar. He says that he'll be here on Sunday week and will stay until after Christmas, and Pip leaves us after Christmas. We have to try to make it a happy time for them, my love.'

'Did you tell Dad that I'm living here?'

'I wrote and told him everything. He asked me to tell you that he's sorry for everything and is looking forward to seeing you and Maggie.'

Janet blinked hard but the tears fell then and she was suddenly sobbing, held in her mother's arms, overwhelmed by a maelstrom of feelings that she hardly understood; there was relief and joy that Mike was alive, uncertainty of her feelings for Ryan and touched by the hint of despair she'd glimpsed in his eyes as she'd let him go – and weakness. For a little while she was a child again and her mother's arms were her world, holding her safe.

'I'm an idiot,' she said and forced a laugh as she drew away. 'I should be on cloud nine. Mike was believed dead and I thought he might be a prisoner of war but he's alive and in a few weeks I shall see him.'

'He will probably remember everything when he sees you.' Peggy kissed her cheek. 'Dry your tears, Janet. You can come and help me in the bar. Nellie is on her own and if I don't watch her she'll get all the prices muddled up again.'

Janet wiped her cheeks, taking a moment before following her mother through to the bar. Every wife and mother in the land was worrying about their loved ones. She'd been lucky.

She had her lovely daughter, her husband was alive, and surely he would remember her when he saw her – and her father had forgiven her for shaming him.

She lifted her head proudly and went into the bar. Somehow she would get through the days and weeks until she could see Mike and she would pray that in the meantime he would remember their love for each other.

*

Peggy looked at her husband as he walked into the kitchen and placed his case on the floor. There was something different about him, she noticed it immediately. He looked younger, more alert, and more alive than he had for years, much more like the man she'd married. Whatever he was doing obviously suited him.

'Laurie,' she said, wiped her hands of the flour she'd been using and went to put her arms about his waist. He smiled, bent his head and kissed her on the mouth, but she sensed immediately that it was not the kiss of a lover. He was greeting her with affection, but not the passion of a man who had missed his wife.

'How are you, Peggy?' he asked. 'Everything all right here?'

'Yes, fine.' She kept her tone light and careless to match his own. 'We're getting our fair share of beer from the brewery. I've only had one weekend when I ran out of draught bitter. I rang the brewery the next day and they sent me a few gallons to tide me over.'

'You've got plenty of spirits?'

'Thanks to you stocking up before the war, yes.' Peggy let her eyes rove over him. He was a handsome man and

327

she suddenly found herself wanting to make love to him. She wished he'd swept her up in his arms and rushed her to bed, as he would have once upon a time after he'd been away, but that wasn't going to happen. Things had been changing between them since before he left and now... there was nothing left of the old passion. Peggy recognised it and felt hollowness about her heart. She'd thought the temporary absence might have been good for their love life, but the opposite had happened.

'Did you go ahead with the party, as I suggested?' Laurence asked. 'If you need more money for anything...'

'Money isn't the problem,' Peggy said. 'It's finding the extra food. I can't use what I'm allowed for the pub or the customers will have to go short next week.'

'Maybe this will help,' Laurence said and handed her a ration card that had none of its coupons marked. 'It was issued to me when I was told I could take leave for Christmas. We don't need them where we are.'

'Special treatment, eh?'

'Something like that, but we live off the land most of the time – a lot of game and stuff, fish from the lake and rivers, salmon and trout, as well as pheasant and grouse, rabbits... that sort of thing. Oh, I managed to buy you a nice slab of farm butter and I got some eggs, and a couple of rabbits. We seem to have plenty where we are.'

'Santa Claus,' Peggy said stiffly. 'You'll have to come home more often.'

She didn't mean it, because she sensed that all this was Laurence making up with gifts for what he was lacking in other ways. She thanked him and put away the butter and eggs; she wondered if there was another woman. Somehow it hadn't occurred to her when Laurence went away that he would have time or the inclination for an affair, but now she knew she'd been a fool to take his loyalty for granted.

*

Laurence groaned inwardly as he watched Peggy serving the customers. A stranger would never know she was upset, but he knew her too well and understood that it was his fault. He'd hurt her. She'd picked something up immediately, even though he'd taken refuge behind his gifts and encouragement for her to have her usual party.

For a moment he reviewed the nights he'd spent in the arms of his passionate lover. Marie was like nothing he'd ever known before and she gave him something special, made him feel young and powerful, more than he'd ever been. Their lovemaking was wonderful. He'd forgotten that sex could be that good, if he'd ever known. Perhaps he was wronging Peggy, but he didn't think she'd ever abandoned herself to sex in the way Marie did. Peggy loved and gave love – but sex with Marie was like a fine wine that lingered on the tongue and made a man feel invincible. Once he'd had her, it was like a drug he needed over and over again.

He'd wished he didn't have to go home for Christmas, but Marie was going away too, though she wouldn't tell him where. He'd been jealous, half-accusing her of having another lover, but she'd laughed and started to kiss him in the way that set him on fire and he'd given in to the pleasure her hands and tongue could give him. Marie knew how to make a man feel like a god.

When they'd parted, she'd kissed him and told him to be nice to his wife.

'Remember you have children together and a life,' she'd

murmured as she breathed gently into his ear and then circled her tongue round it. 'We have just this little time. Make the most of it, my Laurie, and remember always that it was good, no?'

'Wonderful,' he'd said, wishing he could stay with her. 'But it's not over. I'll be back in a few days and I'll need you badly by then...'

Marie had laughed, shaking her long dark hair back, her eyes seeming to tease and torment him. 'You should know that in this world nothing is forever, my heart. Remember how good it was.' And then she'd walked quickly away, leaving him with nothing to do but board his train and come home to Peggy and his children.

He did care about them all, of course he did, Laurence thought as he served the next customer with two orange juices, a half of bitter and a whisky, taking the note and giving the soldier change.

He was glad that Janet was home and that her husband was alive, even if he was badly injured, and he was proud of his son for joining the RAF, even though he wished he could stay safe at home and not risk his life fighting for his country, but he wasn't the only father thinking that way these days.

Laurence looked at his son as he talked with one of his school friends; the other youth was wearing the uniform of a soldier and they were laughing together, sure of themselves, excited by the thought of being a part of the war. As yet they had no idea what it was all about, but they would learn. He'd wanted to keep his children safe, but now he knew that you had to let them go. Nothing was for ever, even Marie. He'd sensed that she was saying goodbye to him when he left and he'd given it some thought since then. Now he suspected that she was going over there. No wonder she'd laughed when he'd been jealous, imagining her in the arms of another lover. Of course Marie was that sort of a woman. He'd always known that he wouldn't hold her for long; she was too bright and beautiful for him, but he'd basked in her warmth and he'd benefited from the experience. He knew that he would probably never see Marie again and the thought hurt, but he couldn't forget her or regret that he'd known her.

Seeing the way Peggy forced a smile, Laurence was sad that he'd hurt her. He would have to try and make it up to her, but he couldn't make love to her, not yet, not with the memory of Marie so recent and vibrant. Best just to pretend to be tired. Perhaps one day, when he was sure that Marie was no longer available, in the future when he'd forgotten the taste of her skin...

Chapter 31

'Happy Christmas, ma'am,' the American voice said and Peggy turned round to see the good-looking officer smiling at her. 'I guess you've forgotten me after all this time.'

'No, I haven't; you liked my apple pie,' Peggy said. 'How are you, Able – and what are you doing back here?'

'I've come over to liaise with your Mr Churchill again,' Able said. 'I expect to be here several months this time so you'll be seeing me often, ma'am – and if there's anything I can do for you...'

'Well, we could always do with some of that delicious coffee you gave us last time,' Peggy said. 'Of course I expect to pay for it – but I'm having a party on Christmas Eve. It's not for general customers, but for friends and family – and I think it would be nice if you came. I never thanked you properly for that coffee last time, and everyone appreciated it so much.'

'Well, that's mighty nice of you, ma'am. I should like it fine, but I have a dinner engagement that evening. How about I visit that morning and bring a few things you might need for a party?'

'Oh, you mustn't feel obliged, but of course we always need extra – and as long as you let me pay...'

'That wouldn't be right; I'm not allowed to sell the stuff we're given,' Able said, 'but I can give it as a gift – and I'd like for you to have it, Mrs Ashley.'

'Then you must allow me to give you some apple pie to say thank you,' Peggy said. 'And please, call me Peggy.' She served him with the whisky he'd requested and told him she would look forward to seeing him on Christmas Eve and moved on to the next customer.

Peggy was busy all the evening, and when she looked round later Able had gone, but she was pleased that he'd promised to call on Christmas Eve, because he had a lovely smile and there was warmth in his eyes when he looked at her. She'd been wanting to cry ever since Laurence arrived, but somehow the American's smile and his generosity had made her feel better.

Life was never going to be the same, but perhaps it didn't have to be all heartbreak and regret.

'Peggy…' Hearing Maureen's breathy voice behind her, she turned to greet her friend. 'I had to come and tell you – I shan't be able to come for the party on Christmas Eve.'

'Oh, I'm sorry. I was looking forward to having you here.' Peggy kissed her cheek. 'Anne won't be here either. She's being sent to Coventry to help out in a temporary school there. The awful blitz they had in November caused a lot of damage and she's helping to set something up – but she'll be home sometime in January next year.'

'Yes, I've just seen her. She's so busy these days, but she brought a gift round for me. I'll pop round on Boxing Day to see you before I leave London, if that's all right?'

'Yes, of course. Are you going somewhere special on Christmas Eve?'

Maureen's smile lit up her face. 'I've had a card and a letter from Rory. He's told me where he is now and asked me to visit.'

'Oh, I'm so pleased for you,' Peggy said and her friend's happiness lifted her spirits. 'You can see him before you start working for the volunteers.'

'Yes, thank God!' Maureen blinked as the tears hovered. 'I have got three days off now and then I start work at the military hospital. I have to visit Rory while I can, because I don't know when I'll get time off again.'

'Well, it all sounds lovely,' Peggy said. 'What about your dad – has he recovered from the wedding yet?'

Maureen shook her head. 'I went because Violet asked me but I only stopped long enough to toast the bride and then I left. I haven't seen them since. Gran said they've got a girl in the shop, but she's useless. I expect that's just prejudice but if Dad shouts at her, I don't think she'll stop long.'

'It isn't your worry now, is it?'

'No, it isn't,' Maureen said and gave her a hug. 'I feel as if I've just started to live, Peggy. I'm out of the shop, ready to start a new job – and I'm going to see Rory.'

'Don't get your hopes too high. If he's been badly burned it won't be that easy...'

'He says he's feeling better and will be better still once he's had his operations, but I don't care about anything except seeing him, Peggy. I know he has to suffer pain, but he has made the first move by asking to see me – and I can't be wrong to hope for a future for us now, can I?'

'No, my love. I'm sure things will be better for you now.'

'Well, I have to go and pack a couple of things,' Maureen said. 'I just wanted to tell you and give you this...' She handed Peggy a small parcel that felt rather like a tin of ham: Maureen must have helped herself to it before she left the shop. 'It may come in useful for the party. Bye, Peggy.'

Peggy watched her leave and smiled. It was good to see a happy face and she hoped Maureen would find contentment at last.

*

'I'm rather tired,' Peggy said when Laurence came into the bedroom later. 'Would you mind sleeping in the other room just for tonight?'

'Peggy...' Laurence stared at her oddly. For a moment she thought he was going to refuse and take her in his arms and kiss her into submission as he had after quarrels in the past, but they hadn't quarrelled and in her heart she knew he no longer wanted her that way. 'No, of course not. You're used to sleeping alone now and I don't want to make you unhappy.'

'But you have, haven't you?' Peggy said and gave him a long, hard look. 'Are you in love with her? Are you going to want a divorce – sell the pub lease and split up?'

'I suppose it's no use lying; you know. I didn't want you to know – it's just a wartime thing, that's all...' he said lamely but the look Peggy threw at him slayed him and he shrugged, staring at her. 'No, I don't want to sell the pub or split up. I'd rather keep the family together, if you're willing?'

'I'll think about it,' Peggy said and Laurence's eyes narrowed, then he turned and walked out, shutting the door softly after him.

Peggy took her make-up off and stared at herself in the

dressing mirror. Was she old, and worn out, was that why Laurence didn't want her any more – or had he fallen for some cheap trollop?

No, she knew him too well for that; Laurence cared or he wouldn't have got involved. Even if he wasn't ready to divorce yet, he didn't want Peggy and if she told the truth she was no longer sure she cared.

For a moment the despair washed over her in great waves, but then anger surged to the rescue. It wasn't her who had almost broken their family by refusing to let Janet marry the man she loved, but Laurence had destroyed her trust and spoiled their marriage. She wasn't going to let him break her, though. She was too strong for that – and she had too many friends and good things in her life.

Maureen was going away, but she would visit and write, and perhaps there was hope for her future now. Anne seldom knew where she would be sent next, but she never failed to send cheerful letters and to visit when she was back in London. At least Janet was living with Peggy for the foreseeable future, though Pip would leave after Christmas to join the RAF. No doubt he would come home with his kitbag full of dirty washing as he'd promised, but it wouldn't be the same. She couldn't hold him back, because it was what he wanted and all their young men had to fight until this rotten war was over. Peggy's world had changed, as it had for so many others, and it wasn't just the rationing, the frequent electricity cuts and the shortages. Everyone had to put up with those as well as the threat of German air raids and the terrible loss of life that went with war. No, Peggy could've taken all that in her stride. It was the people... the faces you knew that would never be seen again. Too many young men were dying out there, and Peggy heard about sons and husbands killed in action from their grieving mothers and wives.

The pub saw them all come and go. Young men in uniform for the first time, their faces eager and bright with pride as they spoke of serving their country, and when they came back on leave, the light drained from their eyes and their cheeks hollow from suffering. She saw young widows and older mothers who had lost their sons, and her heart ached for them all, because they were all a part of her life. A life she'd embraced to the full – and one she feared might never be the same.

Peggy thought about her party. She was glad she'd managed to scrape together enough food and wine to have it, not just because everyone enjoyed it, but because it was one way of showing Laurence that she didn't intend to let him walk all over her. He'd cheated on her, she knew that, but she'd put too much of herself into this pub to give it up and walk away. No, she was going to stay here and fight. She would find a life for herself whatever happened, and for the moment she was staying here amongst the people who were the lifeblood of the lanes.

For some reason the memory of a young officer's smile came to her as she prepared to sleep. He'd promised to visit and bring her some coffee and a few things for the party, and he didn't want her money, just a slice of apple pie. Well, why not? Peggy's mouth curved into a smile as sleep came to claim her after a busy day.

If Laurence didn't want her, she was free to do as she liked with her life and she found herself looking forward to the morning and the visit of her new friend. She would be sure to get up early and make him the best apple pie he'd ever tasted – and maybe after Christmas she would feel ready to face the New Year. Surely 1941 couldn't be worse than the year they'd already endured and perhaps it might hold more for Peggy than she yet dared to dream.